SASHARIA EN GARDE

SASHARIA EN GARDE

SHERWOOD SMITH

PART ONE

ONCE A PRINCESS

ONE

THE RAP, RAP, RAP AT the front door beat a counter-rhythm to the rapping in my skull.

I sighed, and sat up. Remembered that I didn't have anything on as the typical January Los Angeles heat wave had given us a ninety-degree morning.

Rap-rap-RAP! They weren't going to go away.

I pulled my bedspread around me, and my hair swung down over it like a neo-pre-Raphaelite cloak as I lurched out of my bedroom, kicking aside a train of gold silk fringe at each step.

Mentally preparing some sizzling remarks, I yanked open the front door. Instead of somebody begging money for some cult or a door-to-door sales scammer, a pair of older men faced me expectantly, one short and stocky, one tall and lean.

Not American men, oh no. Their clothes didn't fit them right, they didn't stand with the slump-shouldered bend I was used to in L.A. guys, and their eyes were pinkish at the rims in reaction to the smog. I knew that because once, years ago, I had come from pure, clean air to the smog-clogged heat of Los Angeles, though that had not been the sole reason my eyes had been red.

"What," I snapped, my head pounding too hard for thought, or I would have slammed the door at once. Instead I almost lost my grip on the brocade coverlet, and then had to bat my long, frizzy locks of hair behind me.

Both of them stared at the coverlet. The one's eyes widened, and the other's jaw slackened. They were not staring at me in it, they were looking at the pattern of firebirds chasing up and down intertwined vines with little white flowers—queensblossom, it was called.

And it doesn't grow anywhere on Earth.

One of the men exclaimed, "Sasharia Zhavalieshin?"

I hadn't heard my real name for many years. "Wrong house." I winced against the headache.

"You have a look of your father," the other man promptly replied in a very strong accent—one I had worked hard to get rid of all those years ago.

Again an exchange of glances, and one of them said, with a furtive air, "We come with an offer."

"A fabulous offer." The other peeked furtively left and right as though spies lurked in the palm trees and parked cars. "One might say, of magical proportion . . ."

"Wait a minute, wait a minute," I cut in. "So you're trying to tell me that there's tremendous treasure waiting for me?"

Both heads nodded.

"If I take up a cause, one that includes deep magic?"

Vehement nodding.

"And perhaps an ancient castle full of sinister secrets?"

"Yes!"

"And all for truth, justice and honor?"

"Yes, yes!"

My anxiety flared into anger.

"Oh no you don't," I snarled. "I've been there, done that, and they don't even give you T-shirts."

"Tee—"

"Shirts?"

"Let me make it plain. N-O, which in English—the language you are using now—means no mystery offers, no fantastic treasure, no magic and especially no causes. They hurt too much!"

And *then* I slammed the door.

That is, I tried. One put his foot out, and the door thumped into it. He gave a muffled "Ooof," his eyes watering, and the tall gray one glanced back over his shoulder yet again. Still no one there, if you didn't count the string of tightly parked cars belonging to the other tenants of the apartment buildings on my street, and their roommates, boyfriends, girlfriends, and whoever else could crowd in.

He turned back to me. "We must discuss your father. May we enter?" Now he didn't even speak English.

And though I hadn't heard *that* language since I was a child, I understood it. Its cadences, the clear, almost singsong vowels after the flat affect of American English evoked so powerful a memory I froze. My throat hurt. "Is he dead? Just tell me. Yes or no."

"Please." The tall one held out his hands. "We must discuss your—your inheritance."

My heart gave one of those knocks against the ribs that echoes through body and soul with fear confirmed. With the pain of regret.

The younger one said quickly, "That is, we do not know for certain that he is dead, and that is why we—"

So they don't know, either. I pointed past their shoulders. "Whoa, the Winged Victory of Samothrace!"

As they hadn't read *Bored of the Rings*, they peered skyward, shifting their weight as they did so.

This time I got the door to slam.

They pounded, of course, and I half expected them to blast it inward with magic—then realized that if they could have, they already would have. Magic, so untrustworthy on Earth, was on the ebb. They probably had just enough access to whatever magical energy was floating over L.A. to return through the World Gate.

So I hotfooted back to my room and slammed that door, too.

I flung myself onto my bed, which sloshed and undulated, but even pulling the pillow over my head didn't shut out the fact that at last, at last, after all these years, what my mother had warned me about had come true.

They'd found me. Had they found Mom?

"Argh," I croaked, my aching, sleep-deprived brain finally catching up, and I sat up again, so sharply my head swam in a different direction than the water bed undulated. "Oooogh." My insides lurched along with the sloshing water.

But I ignored that, too, and reached for my cell phone, which I'd turned off before work the night before, and hadn't turned back on as my shift had ended at 3:30 a.m. I saw about a hundred calls from Mom. Uh-oh.

She answered on the first ring. "Darling?"

"Mom?"

"Sash! Oh babe, I am so relieved," she exclaimed, as if a month hadn't gone by between our last fight and now. But then it was always that way. After we cooled off we were too glad to hear the other's voice to continue whatever fight had sent me stomping off—Mom's words usually echoing behind me, *You're too much like your father: stubborn, dream-driven, won't compromise* —

"Mom—"

"Sasha." I could hear her breathe. "*They found me.*"

"You too?"

"You—*you* too?" she said, her voice too high with anxiety for either of us to laugh at the echo.

"Two old guys. Something about Dad and an inheritance. I slammed the door in their faces. Mom, he isn't, like, dead, is he? They wouldn't tell me. Or is it the Merindars, and some sort of trick?"

She heaved a shuddering sigh. "I don't know, *chiquita*. The one I got was young, and he isn't any Merindar, unless Canary has mellowed in his old age. If he's aged."

Canary was our private name for Canardan Merindar, usurper to the throne of Khanerenth, on the world Sartorias-deles. It had once been a funny name, meant to ease my fears while we were on the run, back before we'd lost everything but one another.

Mom said urgently, "Look, I don't want to get into this stuff on the phone. It's way too heavy-duty, and I don't know what they can or can't do with magic and phones. Meet me . . . at the old place. Okay?"

"Why not at your house? You've got those security guards and everything—"

"And they got past. Roger's in the middle of getting our tickets, and we are gonna beat feet. But first I needed to talk to you." Her voice roughened, and I knew she'd been worried sick.

Filled with remorse, I nodded, remembered she couldn't see me, and said, "Give me five."

In about a minute and a half, I'd dressed, grabbed my travel bag, and jetted out the door.

"Five" in L.A. traffic is likelier to mean five hours than minutes. An hour later, I'd inched my way across town through the morning commuter traffic to the street we'd first lived on when we blasted back through the World Gate with nothing more than the clothes we wore, a jumble of jewels and keepsakes wrapped in my firebird bedspread, and each other.

My mother drove up from the opposite direction seconds after I arrived in my battered old car. She had the door open almost before she'd turned the engine off. Heads turned on the street as we flung ourselves into the other's arms. Even in L.A. you don't often see a couple of women close to six feet tall hugging—one blond and elegant in hand-tailored haute couture clothes, the other in old jeans and a tee, a hawk's beak of a nose, and butt-length, wildly curly honey-colored hair.

"Sorry, sorry," I muttered into her linen-covered shoulder.

"Sorry, darling," she whispered into my hair.

We backed up to draw breath, caught some smiles and curious glances from people on the sidewalk watching, and remembered why we'd come—I could see it in her face as clearly as I was thinking it.

We looked around guiltily for lurking magical spies as we crossed the dusty L.A. street, Mom whirling to beep her car locked. I didn't bother. No one would want to steal mine, even if they could get it running.

Our "place" was Dinah's, an old fifties diner that miraculously hadn't been axed when the rest of the Bean Fields at the bottom of Sepulveda and Centinela had sprouted into the Hughes Center. We asked for a booth, and headed toward the far corner of the waiting area, me sitting so my back was to the wall and two exits in sight.

Mom hadn't forgotten Dad's training. She'd been on the run for several of my childhood years. What for me had been training had become habit for my mother, the idealist hippie "performance art" chick who met a prince from another world, and crossed with him back to his world.

Dad had never tried to fool her into thinking a "happily ever after" awaited them. There were problems at home, and one of the reasons Dad had left to visit Earth was to think about them, and perhaps to learn how to cope. But my mother had always believed in good causes—even if her prince looked a lot like Harpo Marx.

She said, "This kid came. Young. Your age, I'd think."

I nodded. Comparing in years was almost meaningless between a world with 365 days and one with 441 days.

"He told me your father had set something or other up, some spell. If he wasn't heard from in ten years, they were to activate this spell, and it eventually led to us."

She didn't say *I told you so*. She never did, and I had learned not to either. Our last fight had been over my reluctance to move yet again. We'd run every year since we'd first arrived, after Gramma died. We always returned to some part of L.A. School after school, town after town, getting used to new kids, new rules, new clothes and slang and styles—grammar school, middle school, high school, college.

I'd finally rebelled, declaring I would stay in L.A. and go to graduate school. I'd been grimly slogging my way from work to school ever since, but I had yet to learn to make and keep friends. I got along with everyone I worked with. I just never got close.

She sighed. The waitperson behind the counter called out, "Moira."

We were soon sitting in a booth with drinks before us. I hunched over my latte, stirring in sugar.

"Moira?" I asked.

"My latest name." She made a face. "And yes, they found me anyway."

I didn't say *Told you so* either.

She sighed. "Okay. Roger is getting you a ticket as well. I kept hoping you'd call, and I was going to wait until the last minute."

"Where are you going?"

"New York." That had been our last destination. She added defensively, "Sash, we can get lost in New York City better than anywhere else."

"We can't in *L.A.?*" I waved a hand. "All right. Consider the argument already done, me saying how much I hate running, you with the anonymity, me hating fake names and faker people, you with safety, and me with the fact that we're probably never going to be safe. It looks like we're unfinished business for those guys, and when it comes to tech versus magic, guess who wins?"

"Over there? Magic. But here?" She shrugged. "We've got tech on our side."

"Tech wins only if there's an ebb in the magic. Or a cold spot, or whatever they'd call it. Anyway, they did find us. And even if we run again, those guys are smart enough to find their way to tech if they want us bad enough."

She pushed our cups aside and gripped my hands. Tears slipped down her cheeks as she studied my palms. "You've got strong hands. That was about all I could give you, when your father disappeared." She met my eyes. "But I am afraid. For us both. They can't be tracking us for anything good. If it was good news, your father would come himself. I would rather have you with me."

"Mom, I'd like to stay with you, too. Nothing better. Heck, I even like Roger, even if he does tend to bore on about the stock market."

She smiled faintly, looking young and old at the same time. Vulnerable—though I loathe that word. Kittens are vulnerable. Orchids are vulnerable. When something wants to hurt me, I want to kick its butt from here to Mars.

"Mom, I'm going to stay. I don't see any difference between New York and L.A. for hiding in. Except I can hide better here since I know L.A. But really, I just don't want to run anymore."

"We ran in fear fifteen years ago," Mom said. "Sasha, we're not running from shadows. They are *here*."

"Oh, I'll move. I'll go back to using Gramma's last name, but that's it. I have at least a semblance of a life for the first time. I like my studies, I like my sport. I think I might maybe even learn how to make friends. So I'm staying. If they try to come after me, I know this ground. I'm going to stand and fight."

She held my hands so hard that I had to flex them so her grip wouldn't hurt. Despite her tears, and her elegant, poised appearance, it was obvious she'd stayed in shape too.

She sighed and wiped her eyes on the sleeve of her expensive jacket. "Okay. Like you say, you're good at taking care of yourself. Better than I ever was. There is half your father in you—" Her voice suspended again. We didn't have to say it. We were both thinking, *But he disappeared.*

I zapped her with my index finger, a gesture I'd learned from her. "Time to go back and pack. I hated that apartment anyway."

TWO

TWO WEEKS LATER, THERE I was asleep again, after another night shift. Same time, same weather, same bed—but this time I did not live alone, I had roommates. The apartment was located in Venice instead of West L.A. Fewer palm trees, more sea breeze, otherwise the same close-packed strings of cars out front, same rows of buildings with the ever-present TVs flickering in windows.

The rap at the front door made me bury my head into my pillow. I was sliding back into my dream involving guns, squealing tires, and tomato sauce with oregano, when a knock at my bedroom door startled me.

I jerked upright. "What?"

Leslie, my coworker and new roommate, opened the door and popped her head in. "Sorry, Sasha. Some suit asking for you."

"Suit?"

She shrugged, her beaded dreads swinging and clicking as she glanced over her shoulder, and back at me. "Suit. Tie. Briefcase. Something about legal papers."

A lawyer? Asking for me? This did not sound good. *Take-out delivery lawyer service has to cost a C-note a minute,* I thought. But out loud I thanked her for the heads-up.

Once again I surged up from the water bed and yanked my summer duvet around me. Not the beautiful one. That was now packed at the bottom of my closet in my old karate-gear carryall. This duvet was a gen-yoo-wine cheapo in five garish colors, one hundred percent synthetic Earthwear.

I hadn't unbraided my hair from my work shift, so my braids fell around my shoulders, all six of them, with curly wisps trying to escape; the effect, to my eyes, looked like I'd stuck my fingers in a light socket. Oh well. This was not any visit I'd asked for.

When I entered the living room, the mixed smell of simmering spaghetti sauce and stale marijuana toxins slugged me in my empty gut. The pounding I'd thought was in my head resolved into the boom-crash-screech of an action movie on the TV. So that explained the dream.

The sauce smell drifted in from the kitchen, pungent with fresh oregano. The toxins were from Dougie, a long, lanky guy in a filthy T-shirt and jeans. He lay in the middle of the living room, looking at some book called *How to Make a Million off the Internet* as he smoked his doob. The TV blared unwatched across the room.

Marcie, whose name was on the lease, had to rent out the extra bedrooms in order to scrape together enough cash to support this slob—nobody at the restaurant could figure out why. As they say, love is blind. In this case, blind, deaf and dumb. *Especially* dumb.

Dougie spewed another cloud before greeting me. "Hiya, Sasha." The greeting was accompanied by a leer down my body. I clutched the duvet tighter.

"Dougie." I left off the "hi" or "good morning" or any other word that he could possibly interpret as an invitation to hit on me. Not that that would stop him—as long as Marcie wasn't around.

Leslie jerked her thumb at the visitor and then vanished into the kitchen, firmly shutting the door on Dougie's personal smog bank.

I turned to the front door. There stood a young guy in a suit, carrying a legal briefcase. He looked ordinary enough: pleasant face, wavy brown hair pulled back into a ponytail, dark brown eyes, brown skin. Obviously startled by my height. I don't hold that against anyone—I *am* tall. Not a surprise when you come from two tall parents of spectacular make and model.

"Sasha . . . Muller?" He looked doubtfully down at his paper and up at me again. We were eye to eye.

His using my Gramma's last name was reassuring. "My mother sent you?"

An explosion whacked our ears as Dougie decided it was time to play some trash metal for the entire West Coast of North America.

"Just to sign some papers," the guy said—or I thought he said, not being very practiced at lip-reading.

"Why didn't Mom call me?"

He looked puzzled, cupping his hand to his ear.

Now what to do? Take him somewhere else, obviously, but not while I was practically naked. I couldn't just leave him. Dougie was quite capable of grilling him with nosy questions, and I didn't want this suit thinking Dougie had any right to the answers.

So I jerked my thumb toward the inside door and led the way over Dougie's legs back down the hall to Leslie's room. I hoped she wouldn't mind for five minutes.

I stayed long enough to see him perch carefully on the single chair, and dashed to my own room. I picked up my cell, speed-dialed Mom—to get her answering machine. So I thrashed into some clothes, choosing my most comfortable jeans and my *Got Books?* T-shirt. I braided my six braids into one big one, shoved my feet into my sandals, tried Mom again and got the machine. I waited for the beep. "Mom, call me? You sent some lawyer, or was that Roger?"

There. That took care of it. Right? I frowned at the doorknob as if it had become the Great Doorknob of Power, but two hours of sleep prevented me from getting any vibes about what I'd forgotten.

So I turned around, surveying my room. About the only furniture I owned was my water bed, my one indulgence, because it reminded me of my hammock when I was a kid on board a ship with Dad and Mom. But in Los Angeles, hammocks caused too many questions, and I had learned to compromise with things that raised no questions. Water beds raised no questions.

Everything else was garage-sale rejects, or survival stuff like clothing. I had gotten into the habit of always choosing things for practicality and invisibility.

There was another equally strong habit, being ready to jettison everything and run. I set my cell on my bed and reached into my closet for the gear bag I'd mentioned before, which contained my few important items. It went with me to work every day. Figuring a lawyer might need to look at my legal stuff, I hitched the bag over my shoulder, then eased the door open.

The walls reverberated with Dougie's thrash noise, jarring my teeth and bones. I whizzed across to Leslie's room and threw open the door, braced for action . . . to find the lawyer guy sitting where I'd left him, his briefcase on his knees, his brown eyes tilted up toward me in question.

"Okay." I shut the door. "What've ya got?" The screeching noise diminished to the mindless thud, thud, thud of elementary percussives.

The young man opened the briefcase and sorted through his papers.

"Several items of import," he murmured, the thump of the distant synthesizer drums and the hiss and rattle of his papers muffling his voice.

Import. Did he have an accent? Hispanic, maybe?

"Here."

He held out a sheaf in one hand and a pen in his other, his manner earnest—maybe nervous. Like he wanted to get this done and get out. Who could blame him, with that noise pounding our brains?

"Can you give me a quick overview on what this stuff is?" I was thirsty, hungry and functioning on under two hours of sleep.

"Yes." He stood and obligingly turned so that the papers were not upside down. "Here." He held them under my nose.

I bent to peer at the print. Just as I registered what appeared to be an old rental agreement, five fingers closed hard on my arm. My muscles tightened to whip off a forearm block, light flashed—

—and my body turned inside out, my bones snapped like rubber bands, my head exploded—

Then it all reversed.

Though it had been many years since I'd been wrenched between worlds, I knew instantly what had happened: I'd been thrust through a World Gate.

I dropped with a splat onto a tiled floor, gasping for breath. The lawyer plopped next to me, the briefcase spilling papers all over. He groaned as he struggled to sit up. As I tried to recover my wind-scattered wits, I stared at the papers. They were flyers for local sales, a couple of rental signs and—

"You're a fake." I glared at the guy, who ran a shaky hand through his hair, which had jarred loose from the ponytail. Then, as a few more wits moseyed back, "Of course you're a fake. What could be more unmagical than a lawyer?" Hadn't Mom said a young man had come to her? *About your age.* "Well, this is *totally* craptastic. I can't believe I fell for that."

The guy grimaced, rubbing his temples. He looked confused and upset, and a lot younger than I'd first thought. He probably wasn't much more than twenty. "I feel sick."

"Good," I snarled. "I'm so glad your rotten spell gave you the world's worst smackdown."

"Gate . . . very edge of its reach."

I sighed, disgusted with myself. I'd been braced for the old guys, or if not them, some sinister geezer like Saruman—one glance and I would have slammed the door in his face. But a young, cute guy with puppy-dog brown eyes wearing a tie and a L.A. liberal ponytail, toting a briefcase and talking about legal papers had completely suckered me.

Stupid! I wanted to stomp and yell, but I didn't have enough energy for that, so I settled for a snarky question. "I take it you're one of Canary Merindar's goons?"

We were still speaking English, though his translation spell would probably wear off soon. He winced again, frowned, mouthed the word *goon*, and flushed. "I am not!"

"Only Merindar," I said with false cordiality, "would be slimy and disgusting enough to force me against my will, without my permission, without warning, through that blasted World Gate."

He gulped in air and scrambled to his feet, leaving the briefcase lying on the magic-transfer Destination tiles. "Emergency. They were right behind us." He pointed at the tiles. "Come on, we've got to go."

"Home." I sat where I was. "Now."

The ex-lawyer tugged impatiently at the tie. "How can men wear these things in your world? I feel like I am strangling. No, you are not understanding. If I take you back, Canardan Merindar's mages *will* get you. They had a tracer out, and after we performed the ten-year spell your father asked us—"

"So why are you any better? Anyway, I don't believe that about my father. Those two old guys brought up his name, too. Going for the ol' sentimentality, pretend you're from my dad? No chance, Lance."

"Lance?" He looked around, as if weapons had sprouted somewhere in the little chamber. The English spell seemed to be fading.

"The point is, I don't recall anyone asking my permission to bring me here." I hugged my bag to me.

By now my other senses were waking up, and the smell of the air coming in the high windows, the sight of stone walls, even the rich colors—so much more vivid than those in L.A.—all made my throat hurt and my eyes sting.

I don't do sorrow well. It makes me surly.

"I—" He flapped a hand, shook his head, and opened the single door. "I believe I had better let you talk to Elva." He was now speaking in Khani, the language of my childhood, which I had not used for years.

And, like I said before, I had not forgotten a word.

He lurched dizzily through the door, throwing the tie in one direction and the suit jacket in another, leaving me staring through the doorway at a young woman about my age pacing impatiently. As the guy launched clothes right and left, the female stopped, gaping from him to me.

"You *found* her?" she asked in Khani. "Oh, well done, Devli." Another fast, puzzled glance. "Ah, which one is she?"

"The daughter. Grown up." The kid—Devli—vanished behind a folding screen painted with a highly stylized series of raptors in flight against a starry sky. Grunts and rips from behind the screen indicated he was getting rid of the last of his Earth clothes as fast as he could.

I shifted my attention back to the female, who had to be Elva. She wore a homemade shirt and trousers, her brown hair wrapped up on her head. Her dark eyes, so much like the guy's, quirked in puzzlement as she studied me.

"Send. Me. Back." I tried hard to sound polite. "Please."

"Why?" Devli shouted from behind the screen. "When we tracked you down, it was to discover you were not living as a queen and princess should—"

Anger burned through me. "And when I was last here," I interrupted, "the would-be queen and princess were running for their lives, grateful for stale bread, and eating it with one eye to the door that might come crashing in. How is that any better? My waitress life might not be prestigious, but it didn't include any weapons or death threats."

Elva flexed her hands. "But—"

"And I am not a princess," I added, more quietly. "Sounds to me like Canary is still king. My father is dead, near as I can tell."

Elva said on a hopeful note, "But we have not determined that your father is dead."

"Either a person is dead or is not dead," I retorted. All these years of wondering, and there still was no answer.

"Or is missing—"

Voices shouted from somewhere outside. Elva whirled around.

I scrambled up, still woozy from the world transfer, and

staggered out of the Destination chamber into a big room. I was obviously in a castle. Moss-splotched stone walls, arrow-slit windows down one side with age-darkened, rotting tapestries between them, and two very dusty, spider-webbed huge tables testified to a place abandoned for an appreciable length of time.

"Devli." Elva dashed across the room toward the farther table. "I hear trouble."

"Coming!" Devli squawked, amid increased sounds of frenzied dressing.

She turned back to me. "You need more seemly clothing."

"These are seemly where I come from. And if you send me back, they'll continue to be seemly."

She frowned. "Did I misspeak? You attract attention dressed thus, and it were better if—"

She halted at the ring of iron-shod boot heels outside the main door.

Devli hopped out a second later, trying to fix the ties of a greenweave shoe. Elva reached the table. She picked up a rapier and a saber and tossed the latter to Devli, who let go of his shoe just in time to catch the weapon with both hands.

"Hey," he protested. "That almost knocked me in the head."

"No loss," Elva cracked, and I knew then they were brother and sister. "Now pick up those outlandish other-world clothes, lest you want to signal to every villain within a day's ride where you were."

As she nagged, she picked up the tie and the coat and tossed them to him. He bundled them with the other things into a kind of knapsack, which he slung round behind him. "Table," he said to her.

Together they sprang to the closer table and shoved it against the wooden door about two seconds before the latch rattled. A muffled curse prefaced thumping and kicking.

My two hours of sleep left me struggling to catch up. "Wait—"

"This way." Elva used her sword to flick up the single tapestry on the inner wall.

Her gesture sent up billows of dust. She sneezed.

"Why should I follow you?" I demanded.

Devli said, "It's either us or King Canardan. I am afraid there is no choice left."

Canary? I'd already made one big mistake. I did not want to risk another. I crowded behind Elva and Devli into the narrow passageway previously hidden behind the tapestry.

An ancient magical glowglobe, dim enough to shed faint light, revealed a narrow, moldy corridor.

Elva had pressed against the wall, and when I passed, she closed in behind me. Except for our breathing and footsteps we were silent as we dashed down the passage, which abruptly jolted right. Another ancient glowglobe revealed a steep, cramped spiral stairway.

We shuffled down into darkness. All three of us trailed fingers against the slimy wall to guide us as there was no handrail. Ech. I was glad of my sandals. The stair mold was even worse than the walls.

Devli thumped into a solid door just before we heard a distant *wham!* from the upstairs room we'd left a minute ago. Devli yanked the iron-reinforced door open. Sudden light blinded us when we galumphed through a stone archway into a courtyard.

Elva pushed past me and led the way, sword up, looking around quickly. "Come on—" she began, motioning toward what seemed to be a stable from the smell emanating from the open door.

A stream of guys in brown battle tunics blasted through another stone archway in the wall adjacent to ours. A few waved rapier-sabers, and several wielded heavy straight swords. These had to be Canary's henchminions.

Devli scrambled in front of me, taking up position beside his sister. The men fanned out, moving in slowly. A few gave me puzzled looks.

Someone barked out a short command. The henchminions raised their swords, some upright, others holding the points outward. A couple waved their swords vaguely. Both those swords looked awfully tarnished.

Devli and Elva valiantly tried to drive the warriors back, but they were outnumbered and not well trained. Neither were the henchminions. From the caution with which they circled in, trying to get past Elva's and Devli's frantic sword swinging, it was clear the orders were to "take" and not "kill" or we'd have been sliced and diced.

Still, the siblings retreated. I also retreated, my bag clutched tightly to me. I was trying to think past my brain fog — and coming up with nothing because I had no idea where we were, or who anyone was. I had no weapons, no sleep, and worst of all, no caffeine to boot the brain.

Just then a cry from across the courtyard caused the leader of the patrol to yell, "Out here!"

Great. Reinforcements.

The henchminions grinned, several relaxing, the rest brandishing weapons expectantly. Their leader said to Devli and Elva, "Put your weapons down."

"Not likely," drawled a voice from the archway behind us.

I whirled around. A tall guy sauntered into the courtyard, sword in one hand, long knife in the other. Neither weapon looked tarnished.

Devli sighed, shutting his eyes briefly. "The pirate."

"Pirate? *Pirate?*" I repeated, trying not to bleat. "Pirates I *read* about. I never wanted to *meet* any—"

No one was paying me the least heed. Elva and Devli gripped their weapons with renewed determination, though they didn't seem to know where to attack first.

"Come along," the pirate invited the henchminions, waving his knife to and fro as he passed me by with no more than a glance. "Come on, men! Here's your chance for glory!"

Canary's goons sprang to the attack.

The pirate wore a fringed black bandana, a gold hoop in one ear, a crimson woolen vest over a billowy shirt like those worn by the siblings, only the pirate's shirt had been dyed robin's-egg blue. The vest was both sashed (lime green) and belted. Full black trousers, high blackweave riding boots. I wondered, despite the danger and my headache and everything else, is there, like, a pirate code, where they have to dress like that? I kinda thought pirates, you know, didn't do rules.

Despite his severe lack of fashion sense, the pirate's fighting style left the siblings in the dust. He broke the front patrol line, leaving Elva and Devli to deal with the outer two warriors. Then, as the newcomers spread slowly out, stepping warily, he glanced back once.

"That her?" A brief head-to-toe from light-colored eyes, set well apart.

"Yes," Elva gasped, wiping her brow on her sleeve.

"Useless, eh?" the pirate commented, not missing a beat as he disarmed two of the brown guys.

"We only had weapons for us—" Devli began. A knife, hitherto hidden in the boot top of the patrol leader, thunked into his arm. "Oooh," Devli finished, staggering back.

Elva sprang to her brother's aid.

I hadn't meant to help anyone. I mean, nobody was on my side as far as I could see. But that "useless" comment stung.

"The invitation didn't include swords." Anger smacked away the last of the brain fog.

I slung my bag behind my shoulder and picked up a rapier dropped by one of the guys the pirate had wounded. I hopped over the guy, who lay groaning, rocking back and forth with a hand at his bleeding shoulder. These rapier-sabers were heavier than the fencing saber back on Earth, but far lighter than the clumsy straight swords.

Straight swords can break a rapier—if they connect. Rapiers are fast. Especially if one knows how to use them.

Ah, there was another. I picked it up as well, and as three men charged at me, whirled both blades around experimentally. Yep, heavier, but good reach and a nice snap to the steel.

Fencing for sport has strict rules. My father had explained to me when I was a child that dueling was also hemmed by rules, but warfare wasn't, a piece of advice that my mother and I had minded when seeking extra training in martial arts. Which also has rules. Different ones, though.

So I used the two blades, the dust on the old flagstones, roundhouse kicks and a fallen cloak, pinking all three in under a minute. It was apparent their training was at best rudimentary—counting on numbers—whereas I was hungry, angry, unpadded, and oh yeah, had been competing on fencing teams for the past ten years. Fencing—and winning trophies. Only my fear of publicity had kept me from doing anything professional with it.

And so I ended up fighting next to the pirate as the rest of the attackers came at us, this time with no hesitation. The pirate flicked a smile in my direction and whacked an attacker over to me.

I returned the compliment a moment or two later by tripping one, who lunged at Captain Color-Challenged, took a slice across one arm and a pink in the other arm, and retired from the lists. I didn't kill anyone—I was far too squeamish for that—but noticed that the pirate only wounded as well, taking them with practiced precision out of the fight, but not out of life.

I was breathing hard and sweat ran down into my eyes when the news clue-sticked me that there were no more attackers. They sat or lay, most groaning, some bemused. There were fewer than I'd first seen. A bunch of 'em had prudently found business elsewhere.

The pirate put his point down and leaned on it. "Sasharia Zhavalieshin?"

"No, Snilch Gritchpea," I said crossly, trying unsuccessfully to wipe the sweat from my eyes, but my arm was as sweaty as my face. "I'd like to go home now."

Devli claimed our attention by swaying, then falling face down. Elva knelt and sniffed. "Pepper-poison!" she cried.

And, despite the many years since I had breathed this world's air, there in my mind was the spell my father had taught me. Before I could think I'd muttered it. On Earth, for a time, I'd practiced my father's spells, but they'd never worked, or barely gathered magic. Here, a sudden surge of power ran through me and zapped over Devli in a faint, coruscating light. He sat up, gasping.

Devli and Elva stared at me.

The pirate gave me a pensive smile. "And you want to remain on a world where there's no magic?"

"Well, at least they have aspirin," I muttered. The backlash of powerful magic hit me. I sank to the ground and put my head on my knees.

THREE

"WE HAVE LISTERBLOSSOM STEEP." Elva sounded subdued.

Steep was tea, that I remembered from childhood. Lister-blossom, my mother had once told me, was probably related to willow. It was remarkably effective as a fever-reducing analgesic.

"May I suggest a strategic retreat?" The pirate saluted us with his sword. "Half those boys are hiding inside, but they might combine and rush out for some more sport."

"Here." Devli drew in a cautious breath, touched his arm, and smiled. Then straightened up. "Hands together. I left a transfer token in a . . . a place of safety. Brace yourselves."

"Are you well enough to do a multiple transfer?" his sister asked, concerned.

Devli's eyes widened. "Oh yes. Better! Because that wasn't an antidote. There is no antidote to pepper-poison. If you survive it, you sweat it out. *That* magic I don't even know, but I recognize the effect. It's old morvende magic, taught to Prince Mathias Zhavalieshin."

They all stared at me, living evidence of the previous generation's problems.

I pressed my hands to my eyes, someone touched my shoulder—

—and we transferred. But this time it was quick, causing no

more than an inward jolt and a twinge of queasiness. A short distance, then.

Dim lighting—smell of damp stone—I knew I was underground before I even saw the small, round cave with several dark archways leading off who knows where. In the center sat a low circular table, on it a neat stack of pressed paper, an inkwell and a quill pen that Devli had obviously set up in case of need. The light came from a glowglobe set in a wooden holder. Next to the paper lay Devli's transfer token, which had given him something to focus on in absence of a regular Destination chamber.

Destination chamber. Glowglobe. More blasts from the past.

"We are safe." Devli bowed to me. "Devlaen Eban, journey-mage, sworn to your father's service."

"Elva Eban, navigator aboard the *Flipping Squid*. I—" Elva stopped, and shrugged. "I'm not a mage, but I joined Devli to help." She scowled at the pirate, who leaned in an archway. "Devli's group has been working to find your father, free him and restore him to the throne."

Devlaen whisked himself away somewhere behind me, but I was too tired to look.

Father. Throne. Plots.

Not again.

"Sit down." Elva peered worriedly into my face. "Cushions over in this alcove."

She carried the glowglobe through one of the archways, which opened into a smaller chamber. On the rock floor someone had spread an old carpet, worked in green-dyed wool, and on the carpet had scattered cushions. I dropped gratefully onto the nearest one, next to a short-legged table set with ink, quills, and more paper in little message squares of various sizes. Elva put the glowglobe next to the inkstand.

"*Flipping Squid*?" I looked up at her, trying not to laugh.

Elva gave me a twisted grin. "Well, I didn't pick that name."

The pirate lounged down onto the pillows with an easy swing

that suggested courtyard fights were nothing new. "Ships tend to change hands rather often, off our shores. It's traditional."

Elva muttered, not quite under her breath, "So says a pirate."

"Privateer," he corrected.

"But you have no letter of marque," Elva retorted.

"Of course not," he answered, amicably enough. "How can I get one from the real king when he's missing? And I don't think I'd like to apply to the current king since it's his ships, along with various other enemies, who are my prey."

Elva sniffed. "Talk about stupid names." She turned to me, with a dismissive back-of-hand toward the privateer. "Ask his name."

"*Zathdar* is the name of my flagship." He smiled. "It works well enough for us both."

Elva glared. "So why don't you tell us your real name?"

"Zathdar," I repeated, wanting out of that argument before it started. My head hurt too much. I gave him a mock frown. "There wouldn't be any apostrophes in it, would there?"

"Apostrophes?" He pronounced the word in English. It hadn't translated out in Khani.

Seeing that Elva had stopped glaring and was curious, I reached for the smallest square of paper, dipped a quill into the ink and wrote *Z'ath'd'ar* in English.

"Flyspecks." The pirate turned the paper this way and that. "The letters seem clear, but the purpose of the flyspecks?"

"Well, in magic stories at home, heroes or villains have names that begin with Z," I said. "And a lot of apostrophes. Just checking. You know, if you're a hero—or a villain."

Zathdar compressed his lips into a firm line, as if he was trying hard not to laugh. "Perhaps the absence of flyspecks will serve as my proof that I am neither. Just an ordinary fellow —"

"—wearing a red vest with a lime green sash—" I interjected, and he laughed.

"—going about my ordinary business."

Elva snorted so loudly her sinuses probably buzzed.

Before she could shoot an insult pirate-ward, I gabbled on. "'Dar' I recall means 'spring' in Sartoran, at least as a suffix." I paused, remembering my father's patient voice as he tutored me in tents while rain poured down, on the deck of a smuggling ship, in an old castle tower. His graceful hands, as he sketched out the Sartoran letters, which Khani had adopted. "'Zath' is storm—"

Elva crossed her arms, sitting bolt upright on her cushion. "It means hurricane. Who but a villain calls himself Hurricane?"

"The spring storms that come down on the other side of the continent are the fall storms up north," the privateer Zathdar said. "They come fast and are hard to fight out at sea. It's a great name for a privateer. So it works for me, too."

I turned to him. "Do you have another name?"

Blue eyes gazed back at me, their expression friendly but observant. "Jervaes is my family name." His features were even. I couldn't see his hair, or even if he had any, because of the bandana.

"Jervaes. Sounds familiar. I think." I turned to Elva. "Anything wrong with it?"

She shrugged. "A common enough Sartoran name."

Devli reappeared, smiling with triumph as he held out a heavy ceramic mug to me. He dropped down next to his sister.

The smell was so refreshing it alone almost banished my headache. It also awoke emotions from my childhood, making my eyes sting. I slurped tea to hide my reaction, breathing in the aroma of a field of rain-washed and sun-drenched herbs waving in a gentle wind. The taste was fresh and herbal. I drank the tea down and immediately felt better.

Zathdar the hurricane privateer said, "Why don't you tell us your end of things, so we can put it together with what we know?"

"Sounds reasonable—" I began, but Elva cut in.

"No," she stated, chin up. "At least, not until *you* find your way back to *your ship*."

Zathdar gave her a quick, challenging grin. "Why don't you find your way back to yours?"

Elva flushed. "Because I know my brother's friends. They are all trustworthy. I know they mean to restore Prince Math to the throne, if Queen Ananda doesn't want to rule on her own. If we can find out where he's hidden. You showed up knowing our plans, followed us to the World Gate castle without any invitation—"

"Saved our butts," I put in, trying to keep things fair.

"Oh, I think the three of us could have gotten out without his sword waving around," Elva retorted with commendable bravado, but even she didn't seem convinced.

Especially when Devli shook his head slowly but emphatically. "Bad as those fellows were, we were no help, and Sasharia couldn't have fought them alone. Without him, we'd be in Prince Jehan's grip right now. Or far worse, War Commander Randart's."

Elva shuddered, then squared her shoulders. "I don't trust this fellow. Too many unexplained coincidences."

"There aren't any coincidences from my end." Zathdar sat back on his cushion and clasped his hands around one knee. "One of my crew heard one of your friends asking questions all around Land's End Harbor, hinting at plots that include mages, World Gates, and the name Zhavalieshin. They reported it to me. Some investigation led me to the mage students. They were quite easy to follow." He nodded at Devli, who blushed.

"It was our fault we kept our headquarters at Cousin Nad's house," Devli admitted.

Zathdar continued. "King Canardan was not too stupid to investigate the houses of the former stewards belonging to the old king, he was probably too arrogant. But obviously that changed. I believe the attack on the old castle—which everyone who knows anything about magic knows holds a Destination accessible to the World Gate—is proof enough that the king's men were right on your heels."

Elva sighed. "All right, so we made some mistakes. But I still have questions."

"Well, why not discuss them on the ride down to the river

where I've hidden my flagship? Prince Jehan's men will be busy searching all over, and we cannot hole up in this cave forever."

Elva looked at her brother, who spread his hands, then at me.

I copied Devli's gesture.

"Let's go," she muttered.

FOUR

SHE SAID THOSE WORDS at the very same moment that, away in time and space through the World Gate, sunshine dancingstar Zhavalieshin (later known as Sun, which was the best damage control she could do with that stupid name she'd made legal back when she was twenty-two, complete with lowercase initial letters) picked up her cell phone.

At the hotel-room door, Roger stood patiently. "Coming? We might not get a cab in time to make the curtain."

Sun said, "Sasha has never ignored my calls before. One more try."

Roger murmured, "Maybe she didn't pay her bill?"

Sun gave him an ironic look. "I may be an old hippie. And my daughter is a child of a hippie. But Sasha's too practical to skip paying bills. You ought to know that by now."

"I know you two are half-crazy, with all your talk of World Gates and what all." He grinned, adding under his breath, "But that's part of the fun of being around you."

"Hello?" Sun stood straight, her brows arching in surprise. "I take it this is not my daughter Sasha."

At the other end of the phone, Dougie quickly recovered his surprise at hearing a female voice. "Nah. I was hoping you'd know where she was." How was he to know it wasn't his dope connection calling back? Stupid old bag—having a blocked number. Everyone knows only drug dealers have blocked numbers.

"I am Moira Muller," Sun snapped. "Who *is* this! And why are you using my daughter's phone?"

At first Dougie had thought asking where Sasha was a pretty cool answer—like, lob the ball back at whoever was calling, if it wasn't his connection. He wouldn't have to explain why he had Sasha's phone. But.

Dougie said, fast, "I'm tryin' to find Sasha. She, like, took off earlier. With some suit. I thought they were in here all afternoon." He snickered at the idea of lawyers doing the horizontal Olympics—and charging people for their time. "But when I tapped at the door, like, it, you know, opened. She ain't here. Or the suit," he added.

The lawyer again, Sun thought. *Stick to the point.* "What I am to understand is that my daughter was visited by, or is visiting, a lawyer, but that does not explain who you are, and why you are using her phone."

"Well it was just layin' around—"

"Lying."

"I am not!"

Sun said with the quick, sharp consonants that made it clear to Roger, at least, she was very angry. "The phone was *lying* there. Unless it was *laying* baby phones? Use the language properly, and tell me why you have my daughter's phone, and *who you are*."

Dougie cursed the old bag, Sasha, and the phone, but only inside his head. He was about to sling her some bull but he remembered a show on which the cops traced cell phones. Crap! Maybe it hadn't been such a hot idea to make his connection with someone else's phone, like he'd first thought.

"I'm Doug. Roommate," he muttered. And, in a whine, "Like I told ya, she like took off with the bozo in the suit, and hasn't come back. Her car's out front and everything. I was hopin' the phone would find her—"

"What is the address?"

Dougie stared at the phone, appalled. What if this old broad really was a cop? He closed the phone and tossed it into Sasha's closet. "Hell." He slammed the door behind him.

On the other side of the continent, Sun looked across the hotel room at Roger. "I have to go back," she said.

"Back to what?" Though he knew the answer.

"To L.A., right now." Sun's eyes were tense with worry. "Sasha would never—" She shook her head. "I have to find her. That strange message she left, and she won't take my calls? Some idiot using her phone, obviously without her permission? I'm afraid I know where she's gone."

Roger flung the hotel keycard on the nightstand. "You're not going to say something easy to hear or to believe, are you."

Sun spread her hands. "If she went out of the world, it means she was taken against her will." And when Roger shook his head, she studied him, saying slowly, "You don't believe me, do you? In fact, you never did."

Roger approached, stopping halfway across the room. "What was I supposed to think? Oh, I never thought you outright lied. And I do know the difference between lie and lay."

The feeble attempt at a joke did not bring an answering smile, only a troubled stare. He half held out a hand, but Sun stood there by the window of their suite in the Omni Hotel, below which the traffic of 52nd Street hissed and honked, voices in at least three languages echoing up the buildings.

He said, "I always thought your story was one of your hippie metaphors. Like your names—the fact that the name you gave me is not the same one as on your passport, which isn't the one you pay your taxes under. All your identities seemed your way of keeping your friends at a distance."

Her brows snapped together. "I was always upfront with *you*."

"I know. I expressed it badly. I've the time, the money, and I've always enjoyed being your *cavalier servente*. No one else likes the same music, the same art, the same kinds of conversations. And it was those things that convinced me, well, you might change your mind one day. You might want more than a *cavalier servente* with time and money. And the same taste in opera."

"You've been a good friend," she said gently.

"So what's the bottom line here?" Roger asked. "What happens if you go to L.A. and get swept off to some mystery place? Though I can't really believe it. Even the king is easier to swallow."

Sun rubbed her hands up her arms, which she'd kept in fighting shape, though she'd ceased to let herself believe she'd see Math again. Nor had she — quite — believed he was dead. Her one steady conviction over all these years was that she couldn't bear to go back, to search, to discover there was no hope. She'd hoped he would find them. Like he'd sworn, on his honor, on his heart, before he pushed them through the Gate back to Earth.

And left them there.

She wiped her eyes. "I can't answer that. Maybe I've been weak. Chickenhearted. Trying to outrun the past." She drew in a long, steadying breath. "But one thing I can promise you. I'm going to find whoever it was who grabbed Sasha, and I'm going to kick them from here to Pluto. Because even if I don't rate many points as an ex-princess, nobody, *nobody* messes with Mom."

FIVE

"TELL ME MORE ABOUT these flyspecks?" Zathdar asked presently. "In your world, the flyspecks on a written record signify someone chosen for a great quest? Or signify someone who chooses to thwart a seeker?"

"'Chosen' by the writer." I laughed.

He just looked puzzled.

The two of us were alone. The siblings had dashed off, Devli pausing only to grab the mug from my fingers. Until he asked his question, we'd just sat quietly, me with my eyes shut as I did my yoga breathing in an effort to get rid of the last of the headache.

I sighed, not wanting to explain that I had actually missed Sartorias-deles terribly, so much that I had read every fantasy I could get from the library, and later, the bookstore. Most of those books were delightful, making me wonder if the writers secretly saw another world and hid it behind the guise of fiction for whatever reason. I'd read for escape and also for answers, hoping someone would set a story here, though I'd never encountered one.

To tell the truth, I'd badly wanted to come back, all my life. But I wanted to come back to Dad and a happy existence, like my early childhood. I did not want to be taken back without my consent, especially to be thrown into what was beginning to sound like the same mess we'd escaped—only worse. Because Dad was still missing.

Zathdar regarded me with that puzzled look. I did not want to talk about my dad to a pirate. So what was the previous subject? Oh yeah, apostrophes. "Even when you love the stories, when you read a lot, sometimes certain, oh, what we call in English 'tropes' tend to show up over and over. I guess some writers read them when young, and think they have to use the same ones. Like the flyspecks in names."

Zathdar nodded, to my surprise. "The same can be said for ballads, and certain types of music. Yet we listen even so, past the familiar, for whatever it is that draws us." He tilted his head. "Sounds like Devli and Elva are almost ready." He got to his feet, and as I followed him into the bigger chamber, he smiled back at me. "The search perimeter won't have reached this far yet but that assurance will become less trustworthy as time passes."

"Ready." Devlaen pounded in, lugging a knapsack full of jutting corners. Magic books, obviously.

"Ready." Elva appeared from the other direction, a bag over her shoulder. She held an armload of clothing, which she thrust at me.

Since they were all standing there, I slipped the voluminous shirt over my T-shirt, and pulled on a wide-waisted coarse-woven riding skirt, hiding my jeans. The skirt promptly tried to fall off.

Zathdar's mouth quirked as he undid the Day-Glo green sash and handed it to me. The silk was warm from his touch. "And *this* makes me less noticeable?"

All three nodded, Zathdar's smile broadening.

I sighed, then tied the skirt up as best I could. "Ready."

Devlaen led the way down a short tunnel to what smelled like a stable annex—the clean smell of fresh hay mixed with horse. Again, childhood memories hit me straight in the heart.

Elva glanced at my head, then shrugged. I didn't have to look down to see that my braids were fuzzier than ever. Apparently many braids were exotic but acceptable here too, even scruffy braids, for she did not speak, only beckoned for me to follow.

The sun was just about to set when we rode out, Devlaen

trying to arrange his bulky pack of books on the back of a skittish young mare, Elva watching in all directions. Zathdar seemed content to glance around once, but I remembered that comment about search perimeters. It surprised me that pirates, or rather privateers, talked about search perimeters. I thought their action was confined to water, which you didn't have to search, since there were no convenient mountains, trees, or castles to hide behind.

No, I thought, watching the fringes on his bandana swing gently with the even pace of his horse. *Don't get paranoid because the guy is competent. Competent is good when it saves your sorry butt.* Besides, privateers had to train somewhere, and maybe it was as easy on land as at sea. One thing for sure, he was ready for action. He carried a cavalry sword across his back and the rapier in a saddle sheath.

Elva wore her weapon, which whapped against her leg at every step of her mount. Devlaen seemed to be entirely occupied with his bag of books, and while I had my gear bag clutched to me, it didn't contain any weaponry.

We emerged from the hillside opening into spring-green leafing trees, similar to beech, and I was stunned by the purity of the color. In L.A. you did not breathe such champagne air, or see such color, unless it has rained for a couple of days—something that happens rarely enough in Southern California that it's always a headline news item.

In the distance, on the opposite side of the river valley, a hamlet lay charmingly terraced up the sides of the rocky canyon. Some of the single-story houses were whitewashed, some colored a warm shade, like honey-butter. No people in sight. Bad sign? Good sign?

"Where to?" Zathdar asked Devlaen and Elva.

Devli opened his mouth, then looked confused. "I guess Cousin Nad's is out."

"Away," Elva said shortly, and pushed her mount ahead of us all, so that she was in the lead.

"My flagship is anchored right here at the mouth of the river." Zathdar pointed downward in one direction. We were as yet too high to see the river.

"We need to get away." Elva sounded a little desperate. It was clear she had no ideas, either, except that she didn't like his.

We rode single file, as the path was narrow, bendy, and the shrubs and trees grew close. I grimaced down at my mount's bony neck, and busied my fingers with untangling the coarse mane hair. Smells, sights, even sounds bombarded me, bringing up memories I thought I'd forgotten. I didn't know which hurt worse, the happy ones or the bad ones.

Zathdar had fallen behind me, going last. When I turned in my saddle, I found him studying me. "So what can you tell us from your own perspective?" he asked, voice lifted so the others could hear. "A summary will do. We know you were small when you left this world."

His slightly tilted head, the faint sympathetic smile, made me aware that I'd tightened up from neck to knees. "Right." I tried for an easy tone. It was a perfectly legit question. "What I remember is King Canary. Uh, that's a joke we came up with, me and my mom, though he hardly looks like any small yellow bird. Do any of you know him by sight?"

"No," Elva said from the front. She frowned back at us frequently.

Devlaen grimaced. "From a distance. In parades."

Zathdar just gestured, his palm turned up, which I interpreted as an invitation to go on.

"Well, he's tall, with reddish hair. Eyes a real bright blue. I remember his smile. My mother says he's handsome, but all I remember is that big smile, and how tall he was. Things at the castle were fun. Then the old king—my grandfather, that is. He finally died. I don't remember him much at all—"

I was descending into the personal memories I'd wanted to avoid, and so I shook my head. "He died, as I said. Next thing I knew we were traveling. Then we were on the run. The grownups didn't tell me much, just that we had to be very quiet, and careful. We hid in a forest, we hid on a smuggling ship. My father got us to that old castle. I remembered some of it, though it was at night, during a heavy storm. He sent us through the Gate. Said he'd come for us. Never did."

I paused when we reached a forked path. Elva scowled, running her fingers along her scabbard. She was clearly tense with indecision.

Zathdar said, "Keep to the right, is my suggestion."

"I agree. Left looks like it goes back toward the old castle." Devlaen turned around in his saddle. "That all?" he asked me.

"That's what I remember. Here's the basics of what I know. My mother said Canary began flirting with her as soon as my father brought her over from Earth. Dad was sent to Earth to see other worlds and gain perspective, since he was a second child. Canary had urged him to do that. Mom and I think now that he, Canary I mean, thought Dad would never come back."

"Magister Glathan thought so, too." Devli nodded slowly.

We'd reached another branch of the trail. Elva cast a quick look back. Devli shrugged in non-answer.

Zathdar said pleasantly, "Left-hand trail goes down to the river. I feel obliged to remind you that if War Commander Randart is anywhere behind us, his searchers will find that cave retreat by morning. If not sooner."

Elva sent a darkling look at her brother, who said defensively, "How was I to know our rescue party would turn into a war party?"

Elva muttered, "Hold my spot on ship defense, that I can do. Not against the king's entire army."

"Let's go left, sis." Devli gave an anxious look at the mountaintops.

I could have pointed out that Randart's searchers wouldn't be stupid enough to make silhouettes if they were really up there, but kept quiet, and Elva reluctantly headed to the left.

"Would you continue?" Zathdar asked me. "You had gotten to

King Canardan and your mother and father."

I shrugged. My story wasn't all that exciting. Maybe he thought my natter was better than sullen silence from up front. "Dad didn't die on Earth. Nor did he carve out a new kingdom, or whatever it was Canary thought he'd do. Along the way on his journey through California, he met my mom, at a Renaissance Faire. Um, never mind what a Renaissance is. Just think of it as people dressed up in costumes. Mom didn't know he was a prince. She was a hippie activist because it was romantic and exciting and seemed destined to make the world better. Anyway, they became friends. Same sense of humor. Then they fell in love, and he wanted to marry her. So he sprang the prince business on her and said that getting married over here in this world would make her being a princess more official in the eyes of the people of Khanerenth than a marriage back on Earth."

A distant shout rang through the woods. Zathdar's hand smacked to his blade. He twisted in his saddle, alert as a greyhound, while Elva was still looking around saying, "What was that? Where?"

A voice answered from much closer — a little kid. "We're still berrying, Papa!" and another even younger voice added, "Our baskets are almost full!"

I stayed quiet until we'd rounded the bluff away from the unseen berry pickers, then looked back uncertainly.

Zathdar made a polite gesture to continue.

"Mom didn't know anything about being a princess except what we get in stories, but she loved him, and the idea of adventure. So they came here. She loved Khanarenth, and people seemed to like her. Canary made a big fuss over her, like I said. She thought it was harmless flirtation. Cracked jokes, hand kissing, never carried it beyond public gatherings. And my Aunt Ananda, my father's sister, didn't seem to mind even though she'd very recently married Canary. Though Mom said she was a couple tacos short on her combination plate —"

"What?" three voices asked, right in a row. At least they were listening, I thought, laughing to myself.

"Oops. Uh, Aunt Ananda wasn't very worldly, which didn't seem to bode well for a future queen. And Dad and Mom were really popular, even though Dad wasn't all that much more worldly, for he'd been studying magic for years. To support his older sister when she ruled."

Elva hesitated again.

Devli slewed around to give me an inquiring look as his sister scowled down into the river valley.

Zathdar's expression was impossible to interpret as he checked the horizon constantly. I don't want to say he was inscrutable—he didn't do Sinister and Mysterious—but his smile was just a pleasant smile, with no clue to his thoughts.

Elva clucked to her horse, and we moved.

"I'm almost done," I said into the heavy silence. "Everything seemed fine to Mom. But she says, what does an L.A. hippie chick know about royal politics? Anyway. When the old king died, Canary stepped forward to rule in my aunt's name because she'd gone crazy from grief over her father. Canary sicced the army onto us, claiming my dad had somehow managed to commit high treason. Isn't that the usual charge usurper kings throw at the good guys?"

Devli spread his hands. "I don't know. I'd just been born."

"My ma says it's traditional," Elva called from the front.

"Don't ask me," Zathdar said when I glanced his way. "The charge I worry about is piracy, even though I'm actually a privateer."

"Okay. So War Commander Randart was apparently Canary's old friend from his youth." Three nods confirmed that. "He'd suddenly been promoted to commander in chief of the military." More nods. "He sent what seemed like a zillion soldiers to chase us."

Elva made a spitting motion over her shoulder. I remembered that pretending to spit was a lot like cussing. Actual spitting was worse than any of the sexual cusswords you hear all around you on Earth.

"Oh yeah. At some point someone told Dad that Canary claimed my father had ruined my aunt's wits with his magery, so he
could get the throne to himself. I do remember that, because it was
right before he took us to the castle and put us through the World
Gate. I guess that was the high treason. Until recently there was no
further contact. Nada."

Devli's mount stumbled on a rock half-buried in the dusty
path, causing Elva's to whicker and sidle. She bent to soothe the
animal, and Zathdar said, "What about the magic your father
taught you?"

"What about it?" I asked.

The privateer lifted a hand. "Anything of use? By which I
mean, to find your father?"

"No."

"I don't know much about magic, but it does seem that spell
you used in the castle courtyard was not parlor illusion."

"It is a strong spell, that much I know. Papa wanted to teach
me more, but we were always on the run. Maybe he thought I
could use that one." I waited for someone to call me a liar. Because
I *was* lying, at least partly.

It was true I was not even remotely properly trained. It was not
true that I knew only that spell. I knew another powerful spell, one
a beginner ought not to have been taught, but Papa had been desperate. And so, though I had yet to discover if he even lived, I kept
the promise I'd made to him before Mom and I fell through the
Gate away from him. I would keep that secret.

Devlaen sighed. Zathdar turned his attention to the path,
which switchbacked down the side of a grassy slope into a forest-
covered vale. Elva, who seemed the least interested in questions of
magic, was digging through her pack, and emerged triumphantly,
holding a roundish shape wrapped in a length of clean linen.

"Bread. Anyone hungry?"

"Yes," I exclaimed as my guts growled a hallelujah chorus.

Elva split the bread into four equal portions, passed it down
the row, and we ate as we rode.

SIX

SUN ZHAVALIESHIN CROSSED THE continent of North America, landing with the rest of the red-eye passengers in LAX on a hazy morning.

She'd had plenty of time to plan out her strategy, since she couldn't sleep. First, a cab. Second, the small mailbox place she and Sasha had agreed on years before, a couple miles from the airport. Nothing much changed in Westchester, along Sepulveda. The constant roar of planes overhead kept the area from becoming too hip and thus redesigned every couple of years, unlike some of the other communities so close to the beaches.

The mailbox place was still there. Sun asked the cabbie to wait, got out in her rumpled suit, and ran inside. Her fingers shook as she rattled the lock. She wrenched it open and sorted through the accumulation of trash mail and ads. There, behind her own postcard with the Omni Hotel info, was a postcard with Sasha's latest work and apartment addresses, dated two weeks before. They had faithfully mailed their changes each time they moved, just as promised, in case their cellphones broke, in case email didn't work . . . They knew it really meant that in case one of them vanished without a trace, there'd always be a starting place for a search.

She gave the cabbie Sasha's apartment address and sat back, eyes closed. The meter was ticking up ridiculously, but she didn't care. Either she would soon go out of the country or out of the world. Whichever it turned out to be, she had to use up these dollars.

The new apartment was in Venice. With the meter still ticking, she climbed out, immediately spotting Sasha's old rattletrap of a car. Sun paused on the doorstep long enough to straighten her linen suit and touch a hand to her hair, upswept as always. She knocked.

No answer, but she could hear the thump-thump-thump of a stereo inside. So she rapped with the metal clasp of her purse, and this time the door was opened by a tall, pretty-faced young man with a carefully tended three-day stubble. His leer turned to confusion when he looked up from Sun's bosom to her raised eyebrows. "Yah?"

"I am Sasha's mother. Is she here?"

Dougie wavered. His first instinct was to slam the door, but then he thought the woman might call the cops, and the place reeked of weed.

The woman cleared her throat. Dougie's single remaining brain cell fumbled its way back to the present. "Naw. But you can look around if you want." He opened the door, pointed toward Sasha's bedroom, and cranked up his death metal so she wouldn't grill him with stupid questions.

She marched inside the room and Dougie forgot her as he lit up another joint.

Sun shut the door against the noise and marijuana smoke, and looked around. Absolutely nothing recognizable except that silly water bed. Sun opened the closet, where a few clothes hung.

Below the clothes, two pairs of shoes sat side by side. Otherwise the closet was empty — no gear bag.

No gear bag.

Sasha never went anywhere without that bag.

Sun spotted Sasha's car keys lying on the bare desktop. She grabbed them up, drew in a deep breath, and opened the door. The noise almost blasted her back inside, but she hustled to the front door, glad the lout seemed as determined to ignore her as she wanted to ignore him. There was no use in asking him anything. She wouldn't trust whatever he said.

She stepped out, closed the door, and breathed again.

After she paid off the waiting cabbie, she got into Sasha's car. First, a search. No gear bag. The car smelled of Sasha's favorite herbal shampoo, a scent that made Sun's eyes tear, but she had to keep moving.

All right. Wherever Sasha was, she'd managed to take her gear bag with her.

So it was time to follow.

Sun drove the car to the long-term storage facility in West L.A. that she hadn't opened in years. She'd driven by once or twice, always meaning to get rid of the past and start over. But she'd never made it inside.

Now was different. Math was no longer the issue. Sasha was. Sun parked Sasha's car in the last slot and walked inside, her heart thumping an anxious drum roll.

From the thin chain she wore around her neck, she took the key she'd carried for all these long years, and found the storage locker. It wasn't very big.

Nobody else was in the place, not in the middle of a working day. She crouched down, glad she'd kept herself in shape, and opened the lock. There lay the outfit she was wearing the day they blasted through the Gate back to Los Angeles.

She took it out and buried her face in the soft, hand-woven cotton-linen from another world. It smelled a little musty, but faint, oh-so faint, remained a trace of the queensblossom rinse she'd always loved to use on her hair, and even fainter, a trace of Math's musky, male sweat, left from that last desperate clinging hug and kiss.

A zap of pain tightened her jaw, but two deep breaths and she had control again. Sasha had vanished, maybe against her will. The longer Sun messed around, the longer her search might be, for who knew what time was doing between here and there?

She looked in either direction. No one. So she stripped out of her middle-aged lady suit and pulled on the old clothes. Their softness and scent were nearly as powerful as magic in sending her emotionally back to her confused younger self, who stumbled through the World Gate into Los Angeles with a grieving child at her side, no money, nowhere to go except home—decades in Earth time after she'd left.

"Mom," Sun whispered, leaning her forehead against the cold metal of a locker.

Her mother had taken them in, though she was old. And trenchantly conservative. You don't change women of eighty, you upset them. Sun thought of her mother's wrenching hands, her angry tears, during their last fight—over her giving Sasha fencing and martial arts lessons. *She needs to be a lady, not a boy-girl, or she'll turn out like you!* At least Sasha had known her grandmother for a year, long enough for Sun to get on her feet and find work, before Gramma slipped away after a massive stroke, leaving them on their own yet again.

Time to go.

So. A quick look down. The shirt was roomy and long, the riding trousers voluminous. She tied an old, faded sash, belonging to Math, around her middle, then sat on the dusty floor and pulled off her sensible pumps. There was no leather where she was going. And no one had ever seen nylon stockings.

Her old cotton-wool socks fit over her feet, and then the soft greenweave mocs, cotton-lined inside, nubbly outside where the waxy leddas strips were woven. She stood and bounced lightly on her toes, loving the feel. The shoes were flexible, yet gripped the ground. A person could fight in those shoes. Or run. Or sit comfortably through a rainy night listening to ancient ballads—

She shook away the memory and bent down, her first instinct to bundle all her American clothes into the locker. That would not do. Who knew when she'd be back, and under what circum-stances? Maybe tomorrow. Maybe never. If so, in twenty-five years (for she was paid up that long) whoever emptied it out would find things tidy.

She pulled out the last item, a short knife her husband had given her. She hadn't brought her sword. It would have gotten her arrested in seconds. But the knife she could tie on under her trouser leg.

When she was done she straightened up and opened her purse. Nothing in there was needed except one item, which she slid out and held tightly as she put the purse, with all her money and papers, into the locker. Shut it. Locked it.

And without allowing herself time to worry, she spoke the words she'd never thought to speak, stared down at the gleaming gold transfer talisman in her hand —

Magic ripped her apart and reassembled her on the other side of the World Gate, with all the sensitivity of a giant swatting a gnat.

She landed painfully on her knees and bowed her swimming head. Yoga breathing, in, hold, out, hold. In, hold, out, hold . . . When her stomach settled, she performed some cautious yoga stretches. Very slow stretches, for fifty-year-old hips and ankles aren't as forgiving about sudden jars as twenty-year-old ones.

Gradually sound and sense returned. She picked up the transfer talisman that had fallen from her fingers and tucked it into the deep pocket in her trousers, then looked around the tower Destination chamber, apparently unchanged all these years, except by wind and weather blowing through the narrow arrow slits.

She stepped cautiously into the ancient dining room, and there were all those age-darkened tapestries hanging on the walls, as she remembered. Let's see, the old shortcut — hardly a secret passage, as everyone had used it — lay behind the middle tapestry. On the opposite side of the room, the big carved doors led to the grand stairway, and the great hall below.

Where she heard voices.

She paused. Male voices, exasperatingly blurred by the lousy acoustics of stone. She scanned. The dust and spider webs in the corners indicated that no one had been around for years. Yet here and there the dust had been disturbed. One of the old tables lay on its side, and the other had been shoved into a corner, its top mostly dust free.

So who'd been here? Sasha? No female voices —

As the speakers became more distinct, she realized two things. One, they were coming up the grand stairway, and two, she recognized Canary's voice.

Was it really Canardan Merindar? She shook her head. No, she would not mistake that charming baritone voice, the musical laughter. And they were coming *straight here.*

She tiptoed to the middle tapestry and slipped behind it, poised to run.

Moments later the voices abruptly resolved into audible clarity, meaning the speakers had entered the room through the main door.

". . . they had that door locked. Signs they'd been in here. But by the time my men got the door opened, they were gone."

"There's supposed to be another entrance," Canary said. "Probably behind one of these rotting rugs. Leave it for now. Where is the Destination chamber? Ah."

The voices diminished slightly as the two passed into the tower, but Sun heard Canary say, "There's still a strong sense of magic in here. I don't know enough about transfer magic to gauge how long it would linger. There's nothing else here. All right."

The voices got louder. "Tell me again about the fight in the court. Samdan said it was two men who'd joined those Eban brats."

Eban brats! So Steward Eban, or at least her children, are involved, Sun thought. *She was Math's most loyal —*

Listen!

". . . the pirate or the other?"

"The other, fool. Why do you hesitate?"

The second voice lowered into embarrassed formality. "Pardon me, sire. But the reports did conflict. I report only what I heard. I did not witness the fight myself. Samdan maintains he was at the front, but he was first down, a cut over his eye, then another in his knee. So his glimpse was merely that. But he insisted that, beside the Ebans and the pirate Zathdar, there was a young man in strange garb, a white shirt with odd letters. Tall, with a hawk nose, like the old king. Hair worn back in many braids."

They had stopped. Sun turned her head, gauging their position by sound: standing by the old refectory table that had been shoved into the far corner.

"Well?"

"It was Lankinar who insisted this person was actually a female. He said that the clothes were quite strange. Trousers much like deck trousers on ships, yet different, the shirt made like body singlets, but worn with nothing over it. So it was revealing, ah . . ."

Amused despite herself, Sun wondered how Mr. Official Voice was going to get around the sorts of personal details that no one ever seems to like discussing in official reports to your superior, whatever world you are on. Especially when the personal bits belonged to the likes of kings, queens, and so forth.

The man cleared his throat and tried again in a tone utterly devoid of human emotion. "Lankinar insists there was no male body in those clothes, and most of the others now agree. They saw a man possibly because they expected to see a man, possibly because she was tall, possibly because she fought as well as the pirate."

"Hawk nose, you say?" Canary let out a long breath. "Damnation. They're back. Or at least one of them."

"Who, sire?"

"Never mind. Now, my last question. Where is my son? All of you have been avoiding that question," he added grimly, with a hint of the old laughter Sun remembered. "Which is why I had to drop my own work to oversee his. Is Jehan drunk in a tavern somewhere? Or holed up with some pretty minstrel girl who caught his eye?"

"Uh, no, sire. Prince Jehan did detail the extra ridings to us, you'll remember."

"Don't excuse him. Tell me where he is."

"He rode down to Sarendan. A sculptor. Famed, he said. Wanted to pose for him. Present you with a marble bust as a surprise."

Canary gave a bitter laugh, and Sun remembered him long ago saying, *My boy is too much like his mother.* His heels rang on the floor as he moved through the door. "Finish the search, and send someone to remind Jehan that art, though no doubt admirable, must wait on events . . ." Their voices faded.

Sun leaned against the moldy wall. *Tall, many braids. Hawk nose.* Sasha was here. She was alive. She was also free, and had escaped Canary's clutches, in spite of a fight.

All right, then. Food first. Sleep. Where to begin the search? The brief reference to a pirate made no sense, but "the Eban brats" did. Obviously Sasha was on her way to Steward Eban. *And so thither go I.*

SEVEN

ONE OF THE MANY euphemisms for chamber pot is 'necessary.' I can introduce the necessary topic once and then never again. It was a relief, oh, what a relief, to be able to use the Waste Spell.

When I was ten and new to Earth, I had to learn about toilets. Let me sum it all up in one word: yuk. The Waste Spell did work—sometimes—as magical influence ebbed and flowed through the Gate. But since using the spell involves saying the word at the same time you let go, well, you can imagine how trustworthy that spell turned out to be on Earth.

We paused and drank from a stream, after which I used the spell, celebrating inwardly at the notion of no more restroom hunts.

We rode on.

Conversation was tense and desultory, mostly between Elva and her brother as they brangled about where to go. I was so tired I only wanted to sleep, so I was content to follow, listen, and breathe in the fresh air. Zathdar seemed busy keeping watch.

When it was too dark to travel, we camped in a small clearing under a clump of low-hanging willow. When Elva and Devli began yet another argument about whether or not they could risk a fire, Zathdar said, "You have a Fire Stick, right?" And on their twin nods, "No one will search for the same reason we're camping. They can't see to travel at night any better than we can. As soon as we get these animals rubbed down, I'll pace the perimeter, make sure the fire isn't visible."

Elva pulled the packs off the horses before Devli and Zathdar led the animals a few yards away to where a stream trickled. Elva took a Fire Stick from her pack. She snapped it into flame and made a gesture that would keep the flame low.

Presently Devli returned and sank down with a sigh. "Horses are fine."

Zathdar returned shortly after. "As I thought, these woods are dense. Fire's invisible on all side but from up the trail. Whichever of us is on guard could probably hear any pursuit before they could see the glow."

Devli mouthed the word "Guard?" and Elva scowled again.

Zathdar hitched the rapier over his shoulder on a baldric, checked the other blade, then chose a grassy spot from which he could see the trail and us. While the siblings exchanged low-voiced talk about bedrolls, feedbags and stored food, I took out my splendid embroidered blanket to spread on the soft green grass.

In the sudden silence, foliage rustling in the summer breeze and the snap of the low fire were distinct. The ruddy glow revealed three faces staring at the glinting firebirds embroidered in gold thread on the scarlet background, surrounded by silver-edged white blossoms.

"If anyone wants proof of who you are," Zathdar commented, "that banner is it."

"Right now," I said, fighting a yawn, "it's a bedroll. In the morning it goes back into my bag. And no, I won't ditch it. My father gave it to me."

Devlaen stared at me, Elva stared at the firebird blanket, and Zathdar glanced in the direction of my bag, then away into the darkness.

Nobody spoke.

I fell asleep so fast I don't even remember stretching out.

Crackling twigs woke me, and the smell of fresh tea. The sky through the trees was low and gray, the air cool and misty. I sat up, shivering, and accepted gladly a somewhat-battered travel cup from Devli, whose face looked as grimy as mine felt.

The tea tasted like a fine Gyokoro green tea at home, refreshing and above all, warm. I'd forgotten that summers on this world were usually cooler than Earth's. Khanerenth lay at the eastern end of the enormous continent that stretched a good way around the southern hemisphere. Most people lived on this continent, I'd learned, in part because there was more sun, but in part because some of the northern lands were weird and wild, not conducive to humans building cities.

Elva snapped the fire out, and picked up the Fire Stick to stow away in her pack.

"Where is Zathdar?" I asked.

"He was gone before we woke." Elva grinned. "Hope that means he's gone for good."

"No." Devli cocked his head.

We all heard the thud and crunch of horse hooves on the trail.

Elva flushed, though we could all see that he was as yet too far away to have heard.

Zathdar appeared, leading his horse by the reins. "Time to move briskly. The king investigated the tower himself last night. And he knows you are here." A glance my way.

Elva put her hands on her hips. "You found this out how?"

"I dispatched watchers before I met up with you. I also set up a possible rendezvous, which I kept while you were all asleep."

"Watchers." Devli said only the one word, but the look he gave his sister made it clear that once again they'd forgotten an important detail in their own plans.

Elva scowled as we mounted up. The horses, refreshed after a night of rest, trotted with head-rocking enthusiasm down the narrow trail.

We were low enough now to see the broad stream that all the mountain trickles were feeding into. The constant rush of white water paralleled us as the trail twisted between steep slopes, green with tough grass, gnarly pine and moss-covered rocks. The mist increased to drifting streamers of fog; the forest canopy was so thick we heard the constant splat, splat, splat of water on leaves.

I stayed out of their sporadic talk, which was mostly about the trail and where the searchers might be.

I was awake and alert enough to consider my options. The day before all I could do was follow along and try to keep my eyes open. Now, though I was hungry, thirsty, and still tired, at least I could think.

So . . . what should I do? No use in going back to the castle. Even if I knew any World Gate transfer magic, which I didn't, if the king's men were there, I'd walk straight into their clutches without them having to break a sweat. And while we'd managed to fight our way free of yesterday's guys, I wasn't going to count on that twice. Especially alone.

That left me with my companions. Should I ditch them? Good thing: they had rescued me from capture in the courtyard. Bad thing: at least two of them had been part of forcing me through the World Gate in the first place. Therefore I did not owe them anything.

We paused once on a cliff, and I drew up beside Zathdar. He slanted a questioning look at me. I said, "I assume the World Gate tower is guarded."

"You can't go back. They're watching for you to do that."

I laid the reins along my horse's neck. The animal obligingly swung round and stopped, blocking the trail so the brother and sister drew to a halt. "Before we go on, I wish you would tell me why you forced me through that Gate."

Devlaen sent a pleading look at his sister, but she studied her saddlebag as though it held the One Ring.

"I told you." Devlaen fiercely rubbed grit from his eyes. "It was a promise made to your father. If he vanished we were to wait ten years, then perform a specific spell. It brought us a letter he'd written, telling us where you and your mother were. But the letter disappeared, and we were afraid the king also got that information. We thought it best to get you two safely back here, where we could guard you." His face reddened. "I know what that sounds like. But we were going to bring you only for your own good!"

I decided against a pithy opinion about what they could do with their notions of 'my own good.' "Go on."

"My mage tutor was certain they were ordered to offer you anything you wanted if you would go back with them. They were not well prepared. I don't think anyone was surprised when they came back empty handed, but rumor has it the king demanded that they cross over to that world before we could. So when they returned without you or your mother, they had the World Gate transfer magic to build all over again."

My father had told me that transfer magic took weeks and weeks to make. It was actually a complicated layer of spells put on those transfer tokens. "The king's mages being two older guys? One gray haired?" I asked.

Devli grimaced. "Magisters Perran and Zhavic."

"My mother mentioned them once or twice. It seems weird that they knew my mother, yet came after me first. And tried to trick me! Truth, honor, sinister castles, secrets—"

Devli shrugged. "All that is in the records. When your mother first came, she said she liked such things. So the mages tried to lure you with them, the fools."

"Yes, but at least they tried truth and justice. They didn't pretend to be a lawyer!"

"Heh." Devli's shoulders now shrugged up around his ears, which were as red as his face. He said with the air of a guy picking his way over a minefield, "When your mother wouldn't come with me, I had to find you. It took some time, because you'd changed location. And, see, we've notes from your father. About what he really saw on that world. So I had to find you, lay a false trail for Perran and Zhavic, and put together a plan. And. Um."

"Lied and tricked me. Yes. As I just said. What I'm trying to get at is why."

"I told you, they're *after* you—"

Zathdar had been watching the sky, the fog-blurred treetops, and the shadowy trail that vanished under the forest canopy. I couldn't see or hear anything amiss, but apparently he heard enough to cut in, "I think the rest of the explanation should wait on more trustworthy surroundings."

Without waiting for an answer, he urged his horse down the trail, and we followed, Elva with many backward glances. Beyond the next bend we found the white water of the river where our mountain stream poured in. The bend after that revealed that the river had smoothed and widened. We rode along its bank. I clutched my gear bag to my side, wishing I had more answers. One thing seemed certain, on land I had more freedom of movement. On a ship, I'd be stuck.

We rounded the last hill and there, anchored fore and aft in the middle of the river, lay a pirate ship.

I had the haziest memory of ships from childhood, due to nighttime smugglings on and off, and being hidden in holds. Since then, I hadn't learned much more beyond what I'd read in the novels of Patrick O'Brian, but when I saw that graceful, wickedly lean schooner with its tall, raked-back masts, the long gaff mainsails and the reefed topsail, the narrow hull with the half-deck forecastle and aftcastle, I knew instantly it could be nothing but a pirate ship.

And I longed to be on it.

"Like my *Hurricane*?"

Reluctantly I shifted my gaze, to find Zathdar riding beside me, smiling. I asked, "What chance would you give for me sneaking back into the tower?"

"Why?" he countered, his smile fading, his eyes watchful.

"Because at the very least I need to send a message to warn my mother. I vanished without leaving any word. I know she'll be after me, soon's she figures it out."

He stared down at his ship, brow furrowed. "If you go back to that tower and transfer between worlds, I'd say your chances of leading the king's mages straight to her would be high."

"Oh." I didn't bother telling him I couldn't even do a transfer.

He moved forward again, a kind of nonverbal coercion, and to test it I said, "Aren't you in a bit of a hurry to get us on that ship? I mean, I don't see any danger on the road back up on the hill."

Elva's head turned sharply, her mist-washed face wary.

"Just because you don't see it doesn't mean it isn't there." Zathdar lifted a hand, indicating the forest-covered mountain we'd just ridden out of. "The search will be going out in rings. With the king there himself, instead of War Commander Randart, they will be even more determined to be the ones to nail you down. Then there's the fact that they will have heard from the defeated warriors that I was there."

"And?" I winced, realizing the implications at last. "Oh, I didn't think of that. What, a blockade?"

"I expect the king's messengers are riding belly flat to the ground to all the signal points right this moment, yes. And while I don't mind running a blockade, I prefer to choose the time, and the place, if I can."

"So what you are proposing," I said, "is that we all take ship, and you'll let us off somewhere out of the range of the search?"

"Yes."

"Sounds fair to me." I was relieved at having made a decision. "Lead on."

Elva sighed in disgust. Devlaen did not hide his relief.

We soon reached the pirate ship, which the crew had edged downstream while we were closing the distance. The lee rail had been anchored fairly close to an outcropping. A gangplank had been extended to a broad, mostly flat granite rock. A young boy ran over experimentally as Zathdar rode ahead of us.

Zathdar dismounted and handed his reins to the boy. He hefted his travel pack from the horse and slung it over the opposite shoulder from his sword as he waited for us to dismount.

The boy, maybe twelve, grinned as he collected my reins. The other two left their horses with him and retrieved their packs. I tucked my gear bag tightly under my armpit.

Devli trod first over the gangway. One by one we jumped onto the deck, Zathdar last. Behind us, the boy mounted a horse and led the other animals back up the trail, where they were soon swallowed by the woods.

"That kid going to be okay?" I asked.

"Okay?" Zathdar repeated the English word.

"Safe. Fine. Good."

"Ah. Yes. He's my local eyes. His uncle runs an inn, so the horses will become part of his lending stock before we clear the estuary."

As he spoke the sailors divided into work parties, some pulling in the gangplank, others going to the sail ropes. Zathdar indicated we should go aft, down a few steps with a carved handrail, and into a cabin that spread across the back of the vessel, the walls and stern windows slanting in at a graceful angle. This had to be the captain's cabin.

Elva looked around with the air of an experienced sailor. Devlaen seemed more anxious to keep his balance as he clasped his bulky pack to himself. The siblings halted just inside the door of the captain's cabin, blocking the way.

So I turned my attention back to the smooth, slightly sloping deck. The crew seemed to be mostly made up of young people, females as well as males. Here and there a gray head was visible among the varying shades of brown, black, red, and blond. Some dressed gaudily like their captain, others wore plain homespun shirts and brown-dyed deck trousers. These were like hip-hugger bell-bottoms of my mom's day. Almost all of the crew went barefoot.

On a signal the sails loosed, placketing loudly until the wind caught and filled them so they belled in the slow-moving breeze. The ship surged on the river, water chuckling down the sides.

"Go inside." Zathdar's open-handed gesture was just a tad ironic. "I assure you, there are no trapdoors."

Devli and Elva shuffled farther inside the cabin, gazes flicking warily this way and that. Zathdar's head barely cleared the bulkheads, as did mine. A circular table had been built into the center of the cabin, around which were set cushioned low chairs. I chose the empty one between the siblings. Zathdar left the only vacant chair and moved to the stern windows, through which he peered out at the trail we'd descended.

No pursuit appeared before we rounded a bend and a hill hid the trail from view.

Zathdar faced us. "The short version of what I discovered at my rendezvous is that the king sent his son with a sizable force to take anyone found in the tower. Apparently the prince changed his mind when they arrived just ahead of you and found the place empty. He left the two ridings we met—all inexperienced men— and took the better ones as an honor guard on an art quest southward. He seems to have heard about some famous sculptor—"

Devli snickered in a familiar teenage-boy way.

"—or we'd all be guests of the king right now." Zathdar made an ironic gesture, putting his wrists together as if shackled.

"Art quest," Elva repeated, laughing with her brother. "I've heard all about those art quests of his. What d'you want to wager that sculptor is pretty?"

Zathdar spread his hands, obviously uninterested in sculptors, pretty or not.

"What now?" Devlaen asked.

I said, "Canary has a son? Why would he put a boy in charge of warriors?"

Elva waved a hand. "He's older than all of us. Didn't you know? Canardan Merindar was married to someone else before he married the queen. A morvende. They had a son before the marriage ended. The gossip is, he ended the marriage so he could marry Queen Ananda, and the prince's mother went back to the morvende."

"Well that would explain the prince's interest in art. I mean, what I remember is that the morvende are the deep-cave dwellers who don't have governments, but do lots of singing and painting and archive keeping. And magic."

Devlaen's wistful expression made it clear where his own interests lay.

"I never met any son, though." I shook my head. "I wouldn't have forgotten that."

"But he wasn't in the country for a long time." Elva jerked her thumb toward the west. "He got sent off to those barbarians at the other end of the continent to some military school. When he was done with their lessons in marching, he got sent off somewhere else, I don't know where, but that's not important. The important thing is that he's about as sky-eyed as the queen. Won't set foot on ships. Gets sick. Hates getting dirty, so he won't drill with the castle guard, though he supposedly commands them. The king tries to get him to take charge of guard business, but if he passes by some house with a good mural, or some fine weaving, or hears a new melody, he's as likely to leave the army sitting there in the sun while he chats with some old bard or sculptor or weaver. Especially if the artist is female."

"I'm surprised Canary hasn't killed him," I exclaimed. "Unless he's mellowed since the days he wanted my parents dead. Probably me, too," I added.

"Oh no." Elva waved her hands. "He wanted you alive. To bring up and then marry off to the idiot prince, according to the gossip my mother was hearing from castle people, before she was turned off. Then nobody could complain about your father being ousted."

"What?" I jerked upright. "I never knew that!"

Zathdar said, "It's true. That's why your father had to hide you before he could act."

Devlaen smacked the table. "My mage tutor says the king probably would have killed off Prince Jehan a long time ago if there wasn't a severe shortage of heirs."

"There's also the fact that though he's an idiot, the prince managed somehow to make himself popular." Elva made a disgusted face. "Even though he never gets anything done."

"Maybe *because* he never gets anything done. He never gives orders, just hands out money, and follows after any pretty bard or artist. Our mother says that the government is a mess," Devlaen put in. "Ma told us the king is now trying to arrange a marriage to any suitable princess who will accept a bumbling fool so he can get grandchildren and train *them* in his wonderful ways."

"Ah, speaking of wonderful." Zathdar indicated the cabin door. Three sailors entered, each carrying a tray. Good smells filled the cabin as they set the trays on the table.

Zathdar slapped together a sizable sandwich between slices of very fresh bread and ducked out. His voice drifted from the deck as he issued rapid orders.

The thundering sails and the groan of wood smothered most of his words. I caught a few: lookouts, signals, line of sight. I suspected that the rest of Zathdar's fleet was guarding the river mouth from the sea. As soon as we joined them, they'd be running for open water, spread as far as possible so as to spot any fleets on the horizon.

"So what do you want to do?" Elva asked, recalling my attention. "I mean, after he puts us ashore again."

I needed time to consider my words. I took a bite of a rice-and-cheese stuffed cabbage roll. It tasted like a pot sticker or spring roll.

When my father taught me that last bit of magic, he'd told me there were two plans. The best one was that he'd come himself to get us. The second best would be his old teacher, Magister Glathan, coming for us. That would mean Dad had had to hide in a certain place, but I had memorized the release spell. The magister wouldn't know it in case they caught him and tried to get it out of him.

The worst would be that no one came.

And the worst had happened.

Nobody had said if Dad or Magister Glathan were alive, but I knew where to go to find out about my father. I also knew what to do. What I did not know was whether or not I could trust these people. If Dad was alive but under protective enchantment, what good would it do to perform the spell, just to bring him back straight into danger? "I wish I could contact my mother. She is going to be so worried."

"If they find her, she'll be a prisoner," Devlaen said soberly.

I sighed.

Zathdar reappeared, the fringes on his bandana dancing in the freshening wind. "Soon's you're done I'll show you your cabin." He turned from me to Elva. "If you don't want to bunk in the crew quarters, you can share with her. There are two bunks in the forward cabin."

Elva looked mutinous, but Devlaen half raised a hand as if in supplication. Elva scowled at Zathdar. "I'll stay with the princess. Since you already have a navigator."

Princess. I laughed.

Everyone turned my way.

I waved a hand. "Never mind. It's the princess thing. Took me by surprise. Not that I actually am one. My dad was replaced by a new king."

"But people remember. Your father was very popular. That's why we've found so many people to help us." Devlaen pointed to his sister and himself.

Elva grinned. "And so was Princess Atanial."

"Atanial." Sartoran for "shining sun". I'd forgotten that. My throat tightened, causing me to breathe deeply the way Mom had taught me. I didn't know if I wanted her to find out I was here or not, and have to deal with all the memories and the pain of the questions we could not answer.

So I rose and Zathdar led us forward along the gangway. We dodged around busy crew members. I noticed that nobody stopped or saluted or any of that. Some of the sailors (and they looked to me more like sailors than like my idea of pirates) sang as they hauled on halyards. Others high on the masts talked cheerily.

The forecastle cabin was narrow but pleasant, two bunks built into the sharply curving bow with storage built below each bunk, scuttles for air, and two little fold-down tables on either side of the door. Someone had set neatly piled clothing on one of the bunks, both of which had soft cotton-wool blankets on them.

Zathdar stood on the deck immediately outside the door, for there wasn't much space inside. He ducked his head under the low, carved lintel and indicated the pile of clothing with an open hand. "Donations. Hope something fits."

Elva threw her knapsack onto the other bunk.

"There's a cleaning frame down in the crew's quarters. We all share it." Zathdar nodded at my bag. "If you want that stowed below, I can take it."

"No thank you." I kept the bag gripped in my arms.

They looked at me, and Elva said diffidently, "What do you have in that thing, anyway?"

"Just a lot of boring paperwork of the sort you need on Earth. And a few childhood keepsakes."

"Oh." Elva turned away and busied herself with unpacking her knapsack—all three things.

Zathdar leaned there still, arms over his head and braced against the lintel, one hand dangling beside his fringed bandana. He didn't look the least bit threatening, but Elva set aside the knapsack and scowled at him, her shoulders tight, arms crossed and held close.

"I'll send over the remains of the meal in case you get hungry." He turned away, letting sunlight stream into the cabin, and ran up onto the aftdeck to oversee our emergence from the river into the sea.

EIGHT

SUN REMEMBERED THE ANCIENT castle. It had belonged to the crown (whatever family was currently wearing it) for centuries, with occasional zigzags into the hands of rebellious dukes and princes, and once it was a mage school, established by a princess whose older sister was the heir.

On their very first arrival through the World Gate, Math had conducted her all over the castle, relating its colorful history and pointing out with boyish delight various sites of magical traps and illusions. *Ever since the old mage school was closed,* Math had said, *the mages keep insisting they got them all, but then people discover new ones. In fact, Magister Glathan — he's my tutor, I hope you will come to love him as I do — made me go through until I discovered one, as my own master's test.*

The one Prince Mathias had discovered lay behind what appeared to be solid wall. Beyond that illusory section of wall, Sun remembered, someone had built a cozy little room. There they spent their first night in this world, and their last. The first in a fire of young and ardent love, the last in close-hugging sorrow at the imminence of parting, their tired, bewildered ten-year-old daughter pressed between them for comfort. That they gave. They also kept her between them for safety, which they could only try to give.

Sun turned away from the dining hall, and lifted the tapestry, peering into the mold-walled passage. Even dimly lit by the weak glowglobe, it clearly had not been disturbed for a long time. She trod carefully to the end, avoiding leaving footprints on the mold splotches, but instead of passing down the narrow circular stairs, she turned to the left and cautiously put out her hand.

Cold, damp air chilled her fingers. Yes, the illusion was intact. She held her breath and plunged through. Safely inside, she clapped once. The glowglobe lit, though it, too, was very dim.

Thick, rotting cloth hung on an old rod over the illusory door. She pushed the curtain along the rod, which would block light breaking the illusion, and turned around.

The windowless little room appeared to be untouched. There was the narrow cot on which Sasha had lain her last night in this world, after Math taught her some spells. Difficult spells—far too complicated, one would think, for a child. But Math and Glathan had been desperate, and Sasha brave and determined until she could stay awake no longer.

Sasha had curled up on the bed, and the mage left to walk the perimeter as well as to give them privacy.

Math and Sun had sat shoulder to shoulder, guarding their daughter's slumber while they talked and talked, making promises and contingency plans.

All in vain.

Sun turned in a slow circle. There was the old carved chest, its pattern of running horses so heartbreakingly familiar. She lifted the lid, sniffing in the scent of cedarwood, and pulled out one of the soft yeath blankets, and a sturdy tunic of Math's that she herself had packed away. It was brown livery, the silver-and-crimson firebird of the Zhavalieshins stitched on the front.

No more sorrow. You've wept enough. So you are back at last. Find Sasha. And then find out what happened to Math instead of wasting the rest of your life wondering.

She lay on the cot under the blanket, clapped the globe out and fell asleep, waking suddenly when men's voices brought her sitting up in alarm. She pressed her hands over her mouth, then remembered the illusory wall. She could hear anyone in the passage outside, but if she made noise, they'd hear her.

"...not much of a secret, if you ask me," came an unfamiliar tenor voice.

"More of a shortcut." That deep, slightly husky voice was familiar, a voice from nightmares. It belonged to Dannath Randart, Canary's right-hand slimebag. "But the king said, add it to the patrol sites. It and the main stairway through that old refectory are the only way to the Destination chamber, and he seems to think someone is using magic to come or go."

"All right. But what are we watching for?"

Two sets of footsteps started down the narrow tower stairs, and Sun knew the voices would soon fade. She hesitated, then eased the curtain back and plunged through the icy illusory wall. She tiptoed barefoot to the stairs, grimacing at the feel of cold slimy moss.

"Anyone. Anyone at all. But the king mentioned females."

"Commander? We were all shifted from badly needed coastal patrol to watch a castle for . . . women?"

Sun followed down two, three more steps. *Come on, Randart, you know you want to tell him*, she urged mentally.

"Yes," War Commander Randart said shortly as he reached the arched tower door. "And if any appear, bring them straight to the king. To no one else. No matter who they are. No matter what they say."

The creak of the heavy door caused Sun to crouch on her step and peer around the angled stairs. A shaft of early morning sunlight outlined Randart's tall, broad-shouldered form. Except for looking older and even tougher, he hadn't changed much. His shaggy dark hair was graying, his hard face lined. The other man was also tall and broad, as you'd expect from the king's own men-at-arms. Younger than Randart, though.

He thrust the door open and morning light lanced halfway up the stairs, stopping just short of her toes. The men thumped the door shut behind them and the poised bar *thocked* into place.

Sun slipped back upstairs to the secret room. She ripped the tarnished silver stitching from the brown tunic, and the bits of rotted red silk. Mentally she heard Math's laughing voice. *Livery was supposed to be gold. Silver and gold. But for a long time they couldn't get the dyes to match, and so the runners and warriors were galloping around in pumpkin orange, rust, even pink and yellow, if the sun changed the dye. Not exactly impressive! Finally they settled on brown.*

They were still wearing brown, she'd seen. But with the Merindar cup over the heart, and not the firebird of the Zhavalieshins.

She packed her things together, dug underneath the folded clothes, and brought up the rapier she'd laid in the chest that last night.

Her hands were calm as she pulled the baldric over her shoulder and shifted the sword to her hip. She undid the knife from under her trousers and strapped it on outside. The little knife came next, tucked sideways into her sash the way Math had taught her so long ago.

She knew who the enemy was now, and where to go. But first she had to get out of the castle without being seen.

After a quick listen at the false door, back she trod down to the tower door that led to the courtyard adjacent to the stable. From the courtyard outside came the muted clatter of horse hooves. Ah, that would be Randart's departure. The watch had changed, and the patrols were just beginning. Now was the time to slip out, before the newcomers had discovered all the blind spots and had deployed watchers to cover them.

And hopefully before they'd had their morning coffee and were awake.

As she eased the door open, she smiled, remembering her discovery so long ago that this world had coffee. Proof that the humans here were indeed from Earth—coffee and chocolate. Her smile was a little sad. She could remember thinking, What can go wrong, if a world is beautiful and has magic, coffee and chocolate?

Answer: it also has humans, with all the familiar greed, ambition, and intent. Ah well.

Courtyard. Open. With no better route out of the castle, she eased along the inner wall, watching the sentry walk opposite. So far, no one in view along those crenellations. Randart had probably concentrated the guards around the Destination tower on the other side of the courtyard, inside as well as out.

She slunk farther along the wall, one hand on her sword to keep it from scraping the stone. A flicker in her peripheral vision made her duck behind a hay cart tucked in the corner next to the stable door.

She crouched down and peered between the hay mound and the cart's seat up at the opposite wall, along which walked two guards carrying spears, one of the men wolfing down a bread-and-cheese sandwich, his spear tucked in the crook of his arm. From their shuffling gait and their desultory conversation, she figured they'd just been woken up. The real go-getters were probably searching more methodically inside.

Good. Her job now was to keep it that way.

As soon as they passed beyond the lower tower, she slipped around the cart and into the stable. The animals paid little attention. Heads bobbed in the loose boxes as stable hands rubbed down the mounts that had galloped in that morning. She ghost-footed past. Some of the horses twitched ears at her, and one snorted, but the stable hands were too occupied to pay attention.

She found another door adjacent to a tack room, and sneaked out. The long early morning shadows stretched westward, with two silhouetted guards standing at either end of the wall. The road leading up to the stable entrance bisected a broad grassy expanse, no cover whatsoever.

So she hugged the wall until she reached the north side, with its rough terrain overgrown with weeds and brush. None of it had been cleared away for decades.

Picking her way with care over the rough, rocky ground—she did not want to rustle the shrubs—she eased away from the castle until she reached the shelter of a stand of young maples on a ridge. Now hidden from the castle's walls by their thick canopy, she slipped onto a narrow animal path and hurried downhill to the stream that fed the castle's water supply, and thence along the stream until the castle slid out of sight.

The stream zigzagged steadily downhill. She paused to drink from the cold, clear water from time to time, then clambered awkwardly parallel to the stream, toiling uphill when the ground rose.

Her stomach roiled with hunger by the time she reached flat ground. But no convenient fruit trees grew in the middle of that blossoming forest of mostly cedar, maple, with chestnut trees here and there. The season was early summer, from the look of the bright green growth and the heady sweet smell of bloom. Birds twittered, cheeped and warbled everywhere, hidden by the green canopy overhead. No nuts would fall for months.

At least she'd stumbled upon an old road, shaded by massive oak and maples. Here the air was considerably cooler, and she was no longer being scratched by shrubs, all of which seemed to grow prickly leaves. She stretched out her legs, forcing herself up to a rapid march. The plain brown tunic would mark her as a runner. If she came upon any of Canary's men, she would lie like a rug about being a messenger, and hope that old names and castles matched up with present owners.

The sun glinted high overhead when her ears registered a sound that didn't belong in the rustle of a midday forest landscape. Math had told her, *Don't try to identify every sound and sight, only those that don't belong.*

Instinct got the message first. When her mind caught up with the Danger Flag, she discovered both sword and knife in hand. She hefted them, regretting the two years since her last fencing lesson, and faced the three scruffy highwaymen.

Two feints from either side and she knew they were used to working together, though they moved slowly, their strokes perfunctory instead of precise. She'd instinctively turned her back to an enormous thornberry tree, so the three could not surround her. They stayed well out of one another's range as they tried to close in from either side.

She used her old backup tricks: kicked dirt up into the face of the first, lunged at the second, and while he was shifting his weight to block and the third side-stepped to back him up, she whirled and cut low. Her point stabbed the knee of the third guy, who'd shifted to back up his pal.

He let out a howl as his partner slashed down at her. She flourished her blade into a spiraling downward block, turning the strike toward the ground.

By then Dirtface had recovered, and switched his sword from one hand to the other. The angle of his wrists, the set of his shoulders, caught at memory. She flicked a look at his face. About her own age, heavy chin, big jug-handle ears—

"I know you," she exclaimed, backing up, her point hovering midway between the two on their feet.

The pair also halted, Dirtface squinting.

"You were one of Math's men." She waved her sword for emphasis. "Robbing people?"

Dirtface gaped. "Your—your highness?" He turned to the others. "That accent. It's her highness. Princess Atanial!"

Atanial! The name Sun hadn't heard for fifteen years, the last time being spoken by Math, just before kissing her goodbye. *Atan—bright sun—my darling.* With his kiss warm on her lips, he'd pushed her through the World Gate.

"Hoo." The second one looked away guiltily.

"Still in . . . practice," the third whispered, voice tight with pain. He sat in the dirt, hands pressed to his knee as blood seeped nastily between his fingers.

She flung down her sword, heedless of the others holding their weapons. "Let me look at that knee. It felt like my point went in too far."

"Oh yes. Oh yes," the man muttered, teeth clenched.

"Well, what are you idiots doing holding people up? Math

must be dead or he'd die of shame."

Three variations of upset and dismay faced her.

Dirtface, he of the ears, said, "We never heard he was dead. But he isn't here, either."

The second man, the leanest one, with a thin ferret face, had been silent a while. He jerked his thumb at his taller companion. "Ye recognized them ears. Didn't ya?"

Sun laughed. "Yes. I don't suppose you fellows have anything to eat?"

Dirtface had pulled a length of mostly clean cloth from the pouch at his sash, which he handed down to her. She helped the man she'd wounded to shove up his trouser leg, and she bound his knee snugly.

Dirtface nodded approval when she was done. "If we did, we'd be eatin' and not robbin'."

Sun laughed again, winning rueful smiles from the others. "So here we are. Four middle-aged folks starving in the middle of the forest. Three running from the law one way and one running from the law the other, I guess? Come on, let's at least find a stream. I badly need information." She added wryly, "And to rest my bones."

The two helped their companion up, and they made their way off the road to the river, which ran more or less parallel. They washed faces and hands, and the wounded man soaked his leg in the water, then rebound the bandage. They sat on the grass, Sun with shoes and socks off. She hadn't walked so far in ages. Her feet hurt. It felt wonderful to soak them in the cold stream.

She kicked her toes in and out of the sparkling water, sensing that the armsmen—former armsmen—were uneasy. "I arrived in Khanerenth last night. My daughter is here, apparently in the company of some pirate."

Dirtface pursed his lips. "If it's Zathdar, she'll be held for ransom from the king. If someone else, no telling what's going on."

"What can you tell me about this Zathdar?"

Dirtface shrugged. The second man said, "Rumor from the coast has it he attacks the king's fleet. Keeps 'em in a stir. Messin' up trade. Randart has a prince's fortune on his head as bounty. But no one can catch him. They can't find his lair."

"I mean to find my daughter, lair or no lair." Sun smacked her hands on her knees. "First I need to know a few things. Like, what year is it? What is the last you heard about Math? And—forgive me—but why are you robbing people?"

Dirtface looked at the others, who all deferred to him. "The year is '54. No word of the prince for ten years, now. And we took to the road because there is no other way to fill our bellies."

"Of course the times don't match up," she murmured. "I should have known that. But what's this about no way to earn a living?"

"The King." Dirtface made a spitting motion to the side. "He threw us out of the castle guard. Said lay down arms and disperse or he'd hang us all, meaning Prince Math's guard, man and woman. Some found work. Others found closed doors and threats. *We* got the doors and threats. Not even a stable would take us."

"It's them ears, see," put in the second man, with a thumb toward Dirtface. "Everyone knows the Silvag family. Personal guards to Zhavalieshins for time out of mind. Big ears, every one."

"True." The third man winced. "And we don't know anything but sword and horse."

"What about teaching at that war school?" Sun asked. "Though I remember it was mostly maritime, still—"

"Closed in '34." Silvag lifted a shoulder.

"Opened again after the Siamis War," the second one said. "But Commander Randart made certain none of *us* can poke a nose near the place."

Siamis War? Who or what or where was that? Obviously she had some history to catch up on. But that could come later. "All right, then answer me this. Do you know where Steward Eban lives?"

"Everyone knows that. Everyone from the old days," Silvag

scrupulously amended. "But they watch her place day and night. Especially since spring."

"Well, good to know." Sun forced herself to be cheerful. "Then we'll have some time on the walk to figure a way in, won't we?"

"We?" Silvag said, and Sun saw the wary hope in his face, and heard it in his gruff voice.

"Unless you'd rather stay around here and rob people. I want to find my daughter, and then find Math. It looks like he's needed."

Nine

WHEN I SAW ZATHDAR the next morning, I actually stopped right in my tracks. Poor Elva thumped into me from behind.

She peered around my arm, then snorted. "Ugh. Talk about swagger."

Zathdar flicked his crimson silk shirt, turning this way and that. That shirt was so gaudy it was barbaric with its black and gold embroidery in highly stylized patterns of raptors on the wing. "Handsome, isn't it?" He preened, grinning at Elva. "Bought it in an old pirate cove on the other side of the world. Couldn't resist."

"But . . . couldn't you have found a bandana to match?" I pointed at the glorious green and gold silk tied round his head. This one had even longer fringes than his last. His trousers were sturdy black cotton-wool, but he made up for that lapse into sobriety with a purple sash. "And . . . purple with crimson? Wait, I'm asking that of a guy who wore orange and green together yesterday, with a crimson vest. Never mind."

He spread his hands. "My captains on the other ships have to be able to see me."

I turned to Elva. "That does kind of make sense."

"Signal flags make more sense." She eyed the grinning privateer.

"Not in the middle of battle when everyone is too busy to hoist flags. Speaking of which, since the winds are contrary, we're about to conduct morning drill. If you'd like to watch, feel free, but I must warn you that the gangways here will be busy." He indicated the deck running along the rail on either side of the masts, curving in toward the bow.

I pointed at an elegant rowboat on two hoists. "Shall we watch from there?"

He extended a hand and we clambered up into it.

Someone rang the ship's bell in a fast pattern—*ting-ting, ting-ting, ting-ting*—and the crew stampeded to battle stations, some with smoking firepots, others carrying arrows dipped in oil, and bows, and the youngsters with buckets of sand, presumably to put out any fires the enemy started.

There were no cannons, of course. I remembered that from childhood. My mother had explained that gunpowder did not work on this world, whether because of the cooler, wetter climate or because of some magical influence, she wasn't clear. But no cannon meant longer, lighter, faster ships than those of the Earth age of sail—and completely different fighting tactics.

The crew hauled expertly on steel-edged booms—like long knives on poles—to be swung out to cut enemy rigging, and sweep along the rail of the enemy to lethal effect. Archery parties in the tops went through the motions of shooting arrows, and the sail crews practiced snapping sails out, up, around as the captain called orders. The people at the helm caused the ship to veer and yaw.

"Not bad," Zathdar called out when at last the ship rocked in the water, sails reefed, crew watching him expectantly.

He flicked up his eyeglass and trained it on the closest of the consorts, the *Jumping Bug*. Their crew was still running about the deck.

"But not good, either. Again."

The first mate drowned mutters and groans with a high, tweeting whistle. Once again they ran to their stations.

Next he had the other two of his ships attack. This time the bow crews shot blunted arrows with what looked like paper twists of jelly or some red, sticky substance at the tips, which scored hits on crew and ship alike. The ships yawed and slanted even faster, each trying to board the others, to be vigorously beaten back with wooden practice weapons. By noon they were all red-faced and sweaty, but their motions had tightened to a smoother speed. They had shifted from thinking about what to do to automatic reaction. That's the point of drills, I'd learned during my years at the dojo, and on the fencing floor.

The bells rang a slower pattern, and everyone relaxed, talking as they put away their practice weapons and lined up for water. The captains of the two other ships rowed over and climbed up, then vanished into Zathdar's cabin for a conference. Zathdar kept the door shut, and the helmsman made certain no one walked about on the little half-deck where his scuttles opened to the air.

We climbed out of the lifeboat as the crew returned to their regular duties, the night crew going below to their rest.

Elva scowled and prowled the deck. When the sounds from below the open shuttles indicated the crew had all been served their midday meal, I asked Elva to join me in the cramped wardroom. I was starving.

The cook, a woman my own age, cheerfully provided us with two lipped wooden plates and a helping of what the crew had had. The way Elva dug in, I suspected that these biscuits stuffed with cabbage, savory beans, and cheese were common fare on ships, along with the orange wedges. We ate with our fingers.

"We need to get you safely to land," Elva murmured, after the cook vanished back into her galley.

The mates' wardroom was empty. Everyone had gone to their watch duties or else to rest for a later watch. But I was aware of the canvas doors running down the sides, dividing off the mates' cubbies. (The rest of the crew slept forward and some below.)

"You don't think we're safe now?"

"Oh, I am. I think. I hope." She lowered her voice, glancing at those canvas doors. "But what's to stop *him* from ransoming you for a smacking sum from the king? Or for a pardon and other concessions?"

Ransom! I hadn't thought of that. Uneasily I considered it. Then I said low-voiced, hoping the slap-thump of water against the hull and the creak of mast and deck would cover our conversation, "He has a price on his head, right?"

"That's true."

"So he risked his life to come inland to help you out, ahead of the king's men, and he's against Canary. Those are two points in his favor."

She knuckled the sides of her forehead. "That's what my brother says, too. But I think something's missing. I feel like, oh I don't know, we're on the coast with a strange chart. The big landmarks are all there, but what about the little ones?"

I looked at her puckered brow, her unhappy posture, and wondered if Elva was a math mind. The navigation career sure pointed that way.

"Listen, if you find any reason to distrust Captain Hurricane, I'll listen. But I do feel obliged to tell you that I'm going to make my own plans as soon as we reach land. That doesn't include your brother's mages or magisters, or whoever sent him."

Elva flushed. "That's fair."

We finished our meal and dipped our dishes in the bucket set aside for them. I watched the brief flare of magic cleaning my plate as it hit the water, and I remembered the cleaning buckets from my childhood. It had actually been such homely little magics, and no grand and spectacular spells, that had caused me to ask my father to teach me. On this world no one had to wash and rinse dishes—or clothes, if you had a cleaning bucket or frame. And the cleaning frame not only cleaned your clothes, but your body as well, right to your teeth, when you stepped through. It felt like the snap of electricity all over you, leaving you feeling as if you'd scrubbed with a loofa and rubbed all over with a thick towel.

I stacked my dish on the waiting pile a moment before I heard a step behind me. A young woman as tall as me appeared from one of the little cabins. I ducked out of her way, murmuring a word of pardon.

She bent her head, giving me a quick, almost furtive look without meeting my eyes, and climbed with practiced speed up the ladder to the deck. I followed more slowly, trying to get the feel of climbing a ladder when the ship swings you out, then back, and bucks suddenly from side to side.

On deck I discovered yet more drills going on among those not on duty. This time it was personal combat.

The weather had changed dramatically while Elva and I were below. A heavy mist grayed the masts and the sails overhead, turning the blue sea to gray-green. It made the deck slippery, but that did not stop the practice on the forecastle, directly outside of our cabin, where most of the crew gathered round a clear space.

Devli sat on the rail along with several other young men. He'd accepted a bunk below in the crew's quarters, and these were his messmates. That is, the fellows he shared a table with. The pirates seemed like sailors to me. Nobody was cursing and spitting, or teaching parrots naughty songs. In fact, I wasn't sure if this world even had parrots, though I knew that many Earth animals, birds and other fauna as well as flora had come, or been brought, through.

Devli beckoned to his sister, who walked to the rail where he sat, her arms crossed. Next to the sailors, her uneasiness made her seem out of place.

A short girl with bright red hair tapped her sword point on Elva's shoulder. "Want to join in?"

Elva jumped, and shook her head warily.

Her attitude seemed to puzzle the redhead, and I wondered if her feelings were hurt by Elva's attitude. But she turned my way and said more tentatively, "Would you like to get in some practice?"

After years of dojos full of strangers, I was used to this situation. Thinking that rest, food, and a workout were the three things I needed most, and I'd gotten the first two, I said, "Sure, thanks."

A big grin was my reward. "I'm Robin, second mate. Why don't you grab yourself a weapon. You'll get a turn anon."

She indicated the weapons locker. It was an admirably neat arrangement that rolled back against one side of the half-deck wall and lashed into place. The locker held three rows of neatly stored steel weapons, ranging from light rapiers to very heavy flat swords of the sort infantry carry. There was one curve-tipped cavalry sword marked off with a red tie.

I picked out a dueling saber, buttoned on the end, and began warm-ups as I watched the two in the center.

It was immediately apparent that they were more enthusiastic than trained. The bout only last a few seconds. One dropped his sword. The watchers crowed and catcalled with good nature, then the pair recommenced. This bout lasted longer only because they circled two or three times, watching one another—but not well enough to actually spot openings.

The winner of that bout turned around. His eyes briefly met mine, and the fellow flushed. I wondered if I'd managed to come unbuttoned or unzipped anywhere. No, the sturdy shirt I'd borrowed was laced up to my collarbones, sashed with a plain berry-brown-dye sash. The drawstring of the deck trousers remained securely tied, so I wasn't flashing underwear. My feet were bare, as I'd kicked off my sandals almost first thing on coming aboard.

An older, gray-haired man said, "You keep pickin' the easy ones. Come on, let's see you work up a bit of a sweat." And he stepped up, swinging his sword from hand to hand.

More catcalls, and the gray-haired fellow promptly and gleefully trounced the younger, taller fellow. Then it was his turn to pick a partner, and he pointed straight at me. "Let's see what your father taught you."

"Well, he started teaching me, anyway." I stepped into the ring of watchers. "I got most of my training elsewhere." I felt self-conscious, but no more than one did during a sparring match for a belt test.

I didn't say, because I thought it would sound arrogant, that

I'd seen his own weaknesses when he fought the tall, young fellow from Devli's mess, and so I knew where to get inside his guard as soon as he lunged at me in a feint.

I tapped the button against his chest, and he looked down, blue eyes wide in surprise. "Well! Try it again?"

I swept my sword up in salute. The second bout lasted longer. He had the edge on me with strength, but I had it on footwork, speed, and far-better training. Once again I tapped him, this time just above the collarbones, and a whoop went up from the watchers.

"Pick me! Pick me!"

"Hoo, how would you like to die?"

Laughter and more catcalls surrounded me as Zathdar and his two captains on the half-deck aft watched. A short, wiry man with waving dark red hair leaped over someone and confronted me, his slanty eyes slitted with laughter and his grin wicked. Like Zathdar, he wore a golden hoop in one ear. "Try me, Prin—ah—"

I'd forgotten the princess business. Was that why some of them stared at me so much? "Sasha will do."

"Owl. First mate." I saw a sort of family resemblance to Robin, and later found out they were cousins, though almost a generation apart in age.

"All right, Owl, bring it on!"

"Bring?" He looked around. "It? On?"

"Slang for have at it!"

As we squared up, whispers of *bring it on* went through the watchers. Owl attacked me and I closed out everything else.

I won that first one, only because I whipped a hook kick up and nailed his wrist after I dodged a lunge. The crew sent up an appreciative cheer, Owl flashed a grin, and we went at it again, this time faster and harder. I was soon drenched with sweat, several times nearly losing. I recovered a heartbeat ahead of defeat, and then returning an attack which he parried, almost too late.

But finally he launched a complicated strike that I couldn't deflect without straining my wrist. I was just enough off-balance to take the brunt of the hit in my hand and arm. I dropped my blade, wringing my stinging fingers. "Yi! Yi! Yi!"

"We'll call that a draw." Owl lowered his point to the deck. "Do you usually fight with gloves?"

"Yes," I gasped. "And that's something I'll have to see to right away. But that was a win. It was as fair as my hook kick, right? All's fair in war, but not in dueling? Is that true here?"

A silence fell, at first I thought because of my question, but I saw that Zathdar had joined the circle. "More or less. Depends where you are." Zathdar swung his sword experimentally.

Someone returned my blade. Others made room for me to sit on the deck in the first row.

Zathdar and Owl squared up, and began a long bout that was sheer pleasure to watch.

As they traded feints, Elva slid up next to me. "I think you should thump him." She jerked her chin toward Zathdar. "Do him some good."

"Nope," I said, after a flurry so fast I nearly couldn't follow it. Zathdar staggered back, Owl's sword flew, and he rolled on the deck. The sword was caught in midair by the tall, blond young woman I'd seen below. She had a strong face, with a Kirk Douglas chin. She returned Owl's blade as she said to Zathdar in an oddly shy manner, "That trick. How do you do it?"

"On your feet, Owl. Move through it slowly."

Owl scrambled to his feet and took his sword in hand. "I pressed inside like this." He made a slo-mo lunge.

"And I blocked here, using my shoulder to blind him." Zathdar whipped his sword in a tight circle, shifting his weight as he came out of the turn with his blade low.

"I saw it almost too late, blocked —"

The two reenacted the exchange, their method recalling good bouts from my dojo days. Most of the crew intently watched each pass.

When they were done, people shifted about, and again Elva

said, "Go on."

I shook my head. "He's better."

Elva made a noise of disgust.

Zathdar said in a quiet voice with considerable amusement, "She's right, you know. Not by much, though. It's those upward blocks."

So he'd heard. While I shut out everything when I engage in a bout, he was aware of everything around him. This is the difference between a lifetime of just dojo-floor practice and a lifetime of using what you learned, I thought. But aloud I only said to Elva's flushed face, "We don't hit above the collarbones in competition fencing, which is why I'm unused to blocking upward."

"Nor do you defend against a mounted attacker, is my guess," Zathdar observed.

"True enough. Plus he's a tad taller, and definitely bigger through the upper body than I, so he's got a longer reach. That makes a difference even when the training is the same, but his is better, I think."

"Practical experience." He gestured with a mocking air of apology and flashed a grin. "However. As this is supposed to be learning, want to show them some tricks of the trade from the other world?"

"All right." I scrambled to my feet. "But I saw those hits you scored on Owl. Anyone have a pair of gloves I can borrow?"

Several women offered, but their hands were all smaller than mine. Only the blonde did not offer, though she was my size. A gangly fellow passed me his, and they fit perfectly.

So Zathdar and I squared off, and the entire crew fell silent, even those in the tops, who leaned out to watch.

We began by making a few passes to test reflexes and strength. On the former we were roughly equal, but he had the edge on the latter. Also, his drill hadn't been confined to the rules, and while I'd seen opportunities to use street-fighting techniques with slower fighters, he was too well practiced high, low, behind—all the places sport fencing forbade. He seemed to be holding back. He was demonstrating. Gradually we sped up, until my arm felt like string and my eyes burned with sweat, and then came the inevitable tap of the point lightly in the hollow of my collarbones.

The crew burst into cheers. "That was fantastic," I exclaimed and flourished a salute.

"Want another?" he offered.

"Nope. I can already tell I'm going to be sore and stiff by nightfall. I haven't had a workout that good in much too long."

He turned away to select another volunteer as I returned the gloves to their owner, apologizing for their dampness. At least there was a cleaning frame below, I thought, sitting gratefully.

We observed two more sessions before the watch bell rang. In the general movement Zathdar appeared at my side. "Come to the cabin?"

"All right." I swung to my feet. "I have some questions."

"I thought you might." He twitched his eyebrows at me before leading the way. I followed that silk, no less blinding for being sodden from the increasing mist, as around us the day watches changed, people talking and laughing, the armorer keeping up a running stream of insults if weapons were not wiped down and put back in the racks to his exact specifications.

The other two captains had long since rowed back to their own ships to oversee their own combat sessions. Zathdar waved me into the cabin, and I ducked my head absently as I passed inside. This time I noticed things I hadn't before: the neatly made bunk, and the coverlet dyed various shades of green from pale silver to deep forest. Green was green, but somehow the thing radiated masculine vibes.

Above the bunk at the head end, someone had built shelves, which were crammed with handmade books. Next to the shelves, a silverwork crane taking flight rested on its own little shelf, jury rigged between a bulkhead and the hull. Stacked next to that, in eye-pleasing array, a series of maps—Khanerenth, Sartor, Colend. Chwahirsland. Some of the western lands that I did not recognize.

Above the foot of the bunk, a shelf held an exquisitely rendered tiny carving of a tree, the bark indicated by the grain of the wood, each branch curving up into impossibly tiny and intricate twigs, attached to which were tiny five-point leaves made of green silk.

"I didn't steal that," Zathdar said from right behind me.

I jumped and whirled around, unsettled, as if I'd been caught prying through someone's personal things.

Zathdar did not glance my way. He shifted around me, the crimson silk of his shirt shimmering in the diffuse light from the stern windows. The fabric shaped smoothly over the contours of shoulder and arm as he reached up and carefully took the carved tree from its shelf. "There's a spell that goes with it. You say it, and the leaves rustle. You can listen to them. Very pleasant, I assure you, if you happen to be caught windless out in the deeps, the ship wallowing and no breath of air."

He faced me, holding out the tree in both hands. I shook my head. "It's too delicate. I'm afraid I'll break it."

He turned away again and I whooshed out my breath, trying to find the cause of my absurd reaction. This was a captain's cabin, and little as I knew of ship matters, I did know it hardly constituted personal space, not unless the door was shut (it was not) and the scuttles all closed (they weren't).

He leaned a knee on the bunk and settled the tree just right, the fringes of his bandana swinging against his cheekbone. The books, the green coverlet, the precise slant of the handwriting on those maps, the tree and the silver bird. I'd seen all these the day previous, but then they'd been just things, scarcely noticeable. Now they were *personal*.

Rain began hissing on the deck overhead, which somehow made the space feel even more cramped. Though the rain made a steady thrum, I could hear the sound of his breathing. "Did you steal the ship?" I blushed uncomfortably. I hadn't meant to say that at all.

He grinned. "It's tradition, how pirate ships change hands. But pause and think. Where would you go if you wanted to purchase one? To a kingdom shipyard, asking the yardmaster if he happens to have any pirate ships for sale—very fast, preferably with at least one false hold? No. When navies take pirates, they tend to work the ships into their fleet, captains squabbling over who gets command. Then, er, they tend to be spotted and cut out again by people like me."

"You could have one built."

"But it can take years. If one has enough money. Easier to catch 'em, I'm afraid."

"You said pirate ships. But you claim to be a privateer. How do privateers get their ships?" I asked.

"Steal 'em from pirates." He tapped the earring glinting against his jawline. A ruby stone glittered on it. "You wear a hoop after you've survived a battle, and rubies when you've defeated a real pirate. While that won't scare off other pirates—little does— the ruby tends to ward off the would-bes. Saves effort."

He twiddled his fingers, giving me a wry glance. I laughed, as I was meant to. The moment made me feel slightly less unsettled, but far more aware of *him*. Skilled sword-swingers I had known in plenty during my fencing years, and they had come and gone leaving me unmoved. But a guy with a sense of humor?

"So." He thumped his elbows on the table, hands flicking open. "Before I get to my suggestion, what do you wish to do?"

"I'd like to be set on land as soon as possible, thank you."

"Even though by now there is a price on your head?"

"There is? But I didn't do anything!"

"It's not what you've done, it's who you are." He gave me an apologetic smile. "I guess what follows is what they're afraid you'll do."

Annoyance flushed through me; good, much better, much *safer* than interest. "Arrested for a crime someone else premeditates on my behalf? That's got to be a new one even for the local Dark Lord."

"Dark Lord? King Canardan is a king, not a lord. He also has red hair. Or would the 'dark' refer to his clothing? Except that he is reputed to dress well, and the mode, everyone tells me, is light colors. Not that I follow the fashions, as you can see."

Once again he made me laugh, and my annoyance vanished. I couldn't stay mad at him. Zathdar already knew my situation was unfair, and of course he had a price on his head, too.

So I said, "There's a reward offered for laying me by the heels whether I'm on land or at sea, isn't there?"

He spread his hands.

"Well, on land, I'm my own person, so to speak. I'd rather *call the shots*—" The words came out in English. "I'd rather be on my own."

"To find your father?" he asked gently.

I lifted my gaze—and met his blue eyes straight on.

What is it about the mirroring of gazes? Eyes are just eyes, circles within circles. You meet people's gazes all your life. Then, one moment you look across the table out of surprise or question or maybe even a little challenge, and there are *these* eyes. Your nerves zing and prickle, leaving you intensely aware of your heartbeat, your breathing, your toes crunched in your shoes, your damp palms. Distance is so relative. Whether the other person is a foot away or across a crowded room, you have fallen into intimate space.

I flicked my gaze up to the glittering gold embroidery on his headband. No intimate space here, noooooo.

I said to the fringes, "I have no idea if my father's even alive. No one will tell me."

"He vanished. That's all anyone can tell you." Zathdar snapped his fingers. "The Ebans seem to think you know where he is."

"I can't help that." I shrugged and studied the map of Sartor just beyond his shoulder as if a professor was about to slap a final exam before me.

"There's another matter. Something many of my crew are in favor of, by the way, as nearly all of them are exiles for one reason or another. Far too many are new, as the unrest spreads. Sooner or later someone's going to ask your intentions, so it might as well be now, and by me."

"I'm listening." I moved away from the table and confronted the map, poring over it.

"I thank you for that." I could hear his smile in his voice. "But I was hoping you'd take that as an invitation to talk."

Now even his voice sent prickles through me. This was the last thing I needed. Second to the last, I amended, backpedaling mentally. Worst thing? Capture by Canary's goons. But the second-to-the-last thing I needed was any kind of chemistry with a pirate. *Especially* one who had the worst taste in colors I'd ever known, even in the mega-geek world of graduate school. *That's right, Sasha, make yourself laugh. Use laughter as a defense. If you can keep laughing, it's just a silly chemical thing, here today, gone tomorrow.*

"Rumors have to be crossing the country now, however garbled. If you were to raise your family's banner, many people would flock to it."

That surprised me enough to flick a sideways glance, but I stopped at the bandana. "I don't have a banner."

"You do, too."

"It's just a *blanket*. And anyway I have no legal standing."

"You have, let us call it, a symbolic standing in the eyes of many people who want the Zhavalieshins back on the throne."

"So in place of my dad I serve as a figurehead for civil war? No, I hate that, I'm sorry. I don't mean to sound like I'm casting any aspersions here—blood and guts after all was your career choice—but if you're hinting you'd like me to join your fleet here under the Zhavalieshin banner, well, in a word, no. I won't stand by and let my family name be an excuse for someone wanting power to draw brothers and sisters and mothers and fathers and kids, even, to go marching to their deaths. Or sailing to their deaths. Because that's what civil war *is*, when you strip out the rhetoric about who's right and who's wrong." I winced, suddenly realizing that I was giving A-double-attitude to a pirate captain on his own ship. One who could toss me in the brig, and who would stop him?

But he did not sound angry. "Fair enough. Then you must be set down on land as soon as we can. First, though, there's a little matter of a blockade to run."

"Oh. Blockade. Right. But . . . we aren't exactly racing."

"That's because the blockade will be raised guarding the main harbors, on the other side of the kingdom. And if the king issued the order, you can be sure the orders were sent by magic."

I remembered those magical message boxes. Like email, only with real paper. "Right."

"So we'll make speed soon as we get a favorable wind, but we do need to be ready for anything. Though I have an idea."

"I suppose you can't land me on the coast somewhere?"

"Far too dangerous."

I had a vague memory of my father being told the same thing, back in our smuggling-boat days: lee shore winds, rocks, cliffs . . . Khanerenth's coastline outside of the harbors was terrible on ships.

"Thank you." I turned toward the cabin door. He did not stop me.

Outside, I found that tall young woman with the blond hair.

"I'm Gliss," she said, before I could speak. "Captain of the tops, starboard. The mates invited the sail captains to mess. And you. If you'll come." She sounded gruff, almost as if she didn't want me to, but her eyes were more brooding than angry.

"Thank you," I said. "Lead on."

TEN

"CRAP. CRAP. CRAP. CRAP," Sun muttered with each painful step.

"Shhh." The admonitory hiss blended in with the patter of the rain.

Lightning flared, revealing reproach in Silvag's wet face. Sun realized she'd been speaking instead of thinking. But oh, her feet hurt so much, so very much—

Another flare, farther off; Silvag held a hand flat toward the ground. *Sit.*

She sat right where she was, mud squelching under her butt. She didn't care. It meant her feet could rest.

The next flare brought a long, rumbling judder of thunder across the sky, and the patter became a roaring downpour. Folgothan splashed down next to her, his bad leg held straight out. Leaning close, she muttered, "Sorry."

He shook his head, drops flying off his gray hair. She'd apologized at least fifty times by now, but the sight of his pain filled her with fresh remorse.

Haxin, the ferrety one, had been looking around carefully during the flashes. Now he leaned close. "He's gone ahead. If it's clear, we'll have a cart back."

He didn't mean clear of enemies, though that was implied. Silvag had already explained that his wife had expected him to come home with some money. She had said she didn't care how. He didn't know how serious she'd been.

Wincing and grimacing, she peeled off her socks and set her feet out in the warm rain. The sting slowly diminished, and she almost nodded off into sleep when she heard Haxin splash upright, hand on his sword.

"It's us," came Silvag's low voice.

Moments later hands helped Sun to rise. She picked up her shoes and socks, walking barefoot through the mud. Little stones jabbed into her feet, internal lightning flares of agony, but she thought of Folgothan and kept silent. Presently they reached an old cart, pulled by a patient horse. She sat on the lowered ramp, her feet hanging over. Folgothan sat next to her, swinging his bad leg up. Haxin clambered up behind them, sitting by Silvag on the buckboard.

Sun leaned her cheek against the rough wood of the cart and this time she did fall into an uneasy slumber, waking stickily when the cart rolled to a stop. The rain had ended.

She hobbled behind Folgothan, whose breathing was a constant, painful hiss in and out. They entered a low cottage built in a jagged sort of rectangle, obviously each room added at different times, sized according to what materials they'd managed to find.

They passed through two or three small, scrupulously tidy rooms. At last she was pointed to a rough-and-ready loveseat, cushioned by mismatched, homemade pillows. She sank down gratefully, but stood right up again. "I'm wet," she said in dismay.

A square-faced woman her own age advanced, thin from worry and under-eating. Her expression was forbidding, but after Sun's exclamation she said politely enough, "Never mind that. Those pillows dry out nice."

Sun sank down with a sigh. "Here." She twisted off her opal ring and handed it to the woman.

"For?"

"The household, with my gratitude."

Sun watched the woman's brow clear, and relief pooled inside her. She'd remembered right. People in this country had different attitudes toward work, toward charity, toward a lot of things, than Sun had grown up with in L.A. Silvag's wife might have resented it if Sun had expected her to use the ring to barter for princess things, but a donation to the house was acceptable.

"I'm Plir," the woman said with cautious approval.

"Atanial." The old king had declared that "Sun" was not an appropriate name for a princess. At home when she'd changed her name, it meant paperwork, fees, and standing in long lines at City Hall. Here, a king could change names on a whim. He'd decided that she'd be Atanial, a Sartoran name.

"My daughter is fixing you a bath, your highness. We'll have those clothes through the frame while you soak, and then planning. But first here. Lark, bring it in."

A teenage girl stood in the doorway. Lark was short and strongly built like her mother, with her father's jug ears. Sun noticed she wore her braids firmly back behind them, with no attempt to hide the ears. If anything, the braids framed them. That won Sun over at once. Lark had spirit.

She came in, carrying a mug of listerblossom tea, which Sun took with a word of thanks.

Before long she felt human again. The ache of her feet receded to twinges whenever she flexed her toes. Her clothes were still wet, but the evening's warmth mitigated the dampness.

The men joined Sun and Plir in another room with a big table. Haxin was busy repairing what looked like a piece of harness gear. Folgothan sat back, eyes closed, hands loosely clasped around a mug of listerblossom tea. This tea was a pain reliever.

As Lark silently set out bowls and spoons, the others all faced Sun. "Your highness," Silvag began, after a look sideways at his silent companions. "What is it you wish to do?"

"Get to Steward Eban."

Silvag and Plir exchanged a glance—each obviously reading the other for cues—then Plir said, "When?"

"Whenever it's safe." Sun hoped tiredly that would be in a

week. Except these people would be scrounging extra food for a week.

"They're watched all the time," Silvag muttered.

Lark eyed the grown-ups. "I'm the only one who goes through. No one heeds me."

Sun regarded her, hesitating.

"Question?" Plir prompted. This off-worlder princess might have abandoned them for twenty years, or she might not have been able to get back. She was withholding judgment.

Sun said, "If the king's people don't heed you, it means they see you. Or are you able to get by them unseen?"

Lark grinned. "It was the first, early on. Nobody looked twice at a girl coming round to sell eggs in a basket. Our one thing is our hens, see. They're all good layers. But we can't live on eggs. So I sell 'em. Or trade, more like. Anyways, now I think I know where the spies be."

"When would you suggest we go there?"

"Tonight," Lark said promptly. "It's not far."

Sun winced down at her feet.

"I have some salve, and we could wrap 'em tight," Plir offered.

Sun heard that as a hint that while visitors were fine for a short time, they would age as fast as old fish. She forced herself to nod, and to rise. "Thanks. Sooner done, sooner no one worries."

Nobody argued with that.

Afterward, Sun — Atanial — insisted the less said about that trip the better. Yes, her feet had been wrapped after a liberal slathering with salve. The blisters still hurt and her bones ached.

But for all that, the walk was indeed not far. She learned that Silvag had settled outside of the city of Vadnais because his duty rotation back in the old days had him spending five days in the guardhouse, with two days off. And after he lost his job, the house was the only thing they had, so the family perforce stayed there.

Steward Eban had moved to the outskirts of the city when she was dismissed from the royal palace. She'd expected to live relatively cheaply and in obscurity, and indeed it was that way for a time, but over the past few years she'd become the central repository for messages, reports and complaints about the outrages of Canardan's adherents.

Lark led them by a circuitous route, keeping up a running stream of assurances that this hill was easy, that stream shallow, and it wasn't much farther.

The two middle-aged folks reflected on what a strong, energetic young teen regarded as easy as they shuffled onward, the rain sometimes heavy, sometimes light, but always making a sloggy mess for their feet.

But at last Lark said, "There it is."

Silvag looked around, decided it was safe, and vanished into the darkness. Lark led the way over a gentle hill between carefully tended fruit trees and down through fragrant border shrubs to another long, low house built much like Silvag's.

She and Sun crossed the kitchen garden, past the grape vines, and stepped onto a porch entrance where the boots and coats were kept during winter.

"Oh, oh, oh! Princess Atanial." A short woman with silver flyaway hair bustled up. "Is it truly you, highness?"

"Kreki." Sun—no, Atanial. She would have to get used to her name as Math's wife again, and all the assumptions (and the responsibility) the name implied. "Oh, it's good to see you."

She threw her arms around the smaller woman and hugged her, then they stepped back and studied one another. Kreki, blushing at being hugged by a princess, turned her head to call, "Dinner! Anything that can be warmed, and some berries and cream?"

"Sounds wonderful," Atanial vowed with passionate sincerity, her stomach growling.

In the background two servants began taking down dishes and wrapped food, a third servant vanishing through the opposite door.

Atanial turned back to Kreki, whose round face had aged. Her dark eyes were wide and alert, her blond hair now silver. She was stouter, but still moved like a guided missile.

Kreki found Atanial as beautiful as ever, her hair the same wheat color, the fine skin of her face softened by time over spectacularly handsome bones. "All these years." Her brow puckered.

Atanial spread her hands. "Mathias made me promise to stay. But he never came back for us."

Kreki Eban touched her lips and glanced toward Lark, who stood in the corner, smiling with the peculiar mix of smugness and uncertainty that characterizes teens who *think* they did something clever, something adult—but the adults might still turn on them.

When Kreki nodded slightly, Atanial realized that their coming this night had some special significance.

Kreki said, "Would you honor us by stepping into the pantry? I'm afraid that's where we have our meetings."

She led Atanial through a kitchen with its central stove, fueled by magical Fire Sticks. A door opened into an aromatic pantry. Ceramic pots and jars held dried spices and nuts. Below those a row of barrels contained wheat, cornmeal and other foodstuffs.

They walked single file between the goods to the back wall, which swung silently aside and led steeply down into a cellar lit by a glowglobe. The dirt walls were stacked with barrels of ale and carefully angled rows of square bottles of wine.

In the middle of the cellar, two men and two women sat at a rough table. Only one face was familiar, an older woman with gray hair, round of body, who stared at Atanial with angry eyes.

Atanial's mind caught up. It's a meeting of the resistance council. *And they think I abandoned them.*

"Mathias sent me and my daughter back to my world because we couldn't stay ahead of the pursuit. After several very close escapes, we discovered that Randart had far too good a hold over the army. We tried to escape on a smuggling boat and nearly got caught. It was only Magister Glathan's magery that saved us. And that barely."

The woman, another servant during the blissful palace days, nodded once. She remembered that.

Atanial went on, "And we couldn't go west, for there were mage traps as well as the entire army camped all along the coast, and along the border mountains, ostensibly to train."

Now one of the two men nodded. They seemed to be father and son, for they looked alike: brown hair and skin and eyes, big jaws, eyes with a downward turn at the corners.

"So Math sent us to my world. Promised he'd come for us. He never did. After many years, abruptly, I believe Perran and Canardan's other pet mage, what was his name? Zha-something."

"Zhavic," someone murmured.

"Thank you. They showed up and tried to trap my daughter. She got brought over here by someone. I came after her as soon as I figured it out."

They all made little gestures of acceptance. Five days in another world could have passed in twenty here as easily as five hundred years. Or even "backward" in the sense of someone from farther back in history on the one world being propelled into the future of the other.

"I think it was your son who brought her, Kreki." Atanial turned to Mistress Eban, who looked down at her tightly gripped hands. "Canardan himself was at the castle with the World Gate. I heard him mention your son. I also heard that my daughter was apparently in the hands of some pirate?"

Eyes and mouths rounded in surprise. Atanial remembered her husband saying, all those years ago, *They aren't trained warriors, or spies. They are ordinary people, trying to invent ways to stay safe from an enemy who doesn't look different, talk different, who might even be in the same family.*

For in the early days Canardan had built his alliance one by one, courting at least one person in every influential family.

She said, "Look. You don't want to talk in front of me. Why don't I step outside while you decide what you can tell me? My plan is to find my daughter. After that, I will find out if my husband lives." Her lips trembled. "I have waited years without knowing. I can wait a bit longer."

Kreki said in a quick, breathless voice, "We do not know anything about Prince Mathias, except that he disappeared ten years ago. But Magister Glathan is dead. Word is, Commander Randart had him shot in the back. Crossbow. After a truce."

Atanial covered her face with her hands, then heaved a sigh. "All right. I'll wait outside."

She pushed through the back of the pantry. Nobody stopped her. She nearly ran into one of the servants, a pretty young girl with a long red braid busy scooping dried peas into a cup. Atanial excused herself, then slipped through the empty kitchen to the door.

Outside, the rain had stopped. A fresh, cool breeze soughed through the line of pines planted on the ridge at the edge of the property, just beyond the fruit trees.

Atanial stepped out, breathing deeply. Her feet throbbed dully, but the acute pain of walking had lessened.

A faint glow worried at the extreme edge of her vision. She looked up. In one of the recessed attic windows flickered the warm, golden flames of two candles. Cozy. She wished she were in the bedroom behind that window, whether guest or servant's room, large or small. All she wanted was a nice, soft bed —

"Your highness," Kreki whispered from the kitchen door. "They want to talk. Our passwords, signals, what we're doing."

Passwords and signals. Why did that seem wrong? Atanial frowned. The vague sense of disquiet was too quick, undefined. Her mind was too tired and scattered. Her aching feet — Math — Magister Glathan's death — and riding over it all, Sasha and this mysterious pirate —

"Here we are." Kreki opened the pantry again. "You might remember Fereli Kinn, the royal wardrobe mistress."

The gray-haired woman rose. "Forgive me, highness," she said gruffly.

"You thought I abandoned you." Atanial summoned a smile.

"And in a sense I did. I beg your pardon. I take it the queen couldn't protect you either?"

"The rumor is she's mad." Mistress Kinn flushed, curtseyed, sat. "So the king turned us all off, except for her three personal maids. No one's seen her since, except once a year, standing by the king, on Oath Day."

"I don't think you knew Arlaen Sharveshin." Kreki indicated the older man. "He was a herald-scribe in our day. His son Tam is in the king's guard now, as our ears."

Atanial noted Tam's brown tunic.

"We meet here when we dare," Kreki said. "And exchange news."

"Like? I mean, what is the most important thing facing you now?"

An exchange of looks. Kreki leaned forward. "The mustering of the army. We don't know if the king intends some terrible purge here, or to invade elsewhere."

The man spoke up, a low rumble. "My son hears rumors of a possible invasion of Locan Jora. Take our lands back." The boy inclined his head.

"But we haven't any word for sure. We cannot get close enough to Randart. He keeps only his own picked men around him. The king is guarded by Randart, by the royal mages, and finally by the royal valet, Chas."

Atanial breathed out slowly. "I remember Chas. I caught him in our rooms at least a couple of times, going through Math's things. He seemed to have plausible excuses."

"He's a very tricky spy. So anyway, we keep trying to find out the plans. We fear, from the mustering of supplies and the way training has been going, that this is not a vague future plan. It has a date. Probably next spring, judging from the cloth stockpiled in the border castles."

When no one had anything to add, Atanial turned to her own issues. "Tam, you're in the guard. What can you tell me of this pirate holding my daughter?"

"Nothing." Tam spread big, callused hands. "Nobody can figure out where Zathdar came from. He was suddenly there, some years back, attacking the king's fleet. Breaking trade holds."

Kreki said to Atanial, "What I was just reporting to the others is this. I received two notes from my son. One two nights ago. Hastily written and sent by mage-box. It was only two lines, to tell me that their particular group had been discovered long ago by the king, but they had left the tower after a fight. Your daughter and the pirate defeated the guards."

Atanial gripped her fingers together. "That sounds like Sasha."

"I received another note, even shorter, last night. Again just two sentences. The king apparently knows about the resistance group run by my nephew Nadathan, who is also a mage student. The other stated that the pirate—he calls himself a privateer—declares that his family name is Jervaes."

"Common name deriving from Sartoran origin," Arlaen rumbled. "Various versions all over the southern continent here."

"At least that sounds somewhat civilized. I mean, he offered a family name, right? Didn't call himself Slubbertegullion Squid-Guts or Bloody-Skull Liver-Squisher, right?" At the others' puzzled looks, Atanial sighed. "So no one knows his motive, beyond piracy?"

No one spoke.

"Another thing to find out." Atanial's stomach growled. When would that dinner arrive?

"We thought we ought to tell you the passwords and signals," Kreki began.

"Oh! Like the one in the attic window?" Atanial pointed upward. *That* was what had tweaked at her.

The others gazed in dismay.

If only she wasn't so hungry! It was hard to think. "Two candles? Window?"

Arlaen rubbed his jaw. "We did not post any candles."

Tam lunged to his feet, his face blanched. "Not our signal."

Arlaen's eyes widened in horror. "We have a spy here."

Kreki glared at the others. "Who is the traitor?"

They stared back, their faces shocked, angry, puzzled.

Arlaen whispered, "Tam. He has to get out." He gripped hold of his son and muscled him, protesting ("Let me fight! Let me fight!") toward the door. Then he stopped short, Tam stumbling with a subdued, "Ow!"

Arlaen said, "What if the spy is out there? How can I get Tam out?"

"It could be anyone. Even the servants," Atanial added, remembering the young woman just outside the cellar door when she left previously. *But no one pays attention to servants*, Math's voice came, with gentle irony, out of the past, the time they all disguised as cooks when Randart had driven them into a trap . . . "The girl with the red curls. Servant. Pouring peas. She didn't act surprised when she saw me. Did you tell her anything?"

Kreki breathed out. "No. But Marka has been with us for at least five years."

"So how much does she know? You say your nephew was betrayed. And I overheard that Canardan was hot on your boy's heels when he came to Earth. Well, your son told me so himself. Though I didn't believe him at the time."

Arlaen gazed at his son in dismay. "They'll put Tam here up against the wall." His voice lowered, rough and husky. "They'll have to."

His agony was the agony of any parent. *What happens to your child happens to my child*, Atanial thought, but her mind moved rapidly to memory, and then to action. "Tie up that red-haired girl and take her clothes. Tam, you are about to turn into a girl. *Fast*." The order was out before she could stop herself.

This time everyone sprang to action, the men vanishing through the doorway.

Kreki thrust a wad of papers into Fereli's hands. "We have to burn these." She scratched a light, dropped the flame onto a ceramic bowl, and they began ripping.

Aching feet forgotten (well, not actually, but ignored) Atanial slammed through into the pantry, then stopped short at the barrels. She'd left her sword in the wagon back at Lark's house, and had forgotten about it. Now she had no weapon but the knife, and that she was reluctant to use unless her life was definitely threatened.

Math had said once, *I'll keep training Sasha, but no steel in her hands until she knows the cost. Flour and pepper, yes. We'll teach her to blind them and run.*

Blind them and run. Atanial was beginning to sort through the bags when Kreki banged out of the pantry, bearing a long, wicked knife, and marched into the kitchen.

Her nerves firing with warning, Atanial followed her through another narrow storage room, this one full of bed and bath linens, and up a creaky old stairway. Kreki's speed increased until she was almost running. When she reached a narrow doorway, she burst into Marka's tiny bedroom, saw the two candles in the window still burning and raised her knife.

The red-haired girl lay on the woven-rag-rug floor with her hands bound and her mouth gagged. Kreki brought the knife down. Atanial froze in the doorway, a squawk of protest forming in her throat. Then Kreki's hand came up, brandishing the red of a long, curling braid.

Atanial leaned against the wall, and even the Sharveshins, in the middle of ransacking the girl's clothes trunk, reacted with relief. Tam sank onto the bed, and Arlaen pressed back against the slanting attic so he would not make a shadow on the window.

Kreki squatted down next to the terrified girl. "Give me one good reason why I shouldn't kill you now, you despicable traitor," she uttered in a trembling voice.

Atanial looked at Tam, who uncertainly clutched a gown. Her mind was moving again, more rapidly than before. Kreki was clearly too angry to think. Tam's gaze averted from the girl on the floor. If she was a spy and he was a spy, had there been some quiet time between two attractive young people, both willing to hear and receive information, perhaps while exchanging kisses?

Atanial watched Marka's tear-filled eyes flicking between Kreki's knife and the boy on the bed, and knew she had it.

She cleared her dry throat, wishing they'd actually gotten to eat that dinner. Or at least sample some ale. "Marka must have had a reason." She smiled ruefully down at the girl. "Of course she had a reason. I'll bet it was a good one, too. She doesn't look like she did it for evil reasons."

Now Atanial had all their attention.

Atanial knelt next to Marka, who studied her with the tense forehead and squinted eyes of pain, anger, fear. Confusion.

"Let's have that gag off," Atanial murmured. "You won't yell, will you? You don't want to die, and no one wants to kill you."

A tiny nod.

Atanial took out her own knife as Kreki gripped hers upraised in silent warning. The girl gasped, working her lips and tongue as Atanial said, "Your reasons might have to wait. But here's the important thing. Do you really want to see Tam dead?"

"N-no." Marka gulped on a sob.

Tam opened his mouth, but his father gripped his shoulder in warning.

Atanial said, "They probably have us surrounded by now, don't they? You comforted yourself with the fact that they have orders to *capture* us. But think about it."

"They wouldn't—they *promised*—"

"My dear, you've been living a lie. Surely you can understand that they might lie to you? Just like they asked you to lie to the Ebans and the others?" Atanial glanced Tam's way.

Marka licked her lips, fresh tears coursing down her cheeks. "You think they have orders to kill me?" Her chest heaved with sobs.

"If the orders came through the War Commander," Kreki said decisively. "Yes. He hates spies, though he uses them."

"The king?" Atanial asked softly, wondering how much Canardan had changed.

Kreki shook her head. "He hates actually doing away with

people. Which is the only hope *we* have," she added with irony.

Atanial turned back to Marka. "But Tam, they would execute right away, because he's in the guard. Do you want that to happen?"

"No."

"All we need are the passwords to get Tam through the line," Atanial said, and Kreki gasped. She hadn't thought of passwords, but she had not spent as much time around Randart as Atanial had, back in the old days. He'd always used codes and passwords.

Fresh tears welled in Marka's eyes, dripping into her ears.

Atanial brushed the tears away. "We're going to leave you here, but hidden, so they won't find you. After we leave, you can get yourself free, and away. And do whatever you need to do. But at least get Tam through that line, or he will be dead by morning."

"Hackleberry," Marka whispered, her anguished eyes lifting toward Tam. "The password is *hackleberry*."

Atanial looked up at Tam. "Take Lark with you." She nipped the braid from Kreki, shook it so it unraveled, and pulled a sash from the half-spilled contents of the trunk. "That around your head tying on the hair, a bonnet over your head. The skirt on your waist. Get through the lines now. With Lark. She's got to get home and warn her family."

Tam and his father fixed on the sash and hair in a matter of heartbeats, and then Tam dashed out, wrestling the skirt into place.

Atanial used another sash to bind Marka's mouth, but far more gently.

"All right, the rest of us have to cause as much confusion as we can so Tam and Lark can get through."

They left Marka on the floor, her candles still burning in the window. She promptly wriggled under her bed to hide.

Atanial did not see Tam or Lark as she made her way through the house to the front door. The front parlor was dark, which gave her eyes time to adjust. She eased the door open a crack and peered out. At first the night looked peaceful, but as her night vision got better she saw movement among the pines, and heard a sudden rustle in the orchard.

The king's men were advancing into position.

She shut the door as Kreki joined her. "What did you see?"

"We're surrounded."

Kreki breathed out a shuddering sigh.

"What are we facing here?" Atanial asked. "This was a meeting in a private home, no weapons present."

"What I fear is that he'll have us handy to blame for all the current problems," Kreki said. "Economy is in ruins, trade by sea impossible."

"Due to this Zathdar, no doubt, who has my daughter. Well, one thing at a time. Here's what I think. You tell me if it makes sense. If Canardan can make me vanish without anyone knowing, whether by death, magic or throwing me into a deep dungeon, his life is much easier."

"Just what I was thinking." Kreki determinedly kept her voice calm.

"So everyone out there needs to know who I am. Warriors gossip same as anyone else. Gossip is on my side. Second thing, we must buy that boy time to get through the line and well away before they discover the ruse. So . . . why not playact a pair of stupid old women too dumb to see the danger?"

"No playing on my part. I should have been more careful. I should have suspected something like this. It's been too easy." Kreki's fingers trembled as she brushed her hands down her apron. "Let's get busy."

She clapped, and a small glowglobe lit the parlor.

Atanial opened the front door wide, making sure she stood directly in the center, so her entire body was silhouetted. She lifted a hand and made a business of peering outward.

Kreki came up next to her, polishing a candlestick on her apron. "What is it, your highness?" she asked in a carrying voice.

"I thought I saw something. A light."

"Impossible. Everyone is here. Must be a gleam from the stars, reflecting on the leaves of the peach trees. Do you have peaches in *the other world?*"

"Oh yes. But not as good as the ones here! *My husband Mathias* once told me peaches were brought *through the World Gate.*"

"But which way, *your highness?*" Kreki shrilled. "From *your world?*"

"Now, that I do not remember." Atanial laughed as she leaned out, looking around dramatically under her hand, though the light glowing directly above them made it nearly impossible to see anything.

But she heard rustles. One by the barn, another out by the pines. The crack of a twig.

"Rain is gone." Kreki lifted her hand and began peering upward with theatrical earnestness. "Will be a lovely walk if you decide to move on tonight."

"But my feet hurt," Atanial fog-horned, lifting her bandaged foot. A flutter behind her ribs had to be squelched. She must not laugh. But this was almost fun.

"Oh, *Princess Atanial,*" Kreki exclaimed, loud enough to be heard from the pine ridge.

"That's what I get for marching for days after years of no walking at all. But I met so *very* many *nice people* on the way, who seemed *glad* I have returned. If only I'd thought of it years ago!"

"Oh! How many did you meet? I know all the valley families."

"Too many to count! Oh, but I am so very hungry—"

"Dinner," came a wry voice from out of the darkness, "can be ordered day or night at the royal castle. That's the good thing about royal castles. Welcome back, Sun."

Both women whipped around. Atanial bit her lips against a curse, even a retort. The king himself! She was supposed to be surprised. Were those kids through the lines yet?

"Who is that?" she called uncertainly, doing the peering business again. "*Canardan?* My goodness, is it really *you?*"

"I'm here to personally convey a royal invitation, Sun." Canardan Merindar strolled toward the house, stopping just inside the circle of light.

He was taller than Atanial remembered, his hair a dark auburn, the waves ruddy in the light. He had certainly not gone to fat.

She lifted her voice. "I am here to get my daughter. If you try to stop me, well—" She spread her hands.

"But we can find your daughter together." Canardan lounged a step closer. "Come along, Sun. You really don't want trouble any more than I do."

He used the name "Sun" with a humorous, intimate tone that Atanial disliked just a little more each time she heard it. "No," she responded cordially. "I do not. Therefore, if you let these people go on their merry way, then I won't make any trouble. It's not their fault I seem to have come at the wrong time and headed straight for the wrong place. No one here knew I was coming, I promise you that."

Canardan sighed. "Take 'em." He waved a lazy hand toward the house.

A gaggle of old folks had a snail's chance in the salt mines against a determined band of trained warriors, particularly determined under the ironic eye of their king. But at least it was the king, and not War Commander Randart, which meant they had a better chance of staying alive. And so they gave the escaping young pair their very best effort to prolong things by running around, yelling and ramming into walls, furniture, warriors and each other.

Fereli retreated to the kitchen and threw pots of preserves at the ducking heads of the young fellows trying to corner her. Despite the danger, bubbles of humor fizzed inside her chest when she saw how those big, brawny youngsters hunched and covered their heads each time she took aim.

Arlaen got into the act by groaning and clutching his bad hip as he yanked furniture in the way of the dashing warriors, sometimes tripping them up. He'd apologize, reach to help them, and then knock jugs and plates and baskets onto them. They scrambled about amid showers of crockery, beans, nuts, and once a satisfyingly effective dusting with ground pepper.

Kreki shrieked at the warriors to spare her curtains and rugs, disconcerting them mightily, and Atanial ran around the outside of the house twice, bobbing and weaving, until she stumbled over an unseen cabbage in the garden and measured her length on the carrot tops.

Strong hands picked her up with respectful care. Swords rang, and she smelled healthy young male sweat many times over as she was closely ringed.

Fairly soon the others were brought out.

"This all of 'em?" Canardan asked.

"All we found, sire," responded the captain.

Atanial counted swiftly, then compressed her lips firmly to hide the balloon of relief inside. The prisoners were the old folk and three servants.

No Tam or Lark.

ELEVEN

 to describe how I felt the next day.

In the past the only thing to do was work out harder. Over the next couple of weeks—it was easy to lose track of the flow of days on the sea—Owl and I led the personal weapons practices in the mornings, and he conducted drills in the afternoon. Zathdar was there for some of the sessions, and on other days he took his captain's launch away to inspect his fleet, and to scout ahead.

After the first few days, I nerved myself to climb the shrouds—the ropes connecting each mast to the hull on either side—to the platform on which the crew stowed sails for the higher reaches, and crouched with bows during defense practice. This vantage was splendid, the movement of the ship more dynamic, the view farther, the graceful geometry of the sails quite spectacular.

The masts had three levels—mainsails, topsails and topgallants—with a smaller platform at that third section of mast. The morning Zathdar returned, I climbed up there, clinging to the mast as I accustomed myself to that breathtaking swoop and loop. The wood was rough under my cheek, weather-beaten for countless years, the nails all handmade, each therefore distinctive. On the platform and the side of the mast, unknown hands had carved initials and short words, most of them in unfamiliar alphabets.

Finally I dared to lift my head and look outward. Exhilaration rushed through me at the sight of the vast ocean sparkling in the sun. The deck looked so small below!

"Boat ho," called the lookout on the other mast. "Captain returning."

I shifted. There was the narrow launch, its single sail a long, pure curve as it scudded lightly as a gull, water foaming up in an arch down either side.

Gliss swarmed up with the ease of a flitting bird and scowled at me. "You shouldn't be up here."

"Why not?"

"Because you're a land rat. If you fall, we get the blame."

She turned away before I could speak and slid down a backstay to the deck. That was a trick I was not about to emulate.

My exhilaration vanished, doused by a vague sense of guilt. I climbed laboriously to the deck, clinging with iron desperation as the pitch of the ship swung me out over the water.

When I reached the deck, Zathdar had already closed himself in his cabin with Owl and Robin. The crew in the middle of changing watch nodded and smiled at me, most of them familiar now after days of the practice sessions. They were all fairly friendly. With one exception, Gliss.

Elva was deep in conversation with the navigator at the helm. Having seen almost nothing of Devlaen over the past few days, I explored the lower levels of the ship and discovered him shut into a tiny cubby in the hold, busy with his books under the light of a single swinging lantern. The cabin was hot and stuffy.

"Why are you stuck in this rat hole?" I asked.

He blinked at me. "Studying." He placed his finger on a page covered with tiny handwriting. "Trying to design us some transfer-note boxes. It's more advanced magic than I've learned yet," he admitted.

"For Zathdar?" I asked.

Devli flushed, and I suspected his sister had accused him of throwing in with the . . . if not the enemy, with the not-quite-allies.

He said defensively, "Well, if he wants to communicate with us, I don't see why he shouldn't. And if I design them, I can make sure there aren't any suspicious wards or tracers on them. So the king cannot intercept our messages."

I shrugged. "Sounds reasonable."

He relaxed a little. "Why do you want to be on land?"

"Find out if anyone knows if my father is alive."

"And then?"

"I don't know. Depends on what I hear."

"So you won't search out your father yourself?" Devlaen asked, his expression intent. The lamplight threw his face into relief, making him look older.

"I was ten years old when we left. That was long ago." And when he started to speak, I deflected: "I would like to sit down somewhere and catch up on history before making any plans."

Devli leaned forward, his expression eager. "But I could tell you that. We study history when we learn magic. I could *show* you just why we need—" He reached a hand toward me.

Maybe he reached just to gesture, but I backpedaled fast. *He's a mage, Clueless! A dedicated one. What's to stop him from grabbing you right now?* "I apologize for interrupting your studies." I backed out to find Gliss coming down the hatch.

"Captain wants you," she said shortly.

When she turned to climb back up, I put an arm across the ladder to prevent her. "Gliss. I am not your enemy."

She looked down, scowling. Her broad cheekbones glowed with dusky color.

"There is something I am missing here." I sighed. "Please tell me."

"You are blind." Her scowl turned into a glare before she dropped her gaze to her hands. "Or you're making game of me."

"No. Think of me as new to this world. I don't remember a whole lot before I left."

She shrugged one shoulder sharply and mumbled something in which the words, *the way he looks at you*, could be made out.

"He?" But I knew whom she meant. I'd sensed that my zings were not just my own attraction. I'd felt those looks from Zathdar. Though he had done absolutely nothing about it, the vibe had been there just the same.

"Zathdar's bright blue eyes." If I expected her to be honest, I had to be honest back. "I can't help his looking. I promise you I didn't try to get him to look. I don't know if that helps." I fingered one of my braids, which were beginning to frazzle in the sea air, despite being rebraided just that morning. "I don't even know how relationships work on this world. I was ten when I left. And my mother only talked about how rotten Canary — that is, King Canardan — was."

Gliss crossed her arms and leaned against the bulkhead as the ship gave a lurch. "That's pretty much what Zorala says. I was seeing a *princess* coming on board. Showing us all up. Crooking her royal finger at the captain."

Zorala, one of the cooks, was older, weathered, and seemed to find the crew's interactions as good as theater.

"I'm not a princess." I tried not to sound sharp. "You can blame my parents for my being good at self-defense. My father started that when I was this high." I held my palm down. "And my mother kept it going. As for finger crooking, seems to me that neither royal nor street-sweeper fingers will be any more successful than the other if the captain doesn't want to be crooked."

She hitched her shoulders under her ears, up and down.

"Look, Gliss. Here's how my female code works. I should say that there are many female codes on my sorry planet filled with dysfunction" — the closest word was *distortion in conduct* — "but here's how I see it. If there's a she-and-he twosome, and I find myself attracted to the he, then I wait for her to let me know if there's any hope. Otherwise, hands off. She has to tell me, not him. But if they're not a couple, well, fair's fair. Not that I mean to go after your captain. I'm not sure I like anything but his looks. Definitely not his taste in clothes, and I'm not so sure about this pirate business. But, for my information only, are you two a couple?"

She looked down at the deck. "No." She faced me squarely. "Said on hiring there would be no dalliances with the crew. But sometimes they say that, and later . . ." She shrugged.

"Yeah. I know that men change their minds. So do women. Look, I want to get off this ship onto land, and live my own life. Whatever that might be. Fair enough?"

She didn't smile, but at least she didn't look as angry. "Fair enough." She climbed up so fast I don't think her feet touched the rungs but twice.

I followed more slowly. Just as well I would soon be gone. Political enemies were bad enough. I didn't want to make a personal one, just because Mr. Pirate might turn out to have a roving eye.

So I did my own arm crossing and cold manner when I entered the captain's cabin. If Captain Hurricane noticed, he gave no sign. He was in the middle of studying a chart, barely glanced up, his manner absent as he said, "My messenger finally caught up with us. The king sent the navy out to blockade the main harbor, as I'd predicted. We're maybe a day from their outer perimeter. Here's the news. He knows you're here on my ship. The navy is ordered to be on the watch for us."

"How are you going to break through the blockade?"

"By joining a big fishing fleet. We've been running parallel to one these past few days. By morning we will be a different ship. I must request you to spend the rest of today and all of tomorrow in your cabin. I cannot risk you being seen on deck. You are too recognizable."

"Who on the fishing boats would know me from anyone else?" I asked, not hiding my skepticism.

"We're going to run a quick . . . errand before we land." He looked out the stern windows, as if something important was happening on the choppy seas.

"All right." I knew he wasn't going to tell me what his

"errand" was, not after I'd refused point-blank to become part of his plans. "If you have something to read, I would like to try to reacquaint myself with Sartoran writing. Preferably something that might catch me up on local history."

He frowned at the chart table, fingers toying with a quill pen, then shook his head. "Nothing on board." When my glance strayed to those bound books over his bunk, he said with a quick smile, "Not histories. But if you like, when we land, I could scout you out one."

Thus obliquely asking my plans. Right. As if I'd discuss them! "Well, let's get to safety first. And to land," I said with hearty cheer, my gaze drawn irresistibly . . . And when his eyes met mine the inward jolt made me shift my own attention to the open scuttle, then to the statue.

Yet the afterimage remained of his open-necked night-sky blue shirt with the gold and crimson embroidery of leaping dolphins round the hem, the green-and-white-striped deck trousers, and a sash riding loose on his narrow hips. The sash at least matched his headband, though both were purple with yellow fringe. More specifically I was more aware of him inside those clothes, the contours of muscle shaping the shirt, the long lines of his legs looking very good in those deck trousers. I wondered if he had buns of steel . . .

And stalked out, utterly disgusted with myself.

TWELVE

ELVA WASN'T THERE WHEN I woke the next morning. I eased one of the vapor-blurred scuttles open a crack, bringing in a strong whiff of fish. I was surprised to discover the surrounding waters full of boats and ships, tall masts surging slowly on the sea, sails belling in the same direction.

When I peered out at the foredeck, fine rain misted my face. Under a low, steel gray sky, the crew labored at dismantling what seemed to be another ship. The *Zathdar* with its clean lines had transformed into a clutter of barrels, nets, old sailcloth, with the rakish topgallant masts laid along a gangway. The masts looked stumpy now, and the rigging had been altered completely to the shabby triangles of fore-and-aft, which made sense for fishing cruising, where you stay closer to shore and want to maneuver better. These sails were old, splotched with mold, and patched in places.

The crew looked pretty much like always, except the piratical splashes of color were gone. The big surprise was the captain. I almost missed him, but the angle of shoulder and neck, the distinctive stance snapped my attention back to the man tending the wheel.

If those buns of steel existed, there was certainly no sign of 'em now. He wore a grubby pair of canvas trousers bunched up round his waist and tied with a rope, some kind of knitted stockings (complete with gaping holes), and aged deck shoes. His shirt was a sun-faded brown, with a long vest over it containing a lot of pockets. As usual he'd tied a bandana around his head, but this was a narrow length of brown cloth, below which at last he'd let his hair hang down. I could see why he bound it up. His hair was an ugly hank of tangled, matted brown, coarse as horsehair, constantly flapping in his face.

My radar still bleeped, even with the nightmare hair.

Elva appeared from below-decks, brow tense with worry. Behind her, Devli looked excited and happy.

"What is it?" I asked.

"Let's go inside, where we won't get yelled at or knocked out of the way," Elva grumped.

"We were locked below," Devli said to me.

"How should I know he was serious about that? He's never been serious about anything," Elva protested.

"I *love* the idea that we might be famous. Like, our faces drawn onto wanted posters and spread round the fleet." Devlaen grinned like a kid.

"What's going on now? I take it we're not staying with this fishing fleet?"

"A raid," they said together, Elva with eyes rolled skyward and Devli bouncing on his toes.

"What?"

"We joined the fishers just long enough to get inside the blockade. Now he's going to run a raid. On a navy ship back out on the perimeter." Devli hopped again. "Hiding behind one of the little islands."

"Zathdar is an idiot," Elva added.

Her disgust was a candle to the sun of my anger.

Despite the captain's request that I stay in my cabin, I marched out into the fine, cool rain, but not before I saw the triumphant look Elva shot at her brother.

It took me a little time to thread my way between the crew

members busy dismantling the mess so artistically arranged on deck, and forming long lines of rope haulers along the gangway as the topgallant masts were being raised again.

The seas had gone gray, and the mist was thickening fast, obscuring the other fishing boats. The nearest was a blur maybe two hundred yards away.

By pausing, ducking, swerving, side hopping and squirming, I managed to make it all the way aft, where Zathdar stood at the helm, rain dripping off his matted clumps of hair, his eyes narrowed as he peered into the gray gloom that smeared the line between sky and sea.

I stood for a time, struggling to get firm control of my temper. Bitchiness never helped anything, I knew that. So far, being mellow at least got me some answers.

So, when I knew my voice would be neutral, I asked, "How can you see anything?"

"He's out there," Zathdar said.

"Yes, and I was hoping you'd explain about that."

He regarded me with faint surprise. "I told you we had an errand to run. You have an objection to my running a raid on one of War Commander Randart's most poisonous snakes?"

"I thought your errand meant changing the sails or something. Do you" —I tried to maintain a semblance of cordiality —"have an objection to keeping your word? You did say when we broke the blockade we'd land. I see no land, and your errand seems to be taking us farther out to sea."

"We're in the bay." He gestured with one hand, a wide sweep. "And I saw the perfect opportunity. After my raid, we'll land. I promise that."

If we're successful, I thought, but I knew how that would sound, so I retraced my steps.

Devli and Elva waited inside the cabin, she sitting on her bunk, he at the tiny fold-down table. "Well?" she asked, as I sank onto my bunk.

"We land after this raid." I raised my fingers in air quotes, to which they reacted with mute question. "He says."

Elva scowled. "If we are alive."

"He said I could help." Devli chortled. "So I'm gonna wear a disguise."

Elva turned on him. "What?"

"Perhaps I could cast an illusion or two." Devli rubbed his hands. "Anyway, I'm going. When else will I ever get to be on an actual pirate raid?"

"Wear an eye patch," I suggested, aware of my heartbeat accelerating. My brain was catching up on reality. Me, a waitress, whose most accustomed battles were against L.A. traffic, was on board a *pirate ship*, heading straight for a *raid* on a naval ship.

"Eye patch?" Devli broke into my dark thoughts.

"Pirates have to wear eye patches. And peg legs." I got up, and sat again. "I suspect it has something to do with cannon balls, and no, I'm not explaining that."

The watch bell changed, and Devli vanished on some other errand.

Elva hunched on the other bunk, obviously brooding. We left the door open, watching the swift alteration of the ship back into sleek piracy, as the last of the fishers vanished into the gray haze behind us. The crew got the topgallant masts fidded, the sheets rattled down and the sails set, after which our speed increased with bucking surges, a fine spray arcing on the low, lee side of the ship.

The wind had increased with the rain and we tacked at a dramatic slant. An island emerged out of the gloom, a mere shadow at first, one at which we appeared to be aimed. My nerves twisted slowly into knot-gutted tension as the wind and current brought us closer to it with what was rapid speed for ships.

Chasing another ship is not like a movie car chase. It's a kind of hurry-up-and-wait affair. You run around on deck getting ready, while the ships slowly, inexorably sail toward one another.

The first danger was weathering that island, as we skirted much too close to its rocky cliffs on the in-running tide. I could see the individual twigs making up nests on which birds sat; other birds cawed, dived and flapped about. Zathdar stayed at the wheel, speaking to his crew in short, sharp sentences, while we tacked at that rooftop slant close to the island, and about the same time my tension racked up to high anxiety at the sight of those breakers rolling away toward the rocky shore, the last cliff slid by and we were in open ocean again—revealing our prey. It was a three-masted clipper, easily twice the length of Zathdar's *Hurricane*.

Even I, who knew little about ships, could sense the navy ship's anticipation of an easy kill in the way some sails jerked up and others came down, and the ship hauled its wind in every bit as tight a curve as our own. They were coming on the attack.

So imagine their dismay when, vaguely on the still-gray horizon (it was now late afternoon, not that you could tell where the sun was, but the light was steadily more diffuse) two nicks appeared.

The other two pirate consorts.

Zathdar had sent them the easy way, to form the other half of the pincer. We'd been the bait.

We began to close with the clipper. Devli reappeared, looking ridiculous in a blond wig like an old dust mop and ill-fitting striped trousers (yellow and green) with an outsized shirt dyed a taxing shade of orange. "He has enough disguises to equip the city theater down there," Devli exclaimed happily.

"You look like an idiot," Elva retorted.

"Sure, but I don't look like me. In case they have wanted posters issued. Oh, *how* I'd love to see one, if it's really true," he added longingly. "And how much of a price on my head."

"Probably two copper tinklets. Three more than you're worth," Elva said with sisterly disrespect.

Devli grinned, flipping his curls at her. "You're sour because you don't get to go. If you acted friendly, I'll wager he'd have you along in a trice."

Elva wavered, which surprised me. Then she shrugged. "And

leave Sasharia counting her toes here? Seems fair enough that somebody stays to keep her company."

Devli turned to me. "I wish he'd let you come," he said shyly.

"Thanks. I think." I gripped my hands behind my back. "But no thanks."

Brother and sister widened their eyes in surprise. "But you're good," Devli observed.

"Good at practice. I've spent years and years at it. That does not mean I want to let somebody try to ventilate my chitlins. It only means that maybe I'm ready for it if they try to force the issue." I was desperate to keep my voice even. How could I be the only one scared spitless? But from all I could see, I was.

Devli's brow puckered. "You were so *good* in the fight at the transfer tower."

I thought back, remembering only a blur of tiredness that jolted suddenly into a super-powered adrenaline rush . . . powered not only by inept guards trying to capture us, but by the intense awareness of that derisive pirate whose first word about me had been *useless.*

I wasn't going to say that my main motivation had been to show him how wrong he was. Nope, nope, nope.

"Accident," I stated. "I was half-asleep, running on instinct. I am supposed to stay out of sight. Remember?" And in a thoroughly cowardly, absolutely desperate attempt to change the blasted subject, "Elva would you give me a rundown on what's happened in this kingdom since I was taken away?"

"If you like." She looked perplexed. "In a general way, at least."

To keep my hands busy so they wouldn't shake, I began to unbraid my hair and comb it out. One braid at a time, wincing and cursing under my breath at the snags. Back in L.A. I'd be doing this job after a good treatment with a whole lot of conditioner, but there wasn't any here.

"How far back shall I go?" Elva asked, and then, her eyes rounding, "If you'll pardon my saying so, you have a *lot* of hair."

"Oh yeah. My dad was a frizz-ball too. Made Einstein look bald—never mind who Einstein was. Let's say that where I come from, big hair is totally *uncool*." The word came out in English. There wasn't anything close. "I made the mistake of cutting it when I got mad at my mom, not long after we got through the World Gate, and for a couple of years I looked like a walking mushroom. Growing it long at least weighs it down, and I can braid it."

She grinned as I yanked out another braid, which sprang into determined curls adding to the mass hanging down my back to my butt. When I pulled it straight, I could easily sit on it.

"All right. Well, in '36, there was a strange incident we call the Siamis War, but it wasn't a war, it was more of an enchantment, and extended over the world."

"Oh yes, someone mentioned that. I wondered if 'Siamis' was a place or a person."

"Someone from Norsunder. An original Old Sartoran, I mean from four *thousand* years ago." She hunched her shoulders. "He was young-looking and handsome and charming, and he enchanted people by just thinking at them."

"That sounds nasty." I watched the archery teams climb to the tops.

"It was. Though nobody remembered much afterward. It was like we all lost a year. I was a toddler, so I didn't really notice any-thing, but the adults still talk about it, and they're worried because Norsunder is on the move, they say."

"That sounds even worse." The clatter of arrows and weapons from outside brought us to the cabin door as the archery teams took their places on the mastheads and readied themselves.

"Yes, Devli says the mages—" Elva stiffened, her face blanching.

I leaped up and joined her, my hair half-combed in a curling mass, the other half in ratty braids, as the deck crew lined up along the rails, weapons at hand.

Things had changed far faster than I'd expected.

Our pirate schooner lurched toward the navy ship, which looked enormous as it loomed steadily closer. High-hanging lanterns augmented the fading light in the west. Zathdar's crew waited, motionless except for nervous hands on weapons, and quick head-turnings. Ah. So they were scared, too. I could see it in tightened shoulders, in stiff fingers, shufflings, and restless checking and rechecking of weapons.

For some reason the sight of their tension actually eased some of mine. So I was not the only scared person on board. The proximity of violence, deliberately chosen, jetted a mingling of emotions through me, most negative, but somewhere in there was anticipation. Even readiness. I could feel it in the way my muscles tightened along my spine and through my back, a feeling akin to the moments before a match at a big competition, but at a fuel-injected hyper-level.

Zathdar spun the wheel. Sail parties brailed up two sails with lightning speed and the ships thumped together, yards and rigging entangling, masts creaking. We all staggered, then shadowy figures crouched below the rail jumped up and swung over to the navy ship from ropes. More ran across entangled yards to the other ship, roaring and howling.

"Inside! Shut the door!" Owl bawled at me as he ducked under a swinging lantern, sword raised. He and two others took up station in front of Elva's and my cabin, obviously on defense duty. Either that or to keep Elva and me from running to the navy guys.

The mass of surging figures shouted and fought, dashing to and fro. Annoyed as I was with Zathdar, the name Randart had scared me. I had no intention whatsoever of leaping from *Hurricane's* frying pan into the fire of Canardan's sinister war commander.

But Zathdar didn't know that. Where was he, anyway?

The lanterns shone through the ropes in wild spider-web patterns, creating intersecting geometric light patches and shadows, making it impossible to tell the surging figures apart. *At least the darkness has to be hiding blood and guts . . . sure don't see any, don't want to see any —*

I peered around the cabin door.

The tweet of a whistle—a roar of triumph—and twenty or thirty armed silhouettes jumped down from the navy ship's higher deck. A surprise squad of marines held back as reinforcements leaped over the rail onto our ship and fought their way down the deck, outnumbering the defending pirates.

"They know you're here," Elva said flatly, and I threw open the door.

Owl twisted round. "You know Randart does not mean safety for you."

My jaw was locked, teeth gritted. "I'm out here so I have room to defend myself. I. Do not. Want. To be. *Anyone's.* Prisoner."

From overhead a colorful figure swung, and Zathdar landed on the yard directly above us.

A quick exchange of glances between him and Owl, then: "Here!"

Zathdar flung a cavalry sword through the air toward me.

One sharp thud of heart against ribs, and years of kata training took over. I knew sword forms. I knew how to throw and catch a spinning sword. You don't take it standing still, but match movement, and so I flowed into kata mode and clipped the sword out of the air, bringing it down with a swoosh before the first naval warrior reached us.

He leaped back, joining his companions in the brown uniforms. For a split second they all stared at me, eyes so wide twin lantern flames reflected in them, their heads turning slightly as I swung the saber back and forth, back and forth, trying to get the feel for its unfamiliar weight and shape.

"That's the one," the lead man said. "Take her."

My heartbeat shifted into overdrive, drumming in my ears.

Owl, two of his sailors, and Elva (who'd ducked into the cabin and returned with a knife) formed a line in front of me, all of us keeping clear of the others' reach.

"No kill," Owl ordered hoarsely.

Elva sent him a distracted glance. "I thought that was hot air."

"No. True," he snapped. "Why do you think the bow teams are waiting?"

I remembered them, crouched there overhead. I realized no arrows had been loosed.

Yet.

I swung my cavalry saber, which was much heavier than I was used to. I noted the red tassel on it. This was the one from the weapons locker that no one had touched. Zathdar's fighting blade! But he was nowhere in sight.

A short, barked word and the navy guys rushed us. Then time stopped. The universe narrowed to my trembling fingers, my chi breathing, and the cut and thrust of swinging steel.

No kill? No chance to ask. It made me faster, surer, because I fought as I always had in practice, only one step harder. I did not care if I hurt anyone. I didn't want to *kill* anyone—

—and they were not trying to kill me. Disarm, yes. Wound, even. But not to kill.

And so I parried, blocked, deflected, kicked, punched, nicked, thumped (and used my knee once to unfair but effective advantage—sorry, guy) but I never stabbed.

The endless moment stretched into a roaring blur as sweat stung my eyes and my throat rasped raw. Abruptly I swayed there on the deck, whooping for breath, peering this way and that for the next target, but there were no more targets. There were only four people lying on the deck, either unconscious or wounded. The rest retreated fast, vanishing over the rail as a mass of gathered pirates, fresh from the supporting ships, chased them aft.

As the navy guys swarmed back to their ship, the battle shifted to the other deck. I rushed to the side, Owl next to me, in time to witness the end of a saber duel between Zathdar and their captain. The latter's sword clanged to the deck, Zathdar held his point at the man's throat, and shouted something, echoed by a woman at the other end of the navy ship. One of Zathdar's other captains.

The result? Weapons clanking and whanging to the deck,

hands rising in the universal "I surrender. Don't hit me!" The king's sailors were obviously not going to test the pirates' willingness to stick to the rules at the price of their captain's life, and I wondered if that was out of loyalty or fear.

Zathdar flicked a look our way.

Owl moved with the speed of someone who had received orders. As I leaned on the rail, still breathless, the pirates dragged the unconscious navy guys to the rail and attached them to ropes to be boomed over to their own deck. Meanwhile Zathdar prodded the captain and they vanished into the clipper's broad cabin.

The pirates herded the navy below the clipper's decks, then closed and barred the hatches. After that they moved about, some purposeful, most just talking, pointing, and demonstrating their individual battles with their still-bare weapons, the restless rattling about of people shedding adrenaline.

Devli emerged from the hatch, papers clutched to his orange shirt, his unlikely blond mop bouncing as he bounded toward the place where the two rails ground together on the pitching waves.

On a sharp whistle, pirates swarmed aloft to free rigging and spars; others got busy hacking, chopping, tearing, and cutting ropes. They were doing enough sabotage to ensure no chase would be made without a lot of repairs first. Some returned to the *Hurricane*, carrying pretty much anything the navy guys hadn't nailed down. There wasn't much to loot on a navy scout, but they'd done their best.

Elva joined me. "Ow," she said reflectively, binding a length of cloth round one forearm. "I hope that's the last pirate battle we're in. No matter what my brother says."

"Tell me about this no-kill order." My brain had gone oddly numb, and my hoarse voice sounded far away, like someone else.

"Oh. That. It's just, the Fool, that is, Prince Jehan, who is supposedly in charge of the guard, the navy, and I forget what else his father wants to duck the blame for, *supposedly* issued this command to their forces that in any skirmish they can't kill anyone until our side, that is, the resistance, does. He *supposedly* doesn't want our countrymen killing one another if it can be avoided. It seems to be the same for the pirates, too. Anyway, I always thought it lies. Canardan's people trying to whitewash their rotten reputation. But I guess it's true. For the navy and army, I emphasize," she added, her brow furrowed. "Not for War Commander Randart's private guard."

The two ships jolted, staggering everyone on both decks, then parted with a groan of timbers. I wondered if Zathdar had made it back just as a colorful figure emerged from the navy captain's cabin. He climbed up the shrouds, caught a rope I hadn't seen in the wavering light from the lanterns (it was quite dark by now) and swung over lightly, landing on the topsail yard just as two arrows hissed through the air from the other ship.

He caught one of the backstays, and slid to the deck near us. A last arrow thunked into the coaming round the fore hatch directly behind him, then someone on the other ship shouted an order, and no more arrows whizzed over.

Zathdar gave us all one comprehensive glance. "All right?" He addressed everyone, but his glance rested last on me.

"Alive," I said, and Elva echoed me. Then I drew in a deep breath. *Keep it neutral. You still have to land.*

But I had to ask. "Was it really necessary, this raid? Or just, you know, your typical pirate idea of fun?"

"Oh, let's say that this fellow has been doing a bit of piracy on his own." Zathdar tipped his head toward the ship. "Under orders from the war commander."

His manner was too airy, a contrast with that tight gesture. Plainly I was not the only one keeping crucial info behind buttoned lip.

He grinned at me. "And you think I look strange." He took the cavalry sword from my unresisting fingers, stepped back, and flicked the point through the air a yard from my head—a gently mocking salute.

I clutched at my hair, feeling the one side with ratty braids dangling down, the other a tangled mass of frizzy curls, emphasis on the tangled. Total big-hair crisis! I had to laugh, the sheer, squeaky laugh of a sudden rush of knee-whacking relief. It was really over. My muscles turned to Smuckers' finest.

"Well done." He flourished the sword as he smiled at us all. But again I had the distinct sense he was talking to me.

Then he turned away, lifting his voice. "Captain's punch for every hand!"

The sailors responded with a loud, hearty cheer as Zathdar bent to yank that last arrow out of the coaming. He straightened, flushed with triumph. "Come to the wardroom to celebrate?"

Again, he did not quite address me, but the air in my general direction. Owl, overseeing the last sweep of the deck, raised a hand in agreement. This was a general invitation, not a private one. He'd said it would take place in the wardroom. No harm in that.

Then Zathdar turned my way. "Join us, Sasharia?"

"Sure." And to Owl, who was rubbing his hands and laughing under his breath, "Captain's punch?"

"Oh, it's good." Owl chuckled. "But it'll knock you back if you're not careful."

The crew divided up into two parties, with off-duty crew members carrying food up to those on duty. The watch captains crowded around with us at the battered table in the wardroom, roaring again as the grinning cook muscled in a huge tureen of something that smelled like citrus, with hard liquor undertones.

A variety of cups, mugs, and glasses passed from hand to hand, everyone dipping into the tureen. Next came the sounds of slurping and sighing. The punch tasted of berry, citrus, wine and a raisiny liquor that was very smooth going down, with a delicious bite. Warmth rushed through me, smoothing away the aches.

"Good, eh?" Owl dug his elbow in my side.

"Mighty good." I sipped again, then realized they were all more or less watching me. So I lifted my glass to the table. "Great job, peeps!"

The *peeps* came out in English, but no one seemed to care. They gave another cheer. In such a small space, their enthusiasm hurt the ears.

I gulped down more punch, feeling hot and a little dizzy as everyone started talking, the adrenaline-comedown sort of chatter I remembered from my competition days. "Didya see. . . ?" ". . . and then I took my sword and . . ." "He was goin' for Sage, so I grabbed up a stool and . . ."

Everyone wanted to air their own bit, to praise the others and be praised, and—as the punch loosened tongues—more of the compliments came my way.

I smiled and saluted and returned compliments about skirmishes I couldn't possibly have seen, because the flushed, smiling faces and bright eyes surrounding me so plainly expected it. And deserved it, too. They'd won. We were safe.

But as the talk got wilder, the compliments sent my way took on a certain familiarity of expression. "Thought you'd finally take action," the cook said, giving me a friendly nudge with a powerful arm. I nearly fell face-first into the tureen.

"Knew you'd come out fer yer Dad," the forecastle captain boomed from the other side of the table. "He never forgot us that haven't any titles, no he did not."

And after a general (though less energetic) "Hear him, hear him!" one of the top hands thumped her mug onto the table.

Then red-haired Robin declared, "When you raise your banner, Princess, we'll be right behind you."

I tried to force a smile, and shot a suspicious look at Zathdar. He had been watching me. He gave his head the smallest shake, turning his thumbs outward, and I knew he hadn't said anything to the crew.

They didn't act like people ordered to drop hints about my princessly obligations, and anyway, it was all coming back to me, how people thought here. When you were born to a title, you had a responsibility along with the title. Your job was politics.

I left as soon as I could, aware of Elva's unhappy face over at a side table, where she sat with Zathdar's navigator and bosun. She followed me in silence.

I tramped wearily to my cabin, Elva behind me, wincing as she flexed her fingers. Titles—expectations—obligations—politics chased round in my head like dizzy mice.

A long drink of water, then I lay down, shut my eyes and firmly told myself that answers were my dad's job. I just had to find him.

THIRTEEN

WHILE ATANIAL WAS ON her way with her royal escort to the royal castle at Vadnais, back at the Ebans' home Marka, at last free of her bonds, crept downstairs. She'd wriggled safely under her bed by the time she heard the smashings and bangings of searchers in the lower rooms. She hadn't known who was searching the house, but those words the tall, beautiful woman with the accent had said echoed over and over in her mind, *Living a lie*.

Then the tromping feet came upstairs. Two pairs appeared in her doorway, and one pair kicked roughly at her trunk. A young man said in a bored voice, "Here's the room with the signal. But the girl is gone."

"As well," someone else said.

As well. She knew what that meant. They'd had orders to kill her.

Tromp, tromp, tromp. The heavy boots clattered down the stairs. The crashes and bangs below ended. The door slammed on a silent house.

Wondering if she would ever stop crying, Marka resumed working steadily at the knots.

Dawn painted the world in dreary blue streaks when she finally passed through the ruined rooms. She paused in the kitchen to grab some of the spilled food, drink from the water barrel, and then eased out into the vegetable garden, where cold air promised rain. Cold air chilled her newly bare neck, and fresh tears rolled down her cheeks at the thought of her shorn hair — and Tam bearing it away. Maybe flinging it with disgust into a fire. *Stop it. Get home, warn Mama and the others.*

She thought of Mistress Eban's absent kindness. She thought of Tam, his grin, his hands. His kisses. Her beautiful hair that he used to run his fingers through, calling it ribbon-silk . . .

Her chest ached with the sobs that boiled up, but she couldn't let them escape. At least she had never told the king's man Tam's name, or anything about him. She could be glad of that. She would have to be glad of that.

She crossed the boot-trampled vegetable garden and scurried up the trail through the orchard, leaving barely a rustle.

Atanial slept through the next few days, only rising to drink some healer's tea she found waiting (the smell had woken her up), eat the meals she found on a tray, and go right back to sleep. Each time she woke she rediscovered that she lay in a room, not a cell. The bed was clean and comfortable. Everything else could wait.

She let another week go by while she avoided the king's messengers, either pretending to be asleep, or claiming she still was unwell, as she recovered her strength and wondered what to do.

Then came the morning that Commander Randart entered the king's outer chamber, pushed past the scribes and runners, and scowled at the crowd around the king.

Canardan bustled his bureaucrats through the immediate business, and dismissed the rest with a laugh and a joke.

When the last had departed, the king motioned for Randart to shut the door. He sighed inwardly at his old friend's scowl. "What now?"

"Courier from Ellir." Randart sank into one of the cushioned interview chairs. "Zathdar seems to have slipped inside the blockade."

Canardan slammed a hand down on his desk. "Damn! How does a *pirate ship* 'slip' inside a blockade?"

"My scouts think he might have mingled in with the fishing fleet coming back from northern waters. Though no one reported any vessels standing out or otherwise drawing attention."

Canardan sat back, his breath hissing. "What else?"

"Zathdar reappeared on the other side of Mais Island."

Canardan pressed his hands to his eyes. "No. Don't tell me."

Randart waited, smiling grimly while the silence lengthened.

"All right." Canardan sighed, flinging his hands outward. "Tell me."

"The report is sketchy. Just arrived by transfer note." Only small pieces of paper fit into the magical notecases, which made for very short reports. "But he seems to have cut out the *Skate*. Took it just long enough for his rabble to strip it of supplies while he tried to pry details of the mission from Bragail."

Canardan laughed somewhat bitterly. "I wish him joy for his efforts. Bragail has too many secrets buried to hand any pirate a shovel."

"Except, if I read this aright . . ." Randart held up a folded bit of paper. "Zathdar began by flinging at least a couple of those secrets in his teeth."

Canardan leaned forward, hand out. "Let me see that." He frowned down at the paper . . . *The pirate said 2 words, "Chwahir" & "Glathan," so the cptn. endorsed Z's order to leave them alone in t/cabin. We went below, under swords of pirates.* "Glathan. I suspect we will never cease to regret that."

Randart shrugged. "Only way to deal with mages."

Canardan rubbed his eyes, trying to press back the pangs of a burgeoning headache. The kingdom was unraveling under his fingers. It would take a grand gesture of kingly proportion to wrest triumph out of disaster. One possible gesture lay sequestered upstairs, having been left until her blistered feet had healed enough for her to walk.

Giving Canardan time to consider what to say when they did meet again. He'd been reflecting on those blistered feet from a cross-country run that everyone in the castle—the kingdom— apparently knew about before he did.

Bringing him to the present. "What about my son? No message from him?" Canardan flicked his solid-gold notecase.

"Yes, the courier had word about him as well. He sent one of his runners straight to Ellir, promising that the prince would be back by the beginning of the midsummer games." Randart added wryly, "You haven't heard from him directly because he seems to have been caught napping by some highway robbers along his path in the south, and he was robbed of everything, including his notecase."

Canardan groaned. The headache was worsening with every word he heard.

"Well, he did send his guard to the World Gate tower, so he cannot be blamed for a shortage of personal protection," Randart offered, inwardly despising that absurd order about not killing the enemy until they killed first. For Randart, there was no consideration for fellow countrymen, much less pirates or brigands. If you stood against him, you were an enemy. Enemies deserve death. Clear and simple.

Canardan snorted. "No, he can be blamed for being an idiot who cannot defend himself against a couple of bush skulkers. But he will be a married idiot as soon as we lay hands on Math's girl. We'll make it a grand festival, with public pardons handed out like roses."

Randart did not hide his surprise, or his displeasure.

"Carefully chosen ones," Canardan said swiftly, mistaking the direction of Randart's ire. "Anyway, as soon as Jehan shows up in Ellir, we'll know where he is. Send a message to him to stay put for the midsummer games. He can wine and dine the winning cadets, he can hold musical parties, he can visit every poet and painter in the city, but he is to *stay put*."

"I'll send a dispatch as soon as we're done."

"We're done. Go yourself. Hunt down that pirate. I don't care if you use the entire fleet. The Chwahir plan is a disaster, blockading doesn't work, and we can't even get our trade protected, so you, my friend, are going pirate hunting, and when you do find them, kill them all. Make certain not one is left alive to come back here and blab all over about our villainy. Against *pirates*."

Each considered how unfair that was.

"The only one I want left alive is the girl, and you bring her directly to me," the king ordered.

"Consider it done." Randart got up and left.

That night, Atanial awoke abruptly, aware someone was in her room.

If that's Canary, I will scream so loud they'll hear me in Sartor. She sat bolt upright in bed and yanked the covers to her neck.

A shape passed before the faint starlight glowing in her window, a female shape. Stout, with an ill-confined cloud of frizzy hair.

"Ananda?" she whispered, astonished.

"Yes," came the queen's soft voice. "No, do not light a candle. I am believed to be sleepwalking. It's part of my madness."

Atanial gave her eyes a vigorous rub, then she patted the bed, which was large enough to sleep a family comfortably. "Come. Talk to me. I'm glad you're still alive."

"Oh, he would never dare touch me," Queen Ananda said dryly. "After all, it's my name that brought him the crown, even if he put his Merindar chalice on all the shields and carriages. He's no Zhavalieshin. Neither is his boy. Though I wouldn't mind if Jehan were," she added in a reflective voice.

"Jehan?" Atanial prompted as the bed shifted and the queen settled, hands clasped around her knees. "Tell me about him."

The two women regarded one another in the pale starlight. The queen knew she was unprepossessing, but then she'd always been unprepossessing: short, plump, her hands broad, her nose a hawk beak, her hair an uncontrollable frizzy mat of yellow. Her brother Mathias was the tall, well-made version of frizz and nose who'd gone away and come back with this stunning beauty from another world.

"I know him little. What I do know, I shall tell you anon."

Atanial heard the hesitation in her voice and misconstrued the reason. She exclaimed impulsively, "First I want to say this. I never saw you after your father's memorial. This is *years* of your time too late, but I apologize if I ever made you suffer."

"No," the queen murmured. "You didn't. I knew what Canardan was after when he flirted with you. I only fooled myself once, when I believed his blandishments during our courtship. But I didn't know what real love was until I saw you with Math."

Atanial bowed her head until her brow rested on her knees, which she'd brought up under the covers. Her voice was muffled. "Then my flirtation with Canary must have looked doubly bad to you."

"I could see you keeping it light and merry."

"Yes. And no. He is amazingly attractive, or at least was." Atanial sighed. "So flirting with him was fun. Dancing close to the fire. I thought you didn't care, I thought you didn't notice, I thought I could in some way help Math. And oh, I have to admit I liked the danger. But he burned me good, right along with Math."

The queen nodded. "I know that, and I have my own confession to make. I believe it is my fault that you and Math had to run. You see, I told Canardan the night my father died that I was going to renounce the crown in favor of Math."

"You did? We never heard that!"

"Of course not. You only suffered the results. I thought I could deflect Canardan from taking power, but I had misjudged everything. Including his reasons for marrying me."

"Oh, Ananda. I'm so sorry. So that's behind the mad-queen story?"

"When he said I went mad with grief over my father's death and my brother's treachery, for five years he made sure I saw no one in order to deny it. I did not have the wit or ability to resist. So life went on, passing me by. I became a nonentity." The queen shrugged, her voice briefly caustic, reminding Atanial momentarily of Math. "Maybe I deserved it a little, though I never asked to be born to a title. But I finally realized that the guise of madness was a convenience for us both. He gets the power he wanted, and I have my freedom within these walls. However, taking power has not proved easy for Canardan. Things have gone wrong for him, especially in the past few years. Ever since Jehan came back. Canardan's become very determined as a result."

Atanial said abruptly, "Bringing us back to Canardan's boy. Is he good to you, at least?"

"Jehan's not really a boy. Though everyone thinks of him as one. It's that white morvende hair, the dreamy manner, the boyish preoccupation with fashion. He does have a tendency to veer off and follow bards if they sing well enough, I hear, or artists if they're pretty and paint well, but yes, he's always been kind to me."

"Then I won't hate him. But if I can find a way to defeat Canary, I will."

The queen paused, staring ahead. "Canardan's got the castle on double watches. Everyone, *everyone*, knows you are back. And that you are here. So you have become a royal guest. Which is why you are in the royal-guest wing here, though no one at all sleeps in any of the rooms either side of you, and the tower is guarded at all the stairways. It's also warded, I believe."

"Thank you for the warning."

The queen rose. Her voice was soft and dreamy. "He's going to offer you everything. Including my life. He would keep that promise."

She drifted to the door.

"Ananda, wait," Atanial whispered, not daring to raise her voice.

But the queen had had her say. She vanished, and by the time Atanial had wrestled out of the covers, run to the door and cautiously eased it open, no one was in sight.

Atanial wandered back to the bed. That was weird, that was definitely weird. She sensed the woman had more to say, but if so, why not say it?

Because she thinks I might buy Canary's line. Even at the price of her life.

It was jolting, uncomfortable, and if looked at a certain way, kind of insulting, but Atanial would not let herself go there. She herself had misjudged the queen in the past, so she had to accept without rancor that that was a two-way street.

Atanial threw herself on the bed, knowing she should arm herself with sleep, but that seemed impossible. She wiggled her toes. Her feet did feel a lot better, thanks to the salve they'd given her after that first marvelous bath.

She could get up and look around, except if she lit a lamp in order to check Queen Ananda's words, who might be watching?

Remember, you are a prisoner.

She dozed eventually, but that thought was still with her when she woke. Pearly blue early morning light pooled on the spectacular rug in several shades of green and gold with highly stylized flowers interwoven.

Atanial threw back the coverlet and padded to the wardrobe. Her feet no longer hurt. The wardrobe was almost as large as the bedroom, into which someone had brought quite a number of trunks.

Canary had had an entire day to set up this pretty prison before he'd closed his trap on the Ebans. She needed to remember that, too.

But, she thought happily when she threw back the first trunk and saw the gorgeous silk inside, there was no reason she needn't take any armaments offered her.

It was a stylishly gowned Atanial, her hair pinned up with pearls, who received the runner come to invite her to breakfast with the king, as he had every day.

It was time to face the enemy guns.

"Please, tell him I'd be delighted. Or better, why don't you escort me? Though I remember the castle fairly well, I don't know which rooms he uses."

The young man blushed as he bowed.

Atanial placed her hand confidingly on his arm and tripped along the hall. She mentally counted up all the armsmen she saw, sure there were some out of sight.

Prisoner, she thought, at the same moment Canary glimpsed her floating down the big marble stairway to the terrace where he had the servants set up a breakfast. Nothing private. Not that there was any privacy when every single pair of ears was cocked in this direction, and every pair of eyes jostling to catch a glimpse of the famed princess. Let them see a kingly welcome.

With covert appreciation he noted that only her face had aged, but its lines were those of intelligence, of laughter, of hard-won experience. Her hair was the same sun-lit yellow as the old days, and her body under that blue silken stuff formed the same strong, enticing curves that had caught his eye when they were all much younger.

He forced his gaze away and smiled, and she smiled, and he indicated the table, beautifully laid out with the best gold-edged porcelain, the best golden utensils, a crystal vase with fresh-picked rose buds.

She sat, arranging her skirts.

He waited for the silent servitors to set out the platters of hot food. Then he waved them away.

"Feeling better?" he asked.

"Lovely! So catch me up on the news." She tipped her head and charmed him by plopping her elbows on the table.

"Local news?" he asked, with some irony.

"Oh, no. World news. What have I missed?"

"You missed a couple of brushes with Norsunder." He poured out perfectly steeped Sartoran tea for her, and then himself. "All the mages are yammering about a real strike one of these days. But they've been yammering for the past decade, and nothing has happened yet."

"That sounds nasty." She cradled the fine porcelain cup in her fingers, sipped, and smiled over the gold rim of the cup. "Tell me something nice. What is the news in Sartor?"

"From what I've heard, Shontande Lirendi is busy courting the young queen."

"If I knew that Carlael of Colend had a son, I had forgotten. I hope he is not as mad as his father," Atanial said.

"No. Not in the least. He is also a throwback to Matthias the Magnificent." Canardan added sardonically, "Even my cloud-brained son noticed, when I sent him west to Alsais to get some diplomatic experience. Said every female within riding range is in love with him, and half the men as well. Certainly every princess of eligible age seems to be waiting for him to throw the rose, which leaves the rest, like my boy, out in the cold."

"If he's that beautiful, what are his chances with the queen of Sartor?"

"Well, no one knows. But there's been some diplomatic fluttering about the fact that she'd never leave Sartor, and he'd never leave Colend, so the only solution is those two combining kingdoms into one of the biggest empires this world has ever known, even in the old empire days."

Atanial whistled as she set down the cup and lavishly piled crispy-edged oatcakes onto her plate.

"But there are those who don't think anything will come of it." He helped himself, and for a short time there was no sound but the distant chatter of birds as they ate. Then he lifted his fork, watching appreciatively as she got a second helping. "You still have a splendid appetite, I see."

"Of course," she said equably. "When the food is as good as

this. And when I've gone without as many meals as I have." She gave him a mocking salute with her teacup.

He grinned. "Tell me about your girl. She a good eater as well?"

"Yes." Atanial added honey-butter to her oatcakes.

"That's not exactly informative."

"No." She helped herself to some sliced peaches.

"Will you at least listen to my suggestion?"

"Talk away. It's your palace, and your invitation." She made a wry gesture indicating herself there on the chair in her splendid gown, and gave him a lovely smile. "We'll call it an invitation, since you've been nice enough to include a scented walk-in bath and trunks of clothes and a fine room in your durance vile."

"Now, Atanial," he chided. "I'd rather have you as an ally. Much rather."

"In what plans?"

"Recover Khanerenth's past glories." He lifted his hand, taking in the palace. "That's it without embroidery. We're a sinking ship. Trade disrupted, neighboring kingdoms call the prices, and they don't cut us any deals. Threat of war with Norsunder. Chwahirsland has Shnit Sonscarna back on the throne, which has been no good news to anyone."

"I hadn't known he was gone."

"Oh, for a while. But he came back."

She remembered the horrible reports of the king of the Chwahir. Now *that* was a truly evil king, no ifs, ands, or buts.

But he wasn't the issue. Khanerenth was. "Recovering lost glories sounds nice, but what does that mean? Past artistic achievements? Past trade agreements? Surely not lands that have been settled by treaty."

"Negotiating with bad governments, trouble—" He held up a hand. "I know you're about to come at me with some remark about my governing, but you don't actually know anything except gossip from the Ebans. You can sit in on my interviews, talk to my treasury steward, and make up your own mind. At least I've held on. Locan Jora, the others northwards, they keep changing kings like foot warriors change their socks."

"That can't be good." She ran her fingertip round the gold edging on her cup. "So what do you want from me?"

"An introduction to your daughter. Just an introduction. Let her meet my boy. See if they suit. Good diplomacy, join the families, promote peace. Heal the problems here."

Atanial laughed. "How can I arrange that when I am in your castle, surrounded by half a wing of good-looking young men and women brandishing spears?"

"But you are free to go any time." He opened his hands. "Go and find her, with my good will."

FOURTEEN

I WOKE UP FEELING sticky and hot. The ship wallowed like an old tub. There was no wind. Yet I heard a curious scraping sound, too rhythmic to be weather.

I got up, grumpily wishing that they hadn't seen fit to give me this fancy cabin with a (sweltering) bunk, when a hammock would have been so much airier. Second, I wished I'd warmed up before the swashbuckling of the day before. And how did I get *that* many bruises? I didn't remember taking any of those hits, but they sure ached now.

I peered out of the scuttle. Sun dazzle splashed off the water with eye-watering brightness. There was no hint of a breeze.

A party of tired-looking sailors sat on the deck under the shade of a slack sail, honing the weapons. There were two or three kids about twelve or thirteen aboard. They had been hidden below during the fighting, on Zathdar's orders, so they too seemed grumpy as they carried polished, sharpened weapons to the weapons locker and then brought another to each crew member holding a whetting stone. When I remembered how much drinking had gone on the night before, I suspected headaches were also part of the general malaise.

With a total lack of energy I straightened the bunk. I couldn't complain about a generous gesture —

My thoughts fled like frightened birds when I opened the cupboard below my bunk to get out a change of clothes and saw my gear bag had been moved.

Could that have been the ship? No, it couldn't. I'd tucked it just so. And it hadn't moved during that storm early in our journey.

While I was down in the wardroom, someone had come in and searched my stuff.

Elva was already gone from the cabin. I was alone. I yanked out the bag, ripped it open, and unfolded the exquisite embroidered coverlet. There were my things: my Earth clothes and sandals; a carved wooden box containing the jewels Mother and I had carried through the Gate; a child's simple flute (called a *recorder* on Earth) that my father had given me, but hadn't had time to teach me to play; and plainest, but by far the most important, a seashell wrapped in homespun cloth. Just the sort of memento a child would carry, Magister Glathan and my father had decided when they prepared this magical token, and taught me the spells . . .

It was there. It was safe. I wrapped it back up and replaced the things, then replaced the bag.

Nothing was gone, but there remained the fact that someone on board this ship had nosed through my stuff.

I left the cabin, grimacing as the glare and heat hit me. The heavy summer air was thick with the scents of brine and wet wood, half-dried canvas, and sweaty people. I dodged around the work party and wandered to the shrouds, the heavy ropes attaching the foremast to the hull. These thick ropes smelled of sea and hemp and oils. The round wooden deadeyes showed the effect of wind and weather, but beneath, the stroke of adze remained.

I held onto two of the shrouds, staring down at the water plashing gently against the side of the hull as I mentally reviewed the night before. Who had been at the wardroom table with me? I could pretty much remember them all, mostly by images of flushed faces as they deprogrammed, like after any kind of sudden big event, whether an earthquake or a big competition. Zathdar had been in the wardroom all the time I was there. Same with Owl and Robin. Okay. So . . .now what I had to consider was why I suspected Zathdar first.

Movement at my side broke my concentration. Elva held out some toasted bread with melted cheese. "Hungry?" she asked.

I took it with a word of thanks, and she put her hands through the squares made by the shrouds and the horizontal ratlines, leaning her forehead against the twisted ropes. "I know better than to down that punch. I should have drunk the crew's ale," she said sourly. "He gave them the best. Ellir Gold."

"Well, if they're going to raid, why not the best? I take it then you didn't notice who came and went during the party?"

She gave me a glance of quick concern. "What's wrong?"

"Someone went through my belongings last night."

She didn't ask how I knew. She looked away, her shoulders tight, and I said, in blank surprise, "Devlaen?"

She shrugged, her face pink with embarrassment and guilt. "He was gone for a while, and he seemed, oh, like a scolded pup, when he came back."

I let my breath out. So that's why Elva had looked so miserable last night. "I didn't think it of him."

"I suspect his magisters ordered him to. He says they think you have some kind of magical knowledge that you aren't telling anyone." Her tone expressed disbelief and disinterest. She was a navigator, knew nothing of magic, and cared less. "You suspected Zathdar," she added with faint triumph.

"Not because he's done anything I consider particularly untrustworthy. Opposite."

She fingered the taut shroud. "I don't understand."

"Because my distrust makes no sense. I don't trust him because I like him more than not. I, um, grew up, let us say, hearing about handsome and untrustworthy men."

"You think him handsome? I don't. Anyway, you mean kings." She made a thumbs-down gesture.

"Well, yes. Not only Canary, either. For a time when I was about thirteen my mother was angry with my father for not returning. She got past that, but I guess it had its effect." I whooshed out my breath. "I really have to get over it as well. I mean, Zathdar was there all night. I saw him."

"He could have had someone search your things," she said.

"Yes, but is that really characteristic? From what little we've seen, if he wanted to, he would have searched it himself. Right in front of me."

"Yes, that's more his style." Her tone made it clear she did not think the better of him for it.

I wiped my sweaty forehead against my sleeve. At home I would have jumped in the shower. Now I turned away, my braids swinging against my back, and finished the bread and cheese as I made my way below to the cleaning frame shared by the entire crew. It was made of wood, fitted into the door to the crew quarters, but laden with magic spells. I stepped through, enjoying the snap and tingle of magic whisking away dirt and grime and I guess bacteria.

The air was hot and stuffy down there, the night crew swinging in their hammocks, their deep breathing audible. I paused in the companionway, listening to the thump of feet overhead, as I considered Elva's words. I'd completely forgotten those two older men who'd first knocked on my door at my previous apartment, before Devli appeared at the new one and tricked me.

Except those couldn't be his tutors. They had to be Canardan's mages.

Again I'd overlooked the magical side of this struggle. I had to consider it now.

Devli had magical communication, and he'd been sitting in that hold doing magical stuff. He might not have been making a communications device for Zathdar at all, whatever he'd told the privateer. What if he'd been secretly making a transfer token, like to get two of us off the ship and to his magisters?

Also, I'd been seen by the navy guys. Did *they* have magical communications? I had to consider the fact that not only did Canardan know about my presence, but these magicians did as well. Magicians for and against Canardan, busy with their own purposes. And I did not really know what their goal was, once they'd brought me to this world.

"Problem?"

I lifted my head. Zathdar lounged on the ladder above, one arm lazily blocking the hatch so that no one else could come down. He was back to his scarlet shirt. A shaft of sunlight shimmered with a ruby glow down that extended arm, highlighting its latent strength.

I said, "Devli seems to have received orders to search my stuff."

Zathdar made a slight grimace. "I didn't think of that."

"Here's another thing to consider. He could, say, receive a transfer token in a note box. If he cannot perform a double transfer himself. He's a nice kid, but I don't want him anywhere near me anymore."

Zathdar looked up at the bright blue sky beyond the sagging mainsail, the light stippling the dark sweep of his lashes until he blinked. "I can keep him busy down below, if you stay on deck. We only have a few more days of travel as soon as the wind picks up."

"Will the wind pick up?"

"It's already beginning." He tipped his chin behind me. "We'll have to tack and tack eastward, but north should be a swift run."

"East?" I exclaimed. "I thought we were going west. Aloca Bay lies west, I know that much."

"But the king has Aloca guarded by too large a force to slip by."

"So where are we going?"

"Ellir."

"What? Isn't that one of the king's strongholds?"

"Well, it is. In a sense. But have you ever heard the old saying 'hide in plain sight'?"

"I think our version is 'The safest place for the thief is under the sheriff's bed.'"

He grinned. "That's it. I obtained the latest merchant codes from our friends aboard the *Skate* yesterday, and so it will be a sober trading vessel that makes landfall at Ellir, nice and law abiding. The muscle in Aloca will be searching every vessel. We land in Ellir and do nothing to draw attention."

He hoisted himself up, and I followed after. A faint coolness feathered my cheek. A breeze, just as he'd said. The water in the distance ruffled in little wavelets, whitecaps frothing, color more greenish than the deep and placid blue below us.

"What about the blockade?" I watched one of the slack sails stir, then bell slightly.

"Here comes," someone called from above. Owl bawled out an order, and the sail party scrambled to make the most of the rising breeze.

"The blockade is broken." He gave me a quick grin, a long dimple flashing beside his mouth down to his jaw, and a corresponding flash of warmth kindled my innards. "They're on their way to reinforce Aloca."

I took a deep breath. Pirate or privateer, there was no future here. *Move along*, I told myself, and I climbed past him. He did not try to stop me, but launched in the opposite direction, gazing upward and calling a command to the team shaking out the topsails to catch the rising wind.

FIFTEEN

BY THE WATCH CHANGE, the wind had risen steadily, blowing straight along the coast, and so we tacked in a dramatic zigzag back and forth, using the westward bend to propel us gradually northward. The whistle tweeted, feet thumped. Soon came the agreeable roar of voices from below as the day watch ate their meal and the next watch scrambled from the hatches, checking sea, sky, and sails and sniffing the air.

Devli was nowhere in sight. Neither was his sister. I stayed at the rail, out of the way, enjoying the wind. When a hand struck my biceps in a friendly thump, I was startled to discover Gliss there, the wind combing through her blond hair.

"Thanks for not blabbing," she said gruffly.

"No one's business."

She brought one shoulder up, her smile surprisingly shy. "You off at Ellir?"

I nodded, expecting her to express relief, even if covertly, but she said, even more gruffly, "If you change your mind. Till you're—well, until. You could join our watch. Women are good in the tops because we're fast."

"Thank you." I was gratified and surprised. Not even the reminder of my assumed princessly duties implied in that "until" could upset me. I was just going to have to accept that everyone else had expectations of me. That didn't mean I had to raise a banner and lead an army.

I shoved that subject to the back of my brain, knowing it would sit there and leer at me. "May I ask you a question?" On her cautious nod of assent, "Did you set out to become a pirate—a privateer—or did it sort of happen?"

"You didn't know?" She looked surprised. "Everyone's heard of Zathdar's fleet. People want to sign on. But it's tough, first to get an interview, then to pass their tests."

"No, I hadn't any idea. Our invitation was the kind that you don't refuse." She gave my weak joke a perfunctory smile. She was a very serious person, I realized. "So why does he have such a small fleet?"

"He trains people and then sends them out. Other ships're glad to take us on. It's the training, see. And he doesn't keep people long. On account of the price on his head. Except for Owl and his captains and watch commanders."

Odd. Why would a privateer train people and send them away? Training costs money, at least on Earth. You don't train people to be as fast and tough as these and then just send them off, unless . . .

"We've got allies if we need 'em. They know a couple of signals, see. Like when we broke the navy's threatened alliance with the Chwahir last winter. He says three is more maneuverable." She shrugged. "But if he needs a fleet, well, they're out there."

How do you build a fleet when you haven't a king's budget? You train them, send them out with a couple of signals . . .

I forced my thoughts back to Gliss. "So you started with life on the sea?"

She shook her head once. "Born in the hills between what they call Locan Jora and Khanerenth. Fighting all the time. Too much of it. Got tired of all the family alliances bickering, worse, the landholders versus the plains people who have always ignored borders, ignore them now, and will always ignore them. So. Ran away to sea. Fishing boat, ten years. Then got voted in here, a year ago."

I whistled. "Now that I know what your invitation is worth, I thank you again."

She squinted upward, frowned at something going on with one of the upper sails, and pushed away without another word, swarming up the shrouds like she was flying.

By nightfall we were skimming northward at exhilarating speed. The sky was clear, the air balmy. Three of the day crew brought out instruments, sat on the railing of the forecastle half-deck, and began to play. Some of the crew sang songs in round, in which I could hear the difficult but distinctive Sartoran triplicate chord changes and beats. The teenaged crew members started dancing in twos and threes on the forecastle, one boy alone on the capstan, blithely ignoring jeers and even a couple of metal ale cans potted at him, which he dodged without missing a step.

Owl stumped up beside me. "C'mon, Princess, give us a dance."

"Not much of a dancer." I grinned. "I'm afraid if I get up there and swing my hips around like people my age do at home, every single ale pot would be tossed at me."

"You get up there and swing them hips, and they won't be tossing ale pots." He wiggled his slanting brows.

That made me laugh, but I (easily) resisted the temptation to make a fool of myself.

Zathdar appeared at my other side. I was leaning against the rail with my elbows propped behind me. He leaned next to me, his profile etched against the taut foresail as he watched the dancers jig and twirl round and round the capstan. But I could feel his attention on me. He asked in his mild voice, "No dancing?"

"I'm afraid of what it says about my upbringing that I wouldn't know what to do at a grand ball, but put me on a dojo floor and I'm ready to rock and roll."

Dojo and *rock and roll* did not translate, but he didn't question either of them.

I said, "So did you have a pirate mom or dad?"

He looked up in mock exasperation. "How often do I have to remind you that I'm a privateer?"

"Who dresses like a pirate."

He angled that quick grin again, the dimple accentuated by the golden light of the swinging lamps overhead. I was vaguely aware that Owl had gone from my other side.

"A pirate," I added firmly, "who has no sense of color."

He put his hand to his bandana, which was the long green-and-gold one hanging down his back, the fringes blowing around his slim waist. "Who says green and red is not eminently sensible? Why, in the worst rainstorm, in the thickest action, Owl and Robin only have to look round once and find me anywhere."

"Including in nightmares."

There was the dimple again. I looked away, but I was laughing.

I heard his laugh, a soft chuckle, almost under his breath. His elbow companionably bumped against mine as the ship lurched, and again the fire of attraction crackled through me. But he made no moves.

"Here's an added boon. With this crimson shirt, see, if someone nicks me it doesn't show. I can lie and gloat that they missed. Protect my rep that way."

I laughed again. It was an unguarded moment, at the end of which our eyes met, and his smile turned pensive, his gaze held mine—light blue as the water under a guileless sky—and I had to exert all my will to look away, or drown.

Yeah. I know it sounds stupid, but I really did feel like I couldn't breathe. My nerves flashed hot and cold, my entire body tingling with proximity, with possibility. But I looked away, and as the feelings settled down to the glow one gets when the physical self—whose needs are as simple and direct as those of the creatures around us who do not speak—recognizes equal attraction.

Zathdar said, "With this wind, we'll make landfall day after tomorrow before dawn, on the early tide. I suggest you disembark with the cargo and make your way into the town on the other side of the brewery. If you like, I'll meet you at the Gold Inn, which is run by the brewers. I'll give you any news I discover. That should arm you for whatever you decide next."

"Thanks," I said to the planking of the deck.

When I breathed again, he was gone. I lifted my head in time to see him duck under his cabin door, fringes rippling in the wind.

Owl drifted up next to me. "Why don't you go after him?"

He was so direct yet managed to be so unconfrontational I was not tempted to say, *Why don't you mind your own business?* as I might have to anyone who sneered or leered or made some sort of innuendo.

I said, "You have your life here on the sea. Not for me to say if it's right or wrong, but it's not really mine. I have to find out what mine is."

"You don't want to try to find it here?" Owl raised a scarred hand. "Cause is a good one. More than that, or maybe less, I've never seen him tempted to break his own rule before."

I remembered what Gliss had said about his not being involved with crew.

"Maybe that's why I should go away." I tried to summon a smile, but Owl squinted at me, not smiling back.

My mother said when I was about sixteen: *Here's the truth of my experience. Attraction happens, and it's glorious and good when it happens back. For a short time if the body has picked a bore or a brute, long if the mind and the heart can also match. Because attraction, though it might seem to change the world, is not love. Love is the match of all three. Body. Mind. And spirit.*

How could I find a meeting of the minds with a pirate—or privateer—without talking myself into that life, at least for a time?

I faced Owl. "Whether bad or good I cannot say, but I do know a lawless life on the sea is not my future. And I'm not the kind who can have a fling then leave without a second thought."

He looked up at the sails then back at me, his narrow jaw

working. His ruby-set golden earring, won in pirate battle, glinted against his jawline, emphasizing some tension, perhaps some unspoken thought. "Fair enough."

The armorer was singing a bawdy song in a sweet, soulful tenor when I retreated to my cabin. I lay on my bunk, hands crossed behind my head, watching the light-stippled reflections of water on the ceiling of the cabin as bare feet danced on the deck overhead far into the night.

On the day of our landing, I woke to the sound of bawling commands and busy hammers and saws coming through the open scuttle. Not our ship. In the mellow blue-gold light of dawn, a big brigantine slid by, its deck and masts alive with an enormous crew all busy.

I got up. Elva was already gone, her bunk made. I hauled all my bedding down to the cleaning frame, put it through, and lugged it up again to make my bunk neat. When I stepped out, once again the ship wore a disguise, this time as a slightly down-at-heels merchant. Our masts were stumpy, a single sail on each. The barrels (most of them empty) neatly lined the rail. The crew all wore dull variations on homespun shirts and brown-dyed deck trousers.

Everyone was quiet, self-absorbed. I found Elva sitting on a barrel and joined her, turning my attention to the busy harbor as we threaded slowly through ships of every size and type, each a little world filled with people busy doing things.

"This is Ellir?" I asked.

She pointed at the martial outline of a fortress topping the ridge of hills behind the port. "That's the garrison and also the academy. Supposedly—"

"I know, belongs to Prince Jehan. Whenever you start with 'supposedly' I know Canary's son is fumbling around somewhere behind."

She grinned. "Well, truth is, he does seem to preside, though I understand it all is really run by Captain Randart, the war commander's brother."

"Yuk. More Randarts? Ugh."

"I didn't even mention War Commander Randart's nephew Damedran, who's supposedly the best of the academy cadets. Devli says the mages all think Randart wants Damedran as heir instead of the Fool. Except that Randart defends the Fool. Which is another thing against him."

"That doesn't make sense. Canardan *is* the king, right?"

Elva said soberly, "Yes, but whatever Randart wants, he gets. There was supposed to be no killing, that was promised. Yet Randart was angry when they didn't catch your father, and so he made sure Magister Glathan died. He broke his word to do it. Had the magister shot in the back. Bolt from a crossbow. Right after making a truce."

Magister Glathan — dead?

My father had to be either dead or imprisoned by his last-resort spell. A spell he could not free himself from.

That meant I was the only one who could free him.

If he lived.

I grimaced. Magister Glathan was a vague memory, but he'd been kind and patient with me, and I remembered how much my father and he had talked, how much my father had admired the mage. "That's horrible."

"Anyway, no one knows what Randart wants, except Randart. We'll find out when he gets it." Elva rubbed her arms just above the elbows. "I wonder what can be taking Devli? It's like he married those messmates of his. Never was away from them once, yesterday."

"Where is the brewery?"

"See that big stone building up at the very far end of Market Street? Market Street starts at the base of the main pier, which is just past where that yacht is docked."

I peered under my hand, and whistled. "That's gorgeous. I've never seen such a beautiful yacht."

"It belongs to the Fool," Elva admitted.

"I thought someone said he gets seasick."

"The king gave it to him. He's seldom on it, and only long enough to entertain some of his artists." Elva waved a dismissive hand. "But he has a crew complete with a Colendi cook just sitting around waiting all the same. Anyway, you can see how Market Street runs along the foot of the ridge. See the academy on top of the ridge? The brewery is right below the far end of the academy. Sometimes when the wind comes off the land, you can smell the malt being made from the barley."

"Does Prince Supposedly run that brewery, too?"

She looked surprised. "You didn't know? It's entirely run by old sailors. If you get wounded young and can't sail, you have a place there if you want it."

"Beer made by drunken sailors?"

"Oh no! No one is more serious about brewing than an old sailor. Drink a drop on duty and you're out. Which is why Gold is the very best. Ships come here from all over the continent for the year-ale, the darkest. Best barley from the hills, best hops, everything the best."

"So the Gold Inn is good?"

"The food is great. You should have their corn muffins, all slathered with honey-butter . . ." She sighed. "Why, you going there?"

"Zathdar said he'd meet me there, if he hears any news concerning me, and I could go on my way. I thought that pretty nice of him."

She pursed her lips. "I think it pretty crazy. He's probably the most wanted person in the kingdom, and War Commander Randart, they say, would pay almost anything in reward money to lay him by the heels. I thought he'd stay hidden below while we're here."

"Well, the offer is all the more admirable," I said, lightly enough.

She frowned at me. "But you can't be going like *that*."

"Like what?" I fingered my braids. "Oh. Right. I never thought of that."

"I'm sure someone here will at least give you a bandana for the hair." She paused, frowning again, and stared up at the castle all along the ridge, the stone lit with mellow color by the rising sun behind us. "No, I'm sick of everyone yatching at me about my guesses," she muttered. "Never mind, I'll just check on my own. Here's the important thing right now, you do need a disguise."

The bosun tweeted, causing a stampede of running feet. The masts creaked, sails loosened, whacketted, and slumped. A crew got the anchor atrip, then on command let it go. Underneath us the chain roared until the ship jerked. The anchor was down. We stopped moving, except on the gentle swell.

While the sails were bunted, the anchor crew began booming the longboat over the side. I went below for the last time. The sail mistress had told me that I could have anything but they usually traded, and so I left my Earth clothes. I didn't want the extra weight, I couldn't wear them, and they didn't mean anything to me. Let some pirate puzzle over a T-shirt with *Got books?* on it.

I picked out a sturdy forest green tunic that came down to my knees, below which I wore the deck trousers I'd been given, and found some castoff mocs that fit. I donated my sandals. Maybe someone would think the Earthwear an exotic fashion touch. I chose an old floppy sailor's hat that someone had abandoned. It not only hid my hair but half of my face.

By then the boat was lowered, and the ship boy on duty came shyly to offer me a ride in the first trip.

I reached the rail and looked back at the deck. Some of the crew waved, and one or two saluted. Zathdar was not in sight.

I waved, tucked my gear back under my arm, and clambered down the side to drop into the boat. I thumped clumsily onto the sternsheets and sat with my gear bag in my lap as the crew took up oars and rowed for the passenger dock.

SIXTEEN

GO AND FIND HER with your good will — and your worst spies.

Atanial did not say that out loud. She was not certain how much real freedom she had or what Canary might do if she broke the appearance of a truce.

She did know that if she left, it would either be under guard, or else he'd have people following her.

So she smiled sweetly at King Canardan. She smiled sweetly at the two big guards who escorted her back to her chambers when Canary regretfully excused himself to his day's work.

Back in her room she flung the brass jewelry holder against the fireplace stone, counting under her breath until a maid came running in, and she smiled sweetly at her.

Five seconds. The listening ears were close.

Atanial knew better than to confront the servants. They were doing what they were told, whether by will or coercion now did not matter. "Oops." She picked the brass plate up. "I dropped it."

She set it carefully on the carved wooden bureau, next to the pretty ceramic vase that she would have loved to smash. But she couldn't bring herself to indulge her temper that far. At home, where things were manufactured, maybe. Here, human hands had shaped this vase, and another pair of hands had painted the intertwined ivy leaves all around it. If she did any dropkicking, it would be the seat of Canary's fine linen trousers. Or better yet—

"Is Commander Randart anywhere about?" she asked.

The maid's eyes widened, and Atanial realized that not only was she being watched, but every question had to be reported.

"I wanted to ask him if I could witness a military review." Once again Atanial summoned up her sweetest smile, though by now her face ached. "I used to adore watching those handsome young things march about."

"I can ask, your highness." The maid curtseyed, her eyes frightened at the mental echo of Randart's name.

And by noon the word came that Canary was going to escort her himself to review the midday change of the palace guard.

So they stood side by side on the rampart above the great parade court and looked down at all those earnest-faced young men and women sweltering in their faultless battle tunics, and Atanial thought, *Yes, I'm getting the message about who holds the reins here.*

But again she smiled sweetly as they marched, did an impressive sword form, and presented their spears. And that sweet smile was ready and at her command when the king escorted her down the stairs to walk along the row on close inspection. She forced Canary to stop every so often, while she asked harmless questions: *How long have you been in the guard? Where do you hail from?* She took care to listen to every answer as if her life depended on it, and she looked into every pair of eyes, willing the person behind them to see her. She thanked each speaker as if they'd given her wings.

And maybe they would, despite the fact that she did not see Tam among them. Someone would have to help her. She needed to figure out who and how, without endangering anyone, because two things were immediately clear: one, she had to get away; and two, she was about ten years past vaulting over ten-meter walls and castle rooftops in order to do it.

So the next best thing was to get to know as many people as possible—and inspect the castle to see what escape hole might exist.

She ate alone. Neither king nor queen came near. Someone had placed some books in her sitting room—every single one at least a century out of date.

But old as they were, those books still reminded her of the third option, the one she tended to forget because she didn't understand it.

Magic.

She read until the midnight bells rang, then withdrew into that splendid marble bath, locked the door, and glanced at the scented, slightly steaming water.

First things first. She dug the transfer token out of her bra and examined it closely. There were no more Gate transfers left on it. Whether one person or two came through, the transfer energy was spent. That much she knew, for Math had told her as much before their parting.

The question was, did the transfer use up *all* the magic, or could the thing still sense wards? She'd been told not to risk using the token if it sensed other magical presences around it. She held it up, remembering how Math and (at first reluctantly) Glathan had tried to convince her that magic was not the equivalent of electricity. Magic existed somewhere in the interstices between light and molecular movement, but she thought of it in terms of battery storage and voltage and switches. It was the only way her mind could comprehend what it could do, if not what it was.

She walked around the bath with the token, and noticed a tiny flicker of light around its edges, in response to the water cleaning spell. Ahah. So it did work. And what's more, she had wards around her, of some sort.

More than that she could not tell. It hurt unexpectedly, remembering Math's childlike glee when she showed a modicum of ability with some little magical trick, now forgotten. His Albert Einstein hair seemed to bristle and crackle with his delight. But tempering that had been Glathan's obvious distrust during those early days, when they first came through the Gate. Later that altered to grudging acceptance, and finally to a truce, and even a measure of trust.

And now he was dead.

She set the token carefully down and took a leisurely bath. Dressed in the soft cotton nightgown they'd left for her, she took the candle and the token and walked through the rooms she'd been given, watching how the token flared briefly with green color here, reddish there, and once a sharp blue snap.

A network of protective wards, just as Ananda had told her. Maybe only wards to let someone know when she crossed the threshold, but possibly stronger ones, meant to prevent her from doing magic, or to prevent magic from reaching her.

Now she knew where they were, at least. She tucked the token under her pillow and snuffed the candle so she could sleep.

The next morning she toured the kitchens, asked questions about the baking and cooking, tasted and complimented everything. She saw that there was little chance of egress there, as the kitchens lay directly adjacent to the expanded guard barracks.

At noon she toured the housekeeping area and introduced herself to Mistress Eban's replacement. The woman was so stiff, so wary, that Atanial knew immediately she'd received stringent orders about communicating with the king's "guest." So she kept her questions confined to cloth, weaving, sewing and the current styles in Sartor. By the time Atanial had inspected the lyre-backed chairs with the cushions embroidered with queensblossom, the woman had unbent enough to flick a look her way.

Atanial gave her a smile, but left knowing she'd met defeat there.

Canary invited her to dinner.

Again they were alone.

By then she was ready to begin the first tier of questions.

"Where is Dannath Randart?" she asked.

Canardan grinned. "You want to see him again?"

He gave her such a comically skeptical look that she replied tartly, "I was hoping he'd dropped dead. Preferably with a bolt in the back."

"So you heard about that, eh?"

"Who hasn't?" She spread her hands and then grabbed up a fresh corn bun, noting as she did the faint color along Canardan's still-handsome cheekbones. "I find it utterly reprehensible, and frankly hope that he's on the other side of the kingdom."

"He's going out to sea," Canardan said. "Far enough to keep you from one another's sphere."

"My second question is, what have you done with Mistress Eban and the others?"

"Nothing, as yet. That depends upon a number of things. Including you."

"If you dare try to hold their lives hostage in order to force me into something, I will shout it from the rooftops." Her fists thumped on either side of her plate.

He patted the air between them. "No, no. I know better than that. I should be more clear. I believe more lives will be saved if I keep all of you safely here until the kingdom settles."

She sighed. "Even if you do find Sasha, and if by some miracle she agreed to your proposal, how could a marriage possibly settle the kingdom?"

"It would go a long way toward reestablishing good will." He saluted her with his wine goblet. "Join the names, all that."

"But if you do get her, and threaten my life—"

He looked skyward. "What did I just tell you? I might add that my wayward son, who seldom notices a wall until he smashes into it, would probably object as loudly as your daughter. He thinks he's quite a catch. When he isn't following bards around, he's off flirting with every pretty face he meets. And apparently they all seem to like him. No princesses, though," Canary added regretfully.

Atanial couldn't help but laugh. "It sounds like he'd much prefer a minstrel."

"If she's pretty and she paints, he would probably marry her out of hand." Canardan gestured with his butter knife.

"When do I get to meet him?" Atanial put her elbows on the table and her chin in her hands. Math's voice came back from all those years ago, *Jehan's a fine boy. And smarter than his father thinks, despite all the daydreaming.*

To which Glathan had said in his gruff growl, *Maybe because of it. He learned early to keep his mouth shut. But we don't know if what he's thinking is to our benefit or not.*

Which is why I'm going to write him, since no one else seems to be doing it, Math had said, and despite Glathan's shake of the head he'd been true to his word.

Atanial had never found out if the boy all the way across the continent had written back. Math had never mentioned him again, and Atanial wondered now if that was because of Glathan's disapproval, or if the correspondence had ended with the one letter.

The pause had grown into a silence, Canardan frowning into the middle distance. But he was watchful for all that. All she did was look up, and the flick of her eyelashes seemed to release him from his reverie.

"I'll see what I can arrange, but right now he has duties at the academy." Canardan drank, then set his goblet down, his thumb aligning it with an absent stroke just beyond the point of his knife. "Do you remember the midsummer games?"

"The cadets and their demonstrations. Relay races through the hills. And the yacht races in the harbor."

"Well, we've had to cancel the yacht races, but the relays and the rest will go on as usual."

"Why no yachting? I thought the academy is where you got your navy captains as well as your guard captains?"

"Yes, and we'll hold 'em anon. But the merchant codes were pinched by a pirate a few days ago, and we have reason to believe he might try to slip into either of the two main harbors. Those same codes are being used by countless legitimate merchants, so we don't know if he's coming or already there in some kind of disguise. We already know he has a way of stealing in, doing untold damage, and slipping out unheeded." Atanial saw the telltale signs of anger in the tightened skin at the corners of his eyes.

Her brow furrowed. "Is this the pirate who holds my daughter?"

He spread his hands. "How can we know? He doesn't exactly communicate with us."

"Back to your son." She set her goblet down. "I'd like very much to meet him."

As a distant bell rang, Canardan got to his feet. "Speaking of whom. I thought we might see if one of his charities is worth what I pay out. Are you finished?"

Atanial rose, shook out her skirts, and took his offered arm. Canardan led her through the informal dining room, made of pale peach marble, through the formal dining room that she remembered from the old days. Then it was silver marble to match the Zhavalieshin silver-and-crimson firebird. They walked along the balcony above the main entryway to the palace. From there he took her through the private door to the royal box above the private theater, which was tucked behind the palace's enormous ballroom.

Canardan appreciated her surprise and delight when she saw the lit stage, empty and waiting. The rest of the low circular tiers of chairs were empty. Only their box had a single candle. Two liveried servants stood by, one with wine, another with extra cushions, as Canardan guided Atanial to one end of the beautiful rosewood couch with its fine velvet cushions. He sat next to her and nodded at the servants.

They poured honey-colored wine in the goblets on the little tables at either end of the couch, and set out porcelain plates of tiny lemon-and-custard pastries, layered delicately so that one could take a bite without experiencing any gooshes of custard or splatters of crumbs. Next to the plates, crystal vases of just-budding white roses breathed a delicate scent.

All very thoughtfully arranged, she thought. For?

Another campaign.

Down on the stage, a master illusionist stepped out in the black gown of his calling, and sat upon a stool at one side. Prince Jehan's "charity" was a company of first-rate players. The custom for the master illusionists to come forward onto the stage instead of remaining behind had been introduced twenty years before, so people could watch the magician at work making the scenes. The old days of one or perhaps two rudimentary illusions cast and left up for the duration of the play were gone. The subtle metamorphosis of scene sets behind the players had become art, as it had been centuries before.

In the intervening twenty years, the gestures had taken on stylized grace, reminding Atanial of a person on Earth performing poetry in sign language. Hidden musicians played on flutes and horns, evoking a garden of birds. The stage glittered with a rainbow splash of color as a setting coalesced into being.

The setting was a garden terrace, with tiers of flowers at various levels. Atanial recalled something about Sartoran gardens, how they might take a century or more to properly mature. Colendi gardens could take even longer.

The players strolled out, wearing layers of silk fashioned in complicated folds, the colors subtle gradations of shades from rose to gold. They gathered around a young man in layers of celestial blue.

Atanial tightened all over, bracing for some obvious message aimed at her through the performance, but before very long even she, relatively ignorant of this world's history, recognized the legendary story of the brilliant Prince Tivonais of Sartor. If he lived, it was a couple thousand years ago.

This was a musical comedy, about the one woman who did not surrender to his incredible charms. Any message was confined to the varieties of human passion and love. Atanial sat back and relaxed, chuckling at the ancient jokes about human actions and reactions that hadn't changed much in millennia, whichever world you happen to be on. She sipped the wine, which tasted like liquid gold.

Gradually her focus on the stage widened to include Canardan so close beside her. One of his hands tapped out a counter-rhythm to a dance, while players whirled and stepped and leaped on stage. She heard his breathing as he leaned back, eyes shut, during a beautifully sung lament.

As the play drew to its end, Tivonais sang his serio-comic song about loss. The singer revealed just the right touch of mockery in the relative sorrows of a handsome prince who has everything and everyone he wants. He asks for a single gift from his beloved, a white rose.

While Atanial tried to remember if the white-rose custom among new lovers came before the play, or if the play establish the custom, her body was aware of fingers tracing, ever so lightly, along her shoulder. Her *other* shoulder. A well-shaped arm touching her back.

It was pleasant—she had to admit it was pleasant—that despite the years, the dashed hopes and disappointments, the betrayals and chases, he was still attracted to her. Either that, or he was a master tactician.

But recognition of your opponent's skill in battle is not cause for surrender.

For a moment she considered jumping up and screaming, *You're trying to seduce me!* Oh, how fun it would be to see him embarrassed. Except he wouldn't be, he'd laugh. No, the embarrassment would be all those players down there, now taking their bow for their audience of two. They did not deserve to have their beautiful work reduced to a mere hissing of gossip along the corridors.

She stood. The fingers lifted away. She clapped loudly, then scooped up the white roses from the crystal vase and tossed them one by one down onto the stage.

Below, the young man playing Tivonais, perhaps still in character, made a debonair gesture as he bent, swept up a rose, kissed it and saluted her with it.

She kissed her fingertips and flung her hands out wide, and the other players all clapped too.

Tivonais took another bow. Atanial was aware of Canardan standing beside her, clapping as well, his profile sardonic.

The players bowed a last time, then filed off, the exquisite acoustics carrying back the sound of their whispering.

Atanial turned away from the empty stage and walked to the door, perforce Canardan following, his blue eyes narrowed with not-quite humor as he made a gesture dismissing the waiting servants.

She waited until they were gone and said, "Yes, I felt it. No, I won't act on it. Yes, I was a pompous twit when I first came here all those years ago, but I do not have to justify any actions except—" Even here there were pitfalls, for she dared not suggest that Math was alive, that she might know where.

Nothing but landmines around.

The awareness chilled her spirit like nothing had for years. But she was not a girl in her twenties any more, to indulge in screaming stomping fits because she's so very right while everyone around is wrong, wrong, wrong.

She held her hands out to him, palms toward him. "Age builds its own internal cities, you have to admit that. Whatever your castle walls are made of, I don't know. I don't know if I can believe you if you try to tell me, because there lies behind us the matter of the past. Here's what you can believe from me. Between the garden of appreciation of your attractions—and they are there, as they always were—and the road to action is the wall round my own castle, a wall deep and high, called trust."

He had the grace to take her hands and the poise to lightly kiss her fingers. And let her go.

Then he walked away, and the silent servants conducted her back to her rooms.

SEVENTEEN

WAR COMMANDER DANNATH RANDART arrived in Ellir not long after midnight. Two days of very hard riding, sleep and meals scanted while the horses were changed at military posts along the way, brought him tired, aching, and irritable to the west gate, which is where the guard barracks was located.

Randart's vile temper eased slightly when he saw the walls patrolled by alert guards, the gatekeepers awake and speedy once his trumpeter had blown the king's signal.

He jumped off his sweaty horse and left his troop to rouse the stablehands as he strode upstairs to the commander's tower. He arrived at the same time his younger brother Orthan did, Orthan fastening his tunic with one hand and carrying his boots with the other.

"Dannath," Orthan Randart said by way of greeting, blinking himself awake.

"Any word on Prince Jehan?"

"His personal guard arrived at sunset." Orthan fell heavily into his chair behind the desk. The joints in the wood creaked. "But the prince wasn't with 'em. Apparently there's some girl somewhere outside of town he simply had to visit, and they left him there. But he promised to be along by morning."

Randart sighed, and when a hastily-dressed cadet runner arrived, he ordered coffee and whatever food could be made hot the fastest.

As soon as the boy was gone, the war commander shut the door and set his back against it. "News?"

"Nothing." Orthan indicated the darkened window, which overlooked the harbor. Tiny lights bobbed slowly on the water, lanterns legally required on bows, sterns and foremasts. "Nothing."

"As expected. Well, continue mustering the fleet, except for those at Aloca. I'm going out in force. What's the status of the games?"

"Officially or confidentially?" And when his brother shrugged, Orthan smiled. "Officially, everything is in order. Ready to begin. If the prince does show up. As for our business, Damedran will take every prize."

Randart thought of his huge, husky nephew, but did not smile. "What about archery? Is he at the top there?" On the war commander's orders, Orthan had been drilling his son with extra lessons, but though Damedran was a brute with sword, stick, and grappling, he couldn't seem to get the eye for superlative shooting.

"He'll win," Orthan said.

"He's finally good enough to best the Valleg girl?"

"No. But it seems she suffered a broken arm. Won't be competing in the games."

Randart frowned. "He didn't—"

"No, no, absolutely not. He knows better now, he really does. No, apparently she was offered a drink or two celebrating someone's Name Day, while on stable duty. She tripped over . . . her own feet. Damedran handsomely offered to cover for her— gave the watch commander an excuse. Officially there's no disgrace, and unofficially she's in his debt."

Randart smiled at last, thinking, *Now that is the thinking of a good future king.*

His brother saw that smile, and knew what it meant, but they did not say the word "king" out loud.

Instead they turned their attention to logistical concerns—guard rotations, patrol of the harbor, searchers covert and overt as ships continued to come in, though they didn't have much hope of nabbing Zathdar in the act.

The last errand runner left the room. When they were safely private, War Commander Randart said to his brother, "Here's the truth. I don't really want to catch the pirate lurking around the harbor. I've been given a free hand to take the entire fleet, and I mean to sweep the whole sea of all suspicious ships. 'Suspicious' defined as those crewed by names well known on resistance rosters. Zathdar has far too many allies out on the waters. Some judicious slaughter might be salutary to the entire maritime world. At the end of that, if I find the pirate, fine. I'll consider it a job well done."

Orthan grimaced at that mention of judicious slaughter, but he had learned never to interfere with his brother, who was, after all, the king's right arm. Orthan himself was only a headmaster and garrison commander, positions he felt far more comfortable filling. Training boys and running a garrison, he could do. Judicious slaughter?

But Dannath Randart did not see his brother's grimace. He was too busy sorting through the reports on Orthan's desk, reading the headings, then re-sorting them in his own priority order.

When he was done, he said, "So patrols as normal, no assiduous searches. I want the best men rested and ready for the launch of the entire fleet. We'll form a pincer between here and Aloca. We'll gather them all together and get rid of them."

His mood had improved by the time he downed the potato pancakes a sleepy cook had put together. He swallowed his coffee and withdrew into the command suite to catch some rest, waking at the dawn bells.

He'd been through the baths and was pulling on a clean uniform when a runner reported, "Prince Jehan has arrived."

In the commander's office the brothers exchanged brief glances, and then War Commander Randart said easily, as befitted the prince's best advocate in the kingdom, "Request his highness to honor us with his presence, if that is his royal desire. Or we could join him wherever he wishes, to go over the king's orders."

The cadet vanished.

A short time later there was the sheep, the nickname ostensibly chosen for his white hair. War Commander Randart knew his brother liked the prince, despite his fashionably tailored brown velvet war tunic that had never seen any semblance of war, that long white morvende hair hanging down his back, and a diamond in his ear. Popular Jehan was, but he was also more a fop than a commander. Why couldn't Orthan see that?

Orthan sighed. He wanted his son to be king, but he didn't want anything bad to happen to the prince. Somehow . . . somehow, he hoped, it would all work out. Until then, no use in worrying. Dannath would have his way no matter what.

"What color would you call that?" Jehan asked, indicating the pale shade of the ocean.

"Blue," Randart said with obvious patience. "Your highness, forgive me but it might be better if you don't . . . visit civilians . . . when we're under orders."

"She sings," Jehan explained.

Orthan restacked already neat papers, keeping his face hidden. The runner cadet in the corner watched, his eyes wide.

"Have you ever heard Faleth ballad-style?" Jehan continued, head to one side. "It seems to have its roots in Ancient Sartoran—"

"Very well, very well, perhaps another time, your highness?" Orthan soothed, eyeing the war commander uneasily.

Orthan completely misunderstood his brother. The king persisted in believing Jehan might one day wake up and exhibit even a faint interest in the requirements of a future king. The king believed it, Orthan hoped for it in a vague way—and Randart watched for it.

If he discovered any hint of competence in Prince Sheep, Dannath Randart would arrange for a fatal accident. He really did not want to have to do that. Not in a kingdom where every single person who wasn't plotting was busy gossiping. Far better the king suffer one more disappointment, and get so angry he took care of the heir problem all by himself. And there would be a trained heir, at the top of the academy, loyal, strong, handsome: Damedran Randart.

"We can talk about ballads later." The war commander pitched his voice to be heard by the cadet runners on duty outside the office. He was very careful to present himself as the devoted friend and supporter to the prince. For the benefit of all those listening ears, he added in a gentle, coaxing voice, "But your highness, the king has requested me to convey his wishes to you. Now, about the games . . ."

Everything according to plan.

EIGHTEEN

THE SHIP'S BOY ROWED me to the main pier, which was very long, with small boats coming and going to drop off or pick up people whose ships couldn't afford closer-in anchorage fees. This meant a hefty hike ahead of me.

The two sailors at the bows tied us on, and the ship's boy touched my arm. I stared in surprise at his crimson face as he mutely held out a bag that chinked promisingly.

"Thank you," I said.

"Collection took up by the crew." He blushed even more, if that was humanly possible.

I took pity on him and climbed out, confining myself to a little wave, and I began to duck and sidestep my way through all the busy people on the pier.

The long pier led me past the capital ships pulled alongside. One had to be the navy's flagship. I kept my head low, scarcely looking at it, though no one paid me the least heed. But I felt as if eyes crawled over me like bugs as I hustled past its length.

I slowed a little when passing Prince Jehan's yacht. Every line of it evoked the power and arrogance of princes, to the exquisite carving of laughing dolphins all round the rail. This work of art rocked at the best docking spot in the entire harbor. Yet it was obviously empty of any royal butt sitting in its gorgeous cabin. Its crew looked bored as they polished the gleaming wood and reflemished their pristine ropes.

Near the end of the pier the crowd thickened. A few steps more and I'd reach the quay at last. I was finally on my own.

Everywhere I looked walked, patrolled, and lounged brown-clad warriors. Even the ones whose hands held pastries or drink carried a full complement of weaponry.

I didn't know if they were on guard, or about to embark in the navy ships I could see anchored in neat rows along the inner bay, or on leave for the academy games. I didn't want to find out because it was certain to be the hard way.

I gave myself a mental shakedown as I trod down the last few warped wooden boards of the long pier, stumping a little in an effort to get my land balance back. A good look around made it clear that civilian sailors dress in every imaginable style, tending toward the loud when on shore looking for fun. The career doesn't select for the delicate and dainty, so there were plenty of women of my size around.

The one thing that I feared might catch attention was my gear bag. Though I'd rolled it to be as small as possible, the faint sheen of its plastic weave could draw the eye of anyone searching for the unusual, and so I stopped at the very first vendor selling baskets and paid what I suspect was a thumpingly dishonest price for a scratchy, loosely woven affair that I soon hated, but it did its job by successfully hiding the gear bag stuffed into its depths.

This purchase also used up most of the coins in the bag. Either the basket maker was an outright thief or I'd been given enough to cover a day or two's meals. But that made sense. Sailors would figure a day or so on land, and then one hires out for one's next voyage.

Or maybe the Purple-and-orange Pirate would give me some more of his ill-gotten gains when he met me at the Gold to tell me the local news. Did I want handouts? No. I would cash in some of my gems, or work my way along the road. But I was curious about what he might bring.

For now, I'd just enjoy the market street, which wound in a

kind of slightly skewed crescent along the foot of the rocky ridge. Ellir Harbor, overlooked by the combination academy and garrison, was a jumble of old stone buildings and jerry-rigged tents and claptrap houses with doors and window sills painted with bright colors.

The stone buildings housed the long-term businesses, most sea-related. The rest was seasonal trade, set up in colorful stalls and tents between the dilapidated buildings. These people raised half the market noise with their singing and shouting as they waved brightly dyed pennons and sent enticing smells to lure the crowds who made up the other half of the noise, strolling, talking, looking, laughing, flirting, eating, drinking, and shopping.

Once chasing. "Thief!" someone cried and the shout rose around me, spreading from voice to voice.

Moments later the hapless pickpocket slammed to the stone street, straddled by a pair of brown-tunicked warriors. The hapless thief's tousled head bumped the stone a yard from my feet. Who would be that stupid, or that desperate, to try thievery right under the view of that intimidating castle, with a million guards in every direction?

I never saw the culprit's face. A crowd of guards immediately surrounded him or her, and muscled the miscreant away presumeably to some lockup. I'd hastily backed away, looking down as I tried to be unobtrusive, but the guards paid no attention to the surrounding crowd except in a general sense, making sure there was no threat.

They went in one direction and I in the other, thinking along a new path. What kind of courts did they have, and jails, and sentences? I'd asked my mother a few questions over the years, but Canardan's versions of social government might be different from the Zhavalieshins'.

It was my growling stomach that shifted my attention from the general scene to the specific. I found the moneychangers directly below the gates to the castle, which ought to dissuade all but the most foolhardy and reckless of thieves. There were several to choose from. I drifted along until I spotted a moneychanger where not only coinage was being changed, but valuables of various sorts, including gemstones.

For the first time in all those years, I pulled out one of the more modest gems from the box and brought it to that tent, where a short, thin, stylishly dressed young woman about my age seemed to be handling stones of all kinds. I laid it down, my fake story all ready.

She squinted briefly at it. "Colendi cut, what we call the deep-water sapphire." She named a price.

I'd already noticed that though bargaining took place in many of the market stalls, here there appeared to be a standard price for pretty much everything. Not wanting to call attention to myself in any way, I agreed. She counted out three twelve-sided gold coins, fashioned after Sartoran coins, and eleven silver six-siders, then a handful of thin hammered coppers.

I stuffed them all into the bag the ship's boy had given me, and returned to my shopping. Now to see what this money was actually worth.

The sun was directly overhead when I finished buying a good pair of shoes, cotton-lined greenweave that the cobbler adjusted to fit my feet exactly. I traded in the worn old mocs, which would be recycled.

Hunger forced me up the street toward the Gold Inn, a large building whose merrymakers' noise eddied out through open windows and doors. The first smells that reached my nose were baking cornbread and braised onions.

My stomach growled as I passed inside a cavernous space obviously decorated by sailors—deck prisms in the walls, the heavy, pointed glass gleaming with refracted colors, which banished indoor gloom. Old helm wheels high up, bulkheads curving between the alcoves, booths divided off by fences made of worn oars. The chairs round the smaller tables were all cut from barrels and cushioned with old sailcloth.

The heavy, heady scent of fresh-brewed beer underlay the

scent of brick-oven baked chicken pies, and bread, and some kind of pepper-and-garlic savory fish chowder. I sat at a long plank table on which cadets and sailors had carved initials and witty sayings in at least three alphabets. A party of weavers took up most of the table, well into a celebration for newlyweds, judging from the toasts.

The waiter, a kid of about ten, tapped me on the arm. "What'll I bring you?"

"Cornbread with honey-butter, dark ale, and fish chowder," I said.

He dashed away, as one of the weavers made an obscure joke about damask and brocade, and everyone laughed.

Two toasts later the boy returned with a tray on which the cornbread steamed, fresh from the oven. The weavers began singing a plaintive song in Sartoran triplets about a wandering silk-weaver seeking the source of "rainbow colors true."

A sip of a spicy, almost raisin-flavored ale, a bite of sweet cornbread, and I was lifting my spoon to try the chowder when a brief glimpse of a familiar face in the crowd caused me to pause, spoon in the air.

Elva? No, couldn't be—

She vanished behind a crowd of sailors who suddenly decided to dance a heel-toe stomper right there in the middle of the floor. I dropped my spoon when Elva reappeared, braids flying, brown eyes stark in a face so pale I thought she was going to be sick.

"There you are." She clutched my shoulder. "Get out. Get out."

"What?" I looked at my food. "What's wrong with the—"

She pulled my wrist, sending my spoon flying. "You've got to run. Now."

"Why?" I snapped, getting up to retrieve the spoon.

"Because I followed Owl. I had my suspicions." She made a terrible face. "He met up with *him* at the stable—" She waved a hand toward the far side of the brewery.

"Him? Zathdar?" I stared at the brewery, but just saw barrels of ale.

"Zathdar!" Elva repeated scornfully. "Oh, you're in for a storm, right enough, if you don't move." She dropped onto the bench next to me and muttered into my ear, "It was a stable, at the other end of town. Up behind the old castle and the warehouses. I *saw* him. They didn't see me."

"Saw who? Owl or Zathdar?"

"Both. But he—he—he ditched the bandana. And the horsehair wig. He's got white hair—the brown velvet with the king's cup. Crown over it. Diamond—" She touched her ear where Zathdar had worn his pirate-battle earring.

Heat flooded through me, followed by a sudden and dreadful chill.

"Don't you see?" Elva looked wildly around, and while the unheeding weavers sang of love and loss, she growled, "He's *Prince Jehan Merindar.*"

"But that's impossible."

"I thought so, too. But I *saw* him. He went straight to the castle. The guards on the walls gave him the royal salute, clear as anything."

Whoosh! My first reaction was the self-righteous, fire-hot anger of betrayal, followed by the sickening, almost lip-numbing humiliation that comes of realizing one's been taken for a fool.

I grabbed my basket and followed her between the tables, the singing weavers' plaintive melody blending into the heedless roar of voices behind me.

Out in the street, glare and the rising dust of early afternoon nearly blinded us. I blinked, breathing hard as silhouettes resolved into people, horses, carts, dogs, even a family of geese squawking and flapping. Children danced in a ring to the flitting summer melody played upon a pipe. In front of the last booth before the open road, several women teased a handsome fellow in a brown tunic who seemed to be trying to buy an embroidered scarf.

All oblivious, most of them happy, and very much in the way as I scanned and scanned, resisting Elva's tugs. "This way," she urged.

I faced her earnest, anxious brown eyes and *knew* that Devli waited somewhere, a transfer token in hand. "Thank you for the rescue. But I think I'll take off on my own."

Her face reddened. "It's Devli. Isn't it? You don't trust him."

"I'm sorry, Elva, but I just don't trust those giving him orders," I murmured as a cart full of melons rolled toward us, shoved by a brawny fellow not watching where he was going.

She moved to one side. I ducked to the other side of it so I wouldn't have to see her reaction, and dove into a pack of sailors, several of them wearing battered floppy hats much like mine. I still felt outlined in neon, though so far the few guys in brown tunics around were not searching, merely sauntering.

All right, Sasha, you got what you wanted. You're alone. Pick a direction.

My pack of sailors headed toward the brewery. I stayed with them as far as the door. That sense of being watched intensified, so I slunk round the back of the Gold's stables and peered out, scanning with care.

The marketplace lay to my left, a long street of tent booths below the high palisade of sheer rock on which the garrison and academy bulked. The market street crested to the right, below the bluffs on which the academy barracks ended in the furthermost tower.

The road on the other side of the crest stretched in a lazy arc, paralleling the rocky shore against which long breakers creamed and crashed. Lines of wagons inched their way in a string that curved through mellow grassy fields to the horizon, the only tree in sight a single clump of willow growing beside a stream winding toward the shore.

No cover whatsoever, but at least that road lay outside of Ellir and its bazillion warriors.

I slipped away from my crummy hiding place and headed straight for that high point, beyond which freedom beckoned.

But right before I reached the top of the market street, not five hundred yards from the low stone wall that marked the boundary of the city, my shoulder blades itched. My danger sense had gone into the red zone, urging me to turn and fight.

I just knew I would hate what I saw. But I had to look.

Past the dancing children. Past the strolling flirts, the bargaining marketers with their baskets, past unheeding cadets and warriors obviously on leave, past the dogs and geese and sailors. I stared straight into a pair of familiar blue eyes, now framed by drifting white hair.

Too late.

Too late, but I turned on my toes and sprinted for freedom, despite the faster footsteps behind me — much faster.

When I reached the top of the road, the footsteps had almost caught up so I plunged into a crowd of prentices in one last attempt to shake my pursuer, and risked a glance back.

The stinker was maybe ten steps away. He hadn't yelled, and though some of the people he pushed past turned to stare, and one or two began to call out in protest, stared, then quickly backed away, no one interfered.

The oblivious prentices didn't part for me. They shoved past and stampeded toward the brewery, leaving me alone to face the enemy.

Prince Jehan caught up in an easy step, and stopped an arm's length from me.

So for a long, measureless moment we stood there facing one another at the top of Market Street, the last of the prentices flowing around us with exasperated looks and a wry comment or two that neither of us paid the least attention to.

All the things I could say chased through my mind. *You liar! Go ahead and strike me down, see if I care!* And perhaps most useless of all, *I hate you!* But I said nothing for a breathless, anguished eternity, as the market crowd walked, strolled, sauntered, pushed, shoved, talked, sang, sighed past us.

Prince Hurricane stood there, waiting for me to speak.

And so I said, "You must really love making everyone look like a fool."

He flushed as if I'd slapped him. But then flicked his head, as if repudiating my words, and retorted, "You have no idea what you're talking about."

"Oh, so you're not a liar and a poser?"

"I never lied—"

"No, *Prince* My-family-name-is-Jervaes?"

"But it is." He spread his hands and flushed again when I took a quick step back. "My mother's name."

"Oh." Well, that was a nasty little oopsie, but I plowed right past. "So you managed to tell one bit of truth. What did it cost you?" Take that!

"Listen. Just listen." He half-raised a hand in a gesture of appeal, but when I stepped back, he dropped it to his side. His side, at which he wore a sword. And a knife through his sash. Neither of them touched, much less brandished. Nor had he whistled up his brown-coated minions. There were certainly plenty of them about.

But I couldn't bear another terrible, sickening sense of betrayal, and so, without examining the motivation behind that, I said, "No."

His eyelids lifted slightly, giving me half-a-heartbeat's warning. Before I could draw breath to move, or even to yell, a thick winter quilt blotted out the sun and my world was perforce confined to hot, enshrouding darkness that smelled distinctly of mold.

I began to struggle, though it was futile, writhing and kicking until a familiar voice muttered next to my head, "C'mon, Princess. It's your old friend Owl. You can kick me all you like when we get back to the ship. If you can reach me. But you can't be allowed to get us all killed."

Killed? Say what?

I stopped struggling as I considered that, but before I could decide I didn't believe it, something efficiently wrapped me up into a giant cocoon, and *thump!* I fell onto something wooden. Things thudded round me, and a horse clopped. I was in a cart, which jerked and rumbled at a sedate pace back down the street, my face streaming with sweat in that suffocating quilt. I was so tightly wrapped it was useless to yell. No one could hear me anyway.

NINETEEN

ATANIAL WAS CONSIDERABLY SURPRISED to receive a visitor.

This time it wasn't night, but morning. She'd done a long session of yoga and had emerged from her bath to discover Ananda entering her room through the servants' door.

"Please pardon the intrusion. But this is the only way to have private converse."

Atanial wondered how the queen got past the guards on the stairs, then suspected illusion magic. More important was the timing of this visit. "I certainly didn't have privacy during my intimate little dinner with the king, did I?" she asked with some irony.

Ananda laughed softly. "Privacy? With the entire troupe of players watching the only two members of the audience, and one of them is busy staring at the other, caressing her neck? Watched also by the servants who had to stand there all evening with their wine and plates of uneaten food and unused cushions?"

Atanial had hopped onto her bed. She leaned back against her pillows and crossed her arms. "So I take it I passed some kind of test, and you are here for —?"

Ananda's voice was sad. "There was no test. I would have come anyway, if you had been here alone. Whatever happened. But my message would have been warnings. I am going away,

Atanial."

Atanial's nerves prickled with the cold chill of the unexpected. "Going away, as in . . ."

"Transferring to a place of safety. What no one except the prince knows is that his mother, Feraeth Jervaes, and I have been friends for many years."

Atanial whistled softly. "Sit down. Tell me more, please."

Ananda perched on the edge of the bed. "You know that the morvende do not have what we would call a government. But they do have leaders whose wisdom inclines others to listen. One such is Tarael of the Eleyad geliath on the northern continent. He has seen in dreams that Norsunder will move against the world soon."

Norsunder. Atanial had never quite gotten a grip on the whole concept of a place beyond space and time, controlled by inimical minds who seemed to have lived for thousands of years. She'd defined it to Sasha as a kind of hell, one mostly created by, run by and joined by humans who really, really wanted power. Including, she was told, the power to live forever. "Soon? As in days? Weeks?"

"Time is . . . time is different, for the morvende. It's useless to ask that question, because they cannot answer with any precision. But it could be this year, or next. Or in five. Probably not as long as ten, though, Feraeth told me, judging from some troubling events in the world elsewhere. I waited, and waited, but I think . . ."

Ananda paused, her profile briefly turned toward the window. The sunlight slanting in touched her frizzy hair into a halo of gold.

"I think there is no more I can do here, that what must be done will be done, but easier without me. I will go away. I first wanted to offer you the chance to go with me. The world is changing, and only the young will be strong enough to survive what is regretfully going to come."

Atanial impulsively launched herself across the tumbled bedding and hugged Ananda. "You are a sweetheart. I really appreciate that, more than you probably will ever know. But while my daughter is in danger and while Math is . . . missing, my place is here. That might change, and if I only get this one chance, so be it. But I have to stay and turn my hand to whatever I can."

Ananda smiled and stood, her face in silhouette against the bright window. "I thought it might be so. I did wish to ask. The illusion spell waits for two to leave, if you are reconsidering. But it will be impossible to repeat it. Once I am gone, poor Perran will search every stone of this castle, and he'll increase the wards."

"'Poor' Perran? I thought Perran and Zhavic turned into Evil Sorcerers."

Atanial's tone was half-joking, but Ananda did not smile. "They would never turn to dark magic or to Norsunder. There is a terrible rift between our kingdom's mages. Some withdrew completely and live behind wards. The Eban boy is trained by these. Perran and Zhavic felt they had to swear allegiance to Canardan because he was the king. This was to better protect the kingdom, for they feared if they didn't, he might bring in truly evil mages."

Atanial vaguely remembered Perran. He'd seemed odd back then. Now she pegged him as the kind of guy who'd be a star at Apple Computers, designing brilliant software by day, and on weekends entirely taken up with playing *World of Warcraft*.

"I think I see."

"Everything is confused," the queen said seriously. "I would say that Zhavic, having thrown in with the king, has gradually shifted allegiance, but he is still dedicated to the kingdom. Despite Canardan's earnest wish, even his orders, none of the mages really exert themselves to harm the others. There's always some magical reason why the 'traitor' mages cannot be extirpated, as the war commander often demands. Magister Glathan's death was—"

"I know. Randart's example of how to do it properly. All right, I think I see my duty. I think. Anyway, with Sasha out there in the world, I must stay. But again, thank you."

Ananda lifted a hand. "The gift is not mine, only the thought. I will leave you with terrible trouble, I know, but I was never capable of addressing it. However, I beseech you to trust Canardan's son, though it appears there is much against him. He's also Feraeth's son, and she is convinced he walks the knife-edge between seeming and truth, but to a purpose, and his purpose is good."

"I will remember that." Atanial wondered if she could believe it.

"Fare you well," Ananda said softly, and she left as silently as she had come.

Atanial lay back down, staring at the ceiling. The next day there might be a hue and cry, but more likely Canardan would suppress news of the queen's disappearance as much as he could. She would vanish from history as quietly as she'd lived.

Atanial let her breath trickle slowly out. So what about her own history? So far, she hadn't done all that well. But she was here again, and so she had a second chance.

Plan, then? For now, be a model "guest," make friends with everyone in sight, be visible, friendly, keep talking to people in hopes they would talk to her and about her, so that Randart, at least, would have difficulty making her disappear. Learn whatever she could.

And wait to meet this Prince Jehan on whom so much seemed to depend.

At the far end of the castle lay the senior barracks of the Ellir Academy, near the tower above the very top of Market Street. Across from Market Street was the famous brewery. The barracks thus lay at the other end of the row of buildings from all the masters and guards.

It was the place every cadet yearned to live in. By the time you'd attained that pinnacle, though, you had also become aware that there was hierarchy not only in the academy, but among the seniors.

So it was Damedran Randart, the academy commander's son, whose particular group got all the beds down the window side that overlooked the top of Market Street, the brewery, and the harbor beyond. The rules stated that beds were first come first served, but those not part of Damedran's inner circle who had arrived for the senior year weeks before Damedran had either discovered a taste for the dusty view overlooking the practice courts inside the academy, or they suffered a lot of accidents that the masters didn't seem to notice.

And so, when Damedran came back from seeing his father, he found his friends sitting at the open windows, idly watching Market Street below.

He paused in the doorway, his splendid shoulders set off in the brown tunic (his being tailored, not taken off the piles down in Supply), his long, glossy black hair worn loose instead of clipped back according to regs, but who was going to complain?

He waited impatiently, wondering why they were all staring out at Market Street when he was back, especially as they'd been begging him to find out the final word about the games. "Market Street on fire?"

Gratifying, how they whirled around, a couple of them even snapping to attention. He wasn't a king yet, and they were already thinking of him like one. Good. Maybe Uncle Dannath would stop jawing at him, *Think like a king!*

Red, his chief lieutenant, dashed back the pale red hair that made the origin of his nickname obvious. "The sheep managed to waylay a pickpocket or thief."

Damedran's huge cousin Wolfie said in his deep growl, "Least, we're pretty sure it was the sheep." He raised a huge paw to his unruly black hair, which he wore neatly clipped back. Wolfie did not stand on privilege. He was mainly interested in fights out behind the stable. "Sheep-white hair. Not many o' those in uniform brown."

"None of 'em wear their hair long," Red said. "Has to be the sheep. Only I thought he rode off to Sartor?"

"He rode in this morning." Damedran was uninterested in Prince Jehan, except when he was in trouble. "I'm amazed he managed to waylay a single thief. It must have taken at least thirty of his followers." As the others laughed, he strode into the barracks, nodded at two of the boys, who leaped up and sped to the doors at either end, shutting them and setting their backs to the wood.

The room now being secure, he got right to the subject that interested them all the most. "My father said it's the king's own order. There won't be any yacht runs."

"Whyyyyyyyy?" That was Bowsprit Lanarg, who was the best of all the seniors at skiff running.

Damedran saw disappointment to varying degrees in all their faces, except for Wolfie's. Wolfie just liked fighting. End of subject.

Damedran himself hated anything to do with the ocean. Too much work, and anyway, kings didn't go out on the water. But he had to sound like he cared. "It's because of the pirate Zathdar. They think he's got the old princess's daughter, and so my uncle has been ordered to take the fleet and wipe 'em out."

"Even Prince Math's girl?"

Damedran snorted a laugh. "Orders are to take her, but hey, if she gets in the way of someone's sword, problem ended—" As soon as the words were out he saw they were a mistake.

Not all his followers knew the secret plans. Definitely not Ban Kender, who was his only genuine aristocrat follower. Ban's family had been deposed when Locan Jora took over the western portion of the kingdom. *Handle him like a thoroughbred plains runner,* his father had told him in private. *That whole family, they're romantic. To them we're heroic though outnumbered, fighting for ancient rights. See you don't disabuse 'em of that notion.*

"They'd kill her?" Ban said, sure enough. And the rest (except for Wolfie, who never changed expression) reflected his dismay. "She sounded as gallant as any ballad heroine."

The others muttered in agreement.

They'd all heard the gossip about the mysterious appearance of Princess Atanial's daughter at the ancient tower, followed a day or two later by the princess herself, at the home of the ex-palace steward.

Damedran said quickly, offhand, "You heard about her fighting skill, but you didn't hear about her screaming orders at the criminals who brought her out of the other world. Last thing anyone heard was her yelling about them forgetting to bow, and where was her coach-and-six, and did anyone take her father's jewels?"

Damedran watched Ban, relieved at his faint expression of disgust. The others muttered about swagger—idiots—who did she think she was, anyway? Damedran didn't listen to any of them. Ban's opinion was important, maybe almost as important as his own. Weird, when Ban never strutted.

"We don't need that kind of trouble," Ban said at last. "Not right now."

Damedran nodded, and the others exchanged looks. They weren't supposed to talk about the secret plans to retake Jora, but they all knew. That was one of the good things about being in with the war commander's nephew.

Damedran was amazed that his lie actually worked. Then he got another idea. "No, we sure don't. Cowards, those Zhavalieshins. Skipping out and leaving us with the Siamis trouble, and now that things are settled, dancing back and expecting us all to bow down to them."

The boys expressed loud disgust. Then Bowsprit, who always had one eye on the weather and the other on the sea whenever he could, hooked a thumb toward the window. "Why is the sheep's yacht warping out?"

"He can't be going anywhere." Damedran snorted. "My uncle made it clear enough even to him he has to stay put. He's supposed to preside at the games."

As he spoke, he and the others moved to the windows. All minor boat traffic beyond the royal pier had cleared the way so Prince Jehan's beautiful yacht could be rowed out a ways from the dock.

They didn't have to warp far. The tide had reached flood and the wind had begun to shift as well, judging from the lower layer of clouds coming in under the high wispy ones. In silence they watched the exquisitely cut curved mainsail drop and sheet home. It filled, the craft gathered speed, then the sail was brailed up again. The anchor dropped, and the yacht rocked elegantly out in the roads, isolated east of the fleet ships.

"Well, he certainly won't get to sit on it to watch us compete in the harbor," Damedran said, and Bowsprit groaned. "Maybe Uncle Dannath ordered him to anchor out in the trade roads in case the pirate tries to grab him on shore."

Wolfie said, "Or maybe the sheep is so afraid of the pirate that he gave the orders before the water games were cancelled."

Hoots of derision met this suggestion.

Damedran waved a dismissive hand. "Or maybe my uncle is commandeering it for his pirate hunt. The *important* thing is, the games are now confined to ground, and we're going to win, right?"

The boys cheered. Damedran regarded them in satisfaction. The plans were all set, his father had said. Beginning with his win in every competition this year, the songs about them all winter, and on the rising tide of his reputation, his leading all the young aristocrats in galloping over the hills to liberate Locan Jora in spring. He'd be the hero who reunited the country . . . while Prince Jehan did what? Probably sat around watching some pretty girl paint daisies.

With this prospect in mind, he laughed, triumphant, happy, burning with anticipation. As the bell clanged for the midday break's end, and the beginning of afternoon practice, he led the way out at a run.

The others stampeded after. Or most of them did.

Ban followed more slowly. He was thinking hard until he noticed Bowsprit also lingering, his pointy nose pressed against the window. After one last glance out at that beautiful yacht, Bowsprit said, "How I'd love to crew it, just once. I don't care what stupid orders the sheep gives."

Ban grimaced. Truth was, he hated that "sheep" business. It didn't seem respectful. But his father had said, *If our regaining your mother's family lands from those ruinous Jorans means putting up with Merindar boot heels all over custom for a time, then we put up.*

Bowsprit poked his arm. "And you wouldn't care if it was a fish scow. What's wrong?"

"I just now remembered. The other night, when I had leave, it was the night my mother's friend's son arrived in town. He's a patrol leader. Wounded at that old castle the mages talk about. Samdan was invalided home. Got there right before supper, and at the time I was annoyed that he interrupted. I was afraid we wouldn't eat and I'd have to report back hungry—" Ban noticed Bowsprit's impatience at all that explanation, and got to the point. "This fellow was there when Prince Math's daughter came to the old castle. I really wasn't listening, but I heard some of it. How the pirate wounded him, how she was easily as hot with a blade. They thought she was a fellow at first, because she's tall and really fast."

"You mean, she wasn't a coward?"

Ban closed his eyes. "No. She did faint, or almost faint, but that was after the fight. She did some kind of healer's spell on one of the pirate's people, who got a cut on the arm, and there was poison on the knife."

"How about the coach-and-six?" Bowsprit asked.

"Well, that might have been later. But she sure didn't do it at the castle. Samdan said she came out into the court, picked up a blade, and she and the pirate whacked their way through the prince's patrol. Then she healed the boy, who my sister says was probably Devli Eban. She didn't try to kill anyone, either. Just like the pirate. Then they were gone by magic transfer."

"Who's Devli Eban?"

"Son of the palace steward during Prince Math's days. He was a mage student with my sister, though he's out now. Price on his head and everything, for being resistance."

"Oh." They reached the door, and Bowsprit paused. They could hear the thunder of the others' boots diminishing down the stairs below. No one else was around. They were all racing to the practice courts. "So your cousin's friend's father, or whatever, was wounded. Maybe he didn't hear everything."

"Said he was two spear-lengths from them."

Both considered in silence, each remembering times when Damedran's version of the truth hadn't quite matched with what they'd understood. But did it do you any good to point such things out? Not when the liar is the son of the academy commander, and the nephew of the kingdom's war commander. And, rumor had it—but never when Damedran was around—that if anything happened to Prince Jehan, the king was looking his way for a possible heir.

Bowsprit knocked Ban in the arm again. "Let's go."

In silence they followed the others, each thinking without coming to any conclusions. Sometimes it was better not to say what you thought, and other times it was useless even to think.

Jehan paused as the two sober-faced boys passed him on their way to the quarter-staff court.

He was certain they were two of Damedran Randart's followers, though he only recognized tall, dark-haired Ban Kender. But he'd been watching the games, and how the academy had been changing under the Randarts' command, for years.

He waited until they'd rounded the stone archway between command and the barracks, and followed, but instead of turning toward the courts, he continued across the parade ground to the stable, his expression so thoughtful that Owl, who was dressed in stable homespun and lurking around on the watch, pursed his lips.

They were long practiced at deception. Jehan inspected the high-bred horses reserved for those in command, and the scrappy redhead, who looked like so many others in this part of the world so close to Sarendan where red hair was quite common, busily swept out the stalls.

When they knew they wouldn't be overheard, Owl said, "She's all right. Other than mad as fire."

Jehan nodded. "I know. What troubles me more at the moment is Lesi Valleg, who I discovered is on the sick list. The official report is that she tripped, but Elkin tells me one of Damedran's boys got her drunk while on duty and stretched a cord across the bottom two stairs when she ran down."

Owl winced. "What for? I thought he'd outgrown the bullying."

"He stopped doing it for fun. This one might be to a purpose. Its happening right before the games is too suspicious to be accident. So the question is, what purpose?" Jehan shook his head. "Never mind that. What about Devlaen Eban?"

"He's on his way back to his cousin's new hideout, with the mages who wouldn't swear the allegiance oath. Promises to relay the messages to the mages, asking them to shadow Perran and Zhavic."

"And Elva?"

Owl said, "Devlaen told her the news about their mother being held prisoner. That sobered her enough to get her to agree to keep her mouth shut. I think she will. She's stubborn but honest. I left her in line at the hiring office, as she turned down my offer to join our crew. Her parting words to me were that she wanted to get to sea and forget all of us."

Jehan shook his head. "I really stumbled there."

"Maybe." Owl pinched his nose. "But not as badly as I did."

"We can't slip like that again."

They watched past one another's shoulders as they talked, but now they looked around to make extra certain. The stable was empty.

Jehan said, "Back to the games. Damedran's going to sweep all the categories, that much we can predict. What I wonder is if that connects with the rumored order for more weaponry from abroad? The war games ordered for autumn, including a castle siege, expensive as that is. And the requisitions for increased supplies for the guard in spring. Separately, these orders seem a little odd, but not extraordinarily so. Together, they add up to very odd indeed. Has Randart set the time for his invasion at last?"

Owl watched him as he moved dust around on the ground. He'd known Jehan for years, and was used to living life at a run. This was the prince's method of thinking aloud.

Jehan turned his way, his chin lifting. He'd reached a decision. "We have to intercept that weapons shipment. Get Aslo down to the harbor master's to underbid the others for the ships being hired to deliver the weapons. I don't care how much he has to scant his profit. I'll make up the shortfall. It's to be a sober merchant ship hired into that fleet."

Owl grinned. Their success depended on being able to pick the right battleground, and with one of their own ships sailing with the weapons consignment and relaying the position, they'd be able to do just that.

"I'll send a message to Tharlif to signal for a good-sized fleet to intercept that shipment. It won't stop an invasion if Randart really plans one, but at least it will hold him up."

Owl nodded. "You want me back on board the *Zathdar?*"

"No, let Robin take command. She's ready. You need to stay on that yacht. The most important piece of the puzzle is on it right now. The fewer who know who Sasharia is the better, and no one but us must know where she is." He ran his hand over the flanks of a dappled gray mare, and absently held out his fingers to be lipped. "Tell the *Jumping Bug* and *Mulekick* to make targets for Randart to chase, one off Aloca and one here. I want him busy all over the seas, chasing us and not other independents. Keep the navy busy and scattered as long as possible."

"And you?"

Jehan sighed. "I'm going to have to face the fire."

Owl grinned. "Orders for Kazdi to pass on to the Randarts?"

"Oh, let me see. This time it ought to be a painter. She's even more beautiful than my balladeer, and I promised to see her rendition of Lasva Sky Child being crowned queen of Colend. But

I *swear* to be back by the start of the games."

Jehan left to be seen out in the practice field staring at clouds instead of watching the boys practice staff fighting. He waited until he'd spotted War Commander Randart scowling contemptuously down at him from the command tower, and drifted away.

TWENTY

I COULDN'T SEE ANYTHING, and all I smelled was dust, old wool, and mold. Presently the cart stopped jolting, and the sensations changed to a kind of wallowing.

Angry as the situation made me, the moment I realized I was being lowered into a boat I stopped kicking. I didn't want to end up being dropped into the drink, and if I nailed Owl in the beezer, he might not be any speed demon about fishing me back out. Ending my life at the bottom of the harbor did not fit into my evolving career plans.

I will say the pirate—that is, the prince—well, anyway, his guys were careful, despite my having gotten in a couple of solid kicks early on in the abduction. The journey in the rowboat was accomplished in complete silence. I had no idea who was doing the oar work. Likewise the horrifying lift via boom up onto the deck was also silent.

Then people picked me up again and put me on a bunk.

But did they untie me? No. I was left in that sweltering cocoon for what seemed about ten centuries.

First I lay there thinking. Remembering. Lingering over every affront, until gradually the justified anger cooled into question, which in turn begat more questions, until I fell into a nasty sort of hot, smothered sleep.

I woke with the welcome sensation of the bonds easing.

With an inarticulate roar of rage, I fought my way out of the quilt—to discover I was alone, in a cabin I did not recognize. I blinked against the light of a lantern as I gulped in sweet, cool, fresh air. Someone had thoughtfully opened beautifully made leaded glass windows. Actual windows, not just scuttles.

Even the smell of brine seemed sweet compared to the old mold of that quilt.

Someone had set the lantern on a hook inside the door, which was carved out of redwood in a theme of galloping horses.

I rolled off the bunk, lunged to the door, and found it locked.

I lunged back and in another surge of rage gathered up that quilt and stuffed it out one of the windows. It took some effort, but finally I heard the satisfying splash, and for a short time I stood there on the redwood decking of the small but elegant cabin, breathing hard and watching the quilt float on the night-black sea.

Gradually the bubble holding it up diminished and the quilting soaked up enough water to sink. The last I saw of it was a pale blue corner and then it was gone.

As if released from its ghostly grip, I turned around to take in a cabin obviously designed and made for someone with extreme wealth. Carved wood in themes of running horses, entwined leaves, and artsy lilies, the lines enhanced with inlaid threads of gold.

The cabin's shape indicated that once again, I was in the bow. A tiny table had been fitted into the pointy end, within reach of the bunks angled inward on either side. On this little table someone had set a small porcelain tray with a silver pot all bedewed with moisture. A glass sat next to it.

My tongue felt like a sponge left out in the Gobi Desert, and I pounced, drinking down water until I was breathless. I continued my survey more slowly, looking for possible means of escape.

Built-in drawers with gold handles had been fitted below each bunk, the handles fashioned in the shape of two lilies with entwined stems. A shelf containing handmade books and old scrolls tied with ribbon had been built above one bunk. Affixed over the opposite bunk, a hand-drawn and colored map of the world, every river cobalt blue, paler blue for small lakes, different shades of green representing the predominant trees in forests, different browns for types of land. Cities indicated by highly stylized drawings of small or large towns, walled cities with walls, open ones with main roads done in gold.

It was a breathtaking work of art. I clambered up on the bunk to examine the map more closely. It was so beautiful I almost missed the sound of the cabin door opening behind me.

I whirled around as Jehan ducked slightly and entered, carrying a tray. "Like the map?"

When I was sixteen I might have yelled, *No!* Or tried to tear it up. My adult version of the correct etiquette for an abductee was to say, as rudely as possible, "From whom did you steal it?"

"My father." He flicked down a larger table from the wall, a table so cunningly worked into the bulkhead I'd missed it. He set the tray carefully down as he added, "He stole it from his relatives when he was booted out of Remalna after a family fight and sent here to the military school under strict orders to never return. You'll find Remalna northwest of where the Mardgar drains into the Sartoran Sea. Where the gold crown is drawn in."

I glanced at the map, and found the tiny kingdom, far smaller than Khanerenth. Marking it indeed was a crown, a typical piece of Merindar arrogance.

"Go ahead." He leaned against the opposite bulkhead. I noticed he was dressed in dark colors, a linen shirt dyed dark blue, black sash, and trousers. "Get 'em out."

"Get what out?"

"All the insults you've piled up. You've got to have thought up some good ones. Let's hear them."

"Then what, you can laugh from your oh-so-superior position?" I snapped, eyeing the tray. My appetite had woken like a cage of roaring lions. I considered for about one second the moral satisfaction of flinging that tray at him, but figured he'd just duck, like the total and complete stinker he was, and there'd be all that lovely food wasted.

Because it *was* lovely—a tomato soup sprinkled with fresh basil, some kind of incredibly savory cheese making it creamy, and bits of the very good rice this world grows. Next to it fresh bread, with pats of the honey-butter popular all over the kingdom. A spray of purple grapes, a perfectly sliced peach, and a silver urn containing hot chocolate joined a crystal decanter full of wine in making a feast for a king.

I glared at Zathdar. No, Jehan. Those were Zathdar's blue eyes watching me, but the long, fine white hair was unfamiliar. A diamond glinted in one ear. The laces in his shirt were braided silk, with tiny gold leaves fastening the ends.

I was staring. And the cabin seemed suddenly quite small. So I turned my attention back to the food.

"Go ahead," he invited.

"There are too many dishes," I said, scowling.

"Well, I haven't eaten all day, either. If it helps, feel free to fling my share out the window after Owl's mother's quilt."

Unwillingly I had to laugh. "All right. You win. That much, anyway. Sit down."

The table exactly fitted the space between the two bunks, on which we sat opposite one another.

I'd only had that single bite in the Gold Inn, so I set to with enthusiasm. Two goblets of wine plus the meal later, I sat back, trying to decide if I had enough appetite to assay the chocolate.

Neither of us had spoken, though I was very aware of him sitting an arm's reach away, the play of his hands on the goblet, pouring wine, picking up bread and cheese, homely tasks all, but executed with grace. He ate neatly, with far better manners than I suspected I displayed. But I'd been catching meals on the run for years, usually with a book in one hand.

I frowned at my goblet. Was what I felt the same as my mother had felt all those years ago, when this man's father no doubt ate intimate dinners with her while my own father was busy tending to kingly business for my ailing grandfather?

I looked up. Jehan regarded me steadily over his cup of wine.

I said, crossly, "I suppose you dye your eyelashes and brows?"

"No. Darker shade than my father's, as it happens," he replied in an easy tone, as though he fielded this nosy question every day. "For some reason most half-morvende have dark brows and lashes. The ones with white lashes come from families who have lived over a thousand years underground. Some of the more recent family lines have color here." He indicated a thin stripe at the top of his head. "Almost always black. Sometimes red or yellow or brown. A lot of 'em get rid of it by magic," he added. "If it comes in stripes."

A short pause ensued, during which I was hyper-aware of the soft plash of water against the hull of the vessel, of the flicker of the flame in the lantern, and its golden reflection made manifold by the glass sectioning inside the burnished copper frame. I breathed in the rich fragrance of the chocolate, and set my goblet down.

A phosphorescent tingle sparked along my nerves. I gripped my hands in my lap.

"I apologize for the, ah, summary invitation aboard my yacht," Jehan continued, in the same conversational tone. "I'll end it when I can."

I looked up, the flare of anger back. "You mean when you will."

"No one outside of a dozen people know who I am." He lifted a shoulder in a slight, apologetic shrug. "Except the Ebans, now. And you."

"What did you do to Elva?"

"Nothing. Owl tried to recruit her. She refused. Last he saw, she was trying to find another ship to sign onto."

"Devli?"

"On his way to his mage tutors, wherever they're hiding."

I twisted my fingers. "That might even be true. But if it is, why am *I* not asked to keep silent, and set free to go on my way?"

"Because . . ." He looked away, out the window into the darkness, then back at me. "Because too many people see you as a tool necessary to grip control of the kingdom."

"Including you?"

He looked away again. Then back. "Will you listen to my side of things?" His eyes narrowed. "But you won't believe me, will you?" He moved suddenly, not toward me—though I braced for it—but away, to the little alcove at the point of the cabin. The bulkhead below the tiny table had been adapted into a kind of desk that reminded me of a rolltop, with a lot of little drawers.

He opened one and drew out a packet of heavy linen paper.

"You want to read my correspondence with your father?" He held out the letters.

"How do I know those are real?" I felt not so much angry as sick and miserable. "I wouldn't recognize his handwriting. I wouldn't even know his style. I was ten, the last time I saw him."

He dropped the letters back into the drawer and leaned there with hands on the desk, the silken shirt laces swinging, their golden leaves winking with tiny reflected flames in the light of the lantern. I was staring again.

He turned his head slightly, his white hair drifting over his shoulder. His gaze met mine, and fireworks lit off right behind my ribs. *I hate chemistry.* I jerked my head away, half expecting my eyes to make popping sounds like cartoon tentacles. Argh! I scowled at the carved racing horses in the wood panels.

"Why won't you listen? Do you really think I'd go to all this trouble if I was my father's tool?"

I said to the chocolate pot, "Why didn't you answer me when I asked why I'm here, but you let the Ebans go free?" A quick glance, to see the effect of my words. "You are good at deflecting awkward questions, aren't you?"

I could feel him regarding me steadily, trying to read my reactions. "They don't hold the key to the kingdom. You do. I really did mean to let you go, but that was before I found Randart and all his guards right here in Ellir, and then there was Elba shadowing Owl. Elba's mother is under arrest; if Elba, in dashing out to expose me for a fraud had revealed her own name—and you know she would have—Randart would have snatched her. Do you really want to know what Randart would do to her to get whatever she knew out of her?"

"No." I breathed out the word.

Jehan said quickly, "Then we come to you. There are orders to grab you on sight. I don't know why yet, except that everyone believes that you know where Prince Math is." He got up and put his hand on the latch to the cabin door. "I should mention that your mother followed you through the World Gate. And unfortunately my father has her as well as Kreki Eban. No, don't say it." He raised his hand as I drew in a deep breath. "Whatever you believe me capable of, I can promise you this. If my father gets his hands on you, you can absolutely count on him using your lives against one another in order to get what he wants. Chocolate? Yes? No?"

"Lost my appetite," I said wearily.

He took the tray and left. Locking the door behind him.

Pretty soon I heard through the open windows the noises of the booms being used to lower a small boat. I peered down at an angle as a silhouette descended.

I recognized Jehan by the way he moved. He had confined that moon-pale hair in some sort of knitted sailor cap. That and the dark clothing made him unremarkable, one of many people plying little boats to and fro on the dark waters between the boats all lit by strings of lanterns.

Unremarkable if your eyes hadn't memorized the contours of his arms, the line from shoulder to slim hip, the way the light played over the angles in his face. The arch of his brow. The shape of his lips.

I watched until he and his boat blended into the crown of lights made by the market street and the torchlit castle above, and then I dropped onto the bunk and put my head in my hands.

Yeah, that was definitely one of my worst moments.

Up in the Ellir Academy commander's suite, War Commander Randart longed for sleep. He was getting too old for all-night rides and all-day inspections, distractions, orders, and logistics.

He glared at his nephew, gabbling away to Orthan as if he had never heard of sleep, and finished the rest of his ale. At least that was good. He'd have to make certain a few barrels of Old Gold were included in the commander's stores when he took ship.

"...and they were watching him arrest some cutpurse. I never heard of him doing that before. Must have been his followers who actually did the work."

Orthan laughed.

"Red says, maybe he was trying to teach the thief some poetry and the thief surrendered only to get away."

Orthan guffawed louder, making the war commander's head hurt. "What's that? They didn't tell me Jehan took the cutpurse arrested today."

Orthan and Damedran turned twin expressions of surprise his way. "He didn't. I told you that earlier," Orthan exclaimed, and his brow began to lower. "Two of our fellows did—"

The war commander ignored his brother's long-suffering *You don't listen to me.* They'd been through that too many times. Dannath only listened when Orthan's gibble-gabble was to a purpose. He got to his feet. "All I know is, if he's not here at the start of the games tomorrow, I'll strangle him myself." He pointed at his nephew. "You! Go get some rest. You have one order: to win tomorrow."

"Oh, I'll win," Damedran predicted, stretching as he swung to his feet. "I can thrash anyone I know on the list, one handed." He snapped a fist into the opposite palm, muscles bunching. "I got Captain Traneg to show me the roster before I came up here. Some locals have signed up, but we haven't seen any locals win for years."

"People can sign on until the trumpets tomorrow," Orthan

warned, knowing his son would ignore him, but it was better to endorse his brother's order when Dannath was looking so irritable. "You never know, but some day a good one might show up, like the old days, before Siamis came. You do your best when you're rested."

Damedran snorted. "The back of my hand to locals. I don't see why you don't close the games to them anyway. Yes, I know that's how we recruited in the past, but maybe it's time to change all that. Better cadets from the better families."

"Shut up and go to bed," the war commander ordered.

When he used that voice, it was best to obey. Damedran and his uncle slammed through opposite doors, leaving Orthan to finish the ale alone and then douse the light.

TWENTY-ONE

AFTER A SLEEPLESS NIGHT during which Jehan's brain insisted on reviewing, with remorseless repetition, every single mistake he'd made in deed or speech with Sasharia, he got up, drank the hottest, strongest coffee the innkeeper could brew, then left the humble dockside inn where he'd thought to get overdue rest.

He stopped at the bathhouse and paid to use their cleaning frame. No time for a real bath, and anyway it was going to be far too hot, he thought, staring at the knife-edged shafts of yellow early morning sunlight painting the wooden wall dividing the men's side from the women's.

The sun was climbing into midsummer brilliance when he crossed up an old pathway behind the ruins of a castle long forgotten, and now used mainly for its stone. There, in the shade of a web-clogged alcove he paused to change out of the plain clothes and hat, pulling on his brown velvet.

He rolled up his old outfit, tucked it under his arm, and started up the back trail used by locals who hired on as stable and maintenance support staff at the guard barracks and academy. A few steps up past some flowering shrubs, his shoulder blades prickled. Unseen eyes? He stepped to the side, hand going to his sword, then dropping when he saw four cadet-aged young fellows walking behind him single file.

Three walked and one sauntered, a tall fellow with black hair and pale brown eyes of a distinctive shade—flecked with gold—that evoked flame in that strong summer light. His features were sharp, his gaze sharper; memory stirred from somewhere way back years ago, on the other side of the world.

"Do I know you?" he asked.

The tall one grinned, but did not speak.

"Not really," another one murmured, and when Jehan looked his way his breath caught. He was about to exclaim, "Senrid?" when he realized that this fellow was not Senrid Montredaun-An, king of Marloven Hess—and head of the academy to which Jehan had gone to learn war skills so long ago.

Senrid never wore this sort of thoughtful, almost scholarly expression, nor had he grown as tall. Most tellingly, this fellow's eyes were brown, an ordinary light brown, and King Senrid's were grayish blue. And their spoken accents were completely different. The resemblance was nothing more than a slender build, curly short blond hair . . . and the brain fatigue of a hot summer's day.

"I'm David," the fellow said, pronouncing it not Sartoran DAUF-ed, but Marlovan-style, DAY-vid. David gestured at the three others. "We're here to play in your games."

Jehan took in the two unfamiliar ones. First, a tallish, thin fellow with a dreamy expression, wide-set brown eyes and an unkempt mat of curly light brown hair that brought Prince Math instantly and forcibly to mind. The last was a mere boy, scarcely cadet age from the looks of him. He seemed an everyday small boy, dressed in homespun shirt and riding trousers, brown hair clipped back from a high brow, though Jehan almost immediately began observing subtle anomalies, beginning with his stillness, and the steady, observant hazel gaze that seemed far older than you ever saw in any child's face.

"And the rest of you are?" He suspected he would not get a real answer.

Nor did he. "Competitors," David said, and then, with an air of absent courtesy, "You have no objection to a little roustabout, perhaps?"

"What's that supposed to mean?" Jehan recognized that they knew who he was. Where *had* he seen that tall one before? Now it seemed important.

"Nothing untoward," David soothed. "Shall we meet after the day's entertainment?"

"I suspect"—Jehan eyed the tall one again—"that I will want very much to do that. Where have I seen you before?"

"Here and there." The tall one grinned briefly, no more than a flash of teeth. His voice was lower than you'd expect from someone that lean. Low, husky—and again familiar.

Sweat trickled down Jehan's forehead. The morning air had gone from warm to hot, and the sun was still low. "Go on. Sign up. Do whatever it is you're going to do." *Things could hardly get worse.*

The tall one laughed softly as they passed on by.

The small one was last. As he drew near Jehan he said in Sartoran, "Stay your path."

He dashed after his companions and they vanished around the mossy old wall of the ruined castle, reappearing halfway up the trail at a dead run.

Jehan veered between amusement and annoyance at some urchin advising him how to get to his own academy. As if he was likely to stray off the—

Path. In Sartoran. He listened to the words again, thinking in Sartoran instead of just mentally translating the words.

Stay. Your. Path.

In Sartoran, the connotation was closer to *You're doing the right thing.*

Now, that was strange. He paused to peer upward against the rising sun as the four mystery visitors vanished over the lip of the hill toward the public path. He forgot about the heat, his headache, even his hunger, and began to lope up the trail toward the back way into the old, abandoned storage rooms where he usually left his change of clothes. Maybe the day that had promised a long stretch of annoyance might yield some surprises after all.

TWENTY-TWO

LESI VALLEG WEPT FOR joy, shaking her head impatiently so her vision would not blur. She stood with a cluster of seniors at the sideline of the archery butts, and watched the little boy in homespun lift his bow, pull back, and aim in the same fluid motion so he was one line from thumb to the back elbow, and when he let fly his arm snapped out so his arms were a straight line, thumb to thumb. And then his shooting hand swept down, as smooth and unthinking as the folding wings of a swan.

It was effortless, graceful, expert—and the best shot of the day, despite his age, despite the distance and oh, oh, oh, despite Damedran leaning against the wall on the other side of the butts, his bruised face expressionless.

"See that? Arm all the way back," she muttered, wiping her eyes. "It really does make a difference." And the other seniors standing near her, instead of rolling their eyes or sneering or yawning as they always had in the past, agreed with mutters of wonder.

Once Prince Jehan had told her that this was the way he'd been taught to shoot by that academy on the other side of the continent. But that fact had only earned scoffing. Every cadet knew he was a cloud-brain. And everyone knew the Marlovens were mere horse riders, they didn't train on water as well as land.

If you want to shoot you need first to learn form. Aim will then come, she remembered her old teacher saying. It wouldn't do to remind everyone. She'd be accused of swagger. And anyway, that boy had carried off the silver cup. She didn't *need* to remind them.

She followed the crowd, hoping she could talk to him. She wanted to tell him it was a pleasure to watch him. It would have been a pleasure to shoot against him, no matter who won, if only her arm hadn't been broken.

But the trumpet blew the signal to change events, and most of the competitors, locals as well as cadets, swarmed to the tables to get some water before lining up for the last and favorite event of the land games: the relay race, which took all afternoon.

"You don't have to go," Ban said to Damedran as they followed more slowly. He regretted his earlier triumph when Damedran was summarily thumped in the last grappling match, though he'd enjoyed it thoroughly (and privately) at the time.

Damedran turned his puffy face Ban's way, then flashed up the back of his hand.

Despite the insult Ban was not angry. Not when he saw the spasm of pain that tightened Damedran's features.

Ban, Bowsprit, and a couple of others exchanged wry looks. Nothing felt quite real any more; life was no longer predictable. One thing was clear, despite his drubbing Damedran was going to carry on anyway.

The trumpet pealed, and everyone looked up.

"Teams gather here," bawled the captain in charge of the relay.

Damedran limped slowly to the edge of the field from which the sprinters would take off on the first leg of the relay. Paying no attention to the chatter around him, he said, "I'll ride. Can't run or canoe." He gave them a painful grimace that was supposed to be a smile.

Ban saw Wolfie peering intently to one side, his mouth twisted in the smirk that meant either he'd been fighting or was going to fight. And there was Red moseying along, looking skyward, as he passed by the various teams assembling. He slowed near the strangers who had so unaccountably appeared and taken all the prizes. Red stopped as the unfamiliar four talked briefly and quietly among themselves, bent to pick something from one boot, then he straightened up and sauntered with a bit more speed to Wolfie, and muttered behind his hand.

Wolfie beckoned to a couple of their other followers, and Ban suspected what was probably going to happen. He knew his guess was right when Wolfie stepped up to Damedran and said, "The little one is doing the ride." He chuckled the way he always did before somebody ended up getting scragged. "Guess they won't win the relay."

Damedran shook his head.

Ban said in disgust, "You're going to drop on the littlest one."

Wolfie, Red, and the other two turned his way, their faces ranging from guilty to defiant to angry.

Damedran said, surprising them all, "That's not an . . . an . . . a fair scrag. Dropping on a little boy, that's just rabbiting."

"Fair?" Wolfie repeated derisively. For him, a scrag was a scrag. Any excuse served to have one, because he always won.

"Fair?" Red repeated, as if he'd never heard the word.

"But you dropped Lesi Valleg," Ban observed. It had been a guess. He saw from Damedran's quick grimace that he'd been right.

"That was different," Damedran muttered, trying not to look yet again to where the tall, thin girl with the sling-bound arm stood, her straight brows low, watching him with unsmiling intensity. "We couldn't win against her. I wanted, I needed, wins in everything." He dropped his head back, uttering a strangled laugh.

"It isn't different," Ban said.

Damedran's mouth tightened. He opened his hand. "She wouldn't have won anyway. Not against that little brat."

"Who *are* they?" asked Calan Pradiesh, Red's cousin from the coast.

"I don't know." Damedran shifted with painful care to observe the newcomers, who stood in line, the tall one grinning at something the short one said, the fair-haired one looking pensive, the one with the wild, curly hair watching two raptors riding the thermals high up under the flat carpet of tiny puff clouds that promised rain. "But he used moves I've never seen." He fingered his shoulder, winced again. "Or felt."

They all reflected on the grappling. The lazy way the tall one moved to block, to deflect, and his whip-fast, brutal attacks. All without breaking a sweat.

"They won't win," Wolfie reminded them, rubbing his hands.

Ban studied the small boy who stood there so still and poised as he contemplated the stands where the commanders sat with the prince. Neither of the Randarts smiled, and all the seniors knew they were angry. But they could do nothing. The competition was open, and had been for years.

Nobody cared what Prince Jehan thought.

Ban said suddenly, privately, to Bowsprit, "I think . . ." He shook his head.

Bowsprit turned his thin, pointy nose toward Wolfie's huge, muscular form, and then to the small, slender boy who was probably about nine, if that. "I think so, too."

"First-leg runners, line up here," called the captain. "Second-leg canoe, follow Captain Semmeg, third-leg mountain climbers, follow Captain Torvic, and the horse riders for the last leg, you go with Captain Lesstrad to your posts. We've got animals up there waiting for you." The trumpet played the signal, and a roar went up as the relay racers separated.

Ban took off behind Captain Torvic, along with the five other members of cadet teams, two members of the royal fleet, and the blond foreigner with the pensive face, the one who had won every single sword match.

Ban loped in the fellow's direction, questions forming in his mind, but the other cadets reached the unknown first.

"Where you from?" piped a ten-year-old.

"Oh, here and there, you might say," was the answer, with a faint trace of accent. "Never really settled in one place."

"Where'd you learn your sword work?"

The fellow smiled. "Various teachers. They tend to be hard on mistakes, so, you know, we learn to make as few as possible."

"How hard?" asked a fourteen-year-old girl with the squint-eyed distrust of the middle teens.

"Let's say . . . they broke us of bad habits."

Everyone, even the ten-year-old, heard the humorous ambiguity behind "broke."

"Belay the chatter and hurry up there," called Captain Torvic.

That ended the talk until they reached the site for their leg of the relay. While they waited, the newcomer prowled around looking down at the road, up at the cliffs, at the distant sea, at the sky, and though Ban watched him steadily, he never turned Ban's way.

The newcomer with the frizzy hair was first to their post, and the blond one took off. One of their own group was next, crimson-faced with effort, and Ban sprinted up the mountain, hoping he would not see Wolfie or Red, but afraid he knew where they were.

When he reached the last leg, gasping with effort, the little boy was gone, and the blond fellow sat on the grass, smiling at the sky. Ban almost said something, but shook his head and started back down the trail to the academy.

It was a long, hot, gloomy walk. He took the horse trail anyway, but didn't see anyone.

When he reached the academy, it was to find out that the newcomers had won. The small boy rode bareback into the center of the parade ground on a high-spirited charger, his hands not even on the reins.

Prince Jehan was the first to applaud, and then the others joined, but not with any spirit. The river-rush of voices all talking and exclaiming was almost louder than the clapping.

Bowsprit and Ban, having hoped the boy would escape being scragged by Wolfie, Red, and their chosen few senior cadets, said nothing at all as they followed the glum seniors to the parade ground for the distribution of the prizes.

Up in the stands, Dannath Randart was so angry he felt his blood boiling in a drumbeat through his head. But he schooled himself to sit without moving, fists on his knees, as he stared down at the shambles of his plan.

Plans could be remade. He knew that. He glowered at his nephew, who limped from the horse picket across to the senior line. Why did the idiot have to ride in the relay when he could barely sit his horse, just to lose yet again? Now Randart had to consider ways to wrench some kind of victory from the distasteful, no, the *shameful* exhibition.

The blame would go squarely on the shoulders of the staggeringly stupid white-haired fatwit sitting to his right, who was now getting up and flicking dust from his faultless velvet in order to go down to the field to hand out the prizes.

Randart glared at Jehan. "Those newcomers. I want them." And at the shocked look on Orthan's face, he forced a semblance of civility into his tone. "I believe the king would want to hear about their training. Please, your highness, request them to honor us for a celebratory glass up in the command tower."

Jehan, as always, was oblivious to the sudden change of tone —

Jehan. Prisoners. Market Street — cadets —

Randart put out a hand, remembering again what had bothered him when he woke up. He'd been bothered enough to go down to the lockup and ask a few questions, despite the loaded schedule. "You arrested a cutpurse in Market Street yesterday?"

Jehan's thin brows lifted. "I did?"

"Damedran saw you. That is, the boys saw you from the senior barracks. But the only thief in the lockup is the pickpocket brought in by the pier patrol on the morning rotation."

Jehan sighed, looking apologetic. "Well. I did try. But my miscreant got away."

So he *didn't* have any of his followers in the king's guard with him. "Why didn't you call up the guard? There's always a patrol within earshot."

"I thought they were off duty," Jehan said vaguely. "I did not like to disturb them."

Randart sat back in disgust. He marshaled himself enough to say with forced politeness, "I believe they are waiting on their prizes, your highness. Forgive me for detaining you."

Jehan bowed, a court bow and highly inappropriate here, but that was as usual. Everything was as usual, so why did he feel something crucial was missing from that testimony?

I'm seeing conspiracies everywhere, Randart thought. But just the same, before the prince reached the end of the platform and was about to step down into the regular stands to descend to the field, he called, "Remember, after we speak to the winners, the king requires you to remain with us. Your highness."

Once again a court bow, hand gracefully at his heart, and Jehan ran lightly down the steps to the field, where the captains had the cadets lined up in field order. While the seniors looked around for Wolfie and Red and their two cronies, Randart said to his brother, "I want the prince followed. Say it's for his safety. But put someone discreet on it."

Startled, Orthan leaned over to speak to the aide on duty, who hustled along the back of the platform to the hidden doorway leading down to the guardroom.

The brothers turned their attention back to the field, where Jehan stood next to the four small cadets who so carefully held the prizes. Both forgot the prince when they saw why the ceremonies had not begun. It was not Jehan getting himself lost counting butterflies, it was because the recipients were nowhere in sight.

Randart gripped the edge of his seat. "The little one was just there, riding that horse. Where did he go? Find them. I want them. Whatever excuse it takes. I want to know who they are. Why they were here, if it wasn't to compete to get into our training."

Orthan got up. After a glance at his brother's face, he hustled after his own underling.

On the field, Jehan spoke a few graceful words that few listened to, then gave the signal for the captains to dismiss the contestants. The cadets surged toward the mess hall, everyone voicing his or her opinion, or putting questions to the air. Comments and questions mirrored in the watchers in the stands, who filed out the other way and back down the long zigzagging steps into the harbor city below.

As Jehan traversed the halls between the guard barracks and the academy, the morvende part of his hearing, developed for generations to sift human sound from wind and water rushing along stone tunnels and caverns, registered footsteps matching his pace.

He paused at the guard room to get a drink of water after the long, hot afternoon in the sun, nodded pleasantly when the guards on duty leaped to their feet and saluted, and waved them lazily back to their seats. No one entered after him.

He left. Moseyed slowly to the mess hall, hot as it was and smelling of fish simmered in herbs and tomato. Below that he detected the distinct odor of summer-afternoon adolescent sweat. Jehan stepped into the kitchen, nipped a biscuit from one of the trays being pulled from the oven, and exited through the opposite door as he tossed the hot biscuit from hand to hand.

Still there, same distance back.

Down to the cadet stable, which was built into the oldest part of the castle. There he asked about some of his favorite mounts and ordered Clover to be saddled up. "I want to ride back along the relay trails," he said clearly. "I hope our mysterious visitors did not get lost somewhere along the way."

While the duty cadets and the shadow busied themselves with horse saddling, Jehan slipped through the tack room into the old storage room, which smelled of mildew and stone. He slid the bolt, then keyed the entrance to a passageway that Prince Math had shown him when he was a boy, the single time they had been there together.

When he emerged at the other end, he was dressed again in the blue outfit, a fisherman's stocking cap on his head hiding his hair, his brown velvet hanging in a net bag over his shoulder. He made his way through the rotting barrels that hid the door to the passage, slipped into the alley behind the old row of shops, and from there he strolled into Market Street as the low sun slanted ochre shafts between buildings.

Jehan didn't trouble to look around. The shadow would be riding as fast as he could for the relay trail, which was sure to keep him or her busy for a while. Jehan suspected that David and his three friends, who had indicated they would speak to him after the competition, would find him if they wanted him.

He was right. A crowd of sailors strolled by, talking and laughing; out of their number appeared two figures who flanked Jehan. The tall black-haired one grinned. "Nice sidestep."

He meant it as a compliment. They were aware of the shadow, and how Jehan had slipped the shadow's vigilance. Prickles of invisible ice cooled his neck and the backs of his arms, as the thin one flicked a hand toward one of the more modest tents.

Inside they found David holding a table, to which a harried young woman brought a loaded tray of chicken pies, cornbread and cold, frosty ale.

Almost immediately the small boy drifted in, unnoticed by anyone else in the tent—the conversations at the other tables being mostly about the fleet being made up for the pirate hunt, and who'd hired on where, and what it was doing to trade.

The boy was wearing an outsized shirt. He slid in next to David, then said with a quiet air almost of apology, "I had to use the other for bindings."

Jehan realized then what he'd known instinctively, that these four somehow spoke mind to mind. He knew now from where he recognized the tall one, and possibly the one with the hair. They'd competed in the midsummer games years before, always well, but previously they'd never quite stood out.

Jehan sat back. "So your roustabout was intended as a general humiliation, or for fun?"

David looked surprised, and the fiery-eyed one grinned. "For instruction."

David put down his fork. "Tell me you didn't see what we

were doing."

Jehan shrugged a shoulder. "So you are giving me lessons in curriculum design why?"

The mock surprise and fake air of helpfulness vanished. "Because you will need to train 'em better," David said. "And if I might suggest an added course of instruction, hill warfare against occupation."

Again the ice, burning with warning.

"Norsunder," Jehan breathed. "What? When?" He knew now who they were, but not why they were here.

Before he could speak again, the tall one flicked up a scarred hand. "Don't say anything." He flicked one ear. "They do actually have wards against certain names."

Jehan studied the four faces. "But—the stories about you—whose side are you on, anyway?"

"What's a side?" the smallest one asked.

"The easiest would be anything or anyone that fights against Norsunder taking land, people, life, liberty. Will and spirit," Jehan said deliberately.

"That would be our side," said the boy, his gaze steady. Meeting it felt strangely like falling and falling through the air.

"Not what I've heard about you." Jehan looked away, steadying himself with his hands flat on the table.

The one with the hair looked down, the tall one flashed his sharp-edged grin. David said, "Is everything said about you—action, motivation—true?"

"No."

The small one murmured, "Some of what's said about us is true. But we bring no intent to harm here."

Jehan believed that because he knew what they were capable of.

The tall one had gone on eating. He looked up. "Damedran. Bad bridle training. You take the reins." He gestured, meaning qualified approval, and returned to his meal.

Jehan let out a soundless laugh. He couldn't quite point out that he had no reins to hold, not with Randart hunting him in phantom form and now, possibly in real, all because of that hasty abduction. It was only a matter of time before he slipped and Randart penetrated the tenuous disguise. When seen in the perspective of world politics—the sinister powers hunting the blood of these four and the infamous figures who had trained them—his problems seemed small.

"Everyone is going to have to pitch it together," the one with the hair spoke for the first time. "Everyone. To the best of their ability. War is coming, we cannot avoid it, but we can resist if everyone works together."

David turned his head sharply; Jehan heard a cadenced march above the general noise of the tent.

A search party of guards halted outside the tent. The patrons fell silent and the harried girl ran to the canvas door and lifted it, exclaiming in question and alarm.

Jehan turned back to warn his companions. They were gone, the bottom of the tent reverberating as if just dropped.

He was alone at the table. Even their food was gone, leaving him to hunch over his meal. He felt the hot, weary, exasperated gaze of the search captain sweep past him, and then came the sounds of the searchers marching farther up the row of tents.

Jehan sat there thinking, while he had this precious time to think. War, imminent. *I'd better have Tharlif stockpile those weapons she took off Randart's fleet.*

He slipped out to make his way to the boat as the sun vanished at last and shadows merged.

It was time to go try to make amends with Sasharia. And despite his headache, his regrets, the new threats to his kingdom and to the world, he looked forward to seeing her. Maybe, just maybe, he could get her to laugh.

On the other side of the castle, while riding the last leg of the relay without finding Prince Jehan, or anyone else, his shadow came across four cadets making their way slowly toward the parade ground. In amazement he recognized Wolf, nephew of the commander, and three others. All with broken bones — a wrist, an arm, a shoulder, and Wolf with a broken leg. Each wound thoughtfully splinted and bound up with neatly torn strips from a boy-sized shirt.

No one spoke as he helped them back to the academy.

TWENTY-THREE

THE LAST OF THE day's light glowed deep blue on the western horizon behind him when Jehan reached the yacht. He'd left orders for a single lantern at the stern rather than running lights, so he was surprised to see lanterns swinging and winking as silhouettes crossed back and forth, the sort of movement you expected to see during work aboard a ship.

What work? The sails were furled, the yacht riding at single anchor on the out-flowing tide. He smothered his lantern and waited, oars at rest, until his eyes adjusted enough to determine that the yacht was not being attacked. He'd first seen climbing figures. Now the crew was at the falls and tackle, bringing up the second boat.

There could only be one reason it had been let down. He uncovered his lantern, once again shielding it from the shore side, and pulled hard on his oars, occasionally peering over his shoulder until he could make out a shivering figure with long dripping braids huddled in a blanket on deck as the other crew members finished stowing the second boat.

"*Dolphin*," he called.

"*Dolphin* ho. Falls ready," came Owl's wry voice.

Jehan climbed up the side and crossed to the captain's deck. As he passed Sasharia, she lifted her chin, her face pale and defiant when she recognized him.

"I would have tried it, too," he said.

She laughed, and his breath caught. "You. W-would. Have. G-gotten. Away." Her teeth chattered so hard she almost couldn't speak.

A step nearer, and he saw her blue lips. Angry, he turned his head. "Where is something hot —"

"Right away. Gave the orders when we got back." Owl worked in tandem with the other crew, pulling up Jehan's boat.

"Here I am," came the accented voice of Kaelande, the cook, and a heartbeat later he appeared with a tray of hot coffee, which he set on the capstan. "Dinner," he added after an inscrutable glance at them all, "will be ready anon." He vanished back down to his galley, a tall, stocky man who had been trained in Alsais's royal palace, the most exclusive cooking school in the entire southern hemisphere.

Owl turned a slant-browed, assessing look Jehan's way, and then toward Sasharia. "Looks to me like we could all use it."

Sasharia took her mug, her eyes closing as she cherished its warmth. She carried it toward the guest cabin in the forecastle, and Owl followed Jehan down into the main cabin. They sank onto the fine-carved chairs bolted to the deck, and Owl sighed. "I didn't think she'd try a swim for shore from out here."

"I didn't either. We were wrong. But that's one more tot in the day's total." Jehan tried to shut out the image of Sasha's tall, strong body in that wet clothing. His life was complicated enough, and he knew she didn't want any part of him. But there she was, somehow larger than life in all the ways that were good, with a sudden smile like the sun on the world's first day.

He pressed his thumbs into his eyelids, trying to shutter away Sasha's image. "Randart will probably have a search team out here by morning, soon as he can figure an excuse."

"He's onto us?"

"I think he suspects. And I'm coming to believe, despite his former friendliness, that he would like any excuse to help me suffer a fatal accident. But that's not our biggest problem. Not nearly."

Owl grimaced. "If there's something worse, I'd rather get a meal in me first."

"We'll all do that."

Owl jerked his thumb toward the front of the ship in question.

Jehan said, "Invite her. Then I don't have to explain twice."

Owl waited, but Jehan's gaze had gone diffuse the way it did when he was evolving plans, and so he left.

I stood in the cabin while my core temperature gradually achieved something resembling human levels, rather than penguin, and stared into the coffee.

I hate coffee. That is, I love the smell but find it bitter to drink unless I doctor it with honey and milk. Lots and lots of milk. But I wasn't going to complain about it now. First of all because I needed the warmth, and second because they very definitely had the high moral ground.

Human nature, or maybe it's my own nature, has mule-kick stubbornness beat hollow. If they'd yelled at me for my stupid act, I would have been planning another try. But they'd been nice about it, so I felt guilty. Guilty for simply trying my best to get away, on my own, until I figured out what was right? No, guilty because they'd gone to a terrible amount of trouble to search me out in the ocean, their faces worried sick when they found me about two nanoseconds before my numb body was about to give up.

I felt guilty and cold and waterlogged. All my gear was soaked as well, for the gear bag was not waterproof, and I'd thrown away the horrible basket-weave. Owl had put me through the cleaning frame as soon as I got on board, so the salt sting was gone, but that did not dry anything.

For a short time I stood there staring haplessly down at the soggy firebird coverlet and my other outfit. I let them drop to the deck with a squelch.

A knock a moment later. "Will you join us for dinner?" That was Owl. I knew Owl's voice very well by now. First he'd been on the other side of that hot quilt the day before. Today he'd been calling to me, calling to me, as they sought for me in the boat despite the darkness, as I was about to sink . . .

"No clothes." My lips were numb, my jaw shuddering. "W-wet."

No answer.

I was pressing the cup against my face when the knock came again. "Jehan offers these with his compliments."

I fumbled with still-numb fingers at the cabin door. It opened. Owl handed me folded cloth. "He apologizes for the colors, but says they went through the cleaning frame. If you give me yours, I'll put 'em through the frame and spread 'em near the galley fire."

I silently handed him the cloth things from the gear bag, then shut the door and shucked my tunic and trousers. My undies were wet, too, but no help for those. At least they were clean.

I turned to the clothes. *Jehan's* clothes. The idea whopped me right behind the ribs. I held up a fine linen shirt, the lacing another of those long braided silk things with a tiny gold leaf at the end. Under that, some black riding trousers. Last, a long velvet tunic somewhat like a battle tunic, except obviously not made to be fought in. Brown, with the cup stitched on in real silver—the royal colors. Hence the apology.

I was too numb to care. The shirt was roomy and only slightly large, but the pants, tailored to a very different body, were way tight where it counted most. My wet underwear threatened to make the wedgie of the century, so I took the trousers off again, and slipped on the tunic. Its hem fell below my knees, except for the slits on the sides, but the shirt was long enough to cover me to mid-thigh. Hardly immodest, even here, when during summer many rolled their deck trousers to their knees, especially when working with water.

Still. I felt off-balance, intensely aware of a sense of intimacy in the wearing of Jehan's clothes. The cleaning frame had removed any trace of him, so they smelled like clean cloth, but that curious electricity lingered, the sensory evidence of attraction. I ran my hand down the tunic, which was cut to fit a man—the shoulders hanging over my upper arms, the front reshaped by me. The slim line of the tunic hugged my hips, which are built on the Valkyrie model. If there was a mirror in that cabin, I had not found it. Not that I'd really searched, for earlier in the day I'd only had escape on my mind.

No help for it. I looked the way I looked.

I grabbed up my wet clothes and marched out.

The yacht currently had only four crew members besides Owl: the cook, his wife, and two men, one young, one older. Only one of those was in my line of sight, on watch at the helm. He gazed out to sea.

Owl and Jehan stood near the smooth, elegantly curved stern rail. When the cabin door shut behind me they turned their heads and watched me walk up the half a dozen shallow steps to the deck, the lantern light from the binnacle shining on their faces.

Is that stare universal among het males? Their gazes swept down my body, stopped twice—once north of the equator and once south—then dropped down to my feet and away. Both faces wearing inadvertent grins, a mix of appreciative and slightly embarrassed grins civilized guys show when they get caught staring.

Here's the girl part of that particular embarrassment. If one likes one of the guys, it's not annoying, it makes one feel outlined in light. Well, I do, anyway.

"The pants were too tight," I said curtly, and as soon as the words were out I knew they made everything ten times worse.

Owl turned away, one arm gripping the other arm. He was trying very hard not to laugh. I *felt* the riveted gaze of the fellow at the helm.

"You look better in that tunic than I do," Jehan said, assuming courtly manners, but his tone was genuine. Even enthusiastic.

"Come into the cabin. Supper is ready."

It was a relief to follow him down the broad stairs into the stern cabin. As he stepped with his characteristic quick stride I couldn't stop myself from sneaking a peek at him from behind, that long, slim line from shoulder to — *Stop that!*

I turned my attention to the captain's cabin.

Wow, talk about a sybaritic delight. Whoever had designed this yacht didn't have a rough sailor's life in mind. There were two of everything in the fine wood carvings, shining rich gold in the light of leaded glass lanterns set in graceful golden holders. Two roses, the leaves suggestive of entwined bodies. Two lilies, same. Two dolphins leaping and sporting in repeated motif all round the bunk frame. And what a bunk. Built directly under the broad, slanting stern windows, it enabled one — or two — to lie there and look directly out at the wake glowing in the reflected golden light, foaming away and away under the glimmering stars. I leaned to look —

And felt that neon sensation again.

I whirled around, and crossed my arms when I caught Owl and Jehan staring. Not just staring but checking out my butt in that snug tunic.

Owl looked up at the ceiling as though his future lay written there. Jehan grinned, a laugh barely suppressed in the slightly husky undertone to his voice as he said, "Please sit. Tell me about your day."

Since I'd been doing my own butt-checking a minute previous, I didn't say anything. Just plunked down and thumped my elbows onto the carved table. The chairs were lyre backed, cushioned and comfortable.

"Let me see," I said cordially. "What part would that be? The nice long morning when Owl nearly suffocated me? Or would that be later, when I was still suffocating? Or, maybe after you left, when everyone was busy, the sun sinking. I thought, great time to dive overboard. Straight into an out-flowing tide. Oops."

"What did you plan if the tide had worked for you?" Jehan

poured out some wine into three goblets. "I ask because I've made a couple of ship dives myself."

"Yours being successful, of course."

He grinned over his goblet at me. "I've had more experience with remembering the flow of tides."

"Well, I didn't think I could make it all the way to shore. My idea was to reach another boat. Any boat. I could see them, or rather their running lights, or whatever they are called here. Pretend, if they pulled me out, that I'd fallen overboard on a pleasure cruise, no one noticed because of all the noise, and would someone set me ashore?"

"Except those between us and the harbor are all Randart's fleet." Jehan swept his hand all around us. "Gathering to search for the wicked pirate Zathdar."

"Oh." I sipped the wine, which was perfect, not too sweet, not too tart, a Shakespearean sonnet of subtle flavors. I took another sip, this time pausing long enough to savor it. "Wow, that's good." My annoyance melted away. "All right, so that concludes Sasharia's stupidity for the day. What about you? How did the games go? Was it boring and predictable?"

"No. It was neither." Jehan began with meeting the mystery guys on the walk up to the castle. He ended his report when David and the others vanished through the back of the tent just as the searchers came through the front.

"So I made my way straight to the boat and here I am." He said to Owl, "That tall one. I know I've seen him before."

Owl hunched over his wine. "Really good with his hands? Lean? Eyes a strange shade of pale brown, almost orange in the right light?"

"That's the one."

"Didn't use a name, as I recall. Initials. MV? I think they were MV. Robin was the same age. She said she and the other sprats used to try to guess what they stood for. I remember him during that tangle with the Chwahir and those pirates out of Ghanthur, our very first cruise. Knew nothing about boats when he came aboard us, but he could fight. Don't you remember?"

Jehan leaned tiredly back in his chair, staring out at the sea. "We've had so many brushes with the Chwahir . . . Ghanthur . . . not to mention crew coming and going. That goes way back. Why, it must have been when I met you."

Owl grinned. "Just about. Yes."

They exchanged one of those looks people use when they are thinking of Past History, but before anyone could say anything the Colendi cook appeared, and with a flourish set out the dishes, delicate poached fish with fresh herbs and a dash of wine sauce, steamed carrots with a dash of another herb, and roasted little potatoes, so savory and tasty I could have eaten a plate of them.

Kaelande served more wine. His style of serving was like what I'd been taught, I noticed idly, in the more hotsy-totsy dinner houses I'd worked at, back in L.A. The same even pouring, the flick of the wrist when bringing the bottle up so there were no splashes.

I was beginning to feel a slight buzz, so I shook my head. I really did not know who was friend and who enemy, or how both could manage to be embodied in the same person. I didn't need a wine-glow to further befuddle me.

Jehan said, "That was splendid, Kaelande." He sighed. "I ate well at the tent, but that rowing seems to have woken my appetite."

"You were a few meals behind," Owl commented. "So, what now?"

Good question, *I thought.* And that goes for me, too.

Jehan frowned into his wine. "Those questions Randart asked me. I am trusting to the overwhelming number of tasks that launching a fleet entails to keep him from thinking much about what those boys saw from the barracks window. You had better vanish, all of you —"

"Wait!" I slapped my hands flat on the table. "What exactly does that mean? I'm a prisoner?"

Kaelande flicked me a look from under straight brows.

Jehan pressed his thumbs into his eyelids under his brow ridge. "You are. Not. A prisoner. But—"

Zel, Kaelande's wife, appeared in the door, her short, wispy reddish curls flying. "Biski says the fleet's getting signals."

Jehan was out of his chair fast, pausing only to pluck his spyglass from a holder. By the time I made it out the door behind Owl and Kaelande, Jehan's white hair had already vanished behind the long, elegant curve of the main sail, what we on Earth would call a Bermuda sail. He reappeared in the top next to the younger of the two men whose names I hadn't heard.

They exchanged a few quick words, snapped their glasses out, training them west on the glimmering lights barely visible to us at sea level.

Then Jehan slid down a backstay and landed lightly near us. "They're flanking us. Boats. It's got to be Randart, and he's got some excuse."

"We run?" Owl asked, but almost immediately he sniffed, looked into the direction of the breeze and shook his head.

"We fight?" Kaelande asked, and Zel rubbed her knuckles against her lips. She was a bit older than I, small, weathered, the yacht's bosun. Everyone worked the sails when needed, and obviously fought when needed as well.

Jehan sighed. "I would rather avoid loss of life. He despises the first-blood rule. If he commences a fight, it's going to be to the finish. He won't want any witnesses to tell my father the truth."

Owl grimaced. "So you think he's sprung us at last?"

"Possible. Not for certain. If he's suspicious, he will be looking for the mystery thief the boys will have described. That means the fisher's hat and the forest green tunic. The cadets saw our encounter from the barracks window, and I said I'd tried to catch a thief. Randart brought that up at the games."

Attention zapped my way.

Jehan said to me, "Well? If you want to fall into his hands, here is your chance."

"No. The only thing I am very sure of is this. I do not, and never will, trust Dannath Randart. Especially now that I know he caused Magister Glathan's death."

Jehan let out his breath in relief. "Get out of those clothes. I have to be in livery."

"Hers are wet," Owl said. "And the green will have to go over the side. If any of us wear it, we might be taken as the thief."

Zel measured me with her eyes, and slowly shook her head.

"She's a size one in the juniors, and I'm a size twelve in the Tall department." I pointed to Zel, then myself. "I can't borrow hers."

Kaelande dusted his fingers together. "But you are close to my size. Very close."

Jehan snapped his fingers. "I'll have that Zhavalieshin banner on my own bed. I don't care how wet it is, it won't look wet. The rest of whatever it is you have in that bag is innocuous enough, right?"

My heartbeat had gone into sprint mode. "Mementos collected when I was little."

Owl said to Jehan, "What's the excuse for you being here?"

"Too hot to sleep on land?"

"Stupid," two voices said at once, and Owl shook his head.

Zel sighed dramatically. "Oh, come along, I always wanted to be the girl. Can't I be the girl?"

"When's the last time there was a real girl?" Owl asked the sky.

Jehan laughed. "It seems a thousand years ago. Zel, do whatever you can to become the girl. But you have to be a painter. I told him I was visiting a painter . . . something with Lasva Sky Child. I don't know if he'll remember that."

Zel turned to her husband and said cryptically, but in a triumphant voice, "Told you they'd some day be useful."

"They?" came from three directions.

"Painted fans from Colend. How I met him." She patted her husband on his shoulder, sped by, and vanished down the companionway to the lower deck.

Jehan faced me. "Sasha. Do you mind being a cook?"

I shrugged, feeling about five steps behind. I couldn't find the words to say I knew zip about cooking.

But he took my hapless shrug as agreement.

"Let us get ready to be taken by surprise," Jehan said.

TWENTY-FOUR

War Commander Randart stood with one boot propped on the rail of the lead boat's bow, elbow steadied on his knee, his glass trained on the lonely craft until its elegant lines emerged from the darkness and resolved into the familiar *Dolphin*.

"That's his yacht. Close in," he said with the first evidence of satisfaction he'd shown since his arrival. His personal guard, kept on short sleep and shorter meal breaks, put their backs into their rowing, the outer boats circling outward to surround the yacht as ordered.

Not that anyone expected anything like a good fight. Not on a yacht crewed by half a dozen, if that. And captained by a prince who chased rare butterflies — ones with good figures.

The commander went back to watching through his glass. He would learn a lot by how they reacted when they discovered they were being . . . met.

Mentally veering between suspicion and disbelief, he'd figured that a trained military scramble after the lookout spotted the boats would at least be cause for investigation. The Prince Jehan he knew — he assumed he knew — would never remember to give that kind of order.

However, that possibility diminished with every silent lift of the oars. He could distinctly make out a couple of sailors standing at the helm, drinking from elegant goblets as they chatted. No one else in view, though there was a jerking at the single upper sail, no doubt deployed to keep the yacht pointed up into the wind instead of rolling. Randart applied his glass to the masthead. He saw starlight glinting on red hair, the silhouette a scrawny male. Sailor, nothing military. He certainly wasn't alert.

A movement below caught Randart's attention and he brought down his glass. One of the two at the helm shook an empty wine bottle, and actually peered into it. Then he lurched drunkenly around, and started. Was *that* the lookout instead? Probably. The one up on the mast was apparently asleep.

Randart smacked his glass against his thigh as the now-tiny figures ran about on the deck of the yacht in a manner no proper captain would ever tolerate, as, gradually, lights glowed to life in the open scuttles along the side, revealing a figure or two bobbing about to no apparent purpose.

No white heads in view.

His boat hooked onto the yacht, his guards not even touching their weapons. Damedran sat in the sternsheets scowling. Randart turned his way, gave him a sharp flick of the hand in command, and his nephew rose, wincing. He was probably sore, but mere physical discomfort did not matter in command. He was also tired, but so were they all.

The important thing was, if Jehan turned out to be a traitor, it had to be Damedran to defeat him.

Randart climbed up, followed by Damedran, whose breath wheezed with his effort. The war commander stepped over the rail just as the idiot emerged from the main cabin, his clothes awry, his arm around a petite red-haired woman whose clothes were also awry.

Disgust wrung Randarts innards, followed by anger. He clamped down on a reminder of the orders he'd given this brainless fool not two watches ago. But then one couldn't order a prince. Everyone here knew it.

He must not misstep. He could not be in the wrong in the eyes of the men. The cost was not lives. All except Damedran were expendable. The cost was the kingdom.

"Commander Randart?" the idiot said with his usual vagueness. "Did you want a fan, too?"

Randart fought against the headache he had refused to acknowledge. The pang increased to a hammer. "Fan?" he repeated, striving to keep his voice even. "What are you blather — that is, I fear I do not understand. Honor me with an explanation, your highness?"

Prince Jehan waved a hand around, then indicated the woman at his side. "Artist, paints fans. Needed one, it's so hot. Decided to buy one for my stepmother. Aren't we going back to Vadnais now that the games are done? I want to take a present to Queen Ananda."

There was Randart's cue. "I am going to sea. The king wanted you to stay put. Remember, your highness? I did tell you the king's wishes. Directly after the games."

"Of course. I remember. But we're in the harbor. Not going anywhere. I thought I might pick out a nice fan, return to shore on the morning tide. Be ready for my father's summons. Have a gift for Queen Ananda. Everything in order."

It actually indicated a thought process.

Randart turned his head, summoned his personal aide with a glance, and flicked his gaze fore and aft. The man sketched a salute, beckoned to his handpicked searchers, and they began strolling the length of the yacht, not quite making their search obvious.

Jehan lifted a hand. "Come! Have a drink. Hungry?"

Randart remembered that he had not eaten since morning. And the Fool, for all his lack of brains, did supposedly have good taste in food, wine, and comforts. "Yes. As it happens, I am. Damedran?" He turned to his nephew.

Damedran stood there on the deck glowering. He ached from skull to heels. His gut was indeed empty because why? Because by the time he'd limped his way into the mess hall after the day's disaster otherwise known as the games, there'd been the summons to come up to the command tower and repeat everything the seniors had said about Prince Jehan's attempted arrest of the cutpurse the day before.

He hadn't remembered anything but the barest fact that it had happened, and so, by the time they'd sent someone to fetch Ban—being the most serious and trustworthy of the seniors in his group—and by the time he'd stood by while his uncle and father had asked Ban about a million stupid questions about what he'd seen (and from above! Why not ask people who'd actually been there?) it was already late. Then came the astonishing news that Wolfie, Red, and the other two were all in the lazaretto. Wolfie, the strongest boy in the entire academy, had a broken leg. Given to him when he'd tried to jump a nine-year-old.

Damedran had been trying to reconcile those broken bones with his own experience when he became aware of his uncle ranting on about the fact that Prince Jehan was missing, as was the royal boat from the dock.

Come on, his uncle had said. *If it's necessary to act, you are going to need to be there.*

Well, here they were. So what kind of "act" was expected of someone who probably couldn't even grip a sword? Damedran tried to flex his stiff hands.

For all his uncle complained about the sheep's stupidity, Damedran had discovered during a private challenge a couple of years ago that the training the idiot had gotten out west was very effective even for idiots. Damedran knew he wasn't going to win any duel, no matter what his uncle wanted. He could barely walk.

"Come," a voice said directly above Damedran, as a wine goblet was pressed into his hand. "Come sit down. You've had a rough day. I know. I've been through much the same."

Damedran looked up uncomprehending into Prince Jehan's face.

"I was hoping to talk to you," the sheep went on, not sounding like a sheep at all, though it was exactly the same calm, vague voice. "We really need some changes to the training, and who better to help me figure those out than you?"

"Who worse," Damedran said. Or he tried to say it. His voice was too hoarse.

"Now, now. One thing I learned in Marloven Hess was, you plan better after a thumping than if you win. And I had enough thumpings to prove it. Let's get some food and drink into you, first. Come into the cabin."

Damedran heard his uncle's voice, his forced joviality as he asked to be introduced to the crew, and followed the sheep down into the cabin, gulping wine as he did so. Life had turned into a dream. No, a nightmare. A place where suddenly nothing made sense.

First thing Jehan had said was, "Hide that hair!" before he sped away to make ready, and Zel had taken him at his word.

The floppy hat had vanished unnoticed, and my braids were frizzing like the Bride of Frankenstein, after the time in the quilt, followed by my salt-water conditioning treatment.

First I changed out of Jehan's clothes and into her husband's cooking outfit. At least Kaelande's clothes were roomy, as he was a stocky man. Over them I wore his apron. While I sat on an upturned bucket, Zel's small fingers undid all my braids with lightning speed. She twisted my hair (which would make the most flagrant neo-pre-Raphaelite maiden look bald) into a knot, skewered it with a sail-making tool of some kind, then yanked Jehan's knit sailor cap over it all. It hurt my scalp enough to make my head throb, but it held.

Jehan appeared at the galley door. I straightened up—carefully, as my topknot brushed the ceiling—and his face changed expression. It was the most serious I'd ever seen him.

"What? What?" Zel and I exclaimed together.

"You look just like Mathias." And before anyone could speak, Jehan yanked open one of the cupboards, pulled out a wooden container, lifted the lid. He grabbed a handful of flour and threw it in my face.

I gasped, coughing.

"They're here," Owl's voice had carried softly from the deck.

"Don't touch it," Jehan flung over his shoulder at me. To Kaelande, "She's drunk. Make it look real." He grabbed Zel's hand and the two of them scrambled up the companionway and ducked down low, almost crawling into the cabin as I stood there blinking ground wheat off my eyelashes.

And while the Randarts were busy hooking on, their boats thudding against the *Dolphin*'s hull, their boots loud as they clambered up, Kaelande explained in a running whisper what everything was in the galley, and where the food was stored, his hands gesturing so fast I retained maybe one thing in six.

Meanwhile he splashed wine lightly down my — his — summer shirt of blue cotton and more on the apron. He filled two goblets, and pushed one into my hand. "Drink! We need wine breath."

We each took a good swallow, then stood at either side of the galley door and peered up through the hatch.

The war commander tromped past, followed by half a dozen hulking guards. Though I'd never seen any of the Randarts close up before, I recognized them immediately: huge guys, buff as all get-out, bony faces with tough-guy cheekbones. Thick black hair. The commander's was streaked with gray in a way that any Hollywood hairdresser would charge a thousand bucks to arrange. As for his expression, his armed-to-the-teeth, I'm-in-command-here walk, sinister? *That* I remembered.

Damedran looked like a high-school-aged edition of his uncle, with long and glossy hair. But he wasn't moving like his uncle, at least not now. I knew what had happened to him, but it was quite shocking to see his blackened eye, bruised jaw, one swollen ear, and his slow, painful step. He might strut all over the academy like Mr. I'm-Too-Sexy-For-My-War-Tunic, but right now he looked like he longed for a week's R and R — a thousand miles away.

A touch on my shoulder. "Let's get some listerblossom into

that one," Kaelande murmured, and spoke the soft words that made fire flare up on the little galley stove.

He set a kettle over that to boil and pointed at a cupboard to my right.

Everything was beautifully fitted together like the most complicated puzzle box ever invented. The cupboard door slid up revealing a row of tiny boxes, each neatly labeled with the name of an herb. He touched the listerblossom, and indicated the tea strainer.

Light from the lantern hanging over the companionway ladder was blocked. We turned around to face Randart himself.

He was tall, husky, and absolutely exuded menace, at least standing there in the galley door, a naked knife stuck through his sash, a sword at his side and his eyes narrow slits of suspicion.

It seemed to me he gave Kaelande the briefest of glances and focused all his attention on me.

I heard the sound of the water change to a boil. Yes! It gave me something to do, and maybe even within my limited cooking ability. With shaking fingers, I tried to pinch my listerblossom into the tea strainer—the yacht lurched—I dropped some of the listerblossom. Kaelande's fingers twitched as if to take over, but he reached for his wine instead, and I took the hint, swooped up my goblet, took a swig.

With burning eyes, I finished measuring out the tea and poured the water.

Randart watched all this without speaking.

From behind came Jehan's voice. "Do I smell healer tea?"

I thought of my American accent, and faked a pitiful cough as I cudgeled my brain for any kind of accent. Kaelande was from Colend—this was a prince's yacht—special chef—special accent? But I had no idea how to reproduce that lovely singsong characteristic of the Colendi, which was about as opposite of my plain L.A. accent as you could get.

Well, when in doubt, there is always Pepé Le Pew-style fake French.

Using that, I drawled, "Ze healer brew, it is for ze young mastaire."

Jehan's expression did not alter a whit. "Ah, excellent thought, Lasva."

Lasva, one of the most common names from Sartor to Colend.

Jehan took the tea. "We would like dinner. Is it possible? You seem to have begun your off-duty libations a trifle early. Please serve in the cabin. Kaelande, will you stay on as galley aid?"

Kaelande bowed, and belatedly I bowed, too, the forgotten goblet tipping in my hand. The last of the wine sloshed onto the deck. Kaelande and I reached for the cloth on the little hook over the cleaning bucket, and our heads bumped together. Kaelande laughed, and kissed my shoulder, which made me whoop with surprise.

Randart turned away, rolling his eyes in disgust. From the companionway came his voice, "I don't suppose you have a reason for keeping on hire a drunken cook?"

"Ah, but she is an artist. In all ways, the kitchen and in —"

Randart retorted in a voice of acute revulsion, "Spare me. I'm surprised your entire crew is not made up of women. Pardon, your highness, *artists*."

"Do not think I have not tried to achieve that very thing! But they get bored, they move on to something else. I cannot seem to get them to stay."

"My sympathies," Randart's voice diminished, "I find are entirely with the women. So you've had that cook for a while? Didn't your father mention he'd hired a man, a Colendi?"

Their voices were mere mumbles now, drowned by the lapping of the sea against the hull, and the creaking wood.

While I listened, Kaelande swiped up the rest of the flour as well as the wine, and dunked the cloth into the bucket. The snap and flare of magic restored the cleaning cloth, which he hung up to dry. Then he gestured me into the corner, out of the way while he swiftly retrieved ingredients from this or that cupboard, his hands moving so fast they were almost a blur to my tired eyes.

"Can you cook?" he whispered.

"Mac cheese, tuna melts and PBJs," I muttered. "Uh, all those require boxes, cans, microwaves. You may as well call it magic."

"You'll have to serve. I think he remembers me." Kaelande drew a wicked knife from a nifty holder fitted above his cutting board and began chopping onions and olives. "What you are going to make is a Colendi dish called the Duchess Changes Her Mind—" He named it in Colendi, explaining that the words held two meanings. (Since it was Colendi, I wouldn't have been surprised if it had six meanings. Think French style of the *Ancien Regime*, except with the age and sophistication of the Imperial Chinese Court.)

Then he opened the spice-and-herb cupboard again, and carefully removed a single sprig of a pungent spice.

As he began mincing it with swift chops, the fresh scent threw me back in memory to my childhood.

It's so strange, how smell can be even more powerful at evoking memory than all the other senses. Even sight. Though we always think first of sight.

But I no sooner sniffed that herb than I was right back at the palace in Vadnais, a little kid again, looking up at Canary's big grin, his dashing long hair and heroic stature. Canary . . . my mother laughing at something he said . . .

My mother. A prisoner in Vadnais.

My mother's voice, The thing about Canary was, he always had to be the rescuer, the solver, the good guy. He might even have believed what he said—

Good guy. Canary.

There was some important thought here, but I was distracted by Kaelande, who started explaining how to cook his dish, which was a kind of very, very light crepe, into which wine-and-oil sautéed onions, tomatoes and olives were wrapped. Over it some of that crumbly, delicious cheese was sprinkled.

"Now. You must cook this together," he murmured, dashing wine and the spice over the olives and onions in a shallow pan. He added the tomatoes last, murmured something, gestured, and the flame lowered. He set the shallow pan over it, and I wedged my way in to his left. We stood there shoulder to shoulder, and I reflected on how we were definitely inside each other's personal space, but there was no sense of a boundary crossed. No intimate space. With Jehan, I felt like we were in intimate space when he stood twenty feet away.

Kaelande didn't seem to feel anything either. No furtive looks, and his touch was neutral. Yet I supposed from the galley door we looked like a lovey-dovey pair, so close together. Now, if Jehan had been in here—

Just the idea of being pressed up against him in this tiny galley sent heat from my cheeks to my chitlins.

Concentrate! I began to sauté the mixture, frowning down at the gently sizzling ingredients as I sniffed the scent.

Canary. What was happening to Mom? Canary wouldn't throw her into a dungeon. That wouldn't be the action of a supposed good guy—

That inward tug again, something important, some connection I was missing. Canary, my mother. That wasn't it, though it was related.

Boots clattered back and forth across the deck a few inches above my head. I stirred the ingredients, glaring down at them while Kaelande fashioned perfect crepes with what seemed like preternatural speed, his arm jostling mine, his breath a soft whistle on a plaintive series of three or four notes. No one disturbed us. Every so often Kaelande wiped something on my apron, and even splashed me once or twice, and I remembered I was drunk. I flicked a few drops to my face for artistic verisimilitude, catching a brief grin from Kaelande.

I turned my thoughts inward, considering Canary and my mom, what she'd told me over the years. All the little incidents added up to this: he tried to get her on his side.

Closer, closer. Okay, there was some insight here, instinct insisted.

So keep thinking. Canary was attractive. He was attracted to Mom. He hadn't been faking it. Her so-called free-love hippie days had taught her the difference. He liked her, was attracted . . . needed to be the good guy . . .

Why is this important? Argh! I stirred vigorously. Instinct was poinking and prodding at me now. But why? I wished I had not drunk that wine.

All right, think it through again. Canary, pretending to be the good guy. Canary, attracted to my mother. Wanting her on his side, and so he used her attraction. Heck, he used his own attraction. He used his looks, his charm, said what people wanted to hear, did everything he could to try to get people to buy into his plans, and see him as the good guy . . . *Almost there*—

Canary and Mom. And here I was with his son. Who was doing his best to get me to buy into his plans. Meanwhile lying to everyone. Even his pirates didn't know the truth about him.

So the question now is, how much is he lying to me?

That was it. I grimaced down at the golden onions in my shallow pan. That was a nasty one. *So face it.* How much is Jehan Jervaes Merindar using my own attraction—and his to me—to seduce me if not into his bed, into his plans?

"It looks like it's done," Kaelande whispered.

I started. I'd been standing there with the wooden spatula in the air, and hastily gave the mixture a guilty stir. Luckily the flame had been too low for it to burn.

He took the pan, dashed an even portion of the mixture onto each crepe, wrapped them with nimble fingers, laid out the crepes on plates (lined up along a narrow board that folded down, so he could do six at once), poured in the filling, rolled the crepes, and added a spray of the tiny grapes. "Can you serve?"

I grinned. "I can't cook, but boy howdy can I serve." As his eyes widened, I stashed the plates up my arm in classic waitress carry, hooked four wine goblets with the fingers of the other hand, and with my thumb grabbed up the square wine bottle.

He saluted wryly and I eased my way up and onto the deck,

steadying myself against the rail. I was acutely aware of myself in the clothing of a man I didn't know before yesterday. Here I was, Sasharia Zhavalieshin, pretending to be a cook, and all to support the false role of someone who might be an enemy.

How long was I going to go along with his changing stories, I wondered, leaning my hip against the carving of laughing dolphins running along the rail.

Until he kisses me? And then what?

I cannot tell you how much I hated the thought that he had it all planned, that the dangerous evening would end with the hero prince grabbing the dashing princess for love's triumphant kiss —

He wouldn't. Would he?

I glared down at the plates on my arm and remembered what I was supposed to be doing. At my current rate of travel the food would be congealed into a nasty mess before I even reached the cabin.

The deck was full of big men moving about with either covert or overt purpose, none paying the drunken cook the least heed after a disinterested glance. Dannath Randart vanished into the cabin I'd used, but my stuff was gone, the gear bag over the side (the green tunic inside it as ballast), the mementos and coins stashed in Zel's things.

I descended the few broad steps into the cabin. Jehan and Damedran sat with their heads together at the table, Jehan writing things down as they talked in quick, low voices.

Damedran's wary body language, his reluctant agreements to Jehan's softly murmured questions, were easing as he sipped at the mug of listerblossom.

Zel lounged on the bed like an odalisque, playing with half-circles of myriad colors. A step toward her and the half-circles resolved into open fans, laid like rare flowers against the splendid barbarity of my Zhavalieshin coverlet. Some of the fans were made of lace and thin streamers of ribbon, others a kind of rice paper, gilt in exquisite patterns, and painted. Subtle fragrances arose, carried on the gentle breeze from the open stern windows.

She glanced up at me, then over her shoulder, pursing her lips.

I set the wine bottle on the table, the glasses next to it.

Jehan was saying, oh so persuasively, ". . . completely rethink the infighting—"

"But Master Grescheg wins every competition with Obrin and those fellows from Alsais—"

"Competition. Perhaps there is a difference between hand-to-hand grappling for a medal and fighting in the street? Think about today. That tall fellow broke competition rules, didn't he?"

"He did. I didn't call 'em on it because it seemed cowardice—"

"We all saw that, and it testifies to your credit. But consider this. Would you have him at your back in the street? Or if Norsunder rode over the border in force?"

"Norsunder?" Damedran looked doubtful.

I'd backed up to listen, the plates still stacked on my arm.

"It could happen. You won't remember the Siamis days. It was just before you were born. Did anyone tell you about how frightened people were? The talk of Detlev, Siamis's uncle? We don't know much about him, except that those who held his leash are far worse. And if they find a way to cross into the world . . ."

"Yes," Damedran cut in, his brow a scowl line. "I would want them at my back in any kind of fight. The grappling, and the archery. Nobody could beat that little runt. Not even our best master."

The voices had risen slightly, one with the slightly nasal intonations of late adolescence, gruff with dislike and distrust, the other more tenor, controlled, with that faint humor.

Jehan's trying to win Damedran. What role is he playing now?

"And you saw how he shot. The Marloven bow drill is tedious, that I grant, however the form is unbeaten throughout the world, and you saw the evidence today . . ."

Under how many layers was the truth buried? I stared down at Zel's fans, each a treasure. She must have seen my admiration in my face, for she smiled proudly. Then a glance past me. Her smile vanished. She lay back in a languishing pose.

Boot heels rang on the deck, and the voices stopped. Focus shifted as Dannath Randart filled the doorway to the cabin. He took us all in with a single glance, frowning when he spied the paper before Jehan. He sat, abruptly reaching for it. His hand stopped partway, and Jehan offered it to him with a courteous air.

Randart glanced at it for about five seconds, as I approached the table.

Randart slewed around, watching as I dealt the plates in my very best serving manner. The narrow-eyed suspicion tightening his eyes eased a fraction more each time I snuck a peek at him. By the time I finished playing sommelier with the wine, complete down to the pouring flick of the wrist, he had clearly filed me in the "servant" category, and thereafter ignored me.

The silence stretched into tension, which made distinct the soft slapping of the water against the hull, the creak of wood, the click and ting of silver utensils on porcelain plates. The three ate, the boy and the prince waiting for the war commander to speak.

The power of the moment lay with him, though it was not his ship, but the men up on the deck obeyed him and only him.

Right now the Randarts are the only ones here not faking a role.

Finally Randart leaned forward and tapped the paper. "What's this?"

Jehan said, "My suggestions for new training. Old training to be adapted to new. We all think our own experience best. Why not try what I learned out west? Combine it with what we have here in the east."

"We can't do worse, Uncle. I saw that today," Damedran put in, surly and defensive.

Dannath Randart's slack-lidded eyes flicked from nephew to royal heir and back again. Impossible to tell whether the silence meant surrender or threat. Maybe he didn't know himself. He opened his palm toward Damedran. "Very well. Do what you like. I have to take ship tomorrow. I have pirates to find and destroy." He picked up his fork, then shot a glowering assessment at Zel.

Ahah, he was reassessing her status. Would she be invited to eat? There was that extra plate, congealing fast.

She lay curled up on the bed, the two gold-framed lanterns making a fiery aureole of her wispy ringlets. She uncoiled her feet and stood, drifting in a deliberately provocative, swaying walk, to lean against Jehan's chair, one of her hands playing with one of her fans, twirling it, swirling it idly.

"Sit down and eat, my dear," Jehan invited, pointing to the fourth plate. "It's getting cold. And you know how Lasva threatens to go back to Colend if we do not treat her food with respect."

"I'm not hungry now," Zel said in a crooning voice. She smiled up at me. "The Colendi are forgiving, I know. I will paint you a fan, Lasva."

"Yiss. Iz gud," I sounded more like a TV Russian spy than a TV Frenchwoman, I realized too late.

Randart's face crimped in disgust. He said nothing, though. Just dug in, rapidly finishing his crepe.

No one spoke as they devoured the meal—Damedran surreptitiously helping himself to the fourth plate. For a time the only sounds were those of the ship and of the rising wind, the water.

Once I moved into view to pour more wine. Jehan mouthed the words *thank you*, though he kept his gaze unswervingly on his guests. At his side Zel leaned, one finger twining in his hair in a way that made my insides squeeze, so I looked away. The uncle ignored me as if the wine poured itself.

When his plate was clean he stood. "I have ordered the mages to make you another gold message box, your highness. Do try not to lose it. I'll return now, and send a message to your father. If you discover anything you wish to tell me before morning, I can be found in the command tower before we depart on the morning tide."

He marched out, his boots thumping up the stairs to the deck, where he gave an abrupt command.

That caused the force of brown tunics to line up and climb

down into the boats, a kind of reverse-play of their arrival. I wondered if *they'd* gotten any dinner before the summons to make this trip. From the mutters of some of them and the black looks sent their commander's way, it didn't seem likely.

The crew doused the yacht's deck lights. The ship faded to darkness, except for the golden glow in the cabin, and faint light from the hatchway and the galley beyond.

Jehan moved to the rail to watch them begin to toil their long way back to the harbor through an increasingly choppy sea. Zel and her husband joined him on one side, the two of them holding hands, whispering and occasionally laughing, the relieved laughter of danger passed by. Owl drifted up on Kaelande's other side.

The other two crew were at their posts, one on the mast, one at the helm.

Since Jehan had no one at his left I joined him, peering out to sea as I absently pulled off the knit cap, and yanked free that horrible thing binding my hair so tightly. As there were no lights, I figured we had to be invisible from the boats by now. Even starlight was gone, covered by thick clouds.

The husband and wife moved off, talking in low voices. The last I heard was Zel offering to help dunk the dishes and tidy the galley.

Owl vanished down the hatchway, yawning.

Randart's lights were nearly diminished behind the rising waves when a long purple branch of lightning split the sky, and rain struck with breathtaking suddenness, on us, on the sea, and on the departing rowboats.

We were drenched in moments, but behind us lay warmth, food, shelter. The commander and his force had a very long row ahead of them.

"Perfect end to a disastrous day," Jehan said.

Lightning flared again, reflecting in his eyes so they shone like sapphire, and burnished his hair to silver. He smiled straight into my eyes, and laughed.

I smiled back as my hair streamed into the wind—forgetting Mom, and Canary, and roles, and lies, and all the distresses of the day. For that moment I was proud and triumphant and caught by Jehan's gaze, so brilliant in the flare of lightning, and I laughed, too.

I laughed until his hands caught me by the shoulders, and rain glittered on his eyelashes as soft lips met mine, warm and tasting of sweet wine, and then my thoughts unribboned, my muscles unlaced, and I couldn't think at all, at all.

PART TWO

TWICE A PRINCE

ONE

"PRINCE JEHAN DID WHAT?" King Canardan exclaimed.

Magister Zhavic, one of the king's mages, stroked his gray beard, making sure his voice was detached. Disinterested. Academic. "After the academy cadets finished the midsummer games, His Highness Prince Jehan had himself rowed out to his yacht. In the middle of the harbor. He'd had it moved out there earlier. No one knew why."

"Probably in hopes of a breeze. If it's been half as beastly hot in Ellir as it's been here. Even my son," he added wryly, "is not too dreamy to overlook this weather."

The stars shone in the rain-washed midnight sky over the royal palace in Vadnais, but the palace room was still too warm. Magister Zhavic resisted the temptation to wipe his sleeve over his damp forehead, and got to the important part of his report. "When he heard that the prince had gone out into the harbor for the night, War Commander Randart rowed out with a force into the harbor after him."

Canardan sighed, his gaze straying to the pile of papers waiting on his desk. "Randart's orders are to set sail at dawn, in pursuit of that curst pirate Zathdar. What's he doing chasing after my son? Did he decide to commandeer Jehan's yacht? Or maybe he's taking Jehan out to help catch the pirate?"

"The war commander did not see fit to inform us. He departed without a word to anyone, and was subsequently seen rowing back again, without the prince, just before I transferred myself here to report. They might be docking right now. If the threatened storm did not slow them up. He did not have the prince with him. I made certain of that before I left." He lifted his left hand, on which lay the magical transfer token, bespelled for a trip to the royal palace and back again to Ellir Harbor.

The king's attention flicked from the brassy token to the tall, lean, gray-haired man sitting before him. "You have no idea what Randart was after, then?"

"There is speculation, of course. But the war commander did not inform us directly. All I can tell you is that he took his nephew with him, along with half a company from the garrison."

The king regarded the mage with brooding question. Magister Zhavic sat squarely on his chair, his face stiff, gaze diffuse. But Canardan, used to listening for clues, heard the subtle satisfaction emphasizing certain words. Zhavic was *gloating*. "All right, let's hear the speculation."

"According to Patrol Leader Hathmad, the war commander and his force rowed out to the prince's yacht to make a search."

"A search? For what?" The king leaned forward. "My son's art collection?" Despite the joke, the king did not smile.

"They weren't told, just ordered to search for anomalies. The captain of the war commander's honor guard seemed to have private orders, but the others weren't given those orders."

"What did they find on this search?"

"Nothing. The prince had gone to his yacht to get one of his, ah, female artists to paint a fan for her majesty. The entire force overheard that."

Huh! If Randart was still in the process of rowing back yet Zhavic had this fresh report, that meant one of those men—probably this patrol leader—was a paid informer to the mages. Canardan was not surprised at that so much as at the fact that Zhavic was in such a hurry to tattle on Randart that he revealed the existence of the spy.

"Female artist?" Canardan repeated. Could that possibly be the reason behind the search? There was only one missing female of import—Sasharia Zhavalieshin, daughter of Princess Atanial, whom Canardan had closely guarded up in the tower, ostensibly as a cherished guest.

But if her daughter, who had been captured by the pirate Zathdar at last report, was at large, and War Commander Randart was searching for her, surely, *surely*, the war commander would report that to his king. Wouldn't he?

"What did this female artist look like?" Canardan asked. "Tall? Frizzy hair? Hawk-nosed?"

"Small, short red hair, very attractive. Perhaps Colendi. The only other female on board was the cook. She was quite tall. Hathmad didn't remember her hair, so it must have been unremarkable. She was also drunk, covered with flour and wine, so they couldn't really see her features."

Hathmad was the spy, then. Canardan repeated the name to himself to commit it to memory. He frowned. "I could have sworn last year Jehan treated me to a meal prepared by a Colendi master cook named Kial . . . Kaer . . . ah, I don't remember his name, but in any case this was a man. I can understand that a Colendi master cook might get tired of sitting around on a yacht that sees its owner once or twice a year. Did Hathmad observe the cook working?"

"Said she prepared an exquisite meal and served it like an experienced steward."

"Which the cook has to be, on a yacht that small. Very well, we'll set aside the fan artist and the cook. Randart certainly seems to have. Go on with the report. Does anyone have any worthwhile speculation on why the war commander had them searching for anomalies on my son's yacht in the middle of the night?" Canardan rubbed his jaw, wondering if Randart was ruminating on heirs again. Maybe it was time to send Damedran on a long, long journey, to learn diplomacy or observe armies or whatever.

"Something having to do with the prince having arrested or almost arrested or attempting to arrest, a cutpurse, as near as I can tell. There was very little information to be found out about that. Everyone wanted to talk about the games and those mysterious youths who carried every single prize away from our cadets."

"Yes, just what we needed. Another mystery," Canardan said with heavy irony.

He turned his gaze back to the papers, but he didn't see them. Magisters Zhavic and Perran, the king's mages, both hated the war commander and his brother—a feeling that was mutual. None had any use for the others, which suited Canardan fine. You don't want your military leaders and your strongest mages allied.

The cost was that they spent a lot of time that ought to have been dedicated to his own concerns trying to prove the others false. Canardan knew that Randart was behind recent whispers that the king "should" disinherit Jehan and put his nephew in his place. He blamed himself for speaking aloud in extreme exasperation once, when Jehan had done something particularly fog-headed.

However, the idea had obviously stuck, and Canardan didn't like that. Damedran was a military man's ideal candidate for royal heir: handsome, strong, tough, and courageous. He was also ignorant and bull-headed. His knowledge of trade, of diplomacy, and of all the other aspects of kingship that his father and uncle scorned was even sketchier than Jehan's.

Bothering the king the most? These sporadic secret missions, as though Randart had caught wind of actual treason. Not that chasing a cutpurse was treason. Neither was chasing a cutpurse any reason to take half a company of handpicked guards out for a tedious harbor trip, after a long day spent in the broiling sun. Nor was it a reason to institute a covert search, his target no one less than the crown prince.

Canardan rubbed his eyes. His own ambivalence gave him pause. A part of him *wanted* Jehan to be conniving behind his back. That would mean the boy had his brains after all, and his ambition. Jehan when small had shown a distressing tendency to mimic his mother's impossible ideals, which was one of the reasons Canardan had sent him west to get some sense knocked into him as well as some training. The other reason had been to protect Jehan somewhat when Canardan had parted with his mother.

Jehan had had plenty of time to get used to that. He'd returned beautifully trained, obedient, cooperative... but without ambition.

If Jehan was really conniving, hey, that showed the rudiments of ambition! But why not on his father's side?

Canardan scowled at the papers, still not seeing them. Unlike his own monster of a father (until the old man was killed by Canardan's siblings, who were both far worse) he gave Jehan a free hand. Unlimited money. Rank. Even some responsibility—as long as he followed orders. And Jehan did follow orders ... when he remembered them.

No, Randart had to be inventing shadows to jump at. He'd always had a suspicious nature, which had saved Canardan many times in the past.

Still. Taking Damedran out to the yacht? That was very odd.

Canardan returned his attention to Zhavic. "I want someone trusted on the flagship. Reporting every day."

Zhavic bowed in his chair. "It shall be done."

"Meanwhile, you return to searching for Atanial's daughter. I can't do anything until I have her. The old castle with the World Gate is warded, isn't it?"

"Perran is there himself. No one can possibly transfer between worlds without our knowing immediately." Zhavic hesitated, then made a tentative gesture upward, toward the tower above them. "You are content with matters here?"

"You mean Princess Atanial?" Canardan grinned wryly, thinking, *You mean her magical tokens.* "Oh, I think so. Carry on." He twiddled his fingers in dismissal.

The mage rose, bowed, murmured and transferred by magic,

leaving a puff of displaced air to rattle the papers still gripped in Canardan's hand.

So exactly where was the missing tall, wild-haired, hawk-nosed daughter of Princess Atanial?

I was standing on the yacht in Jehan's arms while we lit up the sky with a supernova kiss.

At least, that's what it felt like.

The thing about sensory firestorms is, there's that rock of common sense sitting somewhere in the center of all the heat. Or so it is with me. Because when I came up for air, the rock was right there inside me with all its insistent weight, and I gasped, nearly choking on rain, and pushed Jehan away.

"Sasharia?" he asked.

Lightning crackled, striking the sea not far away. He held his hands out to me, but when I braced myself to resist, he dropped them to his sides.

In the glow from the cabin door, his light blue eyes looked black, his expression lengthening from passion to puzzlement. "What's wrong?"

I looked at the fine strands of white hair lying across his brow. Tenderness made the insides of my arms ache to hold him, and my fingers twitched, wanting to smooth back his hair, which (I had discovered) was as soft as a bunny's fur, only long. I clenched my hands behind my back, wishing the lightning would do me a big favor and strike me now. "I hate *Fatal Attraction* movies," I snarled.

Of course that made no sense to him whatsoever.

I shook my own wet mop impatiently out of my face, but did not move, despite the lightning and thunder, and the stinging needles of rain. The thunder had rumbled away like boulders falling across the sky to the edge of the world. "I was going to make a joke about sleeping with the enemy and being stupid, but it's not funny, is it?"

"Enemy?" He stepped back, his chin jerking up as if I'd slapped him.

"Oh, Jehan, I didn't mean that. I mean I did, but not—oh, I don't know what I mean." I gave a strangled excuse for a laugh and tried desperately to smooth a horrible moment over with a joke. "So what's your place in"—*my life?*—"Great Events? Did some mysterious mage cast a Shadow of Destiny on you when you were little? Or some weird prophesy turn up with your name in it in reference to a Path of Fate?"

"Fate? Destiny?" he repeated.

The words had come out in English, and I remembered Mom telling me years ago they didn't have any such concepts. Nor did they talk about luck, either bad or good.

My "joke" was about as funny as mud, but I kept trying to turn the most serious conversation of my life into light banter because if you laugh you can't get hurt, right? "I mean do you have a life membership in the Villains' Guild? Now would be the time to zip it from your wallet and get started with the har har har."

"Villains?" He looked skyward. "How can you think that, Sasharia? What have I done? What have I not done?"

Lightning. Thunder. Neither of us moved. We stared at one another, as if anger and passion and desperate questions could reach past locked gazes into skulls and decode the thoughts there. But though people walked in the world who could do that, neither of us had been born with that particular gift. Or curse.

"Call me Sasha." I knew it was inane, and that I was acting like an idiot. But I so wanted to hear him say my name. Just once more. Because I was going to stick to my guns, and leave as soon as I could.

"Sasha." He said my name on an outgoing breath, which sent shivers all through my nerves. "Why won't you let me explain the pirate disguise?"

The rain squall ended abruptly, a wave of slanting gray diminishing over the sea, leaving us standing under the dripping sails on the wet deck. I fought to keep my voice steady. "You. Are. Your father's. Son."

His eyes closed. Then opened. "Didn't you listen to anything I've told you?"

"Oh, I listened. Heard everything you said. Which was, mostly, everything I want to hear. Just as your father talked to my mother twenty years ago your time, using every smile, every charm at his command."

He gripped the rail with both hands, and looked at me over his shoulder. "You're never going to trust me, are you? No matter what I do. What I say. Because of who my father is."

"Let's skip right past the fact that you lied to me about who you really are, when we first met. Privateer or pirate, you are attacking your own side. Your lying to Randart I have no problem with. But you're also lying to your dad. I know you don't want anybody killed, but for whose good? Here's the real question: what would you do with your dad if you won some kind of battle against him? Put him on trial for his life, or stab him in the back?"

"Neither." Jehan faced the sea and let his breath out slowly. "But you won't believe me even on that. Will you." It was a statement, not a question.

"So how do you propose to take away the kingdom? Last I heard he was decades away from a convenient death of frail old age."

"That's not for me to decide, it's for Math," Jehan said. "Don't you see? I am on your father's side. I want Prince Mathias back on his throne. I want the kingdom reunited. Everything I do is to keep Randart on the hop, keep my father busy, which will make it all easier when Math does return. If Math returns, then maybe my father will listen to sense. There doesn't have to be any killing."

"Yes there does, because your father has Randart as his right arm. He likes killing," I retorted. "And your father lets him do it."

"That's why the guises, don't you see? If I can just hold off Randart while finding Math, maybe, maybe, there is a solution without another Khanerenth bloodbath. But as Jehan, I have no freedom."

"A *prince* with no freedom? Then it must be really tough to be a peon!" I could see how much my words hurt him. Or did he want me to see that? "I'm sorry for my sarcasm. I'm not trying to be a crank. It's just that everything you say, I hear my mom warning me . . . and more questions sprout like tentacles in my mind. Like, why didn't my father tell you where he was going, if he really trusted you?"

He did not answer, just stared at me, grim in expression, his mouth a white line.

My righteous anger vanished like the heat in the sudden thunder, leaving me just as unhappy. "Don't you see, Jehan? I *wish* I could believe you. I wish I could *trust* you, because there's no denying we've got some major chemistry going between us." *Chemistry* didn't have a translation any more than *peon* had. He didn't seem to need it. "But all I can think of are my mother's stories about Canary trying to seduce her over to his side. And, well, there we were a few minutes ago —"

"I follow." He flung up a hand. Looked out to sea. "You've said enough."

He lifted the other hand, turned away, and I heard his quick steps crossing the deck and the door to the cabin shut.

Leaving me standing there in the dark, with about as toxic a Pyrrhic victory as anyone ever . . . lost. Because I sure did not feel like a winner.

After a couple thousand years I crossed the deck, which was silent except for the creaking of the wood, the wash and hiss of the restless sea, and the distant mutter of thunder. I shut myself into my cabin.

And sat there, waiting — arguing both sides for when Jehan came back.

But he didn't come back.

The next noise I became aware of was the thump and swish of the boat being lowered. I moved, aching and cold, to the leaded glass window, in time to see him drop down into the boat and raise the single sail, which filled and carried him toward the shore on the making tide.

Behind me, in the east, dawn smeared, a bleak smudge, against the horizon.

TWO

KING CANARDAN WAS STILL thinking about Atanial the next morning, when he was supposed to be looking over Randart's requisitions for the army war game. When an aide announced that Magister Zhavic had just appeared by magic transfer, Canardan decided to use his appearance as an excuse to find her. He was certain he knew where she was.

The aide held open the door and the gray-haired mage dropped unceremoniously into a chair to recover from the sickening wrench of being yanked out of one space and thrust into another. As soon as he drew a deep breath and looked up, Canardan forestalled the usual amenities and said, "Let's take a walk. You get over it faster. Report as we go."

Zhavic was not about to say anything to a king about his theories on recovery from magic transfer. "Very well, your majesty." He struggled to his feet again, breathing deeply against a surge of reaction nausea. "You wished me to report when War Commander Randart departed. He has just done so."

Canardan nodded and walked out of his private chamber.

With a rustling of papers and a thumping of feet, all the aides and runners in the outer office leaped up and bowed. Canardan waved a hand in a big circle, acknowledging and sending them back to their tasks. A very long time ago he'd loved these signs of respect. Showed in outward form everyone knew who was king. Now he wanted them back at work. Work that was *always* behind.

Through the barracks command office he paced, and again the leaps—this time military salutes—the wave of the hand. Into the hall looking onto the back court, and there she was, with the kitchen helpers.

Atanial was laughing, wisps of her hair coming down around her face and shoulders as she churned butter. He grinned, remembering when she first came, and she'd shown a tendency to go around to the servants and lecture them on workers' rights and women's liberation, asking excruciatingly personal questions with the earnest air of a crusader. Math's pride and embarrassment. And her delight and then chagrin when she discovered that whatever "rights" she'd been extolling had long been a part of life here. Delight, chagrin, but no pride, no affront. Skewed as some of her notions were, she really had been an idealist.

"She obviously has no communications device," he said to Magister Zhavic.

"No, we're fairly certain now that the magical object she keeps hidden has to be her World Gate transfer, given her by Magister Glathan."

"As long as she cannot get to the old castle tower she cannot use it, so we can safely let it be, I think." Canardan knew he was disappointing his head mage, who badly wanted that little bit of powerful magic to use for his own purposes. Canardan regarded it as safer where he knew the mages couldn't get their hands on it, but he could if he really had to.

He watched Atanial working away, laughing and chattering, as everyone went about their business. At the sight of her shapely arms and her long body, he was aware of the familiar tightening of desire. He quashed it. *Don't look at her, look at what she's doing*. The problem was, she wasn't really doing anything but talking and being her usual friendly self.

Impulse again. "I think I'm going to give her a party. No, let's make it a grand ball, a masquerade. She used to love those. My chief allies will like it, she can think it's a courting gesture if she likes, but I want them all to see her being obedient and content under my hand." Another thought occurred. "Yes. And let's have Jehan here. That will be the excuse, the two of them meeting. He's supposed to be good with women. Maybe he can win her over for us. Find out where the daughter might be, or at least find out more about her. Let's do it. End of the week."

Zhavic said, "Is that enough time?"

Canardan gave him a wry look. "Whenever I want is enough time. Go back to the harbor. You know your orders. Tell my son I want him here as soon as possible. I'll go get the heralds sending runners out to my other guests. It's a good way to shift the gossip away from whatever happened at those damned games, as well."

Zhavic, seeing that the king had quite decided, bowed and left, sourly thinking of all the extra work that would fall on the mages, warding the castle, the guests to get ready so hastily, and all of it because the king had rediscovered his twenty-year-old hankering for that troublesome woman.

Canardan had already forgotten the mage. He watched Atanial straighten up, arching her back. Was the daughter as smart, as incomprehensible? She couldn't be as beautiful, not if she'd inherited Math's and Ananda's wild wooly hair, and the Zhavalieshin eagle beak of a nose.

Atanial wouldn't talk about the daughter at all. Any questions he asked, she deflected.

Well, maybe it was time to ask again, but not by himself. Jehan, worthless in matters military and diplomatic, ought to be able to manage sweet-talking a woman about her marriageable daughter.

As for him, he might begin their first dance by asking why she liked churning butter.

He walked on, the morning sunlight in the windows outlining his form, shadowing it to silhouette, and outlining it again. Everybody down below in the courtyard had seen him appear in the hall above. They all knew he was there and had redoubled their efforts.

Atanial finished stretching her back and watched him until he vanished into the heralds' wing. If he'd noticed her down here, what did he think? Oh, he noticed. Just as his servants and guards were aware of his presence, very little escaped his eye, she'd learned that much. So if he did ask what she was doing with the kitchen servants, she'd tell him it was fun.

It wasn't fun, but the talk was. The butter churning, she'd discovered, was a splendid upper-body workout without being obvious. She didn't dare demand a sword-fighting session. Canary seemed to be on the watch for her to try something stupid like trying to kiss up to the guards; anyone she spoke to at length was rotated elsewhere.

I wish I had a plan of action, she thought as the second pastry cook tested the butter for color, consistency, and taste.

Guilt tightened her throat, and made her stomach roil.

Everyone seems to assume I'm happy to be here. I've given in, given up. But what else can I do? Yelling about treachery and treason and betrayal would win me a free ticket to a cell all to myself.

No, now she was on sure ground, even if only a few inches of it. Make trouble, and Canary removes the troublemaker. And she wouldn't get anywhere near her friends in the detention wing. Friendliness hadn't accomplished it, but threats and heroic speeches definitely wouldn't.

The kitchen workers headed back inside. Instinct so far had prompted her to make friends with everyone, but then that was an easy plan because she would have done it anyway.

Instinct, not duty. She winced, a sudden memory throwing her back to her very first days in this palace, when the old king was alive, and Math running around doing his jobs. *You don't need to wear those tight dresses with all the frills,* she'd said to one of the young aristocrats at her first ball. *Women are as good as men, and no one will be convinced of it while we're serving as male sex objects in clothes like this.*

But I want to be what you call a "sex object" if by that you mean I dress to attract, was the reply. *I want the attention of the man of my choice. And I want him to dress to attract me. What would be the fun of flirting at a ball if we all dressed in sacks?*

Atanial laughed at herself as she made her way upstairs. How long ago that was! Surely Canary didn't give her this much freedom because he thought she'd go right back to lecturing everyone on self-actualizing and consciousness-raising . . . or did he?

At least if he thinks I'm a fool he won't see me as a threat.

Fool. Threat.

She frowned, thinking over the queen's words.

As she lowered herself into her bath, she thought wistfully, *A threat would have a plan of action. All I've got is a silly reputation.*

Her mood was somber when she emerged from the bath. Feeling she'd betrayed Mathias, Sasha, and everyone else with her total lack of success at coming up with a working plan, she reached for the first gown in the chest, then paused when she saw the heavy cream-colored linen paper resting on her little table by the door.

After pulling her robe back on, she retrieved the note. It was sealed with a silvery wax imprinted with the royal cup. She slid her finger carefully under it, her nails still soft from her bath.

She frowned at the script she hadn't read for years.

His Majesty . . . invites you to honor him with your presence . . . masquerade ball . . . week's end . . . in order to meet his son and heir, Prince Jehan.

Canardan had written this invitation by his own hand.

Zhavic winced away from the brilliant sunlight of a rain-washed morning. Transfers always gave him a headache. At least there didn't seem to be any trouble. He squinted against the dancing points of light reflecting off the deep blue waters of Ellir Harbor, where the fleet was pulling their anchors up and lowering sail as the tide began to ebb.

His mage-apprentice on duty, a trustworthy, sober girl, had informed him as soon as he entered the mage room in the command tower that Prince Jehan had been seen disembarking from his boat after dawn at the height of tidal flood.

"Send someone—no, better go yourself. Find him, request him to meet me, everything polite. King's orders," Zhavic said, and the girl was gone with two quick steps and a swing of rust-colored braids.

Zhavic sent the senior cadet on duty at the door to fetch him some breakfast. He knew by the time anyone found wherever Jehan was moping about and he actually made his way up, the mage could eat a good meal and maybe get rid of the transfer malaise.

While he waited for his food, Zhavic stood at the window and watched Randart's fleet begin its slow departure. He had a mage safely aboard—and at Randart's request, which was far better than having to try to arrange a covert role. Zhavic had chosen a quiet, steady, untoward mage, her area of expertise being woodwork. The commander would not suspect her of other orders.

Everything was as it should be.

Sunlight reflecting off the glass in a merchant's window below in the street lanced at his eyes and he turned away, thinking of Randart's brother in the command suite directly overhead, probably dealing with the results of the disastrous games. The king had been disappointed, but Zhavic, in the safety of an empty room, could permit himself to smile. What could be better for keeping those Randarts busy? One off chasing pirates, the other facing an academy of angry youths who'd been trounced by those mysterious boys from the hills.

Magister Zhavic's breakfast arrived moments later, brought by a breathless weed of a cadet. The boy set the tray down, bowed, and backed outside the door to his post, and that, too, made Zhavic smile. The cadets as well as their masters were all afraid of mages. Good. Healthy attitude.

He'd not taken two bites before he heard the familiar lounging footfalls of the prince. He sauntered in, dressed in his usual brown velvet, his eyes tired, his face tense. Zhavic, looking for mere sulkiness and perhaps the nausea of a hangover, thought he saw the signs. Drunk again. Typical.

But then, if Math turned out to be dead, a future drunken king would be so easy to guide.

Zhavic smiled a welcome. "I am sorry to disturb you, your highness. It was at your father's request. First, would you care for refreshment?"

"No, thank you." Jehan seemed to gather himself inwardly, then he looked up. In his hands he carried something with ribbons dangling. Seeing the mage's gaze go to it, Jehan snapped open a fan with expertise. "I brought this for the queen. Do you think she'll like it?"

"Queen Ananda . . . seems to have departed. No one knows where. Your father has given us to understand that she retired into the countryside."

The prince's eyes narrowed. For a heartbeat he almost looked intelligent. But then a hangover would probably look the same. "I see. But he doesn't actually know that?"

"No one knows where she went. However, your father requests me to convey his wishes. He is giving a masquerade ball at week's end for Princess Atanial. It is his desire to introduce the two of you to one another at this event, which is intended to honor you both. He desires your presence directly back in the capital."

The prince turned his head toward the window, as though the emptiness out at sea would fill the emptiness of his head, the mage thought wearily.

Then Prince Jehan gave Magister Zhavic an airy salute. "It shall be as he wishes. I will depart at once."

THREE

JEHAN'S BOAT VANISHED IN the fleeing darkness of the west along the coast.

I stepped out onto the deck of the yacht. No one in sight except for two figures at the wheel, who looked up.

I said to Owl, "Can we talk?"

He led the way to the cabin, where my coverlet was still spread on the obviously unused bed. I gathered it into my arms, hugging it close. Then I faced Owl. "You've got a couple of choices here. Either you're going to have to put me in irons, and I'm gonna fight you every inch of the way, or else let me dive over and drown. Because I'll keep trying to get to shore. Or you can give me the rowboat and let me go."

"I'll tell Zel to fetch your gear," he said.

Oh. Okay. That was . . . easy.

I retreated, feeling inexplicably awful. I was still wearing clothes belonging to Kaelande, the Colendi cook. I skinned out of those, put on my shirt and trousers, and shoved Kaelande's things through the cleaning frame. It was disguise time for me—a thought that gave me pause, seeing as how I'd just been dinging Jehan for his false faces. But I shook it away. *He* was a prince, after all. *I* was a fugitive.

Owl rejoined me and gave me my little box of mementos and

coins. I checked. Everything was as it should be. "Ready."

Owl indicated the yacht's tiny hold. "He wanted me to offer you your choice of weapons. Anything you think you might need."

"That's all right. Please let me take the boat."

"I'll row you ashore."

"That's all right—"

Owl raised a hand. "The launch is already there. I would really rather not be stranded here without a boat, leaving him with two to bring back."

"Oh. Right."

"I have some shopping to do before the tide turns anyway. You can go your way, I'll go mine."

I felt highly uncomfortable, but was too tired to do much beyond climb down and take my place in the boat. We scarcely spoke on the long row in. When we came to the dock, Owl said, "Farewell, Princess."

"You too," I managed, and I climbed up the barnacle-dotted ladder between the tide-marked pilings, and hastened down the dock without looking back.

Once I reached the street, though, I *did* look back. Not once but several times. I bobbed and weaved, trying to stay as unobtrusive as I could. My rain-washed hair was drying in a massive cloak of frizzy curls, but I left it that way. If they were still going by the description of me at the old castle, they were seeking a woman with braids. Just once I'd wear it down, but next time I was in public it would vanish under a sober cap, foiling any possible new descriptions going out.

I made my way up the street, so tired by now that the sunlight sparkling off glass and metal along the market street seemed to jab my eyes. But I made it to what I was seeking, an unobtrusive-looking inn, where I paused in the doorway, doing one last sweep for long white hair and brown velvet.

Though I didn't know it, Jehan was at that moment galloping to the southwest toward the capital at the head of an honor guard containing his father's servant and Randart's handpicked spy.

Satisfied that Jehan was not lurking somewhere about, I entered the inn. They had rooms to spare (in fact they were all empty, what with the fleet having sailed) and so I bought myself a night, stopped only long enough to help myself from the magic-cleaned water bucket they put out for guests, and then I retreated to the bed and was soon asleep.

I woke at dawn the next day, feeling more human, if not in a better mood. But the inn provided a breakfast of fresh buttered biscuits with honey, crisped potatoes with cheese and eggs, and plenty of hot liquids to drink. My mood altered gradually from *Just kill me now* to *Well I might as well live* as my body responded to the food like a dry garden under a fresh rain, and by the time I was done eating I had a plan of action.

The idea was not to draw attention to myself. So I was quite methodical. I straightened out my clothes (which looked better after a trip through the cleaning frame), braided my hair tightly in a single tail down my back like I saw both women and men wearing, and made my way back down to the moneychangers. This time I cashed in three of the smaller stones, each at a different booth, so no one would remember a handful of jewels or vast amounts of money and equate it with a tall woman yadda yadda.

After each stone, I moseyed up the street, past hand-woven fabrics of every imaginable type and color, baskets, shoes, gear. I stopped to make carefully planned, sober, unostentatious purchases.

After that I retreated to the inn and changed. When I emerged again, my braid was wrapped round my head under a plain scarf of blue, and I wore a long robe of pale blue heavy cotton over riding trousers of forest green.

By the end of the day, as vendors were finishing, I made my last purchases, a sword and a horse, having spotted what I wanted earlier. But now, in the flurry of closing, the tired vendors seemed to be distracted. After a very short dicker and a good price, I found myself the owner of an older cross-country mare who seemed to be mild and well cared for.

I bought her a good saddle pad. Onto it I hooked my new tote bag carrying all my goodies wrapped round my rolled coverlet, which in turn held the box of mementos. On the other side of the saddle pad, I'd hung the saddle sheath containing my new sword, a good dueling rapier.

As the sun began to set, I rode quietly out of the harbor city with the departing marketers. My mare ambled not ten paces from the top of Market Street, where I'd confronted Zathdar—Prince Jehan—what seemed a hundred years ago. Was it really only two days?

No answer.

I rode until well past dark, stopping in a small market town that had its own inlet to the sea. The inn was full of merrymakers celebrating a wedding, but they had a few hammocks slung for desperate travelers and I slapped my cash down before anyone else could claim one. For an extra charge, a stable hand tended to the mare's food, another got out curry brushes, and a third checked her feet.

Satisfied that the mare, at least, would sleep in a good mood, I retreated up to my hammock, and despite the singing, rhythmic stomping, roars of laughter from below, and the sounds of people breathing, sighing, rustling around in the attic around me, I dropped into sleep.

The next day, I began my long journey toward Ivory Mountain, where I hoped to find my father.

FOUR

THE LOOKOUTS ON THE towers at the royal castle in Vadnais sent runners below to announce that the prince was arriving.

More correctly, the dust from the road was spotted by the guards on the walls just about the same time two outriders appeared on foam-flecked horses.

By the time Jehan and his honor guard trotted tiredly through the outer gates and up the streets to the castle, the brown and silver banner indicating the Crown Prince in Residence hung below the king's banner, limp in the humid air.

A small army of stable hands waited to take the drooping animals in hand as the guards dismounted, everyone weary from the grueling pace the prince had kept. (Why did they volunteer for honor-guard duty? Hadn't everyone said he always stopped at every inn to get drunk and flirt with the prettiest girls around?) But no one was more weary than Jehan, who hadn't let himself sleep more than a couple of hours at a stretch for several days.

His mood was vile. Not because he was hot and tired, but because he had tried to outrun his thoughts. He knew better. But the chattering voice in his head had kept pace right with him, whispering all the things he should have said to Sasha to convince her, leaving him with the even more depressing retort: *Doesn't matter. She wouldn't have believed anything I said.*

That was the worst of it. She didn't trust him, didn't believe him. He'd never cared what anyone thought before. There were six people who knew his secret identity—well, nine, with Sasha and the Ebans—but somehow, in a matter of days, Sasha's opinion had come to matter the most.

Canardan, glancing out of one of the windows above the military courtyard, was shocked at the grim tension in Jehan's face. He sent a runner to bring his son upstairs at once, and so Jehan appeared in his private room not long after, bowing his head in salute, his tangled white hair imprinted with the dust of the road.

"Jehan?" Canardan said, puzzled. He'd never seen his son this—this angry, no, this *present*. His mood altered to uneasy question.

"You summoned me, Father."

"You seem to have ridden as if all Norsunder was on your heels. What did Zhavic say to you?"

Jehan blinked, seemed to gather himself, then his face smoothed into a semblance of his customary lack of discernable expression, despite the dust smudges. "A party. I must get to my tailor. I would not dishonor your guest by appearing in last winter's masquerade costume."

Canary was relieved, and irritated. "So you nearly ran the horses to death to get to your tailor?"

"We changed mounts at dawn. Had a race the last way, but it began to get hot," Jehan said, with his usual maddening habit of answering someone else's question, and not the one his father had asked. "The horses were all right, hot but not blown," Jehan added, and Canary nodded. That was true enough.

So Jehan wasn't angry, only overheated from the summer sun. Probably had an aching head. Canardan had had enough of those of late, and not just from the weather. "Well, get yourself some fresh clothes. Eat. I want your report on what happened at the games."

Jehan bowed and left, determined to get a grip on his mood before he faced his father again. He could see questions there.

As soon as he was gone, Canardan turned to his chief valet, a slight man of indeterminate age who went unnoticed by all who did not know him. The other servants, who did, were afraid of him. "Chas. Make certain he and the princess do not meet. Unless I am there to witness it."

Chas did not speak, only bowed and effaced himself, smiling as soon as he was alone. He seldom spoke, but when he did, the other servants listened, for they never knew when it was his will or the king's being expressed. Either way, whatever they said or did was sure to reach royal ears.

While Jehan was taking a cool bath, Atanial moved from the upper reaches of the castle to her own rooms. She'd heard the horns, and watched from the window at the staircase as the boys assigned to banner duty put up the prince's flag in the place she used to see Math's hanging.

She went out onto the nearest balcony that overlooked the courtyard, but all she'd seen was dust and milling horses and military people, with stable hands dashing about in between. Once she thought she caught sight of white hair gleaming in the sunlight, but almost immediately the figure vanished below.

She crossed back to her room and summoned her maid. "If the prince has a free moment, I would very much like to offer him some refreshments."

"If it pleases you, your highness," the girl said nervously. "I can ask permission."

Atanial smiled. "Whenever the king wishes."

Interesting. So Canary didn't want them meeting on their own, then. But what did *that* mean?

Now, for the first time, Atanial looked forward to the ball whose preparations had thrown the entire castle into a state of madness.

She went to the window, looking down into the garden court.

All the servants had brought in relatives to help clean and decorate the ballroom with the summer blooms raided from gardens outside the city. The air smelled day and night of baking, and everywhere one encountered the sounds of brooms wisping, the squeak of vigorous polishing, the slosh of windows being washed. The one time she ventured into the anteroom to the great chambers, a horde of little girls leaped to their feet, flowers drifting into piles on the floor, half-fashioned garlands dropping, as they curtseyed then stared at her in dismay. She made a hasty retreat.

She moved to the balcony again. In all this craziness I bet I could slip away.

Okay. Then what?

Trouble for all the servants, that's what. And maybe threats against those in the dungeon or wherever Kreki and the others were stashed. Meanwhile, exactly what would she be doing, other than lurking around the countryside?

No, much as she longed for it, escape right now would be a bad move. She longed to get away and find Sasha, but she would not risk others.

Besides. She remembered the glimpse of white hair in the courtyard below and remembered what Ananda had said about Jehan. She had to talk to him.

Jehan longed to be standing on the captain's deck of the *Zathdar*. He longed to be asleep on the *Dolphin*.

He longed to be anywhere but here.

But there was no leaving, and certainly no sleep. He bathed, dressed, and drank the hot steeped listerblossom brought to him by servants familiar with his tastes. That at least reduced the headache, at least.

He dressed, making certain his magic-transfer notecase went directly from the pile of dirty clothes into his new, because the moment he left, someone — probably Chas — would be searching his things.

Standard, all of it. Meanwhile his father awaited him for lunch. After that everyone would be expecting him to fuss over his clothes, so he had to find the energy to give them what they expected.

The lunch was being served on the shaded private balcony overlooking the back garden, where stooped backs worked among the roses and other flowers, busy trimming, weeding, sprucing up. Some of the flowers looked withered. There'd been no rain here for almost three days now, and dust rose everywhere, shimmering light brown in the dazzling sunlight, settling to the distantly heard dismay of sweepers, dusters, cleaners.

"Welcome back, my boy," Canardan greeted him.

"Thank you, Father." Jehan bowed.

They sat down to eat, and Jehan faced his father's searching gaze. "Tell me about the games," the king said.

"Shambles." Jehan broke a biscuit fresh from the oven. "We had four outsiders join at the last moment, who took all the prizes they competed for. Then they vanished before the awards."

Canardan rubbed his jaw as Jehan dug into his meal. "What happened to Damedran?"

"Thumped repeatedly. But that did not prevent him from riding in the relay even so."

"And still he lost?"

"Yes."

"Who were they, any idea?"

Jehan had thought this aspect out very carefully. "I know one of them from my training days in the west. He recognized me. Came up beside me when I was going down to visit my yacht, said something about assessment. Said word is out west, Norsunder will be moving against the world soon. Said we should be better trained in defense tactics."

There it was, the truth.

Canardan waved a hand impatiently. "Every court is yipping about Norsunder. I did it myself when I pressed the guilds to up their tax share to me."

"You hold that view despite these warnings?"

"What warnings? It's all rumor, innuendo, nonsense. Excuses for other plans. If Norsunder's mages do start sniffing around, we have Zhavic and Perran to ward 'em. Last I heard, no one has actually seen the Norsundrian army for years, except down there at the southern base, which concerns itself with Sartor and its environs. I want Locan Jora back. We need it. They interfere with Colendi trade, causing me to spend time and energy with these constant negotiations. That's enough to worry about." His voice sharpened, warning that he would no longer listen, only demand.

Jehan deferred yet again, hating himself, the situation, and the entire world. But as usual, hid it. "I had commissioned a gift for the queen. Magister Zhavic told me she vanished. What does that mean, vanished?"

"I don't know myself. One morning she wasn't in her rooms, and no one had seen her depart."

"Magic?"

"Could be, though Zhavic went over her chambers himself, and insisted he found no traces of transfer. But then the magic would . . ." He waved his hand. "Dissipate? Sounds like fog, not spells. Anyway, the residue of major transfers only lingers for a time, they all say. And we don't know when she left. She stayed in her rooms, never came out except to walk in the gardens."

Jehan nodded, satisfied that the queen had gone of her own free will, however mysteriously, and had not been conveniently dispatched. Now that there was a potential queen around.

Speaking of whom, it was time to mention her. "When do I meet Princess Atanial?"

"Officially, at the ball. But if you like I can invite her to supper. She has nothing else to do. I caught her, I might add, having made straight for those fools around that troublemaker Kreki Eban. Who is sitting down in the lockup right now, with the rest of them, awaiting my pleasure."

"What is your pleasure?" Jehan asked.

"That they all drop dead. But they won't. I don't know what to do about them. I can't figure out if I should hope someone runs a rescue raid so I have an excuse to kill them all, or if I should make them disappear. But whether there was dirty work or not, you can be certain rumor would smear me. As usual. So they sit there. And

Atanial here. None of them making trouble." Canardan grinned.

"I am to understand you summoned me here to meet her?"

"To talk to her." The king threw up his hands. "You like women. You chase women. They must like you, or you wouldn't catch them. Atanial is likable, but too old for you to chase. Talk to her instead. Ask about her daughter. What she looks like, what she's been taught. Where she might be. I want that daughter here, and I want you to court her."

"Court her?" Jehan repeated, aghast.

"Court and marry. Zhavalieshin name and ours twined, very romantic and might just settle down this curse-blasted kingdom."

The headache was back, worse than before. "What if she won't have me?"

"Of course she will," his father countered. "You have success with all these artists, surely you can romance her. You're handsome, you're rich, you've got a title. If she's romantic, you give up your artists for a little while. If she's sensible, you don't even have to do that."

From a certain point of view, it sounded reasonable. Kings and queens negotiated just such marriages all the time. But Jehan never felt farther from his father's view of the world than at this moment.

"Do you know where she is?" he asked, thumbs at his temples.

"No, but if the pirate's got her, Randart will soon take care of that. If not, the mages will track her down on land."

"What if she won't cooperate?" Jehan asked.

Father and son eyed one another, striving to understand—and to convince the other.

Was that irony in his Jehan's voice? Canardan eyed his son, then shrugged. Imagination. Maybe the boy hesitated for his usual stupid reasons. She might not be pretty, or more important, might not like art. "She'll cooperate."

They both knew he'd use persuasion, and then threat.

The rest of the lunch was about details—the ball, taxes, decisions. Jehan perceived with a sinking heart that Canardan did not expect any intelligent response. He probably did not want it. He only wanted acquiescence, and that Jehan gave him with his usual air of absence.

Seeing it, his father relaxed. When Canardan was finished, he rose. It was time to get on with his busy day, and for his son to carry out his assigned tasks.

Jehan crossed the long halls to his seldom-used rooms, now filled with people patiently awaiting him: the two tailors, a model his height and build, a dozen apprentices standing ready with swatches of cloth, and servants hovering at the back.

Jehan submitted silently to their ministrations, his thoughts extremely bitter. They stayed that way until evening, by which time his head ached like a hammer on metal.

So he was in no real mood of appreciation when he sat down to dinner with his father and his prisoner, Princess Atanial, who was tall, built on slighter lines than her daughter, though not by much. They had the same magnificent build. They also had the same light hair and the same light eyes, though there the resemblance ended. Sasha, Jehan thought, was a real blend of her parents' features, Math's distinctive bones made beautiful by Atanial's spun-sugar prettiness.

He hated her laugh.

"So *nice* it is to meet you *at last*." She giggled. It really was a giggle. "You *do* have white hair. Not light blond, or what we call *platinum*, it's so white it's blue." And the trilling giggle again.

"All the morvende are like that." Canardan didn't seem to mind the laugh. "You should see a room full of 'em. Like snow statues."

The princess leaned forward and pressed Jehan's fingers. "Oh, but don't think I don't count you as handsome. Woo-hoo-hoo! Why, the girls must simply *swoon* over you."

He tried not to show his wince.

"But I'm told all the Merindars are as handsome as your father."

He braced himself—and there came the laugh.

How could his father possibly admire this woman? But he was staring at her with a peculiar bemusement Jehan had never seen in his face before.

The signal for the servants at least quieted the laugh as food was handed round and everyone ate. Atanial plopped her elbows on the table the same way her daughter did. This breach of manners lessened his irritation enough to make her voice bearable.

Just as well, for she chattered through the entire dinner, running on about masquerades, the castle, music, Math, and ending with, "So what will your costume be, dear?"

Dear? "Not much I can be." He felt measurably better now that he'd eaten.

She chuckled, a soft, even attractive sound that suddenly shifted to the piercing giggle. Jehan's nerves fired. Was it possible she was faking that horrible laugh?

He fought back the tiredness settling like cloud-blankets over his thoughts now that the headache had receded, and forced himself to pay attention. "Not many famous morvende in sunsider history."

"Sunsider? Oh! You mean we who live in the sun and not in your caves. Woo hoo! But you could wear a wig. Some sort of disguise along with your mask—"

And put that idea in everyone's mind? He marshaled the last of his energy and waved a languid hand. "Loathe disguises in any form. Any mask I wear must be a work of art."

"Oh, I *see*." She trilled coyly. "*Art*, yes. I think your father told me you are sensitive to all forms of art. That must be your morvende heritage." And the laugh again.

What a stupid remark! Yet Math had admired his wife's brains, and Sasha thought highly of her mother.

If so, why?

His interest sharpened. Seeing his father gazing at her with a slight furrow between his brows, Jehan said, "Does your daughter like masquerades?"

"My daughter?" Princess Atanial looked around as if a daughter were hiding behind the chandelier or under the table. "Oh yes. That is, she does love a good romp. When in the mood. Though she is not much one for costume. They do so rip and tear so easily. Hee-hee-hee!"

"In the mood?" Jehan persisted, after his father made a motion with his hand, waggling the fingers. *More, more.*

"Well. You know," Atanial said airily, looking at the light through her glass. "Not angry. Or sullen. She does have her very good days, and on those, she can be as sweet as roses, and for longer than many give her credit for. Why, are you interested in my darling Sasha? Oh, you young men, always with the young, but I'm only an ugly old woman, and I don't count. I know, it's the way of life." A bosom-heaving sigh.

Canardan sat back, gazing at her in perplexity. Jehan winced when she trilled again. "Oh no." He forced a smile. "Quite the opposite, I assure you. It's only your beauty that has me hoping your daughter might be a candle to your sun."

He felt a pang of self-loathing, knowing how false he sounded.

She twiddled her fingers at him demurely. "Go along, then. Beautiful indeed! They do say that poor Sasha inherited her father's looks, but we who love her think her beautiful, and as for that terrible Kickpail epithet, well, it's simply not true. Quite unkind, put about by jealous minds."

"Kickpail?" both men repeated at the same time.

Atanial looked skyward. "Oh dear. *Don't* tell me you hadn't heard about everyone calling her Clumsy Kickpail. Naughty me! But how was I supposed to know? I assure you the stories about how ungainly she is are quite exaggerated. Quite. She only broke that table once, and it was already old and ready to fly to pieces at a touch. As for those windows, why, that can happen to anyone. And it's not true she flung the serving maid through one. Stupid girl tripped all on her own, not moving out of the way fast enough." Atanial thumped her elbows back onto the table, chin resting on her laced fingers. "When my daughter has a sword in her hand, it's art to watch her. Though it's better not to watch when her temper is, ah, somewhat peppery. But that's true of anyone. An-ee-one!" She blinked rapidly.

Jehan was stunned. A more false word picture of the Sasha he knew could scarcely be found—except for the sword. *The single true observation reported to my father.* Surely Atanial had to be playing some sort of game, right under Canardan's nose.

"Oh, I do so hope I can introduce the two of you." Atanial gave a coy little bat to Jehan's sleeve. "I can give you some little teentsy hints on how best not to set off, that is, how to please her the most. She is the best company if you don't anger—ah, when in her wonderful social mood."

Jehan was sure of it now, Atanial was lying. To what effect? His father made a surreptitious encouraging motion.

Jehan turned back to Atanial. "Teentsy hints like?"

"Never talk about flowers with her. She hates the sight of them for some reason. Oh, and rain. It puts her in such a dour mood. That's natural, isn't it? Everybody hates rain. She also hates snow, hot weather and wind. Horses. She despises their smell, and their noises. Talking about any other woman will miff her, oooh, the tiniest bit. She's been so sheltered, she never really learned social graces. We were on the run for so many years, and then she had to adjust to another world at the most awkward age, and the awkwardness, I fear . . . Her family loves her dearly, and we don't count any of these faults against her thousands of good qualities." Atanial sighed, looking up again. "But oh, I must admit to the teeniest bit of jealousy myself! That's the way of it. When a young woman enters the conversation, if not the room, the old woman is quite forgotten. I must get used to it, I suppose."

There was more obvious digging for compliments, which Canardan, bestirring himself at last, gave with grace, evoking that head-shattering laugh. And then—none too soon—they all parted, to the sound of hammering and muffled swearing from below as servants muscled garlands out to decorate the walkways leading to the grand chambers.

Canardan put a hand out to keep Jehan from leaving. When

they were alone, he said, "She's never spoken so much about the girl in all the days she's been here."

"Is she always like that?" Jehan asked, too tired to think.

"No." Canardan rubbed his jaw. "But I think, I think she was flirting with you."

Jehan stared, appalled. "That was flirting?"

"What else could it have been? You're young, almost as handsome as I am, and who knows what sort of customs they get up to in that other world?" Canardan took in his son's honest disgust and amazement. "The important thing is, she hasn't said as much in all the weeks she's been here. I want you to take her out for a ride. Let her flirt as much as she likes. Get more out of her, especially about Math."

Jehan forced himself to bring up the subject of Sasha, dangerous as it was. Much as he hated himself for his astounding failure in every particular of their relationship — except for one incredible kiss. Maybe that had been a mistake as well, but one he'd never regret . . . *Focus, idiot.* "Do you really want me to marry someone called Clumsy Kickpail?" And then he had it, Atanial's reasons for the lies. "She sounds terrible. We should be glad she's gone."

But Canardan just grinned. "What could be better? The worse this girl is, the more popular you become. She can always sustain an accident when convenient. From the sound of it, no one would even mind. Better and better."

Jehan sustained a heady, almost dizzy sensation, his emotions veering between revulsion and laughter at how wrong that vivid word picture was of Sasha. How to let Atanial know her ruse was not working? He couldn't. He hated the pretense, the lying, but as he crossed to his rooms, the soft summer air bringing the sounds of workers singing tunelessly a ballad from Sartor, he knew he would lie — cheat — steal, if he had to, if it meant he could protect Sasha from discovery by Randart. Even though she didn't want to be protected.

He also would lie — cheat — steal in order to protect the kingdom.

It needed protecting badly.

Once he reached his room, he dismissed everyone but gangling, tuft-haired Kazdi, his cadet runner. It took only an exchange of looks and Kazdi prowled around watching for spies, especially Chas.

Jehan shut himself in the bath chamber and pulled out his magic-transfer case, which he had not been able to check for days.

Several tiny folded pieces of paper awaited him. The first, from Elkin, his mage-student friend doing his journeywork as a mage-scribe at the academy.

In ancient Sartoran, he'd written: *Damedran put in for changes. Dannath rescinded them. Tension between masters and seniors.*

There was one from Robin, leading the fleet.

The Skate *is leading the Aloca fleet after us. We think they're going to try a pincer. We'll hang them up around the islands.*

One from Aslo, the ally he'd planted in Randart's fleet carrying the invasion weapons, now the liaison with Tharlif, the tough old woman who'd been privateering for most of her life. One of Zathdar's staunchest allies. *Our contact agrees, purpose of shipment is to stockpile weapons. Much speculative war talk.*

So far, as expected.

The last one, the smallest, he unfolded, his heart hammering.

There were no words, only a tiny drawing of an owl in flight.

He smiled for the first time in days, left the bath for his waiting bed, and was soon deep in long-postponed sleep.

FIVE

THE WEATHER DID NOT relent.

In the gardens the blossoms drooped, looking papery and withered, the edges of leaves yellowed, and a silted pall of dust shimmered in the air above the roads. But the night of the masquerade, a couple thousand candles softened the dust and dryness of the city with a forgiving, golden shimmer. Lights were everywhere, candles in cut-glass holders, their flames glittering in infinite reflection against paired mirrors down hallways. Outside, candles glowed in lamps of colored glass that were hung in trees and set along stone walls.

The king watched his guests arrive from his private balcony overlooking the broad entryway to the grand chambers. His son was with him, observing the press of open, light carriages rolling up to release fantastically groomed and glittering guests. Atanial listened through the open doors of her room to the echoes of musicians tuning instruments, servants calling last-minute orders, and bustling about on last errands.

All three knew the setting was right. Why shouldn't it be, after uncounted hands had labored all week to get it that way? All three of them reflected (Canardan briefly, Jehan brooding, Atanial with resignation) how the decorations, the clothes, the starry night with its colored lights, hid the parching drought—as the prospect of a party hid the tensions between people.

The king had to wait until everyone was there, for his appearance signaled the beginning, and afterward arrivals were officially late. Being late to a party given by a king would get you talked about, and not in a good way, for months afterward.

So Canardan stood out on the balcony, which was at least somewhat cooler than indoors. He wished he'd not chosen a heavy robe, splendid as it had looked in the heralds' drawings. Yet his costume was a message, a subtle reminder of his own heritage, for he was going as Matthias Lirendi, the last and most famous (some said infamous) emperor of Colend. Who was a Merindar ancestor. Of course he was an ancestor of most of the royal houses in the eastern part of the continent, but that also underscored Canardan's royal antecedents.

Jehan had chosen the guise of an old Sartoran poet-prince, known for his complete disregard for the invisible boundaries of politics as well as for his visionary works of art. The long paneled robe worn over loose trousers was cool and easy to move in; the colors, sky blue and black, complemented his white hair.

He knew the costume would annoy his father, good as it looked. But its purpose was to deflect interest in him as a political figure. Though in truth, he thought sourly as he reluctantly started downstairs, every single thing he did or said had political repercussions.

The costume and his rank would at least hold importunate guests to discussing any subject he chose, and he chose to stick with poetry.

As his shoes whispered over the marble steps, he considered Atanial. The question was, what would he say to her?

He thought back over their ride earlier that day. They had talked little, both agreeing that the heat was too breathless. In reality, Jehan's planned words had zapped away when he discovered that Chas was to accompany them, ostensibly to see to their needs.

The few words they'd exchanged had been masterpieces of

dullness, punctuated by Atanial's horrible giggle. As Atanial commented with excruciating detail on everything she saw, right to the types of grass growing on the roadside, Jehan enjoyed the jaw-locked tedium in Chas's face.

Obedient to his father's wishes, he'd asked about Sasharia, to be regaled with giggle-punctuated stories not really about Sasha at all, but about Atanial. She'd described little anecdotes even more pointless and tedious than her chatter about grass, often correcting herself several times in the maddening way of the crashing bore. "Was it five? No, no, I state it wrong, it was four. No, it was five, for I remember the moon that night, and I was wearing my new gown . . . four . . . my friend—you should meet her some day—anyway she said, 'Four more times,' I remember it like it was yesterday. Or was it five after all?"

Jehan had kept Chas in view just so he could count the man's attempts to swallow yawns. Jehan was now convinced Atanial's chatter was a performance, and it was brilliant.

More to the point, he saw that Atanial was willing to lie about Sasha when alone with the king and himself, but in front of other ears, she never quite brought herself to say anything at all. And so, mindful of Chas behind him, he'd contributed his mite by boring on until his throat was parched about styles of Sartoran versus Colendi art.

They'd all been glad when that ride ended.

Snapped back to the present by the sweet, brassy peal of the King's Fanfare, Jehan took his place in the grand ballroom. Around him hissed the breathing of far too many people shifting and rustling as they tried not to sweat into their good clothes.

The promenade introductory music prompted the company to assemble, and because this was a masquerade where the customary order of rank was somewhat relaxed, those more bold, more confident or more desperate, all tried to get to the front without unseemly haste.

Atanial, at the king's side, observed the prince's distracted blue gaze as he fell in behind. She raised her hand to meet Canardan's palm at shoulder height, distracted momentarily by the fall of the splendid sleeves of his robe, blue and gold, embroidered with highly stylized, gracefully attenuated lilies.

He did the king thing well, she thought with private humor. He looked good from his fineweave boots to the waving auburn hair brushed back nobly from his brow—not a hint of balding, either. The angle of his chin, his slight smile convinced her he knew it. He was *preening*. That sense of mocking laughter nearly escaped, and she turned it into a smile.

As for arrogance, she knew she looked good all in midnight blue velvet, edged with crimson, and the high medieval headdress like nothing in the room, her mask being (for she knew she was the center of attention, and she'd play along) the sheerest of veils.

It was enough to hide her inch-long grayish silver roots. She remembered that people did color their hair on this world, but it was done by magic, not chemicals. She did not want to risk inviting any of Canardan's mages to perform magic over her. Who knew what kind of spell they might slip in besides the hair color?

Therefore the veil. Even if she was the only one amused, going as Maleficent from Disney's *Sleeping Beauty* definitely gave her secret enjoyment.

The promenade began with a flourish of brassy horns and a clash of cymbals, all the guests pacing in time, chins high, backs straight, toes pointed.

"You look lovely, Atanial." Canardan smiled. "Is that a guise from your world or ours?"

"Oh, mine," she said cheerily, noting the *your world or ours.* "Maleficent is a very, very wicked woman."

"Ah, and by that you are suggesting?"

"Nothing. Do you think me wicked? You know better than that, Canardan. I like her style."

"I sometimes wonder if I know you at all, Sun. But a wicked queen who reigns in a ballroom, it's a fine touch. Danger with dance, without destruction. Would that the world were conducted the same." He smiled, saluting her hand with grace.

And—they were quite aware—every pair of eyes in the ballroom took in that hand kiss.

Snap. The trap she'd helped him to build closed round her, just as she became aware of it. *I ought to have been Clarabelle the stupid cow.* She realized at last what a masquerade *meant*. She was on display, everyone knew who she was, but the very fact that this was a masquerade meant she could not actually speak to anyone about anything real.

She was stuck in a Disney guise, but this was no Disney film, with a handy fairy godmother or blue angel standing by to waft the hapless heroine to a happy ending.

Furious with him, with herself, she stared straight ahead and worked on her breathing, as Canardan looked round to the formed circle of his guests. He caught at least four meaningful glances, people who were going to single him out for A Little Talk.

He faced forward, setting a slower pace. When you're a king you can slow up an entire circle of people and no one will make a peep. The gap between them and the last couple widened. Speaking low so that Jehan and the duchess behind them could not hear—not that they were listening, for he could hear the duchess talking about her daughter's stunning talent in the arts— he said, "I take it you feel more comfortable among those of rank than you once did?"

"Oh, I got over the rank thing really fast in the old days," she responded with forced cheer. "As Math often said, princes have to put on their pants one leg at a time, same as do poets. Or poulterers."

"I remember you brought that up during one of our first conversations. Such sayings sound earnest and egalitarian, but are they really believed? There is such a thing as protesting too much."

"Then I'll drop the sayings. I see your aristocrats as human beings raised to certain customs, ways of speaking and thinking, that become habit. It's partly training that sets anyone apart from anyone else. And training means you're taught to do something, whether it's making lace or running a kingdom, but whether or not you do it well is up to the individual," she said.

Before Canardan could answer, the musicians shifted up half a key, and he realized they'd been patiently playing the same phrase far too many times. He was not being a good host. He lengthened his step, Atanial matched his pace, and they obligingly closed the distance with the rest of the circle.

Atanial turned gracefully to the right as the king turned to his left, and her palm met the prince's. They completed their half turn and began pacing in the opposite direction.

Everyone's attention was distracted by their new partners. She snapped her gaze back to Jehan and was surprised by a narrow, assessing gaze that was, for a moment, startlingly like his father's.

She murmured without moving her lips, "Ananda said to trust you."

And heard him draw in a breath.

No more. Already the couple ahead had glanced back, and she felt the weight of the king's gaze behind her. She turned her attention away from Jehan, smiling vapidly into the room as they trod the measures until the next chord change, half a key up the scale.

Again they changed partners and direction, leaving her facing a man her own age. She recognized a duke from what used to be the west, before Locan Jora forced a treaty onto Khanerenth, dividing the kingdom into two. Thus truncating most of the duke's land. His spare form was barely in costume, more of an old-fashioned court outfit. The "mask" was the visor of his helm, which he'd lifted.

Obviously he was only paying lip service to the masquerade rules. Being a duke, he could. Atanial remembered the unspoken but iron-strong custom: if someone of higher rank broke a social rule, you could too. But you didn't do it first.

It was up to the duke to choose whether he would speak to Atanial or to Maleficent. She wasn't really a princess, not with the Zhavalieshins deposed. It was a mere courtesy title, her privilege (or lack of same) dependent entirely on the king's whim.

"Is Prince Math alive?" he asked, his brows bristling.

"I don't know."

"You trying to find out?"

Step, step, dip—step, step, dip. The music changed, but the duke gripped her hand. "Are you?" He let her go and growled, "Never mind. I think I have my answer." He turned away.

Atanial also turned, not really seeing her next partner. Nausea bubbled in her gut at the certainty that the duke believed she had forgotten her husband and was angling for a king. No time to consider anything except that, so far, the masquerade was a disaster. *I'm a failure without having spoken ten words.*

Her next partner asked who she was.

"Maleficent."

She did not know the man, but he was polite, asking one or two suave questions about Maleficent that were easy to answer, and the dance whirled him on.

The next two partners accepted Maleficent at face value, and embarked on light flirtation with this fantasy wicked queen. She answered in kind, which was easy, but as the long dance wore on she was more and more aware of just how badly she had fumbled.

A new partner leaned close as they placed their palms together. "Do you remember me, your highness?"

She faced him, to encounter her new partner's mask. Through the eye holes she made out familiar gray eyes. Heavy jaw. Iron gray hair.

Resisting the impulse to rip aside her veil and his mask so they could be two real people, she sifted memories. Those eyes. Younger, browner hair—someone around Canary—yes, one of the captains in his own private guard during the old king's days, now obviously titled with land of his own. For Canardan did not invite mere guard captains to masquerade balls in the royal palace.

Above her rank? Below it? What *was* her rank in their eyes, anyway?

Whatever. She was not about to frost him by pretending he'd

broken the blasted "rules". "How nice to see you." She smiled. "You've flourished, I see."

"Old count of Shesba died. No heirs. So I am still in the saddle, but now riding my own lands, so to speak." The familiar voice brought back Math saying . . . *and he's one of the quiet, honest sorts, warrior captains who would carry out their duties no matter who was in charge. If left alone, good, reliable people.*

Atanial now remembered Shesba as a difficult area way to the north, squished between mountains and the vile coastline. She congratulated him, the music changed again, and she found herself with another partner, this one tall, old, unfamiliar, their voices blending with the hum of conversation and the music. Then the entire company sighed as, at last, the unseen mages got their magic spells working and a breath of cooler air teased her already moist flesh, followed by a gentle, steady breeze.

Almost everyone visibly relaxed, some faces turning to the open doorways, through which the mages had drawn their invisible tunnel of colder air from high in the sky.

The short, stout Chief of the Guild Council was her next partner, followed by another landowner of some degree. Other men danced with her after that. Everyone knew who she was, but stayed on their side of the Maleficent pretense. They were all polite, two or three friendly. But, clearly, the king's men. Not allies. And in their eyes, Prince Math's wife was flourishing here in her gilded cage.

Step, step, turn, step, step turn, the promenade sped up, always climbing half a chord. They were nearly at the end of the circle, the talk the most superficial exchanges of politenesses. Her exchange with that duke lingered, making her wary. How many of these smiling men thought she'd abandoned Math to his fate in order to catch a king?

Canardan watched her from across the room. She danced with those entrancing moves she'd always had. Sometimes she spoke, but judging from the lack of reaction in her partners, everything was as it should be. Let her trip prettily around his ballroom and show everyone how well he treated her. He hoped she'd enjoy it.

Thinking about her was more pleasant than listening to the obviously rehearsed compliments and broad hints for returned compliments of his current partner. *Fishing for royal catch*, Canardan thought sourly. Here he'd invited this baroness—old family, good lands, good support, rich—because her daughter might be a fallback for Jehan. He'd forgotten she was a widow.

"May I honor your majesty with a reminder of how famous were your splendid regattas through the city of Alsais? We still read the poems all these centuries later," she whispered, fluttering her fan.

What regatta was she dropping her not-so-subtle hint about? Because it had nothing to do with Colend's past glories, not in that tone. Oh yes. *That* regatta, he thought, smiling into her eyes. Right before he married Ananda, the last time he'd dressed up as Matthias the Magnificent of Colend. What his partner hadn't found out was that she had been one of three dalliances that memorable night.

So. The women already knew that Ananda wasn't skipping the social duty tonight as she usually did, but was gone. *Of course* everyone knew. His worst enemy was rumor, something you couldn't fight with a sword. He'd underestimated how quickly they'd come a-courting.

The music changed, sparing him having to come up with a reply that was agreeable, but not too agreeable, friendly but not flirtatious.

How was Atanial faring? He had almost completed the circle. Atanial was maybe eight or ten men away, talking and laughing with one of his barons. He was aware of Jehan behind him, murmuring something about Sartoran tapestry weaving, and from the tittering, effusive response, he too was being courted.

Where was that daughter of Atanial's? He hoped there'd be a message from either Zhavic or Randart soon.

The dance ended.

Atanial watched how the grand circle broke into tiny circles, each revealing in its numbers, in who moved to whom, who collected company, who stood where.

The biggest circle formed around the king. Of course. But Jehan's was nearly as large—moon to his father's sun—with the younger women forming most of his group. And if they were all doing their best to attract the attention of a handsome prince, who could blame them?

Father and son retreated to get something to drink.

On either side of the room, mirror images, had been set great carved tables bearing rows of tall, fluted glasses containing punch, water, wine. Water! Atanial located the table on her side of the room and made a beeline, her veil fluttering behind. She took one, lifted her veil to drink. Over the rim, glimmering with reflected fire from the chandeliers overhead, she watched father and son meet to exchange brief words before they were surrounded.

The musicians struck up a melody, and both heads turned, for a breathtaking moment poised at exactly the same angle. There was Canardan's handsome profile, in his son planed and refined, Jehan's coloring moonlight and silver instead of ruddy gold. But one thing for certain from their body language: they were fond of one another.

And she, Atanial Fatwit Blitherer, had just tipped her hand to the son. *Why, why, why? Ananda, why did you do that to me, was it revenge after all?*

Jehan chose at random a partner for the new dance. The rest of the young women drifted by, ribbons fluttering, silks glowing richly in the candlelight, no one wanting to ask him and risk being turned down in front of the others, so they eyed him and smiled.

Atanial felt a touch on her wrist and looked up into the face of one of Canardan's aristocratic working men, this one the governor of Vadnais harbor. Numb with self-loathing, she set down her empty glass, curtseyed and trod with him to the middle of the floor. He chatted with cheery ease about his racehorses until the dance ended. The seductive triple beat of a waltz—the first one of the evening—signaled, in straightened shoulders, lifted chins, laughs and shimmering fans, the electrical impulse of expectation.

So strange, Atanial thought. Not just that they had the waltz here, but it apparently was far older than it was on Earth. Chicken/egg.

Canardan watched Atanial look around, her profile behind the veil etched against the wall as she watched—who? Jehan was busy with a very young lady dressed in a stunning gown made up of fragile silk roses of twenty graded shades of pink.

Canardan flicked his gaze back. Atanial was lost behind a long whirling knotwork of dancing couples. When they passed, she was visible again, over by the refreshments table, nibbling a cake—

"Your majesty," someone murmured behind him.

He looked down at the short, balding Chief of the Guild Council, and frowned. No use in hiding behind masquerade nonsense now. His relations with the guilds were already teetering.

"Your majesty, you have not had time to see me, despite my petitions sent each day," the man stated. "But I must and will speak. If I end up with the Scribe Sharveshin in the dungeon for my temerity, despite its being my duty—"

Canardan sighed. "It's not even remotely treason to ask questions, Guild Chief. Why are you pretending it is?"

"Why do you have a scribe in the dungeon? A scribe! May as well be a herald! And the Heralds' Guild Mistress as well as the Scribes' Master, at my office every day demanding to know why. If it's whim, who's next?"

"Asking questions is not treason," Canardan said. "But meeting in a cellar and planning overthrow of the government is."

"Who says they were planning overthrow?" the Guild Chief stated stubbornly. "There has been no public trial. We did not hear witnesses against them. As mandated in the agreement between guilds and crown."

Canardan cursed, mind working rapidly even as his gaze sought Atanial.

She paid no attention to the king. Or his heir. She finished her cake and wondered who would be mortally offended if she left. She should get away before she bumbled even more stupidly—

A flash of blue, and Jehan stepped before her, his partner having been relinquished to another dancer. Jehan's blue eyes were no longer as empty as the sky, but focused. Intense.

It was time, he'd decided, to trust someone. Again, that is.

"I saw her," he murmured, and passed without turning his head.

It was her turn to draw in her breath.

To the Guild Chief (having watched Jehan pass Atanial without stopping) Canardan said, "I will see you after I've had a chance to examine the prisoners myself. Everything according to treaty. But I've not yet had time."

The Chief of the Guild Council had to bow and accept that.

Three men ranged before Atanial. She put out her hand somewhat blindly, smiling her social smile, and triple-stepped, neat and light, with the owner of the first warm fingers that gripped hers.

She did not come within speaking distance of Jehan until the evening was nearly over. That dance was the Khanerenth version of a quadrille—that is, a complicated line dance that broke into whirling and braiding twos, fours, twos, eights, twos, fours, and twos as they slowly moved down the line. One always came back to one's original partner for hands across.

The dance, she had already discovered, had changed only in one regard. There were two dips where there had been two hops, otherwise it was the same one she and Math had drilled down the long royal portrait gallery on those soft spring nights, as they talked and laughed about every subject in the universe.

Once again Jehan appeared abruptly, holding out a hand so they could step past one another.

"You saw Sasha?" she asked.

They parted. Round, round, step, step, smile, dip, twirl, hold up one's hand, traipse in another circle, dip, bow, turn, step step step, and there he was again.

"She's gone. I assume she's seeking Math."

Twirl. Step. Atanial fought impatience. She could feel Canardan watching. A quick look showed benign pleasure, but if he saw them talk, saw them even look serious, that expression could change fast.

I must protect Jehan too. She glanced at the white-haired prince's vacant smile in the next group over, all four with their hands together in the center as they tripped in a circle.

He was thinking the same thing. He couldn't quite see her eyes, but her manner, the way she'd drawn in a breath—the absence of that giggle—had convinced him that he'd done at least this much right. So far. But hurry or furtiveness or even too much said would catch idle eyes, raise questions. They could only speak for that brief time when they met in the center of the square, changing places with hands across.

"She trusted you, then?" Atanial asked, and they parted.

Three, he thought. *We only have five chances left.*

Instinct prompted him to lie, as he always had. But the relief he'd felt on telling her the truth overrode the mere protective instinct, and so when they met again, he said, "No."

Another indrawn breath. Her hand trembled under his fingers, as though she tightened her muscles against betraying expression, and once again he felt relief and alarm.

On the next, when she looked her question as she reached for hands across, he murmured, "Kissed me, yes. No trust."

And he was gone, not seeing her face.

No one could see her face, except behind the mysterious shimmer of her veil, so they could not see the sting of tears. *My fault, my fault,* she was thinking. No use in trying to excuse herself. They'd returned to Earth all those years ago grief-stricken and angry; sunshine dancingstar, she who had left her world a hippie idealist, had come back bitter and afraid. She'd told her daughter over and over, in infinite variation, *Men are pretty and fun to be with, but never. Ever. Trust them.*

Think. Do not make things worse. They had three more exchanges ahead, and the dance would be over.

When they met, both uttered a word at the same time, he blanked his face and she said again, "Is she safe?"

Two more, they each thought as they parted, the pretty melody tripping through the silver flutes and reed horns and harp strings. *We have to talk.*

He trod his stately pace, smiling at the two young heiresses who cast him languishing (and watchful) glances over their fans as he circled them and mentally reviewed the palace. Her rooms, warded. His rooms, warded, and spies in the stable, kitchen and the government rooms —

There she was again, and he could feel her question, but he had no answer, and so number seven passed in silence.

When she neared for number eight, he saw in the rigid line of her shoulders, the tension outlining her veiled head and neck, that the question still stood.

He said, "So far, yes." Knowing that she'd figure out what it meant: that he was having Sasha followed.

SIX

I LEARNED TWO THINGS the first week of my journey.

The first occurred two days to the northwest, on the meandering trade road alongside the Lembesca River. I did not risk any gallop in that withering, humid heat. Shade occurred too seldom as relief, and then only briefly under hardy trees with long thin leaves through which the brilliant sun shone in a lacework of glare.

I arrived at an inn early in the afternoon. I would have liked to push on farther. I'd been careful to walk the horse and to offer water at the two streams we'd passed, but she was looking dangerously droopy as we plodded along the road under what seemed to be a permanent dust pall. Since I had no idea how long I'd ride before finding another village, I thought I'd better stop.

So did a harvest party. And the friends of a journeyman who'd been made master joiner that day, after they'd been working on a building somewhere over the dry, golden hills.

The two parties converged almost at the same time. I had gone in to arrange for a hammock when the harassed innkeeper, who had deployed his entire family for the first party, paused at the door in dismay. From outside came the merry sounds of a crowd turning off the road to the stables as, behind us, the harvesters flowed downstairs into the common room, singing out for food and drink!

Mr. Innkeeper reminded me of my father. Mrs. Innkeeper was a round-faced woman my mother's age who bustled anxiously to the door of the kitchen. Their expressions were a mixture of stun and a kind of helpless horror.

I swerved away from the door, moved to the shelf behind the counter, and took one of the aprons I saw folded there.

The man ran out to the stable to commandeer bodies for cook's helpers. The woman turned her head, her braid half coming down, and stared from the apron to me. Brows rising, she glanced at my arms.

"Experience?" she asked, obviously trying not to hope.

"Four years."

Relief made her face redden. "Here are the choices," she said rapidly. "Broiled cabbage rolls, fresh-water fish, rice, onion, cooked in pressed olive. Rice with melted cheese and chicken with lemon glaze. Lentil soup with yesterday's chicken, and cheese over it if they like. Bread until it runs out, and green-apple tarts."

"Got it. Drink?"

"Don't fret over the drink, my daughters can see to that." She indicated two light-haired girls of about ten and twelve who'd appeared from the storeroom door, both in aprons, one dusty with flour, the other setting down a mending basket behind the bar. "But they are too small to carry more than one plate at a time."

"I can carry six." I flexed my biceps. "On one arm."

She laughed. "You shall have a royal meal when we finish, and our best wine."

"Innkeeper! Wake up!" a man roared, and that was the last time we spoke to one another for many hours.

It was about midnight when I thumped down onto a bench, weary, my arms feeling like string. I had just enough energy to appreciate it. A good workout is a good workout, however one gets it.

The woman entered from the kitchen (from which every scrap of food had been emptied), and took one look around the empty room where the two daughters and I had finished cleaning the tabletops. The younger daughter had fallen asleep on a bench in about two breaths, head on her crossed arms, washcloth still gripped in her fingers. The other girl stood at a window, staring out at the pinpoints of dancing lights as the harvesters wove, singing, back to their homes.

"A bed is waiting." The woman touched my arm. "Follow my daughter."

The older girl led me upstairs. She stumbled in exhaustion. I'd expected a hammock but found myself in a narrow but comfortable bed, the linen sheets smelling of a recent drying in sunlight. Heaven.

When I woke, there was hot water steaming on a table.

I went downstairs to a massive breakfast, which ended as the footsteps of the celebrants overhead began thumping about. The family, still tired, seemed cheered by the father's grin. He'd made enough, he said, to refurbish the stable against winter. Then one by one they turned to me.

So, my two discoveries.

One, in a world without the level of bureaucracy that binds the US of A, you can do things like pick up an apron and there's no worry about contracts, the IRS, etc. That was the good thing. The not-so-good thing I learned is that it's really difficult to make up believable lies when you are a stranger in a strange land.

"Were you inn-raised?" the mother asked me, and as I opened my mouth to lie, the father said, "Where? We know most of the inn families up the coast and a good ways along both rivers."

They were so friendly, and eager for news and gossip. There I was, struggling to come up with lies.

Well, they were not supposed to know I was lying, I told myself sternly. This was the only way I'd get to Dad, which meant a few harmless lies. Therefore my answers had to be short, and boring.

"Stables, mostly." At the surprise in the older daughter's face, I vaguely remembered leaving my mare to be curried, and I said quickly, "Supplies. Cleaning. Helped with the tables, when I was little, down south. Then I became a sailor." I ventured that shot on reflecting how far inland we were. Hopefully they knew nothing of the sea.

"Where did you sail to?" The daughter leaned forward. "I love stories about other places!"

"Why are you so far north?" The mother also leaned forward, ready to be sympathetic if there'd been some disaster.

"Maybe we could get you to run a message, if you're passing toward some of our folks?" the father put in. "Even with things being bad, handing off letters still always nets a free bed for a night, among our folk."

I dealt with all these as best as I could, accepting the message finally, figuring I would pay in the next town I could for a messenger. And I took my leave, feeling isolated, uncertain, afraid my lies would explode behind me.

The route I'd chosen was, I hoped, random enough to keep me anonymous and not make my destination clear to anyone who knew magic. Ivory Mountain lay to the west of Ellir, at the far end of the Bar Larsca Valley, inside of the border mountains. The road to Locan Jora was alongside the river that divided Ivory Mountain from some of the other high peaks.

I knew from childhood that Ivory Mountain had a mysterious rep, having to do with magic. I didn't want to risk going straight to it, so I chose the trade route between the two biggest rivers, where, yes, the most traffic was constantly moving to and fro. I hoped there'd be safety in numbers. The idea was to cruise as unobtrusively as possible to the big trade city, Zhavlir, which lay at the fork of the great rivers. Hang a left to the west. After crossing the Northsca, zap south into the valley.

That was my plan.

I'd also planned to reach Zhavlir in a week—Southern California freeway flyer optimism!

My reeducation began with a high-pressure front squatted over the sweating countryside, forcing all traffic to a crawl except maybe on the military roads, which were beautifully maintained by mages paid out of the king's coffers.

When at last the weather broke I was scarcely halfway to the city, still angling up to the northwest, my butt sore, my clothes soggy, the mare slow. I wished I had my old junkmobile, which (when it was working) at least had air conditioning. Better, I could rev the thing up to sixty miles per hour instead of the two to five I was sort of making now. I'd been on the road a week and a day. That last morning dawned hotter than ever. The sultry stillness began with a peculiar sheen to the light that gradually oranged and blended into shadow as overhead a massive storm boiled up, ready to rock and roll.

And rock and roll it did.

The rain felt good for about the first thirty seconds, until the wind rose. A sudden, cold wind drove stinging hailstones directly into my face and hands. The hail peppered my poor mare, who snorted, skittish with ill temper, and who could blame her? The blackish green clouds barely cleared the lashing treetops. The light vanished, and my mare now plodded, head low, directly into the oncoming storm sweeping down from the northwest.

The road soon turned to muddy slosh, caking her hooves and slowing her so much we seemed to be squelching in one place.

After a couple of ice ages, I realized I was not hallucinating, there really were lights somewhere beyond. I threw back my aching head, peering blearily. Yes. Real lights, glimmering through the downpour. At least the hail had given over to real rain, but so much, so quick, it was like a hose turned onto my head, and I had to breathe behind my hand.

The mare picked up her pace. The lights appeared to recede and I wondered miserably if mirages also came with cold and wet, but then the wind brought the warm scent of horse and hay. A stable! And between one shower and the next, I glimpsed the silhouette of a long, rambling building. Inn? Farmhouse?

Whatever it was, I vowed, they were going to take me as a guest, or discover my frozen corpse on their doorstep come morning, seriously lowering their property values.

Someone called out. The words blurred in the hissing roar. With my waning strength I kept my gaze on that square of golden light, which resolved into a broad, open door, like the gates to heaven.

Silhouettes emerged, one bearing a swinging lantern. I rode past them into the barn, and stopped. Warmth gradually dissolved the grip of cold, and sound returned, the flutter of wings and fretful murmling of birds in the rafters overhead, refugees, like me, from the storm. Around me, the quiet voice of command, and response of obedience.

Gradually I regained sight. Lantern flames flickered in the eddies of wind, reaching into the warm stable, their light stippling with gold the edges of a pile of hay, gleaming along neatly hung lengths of horse harnesses, and on people dressed in uniform color.

I had yet to dismount, though someone held my horse's bridle, waiting patiently. I stared uncomprehending into the faces of a group of young men and a couple of young women. In brown. With little silver cups stitched over the heart.

Sound, sight, and finally sense.

I had fumbled my way into a military outpost.

SEVEN

THE DROUGHT-BREAKING STORM was a major weather front, catching the entire east end of the continent.

All over the kingdom people reacted, either running out to celebrate, or rushing about trying to save things that wet would ruin. Most snugged up inside of castles or cottages, barns or shops, and those on the road sought the shelter of trees or cliff sides.

Out on the sea, traders, navy, smugglers, fishers and pirates alike lay up under mostly bare poles with a scrap of sail to keep them pointed into the wind, and rode it out.

War Commander Randart, having kicked the captain out of his cabin on the ship he'd declared as his flag, sat with his meal uneaten before him, fighting against rage. The king had done *what?*

The report lay on the table, the words mocking him: . . . *promised a treason trial for the prisoners taken along with Princess Atanial.*

Randart shook his head in disgust. Canardan was getting weaker every year. Why not just line them all up and have them shot, in as public an execution as possible? That would end his dilemma with rumors.

At least there was one possibility. Randart could show him how it could be done. Soon as he finished this pirate mission, he'd have those old guardsmen of Prince Math's, Silvag and Folgothan, taken out and shot in a public execution, under military law. That would demonstrate effectively how Canardan ought to handle those fools, and Randart would not have to say a word. It would all be in accordance with military regulations — the ones Randart himself had designed, and Canardan had signed into law.

He balled up the paper and tossed it out one of the stern windows into the storm.

Some welcomed the rain as a chance to escape snooping eyes.

Just outside of Ellir two columns of cadets, riding inland toward the siege war game they'd all been looking forward to, heard the horns call for camp setup, and they gladly broke ranks. Cursing, laughing, calling out insults, they dismounted and stumbled through the furious rain toward their places.

Camp setup was something you began in your first year. The senior cadets under the command of Damedran Randart oversaw the younger students. In good weather, watched by the critical eyes of the adult captains, they were fast, quiet, and bored. The storm freed them from constraint, and though everyone knew what to do, setting up tents in that splashing downpour was an adventure. As the adults were safely busy, there were surreptitious mud fights (the evidence, they knew, would soon rinse off) and some running around. It was fun and also a relief, so strict had been discipline in the temper-exasperating heat of the past three days.

Ban found his arm gripped as he struggled with his team to get the picket line set up. He whipped around, violently flinging off the hand. But he saw Damedran's face reflected in the ruddy glow of a torch.

Damedran jerked his chin over his shoulder. Ban followed. Not to the command tent, which was a misshapen giant mushroom full of snickering, cursing bumps and lumps as the setup crew tried to raise it from inside. Damedran led him to a clump of hardy trees a ways away. They stopped under the foliage, rain rattling the tossing leaves overhead.

"What," Ban shouted.

Damedran put his mouth near Ban's ear. "I think the sheep knows about the invasion."

"What?" Same word, but entirely different intonation.

"I've been thinking. What he said. On that yacht. Not outright. Mostly about what we ought to be doing in training next spring. You know. The hide-and-attack games."

"You told us that. I already told you it's a great idea. Bowsprit, even your cousin thinks so. Everybody does. Except your uncle. Won't let us change the training. So what can *we* do about it?"

"Not that." Damedran shook his head again. "Right before we got off the yacht, the sheep said something about those outsiders who pinched the prizes at the games and scragged my cousin Wolfie and Red. One said something about Norsunder going to war soon."

Warning tightened Ban's shoulders. The wind shifted, bringing a whiff of hot olive oil from the direction of the cook tent, then the cold wind snapped it away. "And?"

"Told Father, who told Uncle Dannath. Before we left. But he just laughed."

Ban shoved his fingers into his armpits. The storm had caught them too fast for them to fetch their gloves from the baggage train. "If the warning came from Prince Jehan, of course your uncle and your father won't listen."

"But I didn't tell that part. I told Father I'd heard it. Gossip. That's one reason why I waited all week. Father reported it to my uncle, then told me Uncle Dannath says I'll hear that all my life from cowards. Slackers. Fools."

Ban shook his head, thinking, *Why am I hearing this instead of Red or even Wolfie?* "Who were those fellows? I mean, how could a nine-year-old have the strength to dust four of us?"

Damedran shook his head. "I asked Wolfie that first thing. I thought the brat snuck up and brained them from behind one by one. Wolfie said they all four tried to take him on, teach him a lesson. Said it wasn't strength, it was that he always seemed to know what they were going to do before they did it, and then he knew exactly where to hit that hurt the most. Wolfie said he could have killed them all if he'd wanted to. The brat didn't even break a sweat. What kind of training teaches an undersized brat to do that?"

Ban shook his head. "I dunno. So why were they even here?"

"And why did they single out the sheep to give their warning to?"

"I think the sheep isn't a sheep at all," Ban said, voicing an inner conviction he'd never thought he'd share.

But Damedran did not scoff. They fell silent, neither quite looking at the other.

Damedran said, "I don't know what to do."

"Nothing."

Damedran frowned at Ban, meeting his gaze at last.

Ban relented. Damedran had been different since that day. He could be setting Ban up, but his instinct was against it. "There's nothing we can do. We're under orders, at the very bottom of the chain of command."

Damedran scowled. Ban was right. What was the good of being senior in rank above all the cadets if the only orders you could give were how many paces apart the tents had to be pitched?

"The real captains don't listen to us," Ban went on. "Your father listens only to your uncle. The king, too. They have their plans. We aren't going to change those." When Damedran ducked his head and grimaced in agreement, he added, "I think it's better to wait. Keep our ears open. Because one of these days we'll find someone who does listen." *Like King Math, if he ever returns.*

Damedran frowned at the runnel of muddy water flowing over his boots, carrying twigs and yellow-edged leaves. The storm was lifting enough to permit some light.

Light. They'd be seen.

Damedran said, "All right. Then we'll wait."

They ran off to resume their duties.

At the same time, not far to the southwest, the proximity of the western mountains caused the air to roil and boil, sending lightning and thunder smashing across the sky.

Under cover of it, Devli Eban and his cousin Nad sped from the mage house where they were staying, circling around and climbing up onto the roof.

There they huddled under the eave of the servants' dormer window, which was shut tight and shuttered.

Ever since Devli had arrived back, they'd longed for a chance to speak to one another, but hadn't dared — not after Nad read the note Devli had slipped into his hand that night:

We have two spies among us, one for the prince and the other for the king.

Now they looked at one another, and as soon as the thunder overhead died away, Devli said, "What is the gossip about me?"

"They told us you got captured along with Prince Math's daughter by the pirate Zathdar, but you escaped. Had to make your way cross-country on foot, as they'd taken your transfer tokens, and you were afraid you were warded by the king's mages so you couldn't use the regular Transfer Destination. How much of that is true?"

Devli looked into his cousin's round face, blotched by cold. At least the worst of the rain was hitting the other side of the building. "Only that I was with them. We were on the pirate ship. When I was let go, I transferred outside of town. I lied to cover how long I was gone, because the king's got at least one spy with us."

Nad pursed his lips in a soundless whistle, knowing how very dangerous it was to transfer anywhere you either hadn't a Destination made safe for transferring, or had laid a token down somewhere in preparation.

"And the prince has a spy with us," Nad prompted. "That's

what your note said."

"Here's what I didn't tell anyone." Devli leaned close. "The pirate Zathdar is none other than Prince Jehan."

Nad's jaw dropped.

"I swore on my honor not to tell, and they let me go. They didn't have to, but he believed me. But I've always told you everything, because we've been like brothers. I won't tell anyone else, and I haven't. So you have to promise, too. And keep it."

"I swear."

Devli let out a shaky sigh. "He's on our side. I'm convinced he's telling the truth, though he's living a lie. He wouldn't tell me everything."

Nad gave a single nod. If the prince had suddenly and readily supplied answers to all Devli's questions, that would have been suspicious. "What convinced you?"

"He wants Prince Math back, and before spring."

"So he believes the invasion rumor is true?"

"Yes."

"And so he'll turn against his father?"

"Said he wants to avoid that. Wants Prince Math back, who is the only one who can stop the invasion, and find some solution with King Canardan."

"If." Nad winced. "If. Two big ifs. What are we supposed to do?"

"Find out who is spying, and what they are reporting. Learn what we can of Magister Zhavic and Magister Perran's orders from the king, though I know Magister Wesec is trying to do that."

Neither had to express what they thought of adult efforts to do anything. They liked Magister Wesec. She was an excellent teacher and a fine mage, but it seemed odd that she couldn't keep out spies, or break the king's mages' wards. But then neither could the king's mages break her wards, and everyone knew they tried.

Adults were just incompetent sometimes.

"And stand ready to aid in the search for Prince Math."

Nad thought rapidly as rain poured between the warped

shingles and down the back of his neck. He still wasn't convinced about the royal heir. But these two orders, they did not require any action from him that was morally reprehensible. Everyone in the resistance wanted to know what Zhavic and Perran were doing on the king's behalf. Everybody dreaded hearing that the king's mages were no longer claiming to be neutral, but had allied with the war commander.

Devli said, "Prince Jehan said we ought to find that acceptable to conscience and vows."

Well, if that was true, it argued for a good prince, didn't it?

Nad still wasn't sure. But he could think it all through later. "What about Prince Math's daughter?"

"Zath—the pr—he took her away. I don't think she wanted to stay with him. My sister certainly didn't. And there's the other trouble. My sister."

Nad blinked rain from his eyelashes. "Elva knows?"

"She discovered the ruse on her own. But she wouldn't believe him and went back to sea."

Nad winced, thinking of his stubborn cousin. "Won't help the prince if she's blabbing his secret all over. Trouble indeed. Royal trouble."

"She won't," Devli said. "Promised. What worries me is that she hired out onto a ship that got commandeered into Randart's fleet. Which is right now chasing the pirate ships. Zathdar's pirate ships."

"Zathdar who is really Prince Jehan."

"Right."

A silvery bell chimed inside, calling the mage students to study. In silence the two young men climbed down, separated and returned to the house via different doors.

And in Vadnais, thunder rolled across the sky, cursed by the musicians, flower arrangers, cooks, and servers who had been hired by the ambassador of Colend for the river-barge party she had planned as a return gesture for the lovely masquerade ball.

Overlooking the bend in the river where the barges rocked—the blossoms from their ruined garlands strewn over the quay in multicolored profusion—was the old audience hall, opened up today because of the mass of petitioners who had arrived on orders of the Guild Council. Safety in numbers was the whispered word, and so they stood all round the walls in a room still slumberous with yesterday's heat as the storm flashed and rumbled, making it impossible to hear the king and the Chief of the Guild Council.

Canardan, oppressed by the heat, the smells of too many close-packed bodies in the still room, and above all by the fact that he could not get around the fool treaty, wished Randart were here to clear them all out at the point of a sword. He wished even more fervently that his son and heir would not slouch over there watching the rain beat against the windows, his profile so obviously bored.

"Yes," Canardan said heavily, before yet another guild master or mistress could belly forward and launch into a bad reading of four or five close-written pages, borrowing the most tedious phrases from old history books. "I see your point. And I promise there will be a hearing, attended by guild representatives as well as those of government, mage and military."

The Chief of the Guild Council bowed. The guild masters and mistresses bowed. Canardan nodded, bending forward to lay his seal on the hot wax of the proclamation the scribe had written.

He noticed, distracted, that Jehan had slipped out, and shook his head. If only the boy had a head for governing.

The room began to empty. Suddenly stifled beyond bearing, Canardan rose, unlatched one of the long mullioned windows and let the wind blow in to cool his face, not hearing the muffled exclamations and curses of his scribes who dashed about trying to catch the flurry of papers that had taken to the air.

EIGHT

LIGHTNING FLICKERED AND THUNDER rumbled like an avalanche of mountain-sized boulders across the sky as Prince Jehan ran up the backstairs, pausing long enough to note where everyone was.

Chas, as he'd hoped, had marshaled all the royal servants to straighten the king's rooms which, because the king had commanded all his windows to be opened that morning, were a welter of puddles, papers, and anything else that was not too heavy for the wind to smite spinning into chaos.

Jehan paused at his own rooms long enough to motion for Kazdi, bent on the same task, to follow. The boy left the other servants working, shutting the door to the outer parlor on his heels.

"Guard the stairs," Jehan murmured.

Kazdi frowned. "Decoy?"

"Do it. Use the rock collection."

The boy zipped inside the room, emerging with a silver bowl of exquisite crystal stones, which he scattered all over the landing, resting the bowl inside the door. Then he took up a stance from which he could see in all directions while Jehan raced up the marble stairs four at a time and down the hall to the tower where Atanial had been isolated. He stopped at the landing of her own stairway, where he suspected the spy-wards bordered — the larger the wards, the harder they were to maintain. He whistled the calls of night birds until apparently she recognized one of them as an anomaly and came herself to investigate.

She ran toward him, fists pressed together under her throat. "What is it?"

"Stop there."

She jolted to a stop, her hands flinging out wide as she pressed herself against the wall.

"It's the wards," he finished.

"I get it." Her brow cleared. "If I cross, the mage spies know. Or if you cross."

"Right. Chas is busy cleaning up the mess in the king's rooms and making sure none of the other servants get a look at his papers. We probably have a few moments to talk."

Atanial clasped her hands again. "You saw Sasha. She's really all right?"

"She's fine, as of last night. Riding west of Ellir. Listen. My father agreed to a hearing for the conspirators."

Atanial did not waste time quibbling over the term. "And?"

"And so it frees you, do you see it?"

She frowned down at her tightly clasped hands, then looked up, eyes narrowed. The expression, so much like her daughter's when she reached a conclusion, acted like a hammer inside his chest.

She said, "He can't use their lives against me, not now. Is that it?"

"Yes. I will see what I can do to get you out."

"Tell me more. Tell me what's happening."

"The cadets from Ellir Academy are on their way to their siege. Most of the harbor guards from three harbors are marching inland, ostensibly to war games."

"That much I gathered. What does it mean? It's not really war games at all?"

"Oh, they'll play their extended war game through the harvest season, right enough. But the games will go on so long that they will be caught by surprise by the first snow, in which case they'll have to winter along the border—"

She drew in a breath. "I see."

"—where supplies will be carried over the next two months, stockpiled against spring, as harvest goods are carried in all directions. They can then launch an invasion over the border at the first snowmelt." Because she not only seemed to comprehend, but was waiting for more, he said swiftly, "Leaving the harbors and coastline all but unguarded. Randart is busy making sure the coast is safe by his definition right now."

"Pirate hunting, right?"

"The excuse is pirate hunting, but what he's really going to do is clear the seas of anyone he deems inconvenient."

Atanial said, "I don't understand. So you rescued Sasha from the pirate?"

"I am the pirate."

She pressed her knuckles against her forehead.

"I've been—"

"Wait. Wait. What were you doing before we showed up in this world?"

"Raiding the coast to keep the army pinned down there. Well away from the border."

"And dropped everything to chase after my daughter?"

"I found out about Prince Math's ten-year spell at the same time as Zhavic and Perran did. I couldn't get to your world to warn you, but I got to the old castle in case they brought either of you back."

She let out a long breath. "Our timing," she said with Sasha's crooked smile, "could hardly have been worse. Though it was not our fault we're here in the first place."

"Yes," he said, because there was no time for anything but the truth.

"Does Sasha know that?"

"No."

Atanial rubbed her eyes again. "I see. She wouldn't listen."

"It was a matter of trust."

"I know. I'm afraid that's my fault—"

A soft whistle from below caused her to freeze, poised for flight.

Jehan motioned her back to her rooms, and they parted, both frustrated to the max.

Voices echoed up the marble stairwell. They belonged to Chas and Kazdi. The boy was busy shuffling gap-mouthed around outside the prince's rooms, cleaning up the stones.

". . . where is the royal heir?"

"Haven't seen him," Kazdi replied in his adolescent honk. "We've been here trying to restore order. The windows were open, and—"

The voices faded behind Jehan as he soft-footed down the hall in the other direction. He slipped into the dusty royal guest chambers, unused for years, and through the servants' door there, as Chas reached the landing where he'd been before—to find it empty.

Chas cursed, ran back downstairs and dispersed with a few curt words his other trusted spies, who had been ordered by Randart to know where the prince was at all times.

When at last they found him, he was sitting peaceably at a table in the heralds' archive where the air was still and cool and the storm a rare low mutter. He was busy translating an old Sartoran treatise on the symbolism of flowers. He began a long, cheerful explanation of the treatise to Chas. "Do you not think this a fine gift for the Colendi ambassador when she reschedules her barge party?"

Chas bowed, effaced himself, and placed a servant on watch in the outer chamber. Idiot!

Hours later Jehan finally was able to get to his rooms and grab a moment of privacy. Not that he expected any messages. Surely the entire kingdom had been grounded by the storm.

But there was one. From Owl.

Lost her in the storm.

NINE

OH, NICE GOING, SASHARIA Disaster Zhavalieshin. I stared in dismay at the cheerful faces surrounding me.

There was absolutely no chance of escape. The mare drooped in exhaustion, and I shivered so violently I didn't think I could walk, much less ride.

They were waiting for an answer, and I hadn't even heard the question.

Not that it wasn't easy to guess what they wanted to know: Who are you and where are you going?

What kind of lie could I possibly tell now that wouldn't just cause more questions? Various stupid scams flitted through my mind, but it was one of the warriors that actually gave me my out.

"Maybe she's a foreigner," one muttered.

"That would explain her getting on the military roads," a woman as tall as me spoke next, tossing back her short, curly auburn hair. "A foreigner wouldn't know about the laws."

"Likely blundered over at the river bend," a fellow behind me said. "It's the only place the two roads are close. Mare probably found the better footing, and there she goes."

So far, they weren't suspicious or angry, only curious. Or resigned, as they briefly disparaged the "river-bend turn," one of them adding in a sour voice, "You know who's gonna be detailed to build a wall between the two roads."

I worked my numb lips, gesturing with my cold hands. They all fell silent. Marshaling all my knowledge of cartoon-character fake accents, I said, "Sheep. Shi-i-i-ip?" I mimed going up and down on waves. "Sailor." I hit my tunic front with a loud, wet smack. I scowled. "Pie-rats."

"Pirates!" the tall woman exclaimed. "Wager you anything they got hit by Zathdar's gang."

The others all made noises of agreement.

She turned back to me. "But what are you doing inland?"

I stared, uncomprehending, and one of the fellows said in a loud, distinct voice, as if loudness magically translated into other languages, "Where-do-you-come-from-and-why-are-you-here?"

I dismounted, my sodden clothing slapping against my limbs. I patted the horse, and pointed outside. "Home. Road." I pointed west, waving my hand in a circle that encompassed most of the broadest continent in the world.

"Her ship must have been grounded by pirates. Or they were raided, and the crew turned off." The woman addressed me slowly and loudly. "Where you from? Not Locan Jora—"

"Naw, they talk like us," someone else said.

"Not Colendi either, I know a Colendi accent," a younger guy spoke up.

"Oh, well, your kingness," the big guy behind me retorted, and they all laughed.

"But I do! I got a cousin in service inside the—"

"Stow it. And your cousin too. She's no Colendi, or where's her coach and eight matched horses, diamonds and the like?"

"They're not *all* toffs. That's not even possible. My cousin's a cook—"

"All Colendi swank," the woman said, and the others made derisive noises of agreement.

The young guy sighed, eyes rolling up toward the ceiling.

Then they all started guessing, naming kingdoms—Devrea, Arland, Sarendan, Gyrn, Deshlen. Recalling some of the names I'd seen on that exquisite map aboard the ship while practicing the

Khanerenth alphabet, I waited until they reached a couple of countries a bit farther west, and when one said, "Melia!" and another, "Couldn't be Tser Mearsies?" I nodded violently, pointing somewhere between the two.

Triumph turned into a sick hiccup when the big guy came round front. He was a full head taller than I, broad face like granite, and a pleasant, helpful expression as he said, "Doesn't Farhan speak Mearsies?"

I tried to hide my dismay.

The woman thumped him on the arm with her fist. I was surprised she didn't break her knuckles. "Don't you remember? Farhan got orders to run with one of the siege attack teams."

They expressed sympathetic disappointment on my behalf. I beamed, unable to hide my relief, and they took it as a complete lack of comprehension.

"Never mind," the youngest one declared to me, loudly and distinctly. "Come. We show you. Eat. Dry out."

"Ee-e-e-et. Dry-y-y-y ou-u-u-ut." I nodded like one of those bobbing toy things some people put in the back windows of their cars.

They surrounded me, everyone using loud voices, as if I were deaf and stupid. I shrugged, smiled, and hefted my pack over my shoulder.

The warriors led me through a side door into a long hall that smelled of old cabbage, the oil they use on their weapons and wet wood. When we reached a big office, they all straightened up.

The woman seemed to be taking a silent vote with her eyes—she was chosen—so she motioned me into the big room, where we found an older man seated behind a desk, a woman maybe ten years older than I at the wall, in the process of sticking pins in a big map. They turned around. After a quick exchange, the commander gave permission to house me until morning in the women's barracks, adding, "Make certain she gets to the civ road at first light."

"Yes, Captain."

Next upstairs, where ten or twelve bunks lined the walls of a steep-roofed room. "Here's where you sleep." My guide pointed to the single bed with no gear hanging next to it and no chest neatly stored beneath it. As I hesitated, thinking of my wet pack, she took it out of my hands, which were beginning to tingle as they warmed, and yanked it open. "Here, let's spread your things out. See? Spread. Out. Make sure dry." She gestured with one hand, as she pulled things out with the other, hesitating when she saw the rolled firebird coverlet. She whistled. "Where did you get *that*?"

I grinned, rubbing my fingers with my thumb. "Buy. Much gold!"

"Oh yes, I'd say. You must have used half a year's pay, unless sailors make ten times what we do. Phew, either you really love your family or you've got one handsome fellow waiting at home. Marda, come here, see this."

"What? You got the foreigner in there?"

Three women entered, all of them exclaiming. "That's a Zhavalieshin firebird! Aren't those against the law?"

"Naw, only banners."

"That *is* a banner."

"And someone who knows it's against the law obviously sold it off. Very sensible. She probably got it for a fraction of the real value. Hey! What's this?"

As they spread the firebird coverlet out with careful fingers the innkeeper's letter slid out and landed on the clean-swept wooden floor.

Another woman picked it up and looked at the address. "Three Falls Inn. Zhavlir. She must be running as a courier, to save the scribe-runner cost."

"I would," someone else spoke up. "You run letters, especially for inns, they almost always give you at least a meal, sometimes a free bed."

"Wonder how they got the idea across."

My auburn companion grinned. "They probably do the same

in Tser Mearsies. Just because she lacks our language doesn't mean she's ignorant about regular life." She turned to me. "What's your name?" She thumbed the front of her tunic, saying, "Britki. That's Marda." She poked one of her friends. "Name! Britki. Marda."

I was ready for that one. "Lasva." I patted my soggy clothes, which made a wet smacking sound.

"Poor thing, she's got to be icy in that stuff. Let's get her before the fire."

"Cleaning frame first." Marda laid my coverlet out on the bed.

The third one put the letter next to it and they led me to the cleaning frame, which zapped away sweat and mud. The women took me downstairs, chattering past me as they decided between them that because of the wicked Zathdar my ship had been raided and the sailors set ashore.

As we gathered round a long plank table, they happily cursed Zathdar, whose raids had kept a lot of their friends on double-duty patrolling along the coast all during the summer, until the fleet recently set sail.

Then out came dinner: fresh cornbread, a thick pepper soup with cheese crumbled on top, and three kinds of layered fruit tarts. They got tired of shouting questions at me while I shrugged and smiled. Gradually they fell into their own conversations.

They reminded me of armed-services people at home — most of them big and buff, cheerful, neat either by inclination or by habit after years of inspections, full of jokes told in their own particular slang, jokes aimed at one another as well as their daily routine. The atmosphere was one of friendly rivalry, but the really creative commentary was reserved for the upper command.

"Didn't I say? Didn't I say?" one guy demanded, waving his fork, after someone commented about the storm. "We're going to end up way out in the field up to our butt cheeks in snow before the rankers wake up and notice winter's here."

"No they won't," a woman retorted, arms crossed. "Because *they'll* be kipped out inside the castle, whooping it up in disgusting luxury. It's only *us* who'll be frozen."

Everyone laughed except the big guy, who shook his head. "Too late in the season for a big war game. Autumn's gonna be short this year. You can smell it in the air. Crazy. Why not in spring, like it used to be? We're gonna end up stuck in the snow."

Bets were exchanged with brisk efficiency while others griped. Not revolutionary stuff. Nobody as much as looked over a shoulder. If anyone questioned the right of the Randarts to order what sounded like a massive siege war game involving nearly the entire army, they didn't do it here. The griping was entirely confined to what seemed foolish timing, and what it would mean down at grunt level.

After the meal most of them vanished on various night duties; those off duty did the usual things people do when there is no television. They talked, mended uniforms, played card games. A couple of people played instruments—a kind of flute-recorder that did not need a reed and a stringed instrument—and one fellow with a good voice sang either love songs or funny marching songs with jokes I did not understand.

Their cards are all hand painted, and though I could see a kind of relation to our deck, it was different. Six suits, for one thing. The most popular game was with cards and markers, reminding me of bridge and chess at the same time. They did invite me in. From their manner, they believed a sailor would know this game so it had to be universal. I hunkered down by the fire, indicating I would sit there and dry out my clothes as I watched them play.

I was forgotten. I meant to listen more, hoping to find out something useful, but as a spy I was worthless. If anything of import was discussed, I wouldn't know how to identify it. Canardan's name had never come up, much less Jehan's or my mother's, or even anything about me. All I got glimpses of were their personal lives.

When I was dry, I was so tired I gave up the spy game and retreated upstairs to sleep. I didn't even waken when the midnight watch changed.

I woke with the others at the dawn bell. After breakfast, two of the women led me to the stable, where my mare had obviously had a good night. She was freshly curried, fed and ready to go. Even my weapon in the saddle sheath, which I'd stupidly left to rust forgotten, had been taken out, cleaned and oiled for me. I thanked everyone in sight.

We rode out into the cool morning air, frost lying lightly on grass and stippling the edges of leaves, drifts of vapor rendering the farmland countryside into a kind of etching. The military road was hard-packed dirt kept by magic as smooth as asphalt. It cut straight through property. But military roads were forbidden to civilians, and so we crossed a couple of meadows, riding under dripping trees, to the regular road—pot-holed, soggy and winding.

The women pointed to the northwest, saying loudly, "Zhavlir that way." I nodded, thanked them, they wished me well in words of one syllable, and I departed, delighted that I'd managed to get out of what could have been major danger. It had not only been easy, it hadn't cost anything!

While behind me, as part of the routine, my hosts wrote me into the daily watch report: *Civilian sailor strayed off the civilian road during storm, female, tall, blond, hazel eyes, name Lasva, from Tser Mearsies. Carrying only personal gear plus a letter from one inn to another, the only item of interest a silken banner in the old Zhavalieshin style.*

TEN

THE NEXT STRETCH OF time brought bands of rain, nothing as spectacular as the storm that broke the summer. The air cooled gradually, and all over the kingdom, harvesters labored madly to get the crops in before another storm came, maybe a worse one, to destroy everything.

So while people concentrated on harvest and storage, and the military were converging on the castle chosen for the siege game, out on the ocean, War Commander Randart's navy chased elusive ships while the war commander cursed.

For several days he'd mostly caught up on his sleep. But after that, time seemed to wear with excruciating slowness. Though he had his magical message case, he hated using it because he was convinced the mages read his messages, though they swore they didn't. It was, after all, what he'd do if he possibly could. Including lie.

That was the worst of it. He didn't really know what magic could and could not do. Even if he asked, he wouldn't believe the answer. Yet Canardan insisted he cooperate with the mages, and even include one on the flagship. "Show good faith," the king had written in a final order. "Who knows? They might even be useful. By whatever means it takes, I want that pirate hanged!"

Randart had obeyed because he must, privately resolving that he would call upon the mage only if there was no other way around it.

That was before several weeks of frustration and incompetence from everyone around him. The merchant ship he'd chosen as the flag seemed incapable of running with proper military order, and the second fleet was always reporting sightings of possible pirates, but no catches. If Bragail wasn't lying, that had to mean the pirates were playing catch-me-if-you-can.

Finally Randart issued the order for the entire fleet to converge. He would stretch the fleet in a net and sweep the entire coast of Khanerenth, as far out into the sea as they could reach, and burn *everything* that had no proper papers.

At dawn a few days later, a scout craft appeared with crowded sail, signals flying. The pirate was on the horizon. Not one of his many underlings, but the *Zathdar*, bold as the sun, riding just within view of the spyglass.

The pirate matched the fleet's speed, keeping the same distance between them.

Randart summoned the merchant captain and ordered him to catch the *Zathdar*, packing on as many sails as needed.

The captain said shortly, "He has the wind. Sir."

"Which means what?"

"Which means he can sheer off any time he wants to, or he can sail down and engage us. He's faster. We can only catch him if the wind shifts."

"Is it likely to do that?"

A shrug was the answer. Irritated, Randart waved him off of his own captain's deck as he stared through his glass at the pirate vessel etched against the morning sky. At last he said without losing sight of the ship, "Get the mage."

Rapid footsteps thumped down the stairs to the companionway and below. Randart watched sailors form a line along the companionway, holding long ropes in order to do something with the sails. He listened to the patter of bare feet around him, the creak of rope and wood, and the whappita-whap of sails being lowered or raised or changed. Somewhere on the other side of the ship, the sailors talked incomprehensible slang as they prepared for an approaching boat. His orders were to chase and close. The sailors were doing the best they could, he could see it, but ships were so *slow*. With a horse under you, you at least moved, and even better was . . .

A quiet step behind and he looked down at the short, stout woman the mages had sent him. She was probably thirty or forty, her expertise was in preserving wood (useful on a ship) and if she'd ever expressed the slightest interest in political power, no one within Randart's extensive spy net had heard it.

He had forgotten her name. "Do you see the pirate?"

She narrowed her gray eyes, pursed her lips so her double chin tripled, and gazed out to sea. He did not offer his glass, nor did she ask for it. They stood there in silence for a moment as the ship rose on a swell, then thumped down, and behind, cries and knocks indicated the approaching boat was hooking on.

The mage finally said, "Just barely."

"Tell me in plain language why I cannot transfer my force to it by magic, since we can see it. I know that magic requires a clear destination. That ship seems clear enough to me."

"First, we can only transfer one or two at most, and the transfer spells must be prepared for. Second, yon ship is not clear enough for transfer," she said.

"Then I'll give you my glass, which I assure you brings details close. I can make out the damned pirates doing whatever it is they do to sails. I can see the planking along the side of the pirate ship. I can see the ropes at either side of each mast."

"But that does not constitute a proper Destination."

"Plain language," he snapped. "I want a concise field report. And if you don't know what that is, I am going to suggest that Perran and Zhavic include basic skills in whatever it is they teach you people before they let you out in the world."

Her cheeks flushed, but her tone was steady, and her gaze stayed on the pirate ship. "You can see the details of the sides of the ship. You can see sails. You can see masts. Is that correct?"

"Yes."

"But you cannot see the details of the deck."

"No."

"If you wish to be transferred"—her tone totally devoid of irony—"you would wish to appear on the deck. And not halfway through a mast, a sail or the side."

Randart thought of the tiled Destination chambers, and nodded. Now he remembered something of an explanation Mathias Zhavalieshin had given him many years ago. Mages memorized the pattern of the tiles, or you could get lost in whatever-it-was between physical spaces. Forever.

"So either you need Destination tiles, or the equivalent on that deck, or you need transfer tokens. And I remember what transfer tokens do: act as a beacon."

"We call it a focus, but yes. However, there is another very important consideration. Destinations must be kept empty. If someone, or something, is already in the space where you transfer, bad things happen. Two objects cannot occupy the same space at the same time."

Randart grimaced. He'd never been able to bring himself to ask Zhavic these questions, and give Zhavic the pleasure of exposing his ignorance. "They don't . . . melt together, do they?"

"No. That would call for a very strange magic indeed. Transfers are just that, but between spaces, so the newly arrived thing impels itself into the new space. It is the impact with air that hurts so much. If the arrival collides with any object it is thrown aside at violent speed. Things break, people are killed."

"It's the same with transfer tokens?"

"Yes, pretty much. They must always be left on floors or open spaces, or on tables next to open spaces."

So much for salting ships with transfer tokens and sending a force by surprise, Randart thought. And, with a brief spurt of self-mockery, *I wonder how many kings thought they invented that idea first, to find themselves at this same impasse.*

He collapsed the glass with a smack. "Back to the crawling pace of the chase." And, because he had to work with the woman and she'd been prompt and informative, "Thank you, Magister." He still couldn't remember her name.

She bowed and withdrew; at once the aide-de-camp on duty stepped to his side. "Commander, Patrol Leader Samdan is here to report."

Samdan. Randart remembered that name. Samdan was the idiot whose entire patrol couldn't stop a pirate, a girl, and a couple of brats belonging to that traitor Kreki Eban. Randart had wanted Samdan and his fools put up against a wall and shot as an example of what to expect for incompetence, but the king himself had pardoned them, reminding Randart that they were a scratch troop, scarcely trained, culled from road-patrol duty when the best warriors had all been shifted to the coast against pirate raids.

Randart remembered quite clearly that he'd concurred on the orders to reinforce Prince Jehan's small honor guard when he was sent to the old World Gate tower. Randart had also agreed to send the prince to the old castle as he himself was busy hunting the pirate, and hadn't those two fool mages made the world transfer once before, to return empty handed?

But that did not excuse the sheer incompetence of an entire troop, however badly trained, defeated or driven off by four people.

By two, really: the pirate Zathdar and the Zhavalieshin girl.

Randart turned back to glare at that distant ship, now a silhouette against the rising sun. On that thing Zathdar now stood, presumably with Atanial's girl. He also knew Bragail of the *Skate*'s secrets, all of them on Randart's orders. Why hadn't the pirate brandished either the girl or the threat of Bragail's exposure yet? No one could accuse him of lacking in arrogant boldness. What did he want, this pirate bestirring himself in the matters of kings? The very idea of pirates and politics did not make sense.

Randart became aware of the aide still standing there. "Well? Cannot Samdan report to his captain on his own ship?"

The aide lowered his voice slightly. "Said he ought to speak directly to you."

Sharpened interest caused him to nod. "Very well."

Samdan, meanwhile, stood against the rail on the weather side of the ship, watching Randart's back. He'd been living with disgrace for weeks, all the more telling because it was unspoken since the king himself had ordered pardons all round.

The looks and whispers and avoidances resulting were, he'd decided bleakly, far worse than the floggings War Commander Randart handed out. At least those, if you lived through them, were then over. And people didn't hold your mistake against you.

Now he limped forward. His knee where the pirate had stabbed him still hurt. As it should.

Maybe he could retrieve some of his old standing, so easily taken for granted before most of his old cronies began turning their backs or not being around when he slipped away from his mother's place in Ellir, where he'd been sent to convalesce. Ever since the king's pardon, he didn't feel welcome in any of the guards' regular haunts.

That lack of welcome as well as the wish to retrieve his honor had caused him to volunteer when the word went out for supply duty on this pirate expedition.

Now the war commander's dark eyes flicked from his bound knee to his face, his lips curled in contempt. "You had a report you thought I should hear?"

Samdan's heart thudded against his ribs. This was it. He licked his lips. "The navigator. On our boat. I've seen her before. She was one of those with the pirate and the princess, in the old tower."

And watched the contempt in Randart's face clear to surprise, then question. "Are you certain of that?"

Samdan licked his lips again. "I made sure of it. They've had her on night duty, see, or I'd have noticed before. But yesterday she had to do a day rotation, I don't know why. And so when Captain Dembic had us out on deck doing our morning drill, well, there she was behind the wheel, and I knew I'd seen her before. It wasn't until I heard her speak to one of the sailors I got it. She was in the court that day, along with the mage-boy who transferred 'em out."

"Did you say anything to anyone?"

"Only Captain Dembic. She said by rights I should report to you myself."

Randart turned around. Captain Dembic stood at the rail. He beckoned her over, and watched the sturdy, gray-haired woman tromp across the deck. She was his head of supply on the coast. She'd been trustworthy for decades, and also close lipped.

With marked approval, he said, "Does anyone on your ship know about this matter?"

Dembic shook her head. "No, War Commander. Patrol Leader Samdan reported to me, and I gave orders for a boat to the ship captain, but told him it was to make my regular report on your orders."

Randart nodded, recognizing the implication: the use of his name guaranteed no questions, even if the explanation was not strictly true.

"Well done," he said, to both of them. What the king had said about Samdan—*It's our fault, not his, that his training has been so slapdash. If they're lazy, it's because we've let them become that way*—now sounded different. Good material, slapdash training. Yes. The words were different, the morning light looked different, the cold air felt different—full of promise. Randart felt his sour mood lift for the first time in weeks.

He almost smiled as he began issuing a rapid stream of orders.

On board the *Clam Dancer*, the mess bell had rung. Elva yawned as she gladly handed off navigation to the afternoon watch. Two yawns punctuated her repetition of the standing orders; the man taking her place grinned in sympathy, but said nothing. Everyone knew what a middle-of-the-night-till-noon watch was like.

She followed the slumping, shuffling sail crews down to the galley, where, according to universal ship rule, the off-coming watch had first serve on food. She loaded her plate, thumped down at a table, and picked up the square-bottomed mug full of soup. Holding it in tired hands, she sipped, so intent on drinking without slopping as the ship swayed around her she didn't quite notice the sudden silence until the fast tramp of booted feet caused her to frown. Sailors never wore shoes unless it was freezing outside—

Hard hands gripped her arms, yanking her to her feet. Her soup went flying. She tried to twist and fight but was shoved violently face-first onto the table. Her arms were wrenched behind her back and rope bound around them while she struggled to breathe.

The brown uniformed guards muscled her past her astonished mates. At first she was stunned. It wasn't until she was flung down into the boat that it occurred to her that she'd been betrayed. By who? All she could think was, *Prince Jehan.*

Anger replaced the sick horror, fury so hot she could hardly wait until she saw the enemy. And could tell her side of the story.

No one spoke on the trip to the flagship, either to one another or to her. She noted the sound of the oars, the jerking rhythm, the wind and the choppy sea, with a remote part of her mind while righteous anger streamed and streamed, helping her shape what she'd say about the Pirate Prince of Liars.

Everyone aboard the flagship watched their approach, the sailors from the relative safety of the upper yards. Randart had told them nothing, but no one could miss the way he'd suddenly ordered up a patrol of heavily armed warriors from his own personal guard and sent them to the *Clam Dancer* as fast as the rowers could pull them.

No use asking questions. The army didn't talk to anyone except one another, and no one wanted to approach Randart, who during the first day out to sea had had four sailors rope-flogged at the foremast for not taking orders from the warriors, or not getting out of their way, even if the sailors were on duty and the warriors not.

It had been made abundantly clear that sailors and ships existed to serve, were in no way equals, had no rights. Even aboard their own ship. The captain had reminded them in a private meeting down in the hold that they were getting a year's pay if the pirate was apprehended, and to think on that if they didn't want to end up dead.

So the sailors invented reasons to be watching from above, and the warriors from the deck as the boat came back, and what they saw instead of a slinking spy or a glowering traitor among their own kind was a slip of a young woman barely out of girlhood, blood trickling down into one eye from a cut on her scalp, the other side of her face bruising fast from where she'd landed after being thrown into the boat with her hands tied.

Samdan's good mood ended the moment he saw that pale face with the obscene trickle of red dripping down.

Randart clapped him on the back, laughing. "Excellent work, excellent. You shall be in at the kill."

The *kill*?

Samdan watched from his place of honor behind the war commander as the girl was summarily hauled to the deck, and muscled into the spacious cabin that Randart had taken for his own. He was thinking, *I don't want to see any more*, when the war commander gestured for him somewhat impatiently. He'd regained his honor. He'd done his duty. Hadn't he?

Yes. So it was probably fair for him to see the results. Grimly he limped after the war commander, the rest of the guard falling in behind. His knee was throbbing by now; he leaned against a bulkhead as the men found room to stand.

The Eban girl was thrust into a chair.

Randart said, "Don't even bother lying to me." He gestured toward Samdan. "He positively identified you as having been in the courtyard with the pirate the day Atanial Zhavalieshin's daughter appeared through the World Gate, attacked the king's guards sent to meet her, and vanished. Using, I understand, magic done by your renegade brother."

Samdan saw the girl's eyes widen and her lips part in surprise. Then a flush of—relief? No, it couldn't be.

Relief it was, followed by sorrow, and anger. Elva, her head aching, her muscles trembling over watery bones, recognized how close she'd come to betrayal. *It wasn't Prince Jehan. He kept his word.*

She hated his guts, but he had kept his word.

So she had to keep hers.

"I don't know anything," she said shortly.

Randart stepped forward and struck her across the face so hard he knocked her out of the chair. He gestured for the guard to pluck her off the floor and plunk her back onto the chair.

She blinked, her cheek now smeared with blood.

"Let's begin again," Randart said pleasantly. For the first time in weeks, he was enjoying himself very much. "Where were you transferred, and where, exactly, did the pirate take the Zhavalieshin girl? What was your part in all that?"

"He dumped my brother and me as soon as we transferred," she said through rapidly swelling lips. "Didn't want us. Only her. For ransom, he said."

"She went willingly?"

"No."

"What happened next?"

"Left us behind. Took her away. Pirate escort."

Randart leaned forward. "You mean I am supposed to believe that the pirate Zathdar happened, without any previous communication with you or your brother, to pop up at the tower the very day your brother crossed to the other world, and you had no idea he'd be there?"

"He had spies. Following Devli."

"Spies, is it? But you fought alongside him anyway, against the king's own? Did the pirate have a knife at your back?"

Elva flushed. "We wanted to save her from *you*. You already know we're fighting to restore Prince Math to the throne—"

Randart struck her again, so hard she lay stunned, gazing up at the bulkhead above.

"Prince Math," he stated in a soft, deadly voice, "is dead. Or gone, living it up somewhere far away. There is, you may have noticed, a legally crowned king."

Randart was aware of stirrings and shufflings around him. He would have loved to beat some sense into this arrogant scrub, but not here, not now. Some of these fools were young enough to be sentimental, obviously.

"Get the mage. Tell her to bring kinthus. We'll get the truth without any further exertion. After that you may take this traitor out and hang her from one of those poles, good and high so all can see. I think our friends working the sails need a reminder of who the lawful king is, and what upholding the law means."

Below, Magister Lorat was expecting some sort of summons. Randart's voice had carried through the scuttle quite clearly, and she had been writing his words as they were spoken. She had enough time to twist the tiny paper up, drop it into her magical transfer case and send it to Magister Zhavic by the time the banging came on her door.

She slid the case into the pocket in her robe and turned to fetch her herbs, including her vial of the powder made from the kinthus plant, carefully dried and ground into a concentrate of dangerous power that could so easily part spirit from body.

There was no time to wait for orders from the king's mage, but then he could not countermand the king's war commander. She would have to do as she was told.

She trod up to the captain's cabin, and said nothing when she found her victim lying on the deck where she'd fallen. She said nothing when she saw the look in the girl's eyes, not dazzlement, but a single-minded concentration.

Her brother is a mage student, Lorat thought. Her own observations had not been commanded and would not be offered. She would do as she was told.

While she slowly and steadily poured water into a waiting

cup, and then measured out the fine powder whose smell was so strong she had to hold her breath — and every man in the room moved back an inadvertent step — she gave the girl as much time as she dared.

o0o

On the third ship out, Captain Tham watched his boat return from the *Dancing Clam* and his trusted first mate clamber up.

Closed in the cabin, the young men stared at one another in dismay — both big, strong, smart, and very loyal to Zathdar. Tham knew his secret identity. The mate hadn't been told, but suspected enough *not* to ask questions.

The first mate said, "Word is, they arrested the daughter of old Steward Eban. Randart is putting her to the question right now."

Tham was writing as the first mate spoke. He sent the message off, and sat back to wait, case in hand. Either the prince got it now, or he wasn't there to get it.

An answer came back almost immediately.

Send notice to Robin: attack, full force. I am on my way.

ELEVEN

Elva lay on the deck, grateful not to be moved. The commander and all his men stood around, looking like brown, frowning statues from this vantage, and maybe it was supposed to be humiliating, and it did hurt with her arms doubled so unnaturally behind her, but lying flat she could fight better against pain, nausea, and fear.

Kinthus. *Focus on the present.*

She stared up at the wood curving overhead. Devli's face, long ago, when he came home on a visit. Took her to the woods, and said, *Did you know there's a trick to getting round green kinthus? The mages taught us, but not all of us can do it.*

Her own voice. *A trick? Teach me.*

She never thought she'd need it, or maybe she did, the way her mother worried every time a messenger came and went. But it seemed fun, it seemed a way to fool *them*, the king's people, and they practiced keeping their thoughts strictly on the present.

Don't think of the past, Devli had said, *or it opens the door to memory. The trick they showed me is to run through all the senses, what you're seeing, hearing, smelling. Right now. If you do it and keep doing it, memory stays locked away. Your mind runs along in the present, and there's nothing they can do.*

She concentrated on the present moment, each sense in turn. When a mage appeared, kneeling down beside her, Elva kept her thoughts on the now. *She's my mother's age, maybe, moving slow — light on the glass — oh, that was a good wave, the lamp swinging, is the wind north by northwest — what grain of wood is that?*

The woman finally slid her hand firmly under the back of Elva's neck and lifted her head enough for her to drink. And she did, because she knew there was no other choice, *Taste — it's actually like chidder-weed and mint, but it makes my nose feel like a sneeze, ugh, ugh, cold, I'm thirsty —*

A blanket seemed to settle over her mind, but she did not examine it. She kept on looking, listening, sniffing, taste, the touch of her fingers bunched behind her, the grit on the deck boards —

"Can you speak?" the mage murmured.

"... the grit of the deck boards feels like sand. Sand at sea, I can't smell it past this kinthus nobody told me it smells like chidweed. We call chidder-weed chid or ..." Elva whispered.

The mage looked up at Randart. "The kinthus has taken hold."

On board the *Zathdar*, Robin, temporary captain, received Tham's note. She carefully slid her magic case deep into a pocket. None of her current crew knew the captain's real identity, though they knew he sometimes had access to transfer magic. Anyone who had enough money could buy transfer tokens.

She placed the one Owl had given her on the table in the captain's cabin, then backed hastily out, closing the door and staring upward, ostensibly watching the set of the sail.

She was wondering how long she'd have to stand there looking stupid when she heard a muffled thump and thud in the cabin behind her. She opened to door to find Prince Jehan getting up from the deck, his complexion the familiar greenish-tinged mask of nausea and pain.

She waited while he leaned on the table, hands gripping the edge of it, as he recovered his balance. Two deep, shuddering breaths, his face flushed red, and he gave the sheen on his forehead a swipe with an exquisitely made cambric shirt sleeve.

That and his white hair were proof he was really a prince in disguise. She always had trouble believing it. She'd always known him as a privateer, until very recently.

"I'm here," he said. "And awake. Status?"

"Fleet downwind, on station in two columns. The *Skate* had been leading the Aloca fleet. They're tacking straight out to sea. They have to be trying to get upwind and close on us, so we've hauled east to keep the wind."

While she spoke, he flung off his clothes, rolling up the expensive linen and cambric. She glimpsed his long, muscular back and shifted her gaze out the stern windows, where she could see the *Jumping Bug* rising on the swell, sails taut. Funny, how when she was small the older men changed in front of everyone, as did the women. You didn't get much privacy on a ship. But when they were little they didn't pay any attention, and Zathdar had always seemed one of the grownups, Owl's generation. Then suddenly — she hadn't really noticed when — he was closer to *her* generation, and, well, you couldn't help *looking*.

So she scowled at the *Jumping Bug*, forcing her mind to shift to the crisis. Attack. Bad enough of a crisis, yes. There's the *Bug* with fighting sail ready, and probably passing out weapons to the fire crews. Ready, waiting for orders to . . . Could even Zathdar take three ships in against half the entire navy?

She swung around, forgetting irrelevancies like personal privacy.

"We're really going to attack Randart's whole *fleet*?"

"Are you ready?" He was pulling on a shirt, brilliant pink, she noted, a flicker of laughter appearing and vanishing back in her mind like a stray sunbeam during a rainstorm. Brilliant pink except for the orange peonies embroidered all over it. The trousers were striped blue and white. "I signaled to prepare for action before I got out the transfer coin. You know how many of them there are?" Strange, how when he was Prince Jehan his eyes were so blue under that white hair. Blue and vague. When he put on the pirate clothes, his face changed. Intense, it became.

"Are we really going to rescue Elva Eban?" Robin asked. "She acted like a worse snot than you'd have expected of the princess. And *she* wasn't a snot at all."

"Elva Eban was crew."

The subject was ended, Robin knew. Even if Elva only actually helped serve a day or so, he'd decided she was crew, and they all knew his first rule: *We never abandon crew to the enemy.*

He yanked a green-striped bandana from the chest, flung his old clothes in and slammed the lid. A few quick, practiced twists and his hair was bound up, the yellow fringes dancing against the horrible pink shirt. Last, he unfastened the diamond in his ear, moved to the little carved box on the shelf above the bed, and she heard the clatter as he tossed it in. "Let's take a look." He grabbed his spyglass with one hand and snapped the clasp on his gold hoop with the other.

Together they strode out on deck, she aware of the waiting tension, the watching eyes, he seemingly unaware as he tucked his glass under one arm and scrambled up to the masthead.

She was right behind him with her own glass.

No sound, no voices, only the endless wash of the sea, and the creak of wood as he eyed the fleet. Then he smiled and lowered the glass. He spoke in a pitched voice, carrying to the waiting crew. "He doesn't have half the navy, he only has part of it."

Everyone was listening.

"Another thing. What we see here is not one fleet, but two. Randart thinks he has one. But one look at those ill-kept columns and it's clear to anyone used to the sea he's got his dozen or so of the Ellir Fleet, beautifully on station, plus a lot of craft that seem to be having trouble staying more or less in a line. Which one is he on? Fleet flagship doesn't seem to be flying the king's banner."

"That's because he's on the biggest merch," Robin said.

"He's what?" Zathdar looked askance, and there was some subdued laughter from the tops. "He isn't that stupid."

"According to the orders relayed among the merches via Tham, he's been there to see that they learn their place. He *says* he's training them navy-style."

"But he doesn't know anything about the navy."

"That's the word."

Zathdar murmured so softly the wind almost took his words away, "Chain of command forged by fear." He nodded. "Then that gives us a bit more time. Even better, my rescue attempt might even work."

"Two fleets . . ." "Two fleets . . ." The whisper susurrated through the crew.

He lifted his voice. "Set sail now, right down the middle. Fire-arrow barrage from both sides. Aim for sails, no human targets. I want every single sail in that fleet on fire. As soon as we draw nigh Tham, tell him to be ready with the sugar bricks."

Randart crouched over his prisoner, who stared upward, a slight frown between her eyes. The rest of her dirty, blood-smeared face was impossible to read, but her bruised lips kept moving as she whispered.

"You were taken by the pirate Zathdar," he said clearly. "Where did he take you?"

". . . and what is that smell? I smell sweat. Old sweat, some mud. Mud on a ship—you don't get mud on a ship—from the swell I'd say the wind is out of the northwest . . ."

Randart raised a hand, then hesitated, not wanting her blood dirtying his hands. So he gripped her hair and yanked her head so she faced him.

Tears filled her eyes.

"Hurts! Pain—stab of needles, hot needles, not on the scalp but down my neck my stomach boils I might puke I don't want to puke I had nothing to eat my head aches feels like a cloth tied around it—"

Randart sighed in exasperation.

"Zathdar!" he said sharply.

"Pirate," Elva responded. "Those colors ugly colors brown,

brown, brown all around am I wearing my blue tunic I need a cleaning frame don't want it ruined—"

Thumping and yells on the deck distracted Randart, who bent closer to hear the continuous stream of whispered words.

"Where. Is. Zathdar's. Land. Base?" he enunciated distinctly.

". . . different pain from my arms, that's red pain, white pain is the sudden sharp one maybe it's like the glow of a dying fire . . ."

"Atanial! Zathdar!"

"Princess. Pirate name." Elva blinked, her eyes losing focus. "Ugly—my clothes are never ugly I don't like choosing clothes blood on my sleeve I can feel the wet against my arm it smells like sweet salt but with iron rust—"

The rumble of feet overhead caused Randart to glare at one of his aides. "Tell them to stay quiet on the ceiling. Whatever they are doing can wait until I am done."

The door whisked open. The noise from outside the cabin was briefly louder.

"Voices," Elva babbled on. "Do I know anyone I don't think I know them my head does hurt so—"

Randart cursed, irritated by the increase in noise from the sailors above. Were they possibly making it on purpose? He'd have them all flogged as mutineers. He was also irritated by this fool of a girl, who should, by rights, be spewing memory, not inanities about whatever she saw right in front of her nose.

His aide returned and took up his position beside the door as Randart glared at the mage. "I thought you people were supposed to be experts with kinthus. I can do better. Have done better my very first interrogation."

She opened her hand as if to say *Be my guest,* but said only, "I am not trained in interrogation. My expertise is wood. However, it appears she's caught in an immediate thought stream. It can happen to some, with green kinthus."

She sat back, hands folded. She had been ordered to cooperate with the war commander, and her oath to the king required that she strictly obey orders. But he made her so angry she would not offer him a single breath of aid beyond what he'd ordered.

So if he didn't know that the girl had managed to shutter off her memory, Magister Lorat wasn't going to offer the information.

For a time the magister watched, impassive, as Randart shook the girl, slapped her again and barked words at her, but all she did was talk about what she was seeing, hearing. Feeling. Especially feeling. When she started commenting on the revulsion she felt at the commander's proximity, and there was a revealing scrape somewhere behind them—probably someone trying hard not to laugh or even to breathe—he flung her down.

"Is there any use in continuing? How about giving her more?"

"She is on the verge of falling asleep as it is," the mage replied tonelessly. "Any more will probably kill her."

"Save the herb." He looked up at his aide and the day captain of his personal guard. "Take her out and hang her."

The guards were in the act of picking up Elva by the arms when there came a rap at the door.

"What," Randart shouted over his shoulder.

"Pardon, Commander," came the voice of the ship's captain. "But I felt you should be informed that we are under attack."

"Lower the cutter," Zathdar ordered.

Robin frowned. "You're not going to board the flagship?"

Zathdar paused on his way to the weapons locker, and glanced back. "Who else?"

"Anyone else. How did that fool get herself caught anyway?"

"I'm afraid it's our fault," Zathdar said.

Robin scowled, for she hadn't liked that Elva Eban, always grumping about on the deck with her sniffy attitude. As if *she* were the princess, whereas Prince Math's daughter had been instant mates with everyone, without a hint of swank. And she could have swanked, not only because she was a prince's daughter, but because she was one of the best fighters in the fleet.

Zathdar could see Robin's thoughts fairly clearly, so he stepped close and murmured apologetically, "Owl's mistake, actually."

Leaving her nothing more to say on the matter.

That is, until he drew out a fine Colendi dueling blade, long, thin, edged but not as strong as a saber. She gasped. "Take the cavalry sword. You can't defend yourself with that!"

"It has an edge, and a point, which is all I ask. Remember, Randart has seen my fighting style with the cavalry sword. But not with this." He swung it, making it whistle. "That might be the only disguise left to me, besides these absurd clothes, so I'll take what I can."

You shouldn't go at all. She kept her teeth gritted as she lent a hand lowering his boat. After he called for volunteers and chose among the forest of hands that instantly shot up, she said, "Orders?"

"As much chaos as possible."

He leaped down into the cutter, which was really a one-masted pinnace, but made to his own design on the lines of larger cutters, lean and fast, its sides painted a camouflaging bluish gray.

They raised the sail, tacking directly in the lee of the *Zathdar*, hidden from view of the oncoming fleet.

Robin returned to the wheel and took over. They were nearly in bowshot. On the enemy ships, naval crews scrambled aloft to the tops, taking up their stations on the mastheads, drilled and waiting. On the merchant ships, sailors scurried about and warriors ran around, all getting in one another's way. She laughed, watching the glint of sun on swords being waved, sails jerking as their unprepared crews tried to figure out how they were going to fight and sail at the same time.

Chaos he wants, chaos we will give him. I'll buy myself a new silk shirt if I can get two of these stinkers to crash bow over stern. She spun the wheel and lifted her voice. "Sail crews, let's make *Zathdar* dance. Bow teams? Prepare for attack!"

The smell of rancid oil drifted down, whipping away on the wind, as the fire crews above dipped their arrows.

Randart shoved his way to the forecastle. All the sailors scrambled back. He had his glass, but didn't need it to see the three pirates bearing down, sails taut against the wind.

"They're moving faster than we," he snapped.

The captain was an old man, weathered from years of sun and sea. "They have the wind. As we reported to you before, War Commander."

Randart gritted his teeth against snapping back a futile question. Obviously the fleet couldn't regain the wind, whatever that meant, not under strict orders to give chase.

But one question he could ask. He glared in narrow-eyed fury into the dark eyes of the waiting captain. "Why did you not report this attack at once?"

"I sent someone, but your aide said you couldn't be disturbed in the cabin. And you did say to give chase, so now we're closing." His raspy voice was devoid of expression, but Randart felt his antagonism.

"If I get even a hint," he said in a low, venomous murmur, "there was any treason in this spectacular exhibition of incompetence, I'll have you flogged to death on your own deck."

The captain's face stayed stony, his gaze steady. "Why would we do that? We were promised a year's pay for a single capture. But you said that the orders have to come from you. War Commander."

"Then your orders now are to defeat these pirates." Randart turned his head. "Signal to use ramming force and fire. I want the pirate Zathdar captured if possible, otherwise I want those ships destroyed, and no survivors."

He caught sight of Samdan limping on the companionway. Behind him his men waited, the Eban girl hanging in their grip, her lips still moving. He wanted the pirates to see her dead body hanging from one of those big pieces of wood holding up the sails. But both crews were far too busy, one dealing with sails, the other getting to their fighting stations, to make the exhibition he desired. There was no point in staging an execution as a lesson if no one was watching.

"She can go in the brig for now. We'll hang her as soon as the pirates surrender, before we fire their ships." He stepped to the rail, glass in hand. "She'll hang side by side with the pirate. After I'm through with him."

The thought of what he would do to the pirate—and how long it would last—brought a grim smile.

The captain of the ship flicked a summoning glance at his first mate, who also happened to be his wife. Together they retreated to the captain's deck. The captain took up station behind the helmsman, making certain his own crew were the only ones in earshot, "I am told that Zathdar never kills."

His wife's gray, grizzled brows rose, then her chin came down slowly. She turned away to supervise the sails and gave her own crew orders for the issuing of weapons. Around them warriors took up the fighting positions they'd drilled.

Above, signal flags rose, fluttering. Along the columns, now breaking apart to encircle the pirates, sails raised and lowered, crews ran about on decks—efficient on the navy ships, full of energy but less purpose on the merchants, for none of them knew what to do when under attack.

As the pirate drew between the first two ships in the column, fire arrows arced in glinting gold pinpricks against the blue sky. They flew in both directions, striking against the fleet's upper sails. Next, the stink of smoke reached the captain's nostrils—the distinctive stench of manure bricks mixed with sugar and set on fire, which burned messily but didn't do much else—and he chuckled softly to himself.

"Here, you, stand guard. You can't fight on deck with that knee," the patrol captain said to Samdan, motioning him to follow down into the hold. The two men dumped the girl into the tiny cupboard the commander had designated as the brig, slammed the door, slid the bar, and one turned, handing him a sword.

The lamplight shone on his grin. "My guess is, they won't get down this far, but you never know. May's well have a measure of safety." He indicated the length of the blade, and then the two vanished, their boots clattering, their curses not quite muffled as a rolling lurch of the ship slammed them back and forth in the hatchways.

Samdan sat slowly on a barrel, listening to the girl's soft whisper. He wondered if he should use the blade on her. That would be better than hanging and whatever other fun and games the commander might be inspired to try first. Or maybe he should just use it on himself.

Randart's smile had faded. He glowered at the mage.

"My training is in helping to help defend the integrity of ships' wood," Magister Lorat stated. "That I can and will perform."

"Can you damage the wood of the enemy ships?"

She rubbed her lip as she stared over the water. "If I can get close enough to focus, I might enable them to waterlog, but that's only if their wood is not warded against such spells. Most well-kept ships, even pirates, are warded as a matter of regular maintenance."

Randart sighed, thinking once again that magic was basically useless for anything but housekeeping. "Do what you can. If I see evidence of your aid in defeating them, I will see to it Zhavic rewards you suitably."

Anger flashed through her, but she hid it. "I will do my best, War Commander."

He moved on, forgetting her within two steps.

She stared down at the water. The best of nothing is nothing.

Smoke billowed from the pirates in grayish cotton streamers, carried by the wind toward the fleet. The three in the cutter watched the navy ships tacking desperately against the wind in order to come around and close on the *Bug* and the *Mule*.

Gray, one of Zathdar's strongest and steadiest crew members, said pleasantly, "You know this madness is going to get us all killed."

Zathdar laughed. "Hinting for double pay?"

"If we're alive to spend it, might be nice." Gray gave his captain a mocking salute.

"Ship ho," Gliss called from the tiller as she came up under the lee of the smoking vessel.

Tham dropped in, sending shudders through the craft, which was already picking up speed.

"Going to rescue the Eban girl?" Tham asked.

"That's the idea," Zathdar said.

Tham laughed. "I would rather die heroically rescuing that wheat-haired princess, if you asked me."

Zathdar said, "It might come to that. If we find her. Right now, consider. Randart, who knows nothing of fleet actions, has had plenty of time to sow resentment among all these sailors."

"You think that's gonna help us?" Tham asked, and the others looked askance.

Zathdar spread his hands. "On land, I wouldn't dare go up against him with four swords, doughty as you are. But now—whatever chance we have, we must take. As for our target, Elva Eban is crew. And you know the rule."

No one argued with that. They all knew it could have been one of them on that ship.

A grinding crash snapped everyone's eyes south as a merchant craft, half-hidden by the increasing smoke from the scattering bursts of new fires, jammed its jib over the taffrail of one of the naval ships. Faint cries of rage carried over the smoke from both ships, creaks and cracks of wood, and the beating ruddy glow of sky-reaching flames.

"Oars," Zathdar said. "There's the flagship."

TWELVE

"IT'S A DISASTER." RANDART wiped his smoke-burning eyes again.

A disaster with at least one mind familiar with siege tactics employed against them. Randart knew the distinctive smell of manure-brick-and-sugar fire, called smoke screen in the military.

He watched in growing but helpless fury the slow, disastrous collapse of order at this end of the fleet. Impossible to see if the naval ships were closing in from the other side. Probably not. The smoke seemed to kill the wind, and the ships had slowed even more, wallowing as fast and furious arcs of flame hissed at them.

The pirates shot a ceaseless stream of fire arrows. He had ordered his men to kill, but they couldn't see their targets.

Randart controlled the urge to strike out at the closest target. Though he could not ride, or bugle for a troop to thunder up and encircle the enemy, he did have one last possibility. All he needed was to spot the lead pirate ship, then he could order down the boats and send his men over to take it. Wrest something from the turmoil.

But the smoke thickened, obscuring even the two ships at either side. All he could see were the tiny pricks of light of the fire arrows. The arcs now went out in both directions. His men were shooting from the topmasts above him, he was glad to see, though he had no idea who they were aiming at. Maybe a defensive measure. They certainly couldn't see any pirates to shoot.

The smoke was making his throat raw. Usually he kept his command center upwind of smoke screens, but the pirates *had the wind.*

He retreated to his cabin, and was downing his second cup of water when Jehan's cutter eased up under the stern, directly below him—and unseen because it never occurred to him to peer out the stern windows.

Gliss, at the tiller, stayed in the vessel to fight off anyone who tried to take it. She'd come aboard if summoned as last-ditch backup. Hoping for a chance, she kept the boat as close under the stern as possible, out of sight from the rail.

The other four climbed fast, Jehan's colorful figure first.

He murmured, "No deaths if you can avoid it."

"Even army?" Tham muttered, though he knew the answer.

"Yes."

Tham sighed, not surprised. He knew that Randart would be angry enough to feel no such compunction when giving orders to his men.

Jehan leaped lightly over the rail, dueling rapier in one hand, knife in the other, the others behind as backup. And as Zathdar paced past the old captain at the helm, raked his gaze down the unarmed man and moved by, the captain flicked a glance at his wife, who promptly went about her inspection as though she hadn't even seen the intruders.

Gray, hefting his sword behind Tham, whistled softly, long and low. Zathdar had been right. Randart had made enemies of these sailors.

They might actually survive.

The breather lasted another ten heartbeats. A patrolling warrior spotted them, and yelled up at the first mate, "Hey! Who's that?" But she was coughing too hard from the smoke, and groped helplessly as she stood at the rail, whooping for breath.

The patroller stared at the slim man in garish colors. He came on fast and the warrior pulled his sword, yelling, "Pirates! We're under attack!"

The ship erupted in cries, crashes, and desperate fights. The warrior detachment boiled up from below, each wanting badly to bag a pirate and the promotion and reward that came with it.

The sailors all yelled "Attack!" and "Defense!" and waved their weapons, running into one another and dropping armloads of sailing gear that suddenly everyone seemed to be carrying.

Tham, backing up Zathdar, found himself pressed against the rail by three good fighters in the king's brown. He was mentally bidding farewell to a good, though short, life, when a cry from overhead startled everyone—and a sailor landed on top of two of the warriors, knocking the third spinning. Tham promptly jabbed his knee and the opposite shoulder, putting him out of action, as the sailor held up a frayed rope end and said loudly, "It broke!"

Three big blocks dropped from above, two clonking onto the heads of warriors. One warrior was knocked out, the other staggered toward the rail, a cut over one eye. Crew members leaped to help, getting in the way of Randart's men who tried to close in on the pirates.

"Get out of the way!"

"Where?"

"Help, help, the boom is about to drop!"

"I can't see!"

The first mate stood at the rail, apparently blind to the chaos as she coughed from the smoke.

A party of five sailors chose this moment to haul up a huge sail between the pirates and the advancing guards. Gray and Tham covered Zathdar, who dropped down the hatch.

He slashed his blade across the forehead of one fellow, nailed the elbow and hip of another, then jumped to the second hatchway. Now the search would begin. Where would they would stash a prisoner?

Randart emerged from his cabin to discover fighting all over the deck, warriors slipping in spilled oil, smacked in the back of the head by swinging blocks of wood from the sails overhead, bumped into by groups of sailors running about, some carrying huge sails, others with long snarls of rope, everyone yelling at the tops of their voices.

"Pirates?" Randart roared. He spotted them, three around the main hatchway. On guard, it looked like.

Why? It *couldn't* be the Eban girl they were after—

A loud rattling sounded overhead, and a sail swooped down and dropped over him, knocking him flat.

"We're on fire!" someone screeched above.

"Mizzen top down! Mizzen top down! Sail crew!" the ship captain howled, and feet trampled over Randart, squashing him flat.

Randart shouted, "Get off me!" but the noise of the sailors bellowing arcane sail jargon at one another, the captain bawling orders, the noise of fighting, of sails flapping, of coughing and whooping caused by the smoke, drowned him out.

Below, Zathdar began grimly on his search, waiting for the inevitable squad to descend from the deck, each intent on winning fame and fortune by some judicious pirate killing. Take every chance to its end, he'd been taught at the academy across the continent, where dying in battle was considered the best end for a warrior.

A cough caught his attention, and he whirled, blades up.

A man's head popped up from the deck below, barely lit by the single swinging lantern. "She's here."

It was one of Randart's warriors.

Expecting a trap, Zathdar hefted his weapon and dropped down to the dim, low third level, which was usually used for storage, to find himself alone with a man with a bound knee. The face was vaguely familiar.

"He's going to hang her." Samdan looked at the pirate dressed in ridiculous clothes, like a traveling player. But there was nothing silly about the narrowed eyes, twin gleams from the lamp flame reflecting in his steady gaze, or the way he held those red-tipped weapons. "Did you kill anyone?"

A shake of the fringed bandana.

"Yes. Well, she's there." A point.

A step, a kick to the wooden bar, and indeed, there she was, on her knees, arms bound. One slash and her hands dropped to her sides, her mouth moving as she chattered a stream of nonsense observations in a low, monotonous whisper.

"You'd best thump me." Samdan turned his back. *And if you kill me, well, it's only just.*

The pirate nodded once, and didn't make the man wait. Tossing his knife up, he caught it by the blade, and brought the handle down behind Samdan's ear.

Samdan dropped to the deck, his weapon clattering out of his hands. Zathdar stared at Samdan's knee, remembering where he'd seen the man last—lying wounded in the transfer-tower courtyard. Bending, he lightly nicked Samdan where it would hurt least but bleed most, the better to make it seem he'd put up a good fight, and cut the rest of Elva's bonds.

"Can't use hands," she murmured, in the slurry voice of someone who was under the influence of kinthus.

"Stop talking." The kinthus would make her obey, and thus she would also be able to halt the weird chatter.

He slid his arm under hers and supported her up one ladder— propping her against a bulkhead to step out and look round. There was only one sailor, with the galley and the officers' wardroom blocked off by barrels. The man looked at them, turned his back, and dropped another barrel onto its side.

"I'm trying to get you out, but someone upset all the food stores," he bellowed to the officers shouting and trying to batter the blocked wardroom cabin door.

Zathdar helped Elva up the last ladder, where they found the deck in chaos, sails hanging loose or dropped altogether, fires being busily put out with water splashing everywhere. And what were these impossible tangles of ropes?

A rush of warriors toward them turned into a mass skid as

someone fell over a barrel of oil that had spilled all over the deck.

There were Gray, Tham, and Vestar, bloody but alive.

They closed around him, Gray pressing up on Elva's other side. Together they lifted her as they mounted to the captain's deck, where the first mate was busy yelling at a disaster with the mizzen topsails. A web of tangle rope jerked upward, blocking off the scrambling warriors who'd managed to get past the oil.

A boom swung out from the other direction, lifting the rest of the pursuit off their feet, to crash onto the mizzen sail still being trampled and splashed with buckets of water.

Zathdar thought he heard Randart's voice adding to the noise somewhere around that mizzen sail, and laughed as they passed Elva down to Gliss.

Then they were in the boat, whooping for breath, weapons dropping from hands, minds trying to grapple with the amazing fact that they were alive after all.

Elva struggled up, her bruised, blood-smeared face lit by the ship fires.

They rowed out, and Gliss ran up the sail, sheeting it home.

On the journey back through the smoky ruin in the fleet, the kinthus wore off, and with it the numbing effect of all those bruises. But Elva didn't care. She had survived. She was alive.

She said nothing, unsure who knew what, until they reached the *Zathdar*. It was the pirate himself who offered his shoulder for her to lean on. She couldn't resist one more test, murmuring into his bandana-covered ear, "Didn't want me talking, huh?"

His quick look of surprise was revealing, but all he said was, "And ruin my reputation as the best-dressed prince on the east coast?" The smile Zathdar gave her was his rare, sudden one, a real smile full of fun.

She contemplated that surprise. He thought she'd talked, but came after her anyway. And though her heart was not fashioned to respond to him, or to any man, what she did feel budding under the miasma of weariness, shock, pain, and unhoped-for reprieve was the green shoot of insight: this was what loyalty was all about.

Prince Jehan had no reason to like her, he didn't even know her, but he'd obviously found her worthy of rescue. A prince who could be loyal to people was worth allegiance.

Randart rubbed his throbbing forehead, but that didn't even begin to assuage the merciless slam of his headache. The day had begun so well, emphasizing all the more strongly the catastrophic results.

He faced the captain of the ship, and his own officers, and the mage, who all waited, eyes steady, some weary, some afraid, most of them with the closed faces of unexpressed anger.

Nothing he could ask was going to reveal the true cause of that sullen fury he saw all around him. How was he to determine if the catastrophe was due to incompetence or to treachery? At home, on land, with the king at his side and the circumstances of well-understood military action at his back, he could probably force out the truth.

The king. He was finally answerable to the king.

He drew a deep breath of the stale air, for the cabin was closed tight against listening ears and the rattle and thud of cleanup. "It is very apparent to me, and I am sure it is to you as well, that this pirate attack and the rescue of the Eban girl are not coincidence."

His words were met with profound silence, except for the shifting of one officer easing a broken arm, and the captain twisting slightly as he cocked his ear upward at some incomprehensible shout up on deck.

"Someone," Randart enunciated clearly, "sent the pirate a message. It has to have been by magic, and it has to have been someone on this ship. Maybe in this room."

The captain cleared his throat. "Begging your pardon, War Commander. But there were more witnesses seeing that girl brought over than just your people. Supply boats were coming and going. Any of them would be carrying word of what they saw. It's the way of the sea, everyone will tell you that. Even your captains, if they are honest." He indicated the Fleet Captain, a thin, morose man sitting opposite Randart, whose ships had accidentally attacked merches, what with the smoke and noise and general chaos. *That* disaster had enabled the three pirates to slip between the ragged, uncontrolled line of merches and sail downwind, hidden by the smoke and the embrace of night.

Everyone turned attention to the unhappy Fleet Captain, who lifted a hand. "It's notoriously hard to keep ears from hearing things on a ship, yes," he said heavily.

Randart knew his Fleet Captain was loyal. That crash had occurred in the smoke and chaos that Randart himself had made no sense of, though he'd tried, once he got free of that cursed sail that had fallen on top of him.

The sail, yes.

He turned on the merchant captain. "Very well. Then the way of the sea will work *for* us." Randart breathed deeply, feeling the slight ease of decision. "*You* will discover who betrayed us. And when that happens—only when that happens, I emphasize—you will be paid for repairs and the month's wages. But until then, you are on your own." Lifting a hand, he added sardonically, "Let that word get out according to the ways of the sea."

He rose. Thus released, the ship captain opened the cabin door and sweet, cool air rushed in as they filed out, defeat and tiredness shaping everyone's countenance, lagging their steps.

Randart caught the mage's eye and raised a hand to halt her.

When the others were gone, he said, "Prepare to transfer back with me to Ellir. We can leave whenever you are ready."

She nodded and left.

He walked up onto the deck, staring at the snarl of ropes and wooden implements whose use he could only guess at, but which probably had something to do with sails. The big sail that had landed on him still lay where it had been kicked, with the jagged cut he'd made by his knife in releasing himself. Bloodstains on it where his knife had caught someone or other who, either accidentally or on purpose, had been trampling the sail while doing something or other to the upper reaches of the ship. He could not know if that had been deliberate or another consequence of the chaos of sea battles. Fleet action, he had learned to his cost, lay too far outside his realm of experience.

Undeniably the sailors were hacked up, several, like his own warriors, with broken limbs, cuts rudely bound. When he asked, they all seemed not to know if pirates or his own men had caused the wounds. Yet the fact was, no more than four pirates had boarded the ship, made it down to the hold, released the prisoner, and retreated again.

Samdan was yet unconscious, but Randart was not going to wait for him to waken. He probably didn't know anything. From the look of him he'd fought his best, hampered by the bad knee and having only a single lamp to see by in the dark hold.

None of them seemed to know anything useful, except that one of the pirates wore garish clothing like Zathdar was reputed to favor. That would mean the pirate captain himself had been here, and Randart flat on his back under a sail as heavy as a horse.

There was no evidence of collusion, but he sensed it everywhere he looked. The sailors were too somber, too weary for the obvious signs of collusion. But the quality of the silence formed a wall between him and these mariners.

Randart let out his breath. Defeat, on unfamiliar territory. But he'd learned something. The pirate had spies everywhere. And he had land ties. Therefore he'd inevitably return to land, and that was Randart's territory. There would be no defeat next time.

But first Randart had to get back, and they were at least a week, probably more, from land. It was time for magic transfer, something he not only detested but distrusted. What was to stop the mages from making him vanish conveniently? He didn't trust Zhavic or Perran for a heartbeat. So he would force the mage to transfer with him. He would never use a magic token himself, though he kept them to expedite those under his orders.

Magister Lorat presented herself with her bag of belongings, and he wondered if she could have been the traitor. No, that was ridiculous. She probably was reporting to Zhavic, but she'd come with a solid reputation, he'd checked that out first thing. She was a wood mage, which meant she would not be a brilliant thinker in the chaos of battle. She'd done what she was told with the stolidity of the wood she worked with.

So he braced himself for the wrench which was no easier to endure than it ever was. He'd avoided eating dinner once he'd made his decision, so the nausea, at least, was easier to fend off if his stomach was not full.

When he recovered, the mage was already gone. He looked about him at the comforting familiarity of stone in the Destination room of Ellir Castle. As soon as he could get his legs to carry him, he forced himself to climb up to Orthan's tower, which was empty.

The entire academy was pretty much empty against the war game soon to commence. Randart clapped on the glowglobe and sat down at his brother's desk to look through the reports stacked there, some annotated in Orthan's neat hand.

Everything looked as it should. Randart was having trouble forcing his increasingly aching head to concentrate. That defeat rankled, the more because he knew, he *knew*, there was deliberate treachery behind it. So he forced himself to be thorough.

He read one report three times without comprehension before he finally found the sense. Zathdar's sometime ally, Tharlif, had swooped down onto his secret shipment of weapons meant for spring, and captured them all.

Fury blinded Randart, leaving him gasping, until he remembered he'd protected himself with a double order, one overland, one by sea. He had planned for this possibility.

His focus sharpened again. There was no report about the overland wagons being molested. All was well. All was well. He would stay on land in future.

He forced himself to get through the rest of the reports, then set the pile down. It was time to eat. Sleep. Forget asking Magister Zhavic for news. The mage would just lie or leave out crucial details. No more magic. Randart would take the extra day or so to ride back to the king, and compose his report on the way — that and his strategy for dealing with kingdom matters as they stood.

But that plan vanished like the sky after the sail dropped on him when he saw the neatly tied pile at the bottom of the reports, a scrap of paper on top written in his brother's hand: *Save for Dannath.*

He pulled up that pile and leafed through it. Most of these would take concentration for it seemed there were some anomalies in supply reports, people where they should not be or missing where they should be. All of that promised painstaking checking, and by trusted aides.

But that third one down, beginning with the note in Orthan's hand: *I don't know if this is important. Looked strange.*

Randart glanced at the heading. It was a weekly report from one of the more remote outposts along the northern river.

He scanned rapidly down to where his brother had made a neat question mark.

Civilian sailor strayed off the civilian road during storm, female, tall, blond, hazel eyes, name Lasva, from Tser Mearsies. Carrying only personal gear plus a letter from one inn to another, the only item of interest a silken banner in the old Zhavalieshin style.

It could be any woman, on the most innocuous of journeys. Except why did the mind immediately leap to the missing daughter of Atanial Zhavalieshin? It was the banner. Randart was willing to swear an oath he had seen it or one just like it, in Prince Mathias's rooms during the old days when he was royal castle commander. The banner had been stitched by Math's grandmother and her ladies for the prince's birth: queensblossom vines around rising firebirds, all in gold and scarlet.

He'd seen it recently, hadn't he? If only his head did not ache so. Banner . . . and he had it. A silken banner, covered with queensblossom vines all around rising firebirds.

It had lain over the bed on the *Dolphin*, the prince's yacht. Were there two of those banners? Because if not, *Jehan had had her after all.* And lied? No. Randart had not told him why he was searching, or for what. The Fool could have been keeping her in order to bring her to his father himself, for badly needed prestige . . . and, being the fool he was, had lost her.

No matter which, she was alone, on the road. And no one seemed to know who she was.

That is, no one *else* seemed to know who she was.

THIRTEEN

SHARP VOICES ECHOED UP the marble stairs from Prince Jehan's rooms. Atanial knew from the tone that there was trouble, but she could not hear the words.

Something had to be wrong in a big way. She sensed tension when the servants came to invite her to breakfast with the king, as had become habit.

She was already dressed, her hair braided up with pearls to distract from the startling silver roots of her otherwise blond hair. The number of guards at the stairways had increased. Of course no one had told her anything of what was going on since her brief conversation with Jehan. She couldn't even ask, because she knew the servants were questioned by that oily Chas every single time they came up to her tower.

As she walked down to breakfast, she wondered if she'd find the usual scene, the prince sitting there staring out the window, Canardan wearily pleasant and sometimes wry as they verbally fenced.

The first surprise of the day was when she found Canardan alone.

"Sent Jehan off somewhere?" she asked as she sat down.

Since the weather had cooled, they'd begun eating in the king's conservatory, a room facing east, mostly windows, filled with potted plants. Atanial had expressed delight the first time she saw it, and had made the mistake of asking if it had been Ananda's chamber. Canardan had talked right over her—pleasant, even funny—as if she hadn't spoken. Oh. Ananda had become one of *those* subjects.

Now she wondered if Jehan had suddenly become another one, as Canardan reached for the fresh bread, offering her some first.

Then he sighed. "He slipped away to visit another female, apparently. No, he didn't tell me. He never does. But a letter was found in his chambers. Perfume. Written in purple ink, if you can imagine. Do these so-called artists really think they will actually marry him? It cannot be his company—" Canardan shut his mouth, a gesture so determined Atanial, watching in fascination, saw his jaw clench.

A letter was found. So the prince was not exempt from searches, either. Definitely signs of trouble in paradise.

"Up all night worrying, eh?" she asked, and when he gave her a narrow-eyed glance, she deflected the flash of anger by shifting from specifics to general. "The price of parenthood on all worlds, I suspect."

"Your girl left you up all night worrying, I gather?"

"Oh yes." That was only fair, since she'd asked first. But to ward any more questions she added, "I was always afraid she might lose her temper with some villain, and the police would come to arrest her for ridding the world of one more slimebag."

He did not ask if that was a subtle hint. He knew it was. Therefore he knew how unsubtle. But he also knew she was being irritating in order to sting him into revealing more, and though he felt the usual surge of laughter and attraction that her ripostes inevitably caused, he was too tired to keep his guard up. He fell silent, only answering when, in desperation, she turned to the weather and the harvest.

Such a limping conversation couldn't end fast enough for either of them. Once she'd turned down his offer of a ride—a picnic—a tour (in other words, another public display of his prize prisoner), she excused herself.

That left her to another boring day. Later she barely remembered it. What she did remember was the faint but persistent tapping at the window long after she'd finally dropped into troubled dreams.

She sat up, disoriented. The tapping had sounded like the brush of barren twigs against a window, the way the bitter, dry desert winds of Southern California blew the tree branches all during the months that elsewhere were called winter. But she was in a tower, not in Los Angeles.

She sat up, and once again heard the faint tapping.

She threw off the covers and ran across the floor of the bedroom, and started violently when she saw a pale face peering in through a dark window.

She stumbled back, then halted when the pale starlight revealed the oval of a young female. She unlocked the casement, swung it open and stared down into vaguely familiar eyes. A hand extended up in mute appeal. Atanial gripped it and pulled. The girl shifted her weight; there was a rustle, a heave, and the young woman tumbled inside the window.

"Sh, sh," she hissed softly, though Atanial had neither spoken or made a sound. The girl looked around fearfully and whispered, "You have to come now. Tam can only vouch for his sentry watch."

"Tam?"

She blushed. "Sharveshin."

Tam . . . one of Kreki Eban's conspirators.

"Marka?" Atanial peered down. Yes, the starlight glimmered softly on short reddish curls ruffling all round the girl's head.

"It is I. Come. Did you know they are getting a trial? The king cannot kill them now. So I'm here to get you out of the castle. Tam and, well, some others, they are all covering your exit. But you have to climb down outside the window, which isn't warded like the doors are."

Obviously young love had managed to overcome political

differences. "Climb down the stones of the tower?"

"There's ivy."

Atanial gritted her teeth. The idea of climbing down a hundred feet of ivy did not appeal, but neither did staying here in this jewel-box prison one second more, now that she no longer had to.

She swung around, dug through her clothes with shaking hands, and dressed in layers of dark, sensible clothing. Into her bra she shoved her magic tokens, and the few bits of jewelry she'd been given. She would probably need them to trade for food.

Marka slipped out the window. "Put your hands and feet where I do."

It felt like four hours later she was maybe ten feet below the window, her hands aching from the death grip on the branches, her muscles trembling, when she felt a familiar nauseous ache behind her sternum that spread outward as heat.

She stopped, leaning her forehead against her arm, and nearly sobbed. *Great. Climbing down a tower wall, and here comes a hot flash.*

"Princess?"

"I'm on my way," she muttered, her voice shaky.

She wiped her sweaty hands on her clothes one at a time, placed a foot, a hand, and eased herself down a few inches. Ivy tickled her nose, but she held her breath against a sneeze. Hand. Foot. Hand. Foot.

Later that journey seemed longer than all the weeks of her imprisonment. But at last, oh, at last her foot encountered stone, and she stepped onto the sentry wall.

Marka took her hand, sweaty and gritty as it was, and pulled her unresisting inside a dank access-way. They flitted down some mossy steps and across a dripping hall that smelled of mold and old wood. Then they continued down, this time to a stable.

"Here she is," Marka breathed, running toward a shadowy corner.

Tam Sharveshin emerged, sword in hand. "Ride out."

A tall, skinny teenage boy with a prominent Adam's apple and tousled cinnamon hair silently handed to Atanial a folded cape, the plain brown of a runner.

"Don't tell us where," Tam added.

Atanial shook her head. "I won't. But I'd like to know whom to thank for this rescue."

Tam and the teen glanced up at the tower where Prince Jehan's rooms were lit, even though he was gone.

"Ah." Jehan Merindar.

The teen said in an unprepossessing nasal honk, "He told us to arrange it. Not to say when. So he officially won't know when or how. His fellows in the guard helped. They're all busy looking elsewhere."

"I understand." Atanial suspected the cost of being caught. They were so young to be in such danger, but she knew better than to mention it. From the looks of him, that teen would on Earth be a computer geek, the type who loved logistical challenges. "What will you say?"

"Nothing, if I get back to my patrol. They know you have some magical device." Tam mimed holding a disc. "I overheard the orders for the search of your rooms when you were with the king, under Magister Zhavic's direction. Rumor was, the magister thinks you carry a token around, but the king wouldn't let him search you. So we figured if there were no signs left behind—and they won't think to check the ivy—they'll figure on magical transfer. And no one on wall duty right now will see anything at all."

Atanial nodded, then the boy gave her a hasty lesson in horse care, indicating the feed bag, rolled blanket, and curry comb in the saddle pack. "Most people will help with a horse if asked," he finished.

Atanial thanked him as she shook out the cape and pulled up the hood. The soft, sturdy woolen garment smelled sun fresh. "All of you—I mean all including those outside this space. Thank you, my dears." She kissed Marka and Tam, laughing silently when they blushed like children.

She hesitated before the teen, whose shoulders had come up to his jug-handle ears. She knew from his agonized face, his defensive posture, that however he felt about kisses from young ladies, he was definitely at that age when teenage boys would rather be tortured by fire and sword than kissed by old ones. So she patted him kindly on the arm, and laughed to herself at the way Marka and Tam's hands came together, gripping tightly.

She mounted up and left at a sedate pace, riding along the military trail they'd pointed out, staying with it only until she was out of sight of the city gates. Then she turned off the road.

Before long the low gray clouds began to drizzle, and she discovered that the runner cloak was warded against wet. The cool, sweet air smelled the better for the sense of freedom.

During the days and days she'd had time to think, she'd decided if she ever won free, she would begin her search at the abandoned morvende geliath Math had talked about, where mysterious mages had once taught him some mysterious magic: Ivory Mountain. Oh, not ivory from animals. They didn't kill mammals for fur, meat, or anything else on this world. "Ivory" was far weirder, a stone that was more like metal, and in ancient histories—so Math had told her once, his eyes wide with wonder—it *sang*.

But before she found her way to Ivory Mountain, she needed allies. Alone, she couldn't do anything. But one thing people in Los Angeles knew was the sheer weight of a crowd.

An inward image of a smart girl with capable hands, jug ears framed uncompromisingly by braids: What better person to go to first than Lark Silvag?

FOURTEEN

Because she rode northwest, she and Jehan happened to be on the opposite sides of the city, one departing, one arriving. Though they would have loved to have the leisure for a talk, they were unaware of the other's movements.

Jehan's mood was sober. Triumph after a successful escapade didn't last long any more, not before the impending storm of trouble threatening the kingdom. At least this time he was spared the necessity that—it was becoming more obvious every day— only he insisted on, the swearing of a new partisan not to himself but to King Math. Elva Eban was already sworn to Math.

Even thinking about it brought Owl's voice back a year or two ago. "What are you going to do if he's dead?"

"I can't think of that," Jehan had responded. "I have to go on as if he's alive."

Owl, who had never known Math, shook his head with some sympathy. "You'd better think of it. Because you can be sure Randart is. Every single day."

Owl's voice echoed in Jehan's ears as he rode through the south gate, waving in response to the salute from the sentries on the wall. He was going to be facing Randart soon, maybe now, more likely later. Jehan had hoped to get back before the war commander, who detested magic as much as he distrusted it. But that couldn't be counted on.

The covert glances sent Jehan's way when he reached the royal castle's stable served as his weather vane. From the silence, the furtive glances, and the tension in hands and shoulders, it seemed his father was in far more of a temper than Jehan had expected. Maybe they hadn't found the fake letter, or maybe they had and had figured out at last that those letters were indeed fake.

He handed over the reins of his mount and walked inside. He was met almost at once by a runner who said, with scared eyes, "The king would like you to come straightaway in, your highness."

"All right. Thank you." Tension gripped him.

His father sat in his workroom. As soon as Jehan walked in, Canardan threw down his pen so hard it clattered to the floor. "Why," he began in a tired voice, "did you see fit to ride out without a word to anyone, not even your own servants?" He flicked the letter. "Was her desire for your company really all that much more alluring than duty?"

"I thought so." Jehan kept his voice even. "But then my duty is surpassing tedious. Not that I find Princess Atanial tedious, but trying to get her to go on rides, or even a walk in the garden, is not much of a duty when she refuses every single day, leaving me little to do."

Regarding his son with a strange mixture of relief and anger, Canardan said abruptly, "Atanial vanished."

Jehan had not expected that so soon. Mentally saluting Kazdi and the other guards, he exclaimed, "What?"

Canardan saw that unfeigned surprise and let out a slow breath.

Jehan comprehended then that his father had feared he'd been involved.

The king said in a far milder voice, "Atanial. Is gone. Missing. Probably used that thrice-damned magic token the mages said she had on her, but which I, being a fool, insisted they not take off her because she assuredly kept it next to her person. She would never have forgiven that."

What that revealed: the king had had her rooms searched, and she knew it. She hadn't trusted him, and he knew it.

Jehan sat down as Canardan walked around the desk, stooped, and picked up the pen. "I don't know where she went. Maybe back to her world, as Zhavic insisted the token was a World Gate one. Maybe she had a transfer spell for this world over it, and went straight to the tower, and then out. Perran, who is there, might not have even seen her. At least he hasn't been here to report anything untoward at the tower. I hope that's the case."

Jehan rubbed his jaw. "Is it a problem to have her here?"

"No. Yes. Everything is a problem," Canardan said angrily.

Jehan's neck tightened. Was his father, at last, going to admit to the secret plans for the spring invasion?

For weeks Jehan had wrestled inwardly about that question — whether it would be better or worse to be told. Either way was going to mean endless trouble, but he had finally decided that if his father kept it secret, it was because the king truly knew that breaking the treaty with Locan Jora was wrong. Whatever excuses would subsequently be offered.

If the king had talked himself into speaking openly about it before Jehan, that brought its own troubles. An invasion of what was legally if not historically another country was royal treachery on a scale that could only be dealt with by a king. Like Math. Otherwise the kingdom would be plunged into the sort of bloody civil war that had happened far too often over Khanerenth's long history.

And none of Jehan's own intensely loyal, dedicated, brave, smart, risk-taking and innovative followers knew about the invasion, except for Owl. He couldn't tell them until he knew for certain it was true.

". . . so you see, though I know what it's like to be young — and I loved assignations as much as the next young man, when I was your age — I need you to stay here. You can grace various occasions, especially those given by foreigners with their constant spies, when my time demands I be elsewhere. We have too many problems. I cannot risk angering the least of the ambassadors or envoys by avoiding their social foolishness, and with winter coming, there will be even more of it."

Jehan signified assent. A runner entered and bowed. "War Commander Randart rode into the stable, your majesty. Requests an immediate interview."

Canardan lifted a hand and she dashed out.

"Let's not say anything about this, shall we?" Canardan murmured, picking up the fake letter and tossing it onto the fire. "I'm certain that Randart has enough on his mind, and we understand one another, do we not?"

Jehan bowed. "I'm certain he will wish to keep his interview private."

Canardan was on the verge of acknowledging the truth of this, then he paused, regarding his son with a puzzled frown. Duty. The boy did seem to be slightly less wool-minded than usual. Was it possible he was waking up to his responsibilities?

"Stay," he said, coming to a sudden decision. "Zhavic sent me a report. There was trouble with the fleet, and the pirate apparently got away. Whatever Randart has to say, you may as well hear it."

The war commander reached them moments later, a tall, husky man whose strong arms strained against the sleeves of his sturdy brown cotton-wool tunic. He scorned velvet. The tunic was also unmarked as any warrior's, except for the silver crown stitched over the golden cup—the device of the king's own man. He didn't need to wear rank markers, because in his own view, his rank was the highest in the kingdom, above mere dukes. Except of course for the king himself.

Randart's face hardened even more than usual when he saw who sat with the king. He hesitated, and Jehan knew that the war commander was waiting for the king to dismiss his son like an errant lap dog.

"Your report?" Canardan asked, with the smiling irony that

signaled to Jehan his father was quite aware of Randart's attitude.

Randart clawed his shaggy, gray-streaked hair back, a rare, entirely human gesture. Both father and son recognized how upset Randart had been by his defeat. "The pirate tangled the merchants with my naval ships, under cover of smoke screen. I'd captured one of the Eban brats, and was in the middle of questioning her when the attack commenced. The pirates boarded my flagship, a merchant, and got her away while my own guard and the sailors ran around getting in the way of one another's blades. The smoke did not help. In short, a disaster."

He dropped a sheaf of papers onto the king's desk. "Here are the details, if you want them, on the top report. The rest are my brother's reports on guard and academy matters."

Canardan did not even glance at the papers. "Why did you make a flagship of a merchant? Did they know naval maneuvers?"

"No. I intended to train them into a fighting fleet."

"In a matter of weeks? I thought our navy trained for longer. Well, never mind, I can appreciate your thinking, but it might be better in the future to set up your flag on the fastest ship."

Randart saluted, lips tight.

"I take it Zathdar himself was present?"

"Description of the leader of the rescue party fits, but I did not see him myself."

Canardan frowned. "Yet you say this happened aboard your flagship. Where were you?"

"Buried underneath an enormous sail which apparently fell due to fires in the upper masts. The pirates kept up a steady barrage of fire arrows. By the time I cut my way out, the pirates were gone, with my prisoner."

Canardan sighed. "And so we have it to do again."

Randart hesitated, looked at the vacant blue eyes of the idiot son, and shut his teeth. His subsequent discoveries and surmises would wait until he could be alone with the king. It made him angry enough to have to admit to defeat before the Fool. But he deemed it just retribution.

Except, what did the sheep know? Prompted by the sudden, unpleasant conviction that the king had told the sheep about the invasion, he tested, saying, "So as for the future—"

The king waved a hand. "All that can wait. I can see from the mud you've been riding all day. Go get something to eat. Get some rest. I can read through the reports while you do those things."

Randart stood up. "I'll give the orders for the execution. We can do that at noon tomorrow, before I—"

"Execution?" Canardan repeated.

"Of course. The traitor guardsmen. Silvag, and I forget the other's name. If we put crossbolts through them, that should solve your civilian-trial problem—"

Canardan was just irritated enough with Randart to resent this summary disposition of his time. "Not tomorrow. I have three interviews, two of those with envoys. Nothing is more awkward than executions, especially when you're trying to smooth things over. It can wait."

Randart had been considering whether or not to tell Canardan about the report and his theory on Atanial's missing daughter. Telling the king would have eased some of the bitterness of his defeat. On the other hand, nailing that girl down first would go even further in removing the bitterness of defeat.

Then there was the matter of Canardan's wavering.

Maybe it would be better to secure her first, and . . .

And see.

Smiling with grim anticipation, Randart withdrew.

FIFTEEN

BORED AND HOT, THE two guards on patrol rode at an idle pace along the established perimeter. You didn't question orders, you just obeyed, but there wasn't much chance of action guarding a bunch of old people, half of whom were in jail.

Atanial watched them from the shade of an ancient, gnarled willow. Through its hanging green curtain, still in the late-summer air, she peered after the patrol, timing them as she waited for the cover of darkness.

She was tired and hungry and thirsty, despite having had a long drink at the last stream. She knew she'd be a lot worse off if she had to let the horse go. That might happen. It's difficult to hide a horse.

So far, she was all right. The animal stood patiently in the shade with her, tail twitching. When at last the shadows fused into darkness, she decided to move after the next patrol. It came right on time, roughly an hour after the last round. She waited until the pair had safely ridden by, then tied the reins of her horse loosely to a low branch, pulled out the feedbag, filled it, and put it on the horse.

This took longer than she'd thought it would, as she and the horse were unfamiliar with one another. The movements were also unfamiliar.

When she was done, she took off running with her head low.

She zipped across the road and over a gentle hill toward the Silvags' orchard. She was thinking of cover, but she almost ran Lark down, out picking peaches now that the sun was gone.

They both gasped, Lark almost dropping her basket. The girl poised to flee.

Atanial whispered, "It's me, Sun—er, Atanial."

Lark whistled. "You better leave, your highness, before my mother—"

"Before your mother what?" Plir Silvag rounded an old peach tree, a basket on her arm. She was only a silhouette in the deepening gloom, but Atanial saw the tension in her movements. "Who are you? You can't be—"

"Sun. Atanial. Whatever—"

"Get. Out."

Atanial sighed, the inner vision of water, food, a bath vanishing. "Please. Just listen to me."

"Last time I listened to you, my husband got taken. He may even be dead for all I know—"

"He's not."

"So you say—"

"He's not. Tam would have told me. They're all safe. The king won't do anything to them because he agreed to hold a trial."

"She's right," Lark said. "Tam said so. So did my cousin in the stable."

"You hold your tongue."

"Ma, Tam keeps telling us—"

"He'll say anything," Plir retorted. "To protect that little traitor Marka."

Atanial winced. How sickening civil war was, the conflict and division from regions right down to the personal level.

Plir's basket whisked against her skirt, a scratchy sound, as she shifted it. "All right. I'll listen. But if that patrol catches you, I'll just stand by and watch. I'm not losing my home too."

"I'll be quick, I promise. I spied on the patrol all day, and I know when they'll come round again. I promise to be long gone before they do."

"Speak, then."

"First, I'm sorry about your husband, and I know they got Folgothan too."

"He couldn't run," Plir Silvag said bitterly. "Because *someone* stabbed him in the leg. And my husband wouldn't just leave him."

"Is Haxin all right?" Atanial remembered the name of the ferret-faced fellow.

"He is," Lark spoke up. "But Kenda—his daughter, my age, well, Kenda was dismissed from the service. She just got promoted to signal flag officer on *Adamant*. But the war commander turfed her out. On account of her dad."

"They went over the mountain back to Locan Jora, where his cousins live," Plir said.

"Oh no." Atanial hadn't meant it to slip out, but both the Silvags exclaimed, "What?" Their voices were hoarse with the effort to keep from yelling.

"That's why I came. Word is, the king plans an invasion of Locan Jora in the spring. No, no, please don't talk. I promised you I'd speak my piece and be gone, so let me speak it. I know you don't want any fighting, not with friends and cousins and so forth over there. I don't either. You saw what happened when I took up the sword. One fight, and Folgothan got hurt and arrested. Even small wounds can have bad consequences."

Lark and Plir gave similar short nods.

"So what I want to do is gather all the women, those who have family in the military. The military have to follow orders, I understand that. And we can't do much against trained fighters, not alone. But what if we were a great number? What if, just imagine it, we had half the kingdom raised, all peaceful, no swords among us, and we begged the king not to invade?"

Plir went very still. Atanial scarcely breathed.

"Randart would cut us down without compunction," Plir stated.

"But Canardan won't. He'd hate even the suggestion. I don't

have a lot to say in his favor, but I know he wouldn't do that."

Plir shifted the basket again. "Yes, we've heard a lot about you and Canardan."

Atanial sighed. "My prison was a beautiful suite. He gave me clothes, and he even gave me jewels." *And how many times am I going to have this conversation? With every single woman, no doubt.* "He wanted everyone seeing me in those clothes and jewels. He wanted people to see me dancing at that masquerade, because he knew what people would think."

"Queen Ananda's servants swore you and he were not lovers," Plir said unexpectedly. "But he could have forced them to say that before he pensioned them off." She turned away. "I have to think."

Atanial backed up a step or two. "I said I'd be going. I'll be gathering at Ivory Mountain," she added deliberately and walked away, her heart thumping hard.

The stars were just emerging, weak glimmers overhead. It was close timing, but she heard no sound of hoof beats on the still air.

She mistook four trees for her willow and had to backtrack to the road before she found the right one. Freezing into place under its sheltering curtain, she watched the riders amble into view, each carrying a bobbing lantern.

Their noise smothered the quiet, steady munch of the horse. Atanial leaned against the animal's neck, arms pressed across her front. She knew she was going to face that same conversation every time she tried to build her protest march.

Or maybe she wouldn't after all, if some angry woman reported her.

No self-pity. She would simply go until she either had her peace marchers a la the sixties, or she was caught. *At least*, she thought, trying for humor, *if Canardan catches me again I'll get another soak in that wonderful tub.*

She'd just mounted up when a furtive step caused her to whirl around.

"It's me. Lark. Ma sent me. I'll show you who's important. She's going to stay here and spread the word."

Atanial's eyelids burned with grateful tears. She wiped her eyes, then helped Lark up onto the horse's back. She mounted, and they vanished into the night, Lark pointing the way.

Mindful of his promise, Jehan agreed to attend a ball that evening, freeing up his father for his private interview with Randart.

Attending a ball was not exactly torture. In fact, one of the duchesses had brought a daughter, newly arrived home from Colend, who was bright, beautiful, witty, and fun to dance with.

A year ago he would have lingered and found a way to visit her again. But now he discovered there was just no spark. Her trenchant observations on the shortcomings of last season's plays in Colend made him want to take Sasha to Alsais to see how she liked Colendi theater. Though the duchess's daughter employed all her arts to attract, Jehan did not really notice her tiny waist, or her exquisite sense of style in gown and hair. The image that compelled him most came from memory, a tall woman with a swinging stride and hawk's beak nose, her braids dancing around her shoulders, her grin rakish and not the least coy.

After two or three dances, the duchess's daughter sensed his indifference to her arts of attraction. Her laughter gradually lilted less and became a lot more wry. At the end of a long night of waltzing and scintillating talk on the subject of art, he gracefully saluted her hand, expressing a friendly wish they would meet again to continue their conversation.

Presently she left with her mother, saying, "Conversation is all he means. I think there's someone else."

"Nonsense." The duchess snorted. "He's notoriously cloud-brained. You'll have to work harder to catch his attention."

The daughter did not argue. She never did. But mentally she resolved to return to Colend, and when she came back again to Khanerenth she would be married. Next time he saw her, this

Prince Jehan—who *wasn't* cloud-brained, by the way—would probably want to introduce his wife.

As for Jehan, he was glad to drop wearily into bed at last. Too tired to plan much beyond avoiding Randart the next day, he slid into slumber in the last watch before dawn.

And woke with Kazdi at his bedside, holding a tray of aromatic coffee. "Randart rode out after the sun came up."

Jehan sipped, burned his lips and tongue, and sighed. "Any idea where?"

"Bar Larsca Valley. The guards were joking about the siege site, and how Randart can't seem to stay away from the game."

Jehan frowned. "Riding off the morning after arriving? There has to be something else."

Kazdi shrugged. He never even tried to understand Randart, much less out-think him. That was the prince's job. His job was to try to deflect Chas and other spies.

"He's suspicious."

"Of us?" Kazdi's voice cracked on the word *us,* but Jehan didn't smile, and Kazdi was too anxious to blush.

"I don't know," Jehan said finally. "Let's accept that as a given and go from there."

SIXTEEN

THE REST OF THE academy and the guards finally joined Damedran and the academy cadets at Cheslan Castle.

By then the senior cadets had a camp set up at the site the baron had designated with planted flags, a stretch of land recently harvested. In the fields beyond the campsite, the work of harvest went on as the newly arrived cadets finished helping set up the permanent camp.

Damedran, as senior cadet, accompanied his father to the castle for the first meeting with the baron. It was a meeting of surpassing tedium, but Damedran didn't care, at first, his mood was a happy blend of anticipation and triumph. After weeks and weeks of stony looks and avoidance, Lesi Valleg had finally spoken to him. It was short and gruff—about watch assignments—but that was far better than being scowled at.

As the baron and Orthan Randart settled what the army could and could not do with the castle, outbuildings and grounds, Damedran thought about Lesi.

He loved war games, he loved commanding and, well, some said Lesi had ears like open clam shells and buckteeth, but he'd liked her ever since they were little. She was tough, smart, and no one in the entire academy shot better than she did.

She was also the leader of the cadets who didn't like him, Damedran knew. When he was younger, that was the perfect excuse for scrapping whenever there was an opportunity. But this year thrashing them had gotten less fun, somehow. He much preferred things when the seniors were all together as a unit. With him at the top, of course.

It was especially clear after this boring ride that having the senior class divided was no good. When half weren't talking to the other half, opportunities for some great practical jokes and some well-earned and entirely fair swank in front of the younger brats went right by.

What was it the sheep had said? Prince Jehan, he reminded himself. They'd have to be unified if Norsunder attacked. And, much as he'd love to believe how tough they were, he and his gang, the midsummer games had sure proved *that* wrong.

Reminded of that mysterious nine-year-old boy, Damedran shrugged inwardly. Rumors had been flying around since the games disaster, most insisting that boy was really the son of the hated Siamis of Norsunder, who had commanded two wars in the previous decade. Either his son or the son of the far worse villain, Detlev, about whom the stories were amazing and chilling.

But Damedran scoffed at such gassing. Even if those enigmatic villains, who commanded vast armies and had their eyes set on world conquering, had children, wouldn't those children be busy in some hidden lair learning whatever it was you learned for world conquering, and not wandering around shooting in stupid contests like the yearly games in Khanerenth?

That much he said out loud when the others brought up the games and rumors. But alone at night, thinking and, well, go ahead and admit it. Worrying. He couldn't help wonder about what Wolfie had said after that fight. And that amazing training.

"All right then, that covers it, Orthan. We're done. I look forward to watching, heh heh."

"I hope we'll show you something worth seeing."

The men stood, breaking Damedran's reverie. He was glad to be interrupted.

Orthan Randart started out, pleased with his son's quiet, even agreeable demeanor, unlike his accustomed slouch and scowl. Not realizing that Damedran had not heard a single word spoken, Orthan rubbed his hands as they descended the main stairway and clattered through the old hall to the front gate, their heels ringing loudly, their mail and gear jingling. On either side of them, servants were busy taking down and rolling tapestries, or carrying off heavy, carved chairs with gold inlay, the style of three generations previous. Windows were being removed, leaving the castle a bare shell, suitable for a satisfactory siege game.

"It's good to deal with one who understands the military," Orthan said. "Here's the boundaries, here's the rules, point, point, point, and we're done. Civs, they argue about every piece of porcelain, every bush, yowling, 'But what if?' until your head aches, and then they've got their hands out. The king's purse might be deep, but it's not a bottomless pit. As they ought to be the first to know, they argue so much about taxes. Heh. Looks like we've got everyone in at last."

They had passed through the courtyard to see dust hanging in the air above the meadow where they had set up camp. The swarms of youth in brown had been obscured entirely by strings of horses, wagons, and a mass of warriors moving about with various duties, a few casting glances skyward at the gathering clouds. The smell of horse and human, of cooking food, hit them with a similar sense of sharp anticipation.

As they got closer, the mass became identifiable as discrete patrols, each with a task. Most talked, laughed, and joked with the geniality that father and son associated with the commencement of a massive war game, the prospect of fun not only for a day or a week, but for an extended period.

Orthan veered to search for the newly arrived captains. Damedran lagged, hoping to slip away to his own crowd to find out how much was finished, and what practical jokes might be possible.

Then a bugle's exciting challenge ripped the air from a distance: the king's signal, but blown once.

"It's the war commander. Riding at the gallop!"

Heads turned, voices sharpened, and that enormous crowd of people—everyone at different chores—parted like the waters of a great river. Down the cleared, trampled grass rode Randart at the head of an honor guard of six.

Damedran's first reaction was the old excitement. That's what command did for you, it parted the way better than magic ever could.

Orthan laughed at his son's avid expression. "Dannath does so love scattering us like chickens in a fowl yard. Always has."

Damedran looked up skeptically. "Uncle Dannath? He doesn't love anything. Except work."

Orthan shook his head, watching the riders rein to a halt. They were immediately surrounded by officers, to fade back again when Randart waved a gloved hand, obviously giving some order, after which he disappeared into the command tent, two of his guard taking up position at the flap. "He loves power," Orthan murmured.

Damedran grinned. "And we don't?"

Orthan grinned back. "I like my power circumscribed. I wouldn't take a crown if it fell in the dust at my feet. Too much work. Think about it. I was upstairs watching my old cadet friend, Trevan Hazhan, now the Baron Cheslan. He was with Dannath and me and the king in the academy. The king handed out titles as he'd promised. We got ours. But are we ever *at* our castle?"

Damedran's lips parted. It was true. He was technically heir to a barony now, but that title had never seemed real. He'd only been in the castle for a few brief visits since he was eight, and old enough for the academy. Wolfie's mother helped Damedran's mother govern it, and Damedran had gradually grown accustomed to the idea that Wolfie would inherit. Because *he* was going to have a much higher rank.

"Would you leave the academy if you could? Go live in the castle?" Damedran asked his father. "I know Uncle Dannath wouldn't. He'd hate that, being stuck inland at some poking-small castle. He's used to being the king's right hand."

Orthan chuckled, muttering under his breath.

Damedran thought he heard the words—*he's used to being king*—but wasn't sure he'd heard right. Wasn't sure he could even ask. Anyway they were nearly at the command tent, and Uncle Dannath appeared at the flap, beckoning impatiently.

The jumble of belongings, maps, papers, swords wooden and real, had been thrust into the far corner of the tent, the folding camp table swept bare. Randart looked up at his brother and nephew, his eyes red-rimmed with tiredness and road dust. "Report."

"Just now finishing up with Trevan. Everything laid out, all in order. First thing—"

Randart waved his gloved hand. "You see to the logistics, Orthan. Where are the other wings?"

"Probably on the road. I haven't had any scouts, but we just got here ourselves," Orthan replied.

Randart nodded once, staring down at the list Orthan had laid on the empty table. It was apparent that he was preoccupied, that he didn't see it.

The silence in the tent seemed to sharpen the sounds from outside: horses' hooves clopping, shouted exchanges, the thrump of marching feet on the cobblestone road, wagons creaking, grunts and laughs and curses as barrels and baskets and boxes were unloaded at the cook tent an arrow shot away.

After a long pause, during which Damedran tried not to fidget or to look a question at his father, Randart said abruptly, "We'll ride the perimeter." And strode out, leaving father and son to follow.

As Randart barked orders for three saddled horses to be brought at once, Damedran sighed. More interminable talk about logistics, had to be. He longed to get back to the cadets' side of the camp.

He turned his attention that way and caught sight of shoulder-length ruddy curls. Lesi. Talking to Ban! What were they talking about? Lesi lifted a saddle and turned, her gaze meeting his. Her expression changed to the remote one he hated.

"Damedran."

The sharp tone whirled him around. His uncle gave him an impatient look, and Damedran loped to close the distance between himself and the two men.

The war commander glared at the senior cadets, then mounted up. They rode out, again everyone backing out of the way, no matter what they were doing.

On the way out of the camp, Orthan talked about the baron's dispositions. Randart and Damedran only appeared to be listening.

As soon as they reached an area Randart deemed beyond earshot of the first perimeter sentries, Randart cut him off with an abrupt gesture. "No one can hear us. And no one is to know what we three discuss. Orthan, you are to be commended for your excellent attention to detail. I have had a chance to think over what you flagged, and I have the same suspicion as you do. That female with the firebird banner who fumbled onto the military road is probably Atanial's missing daughter. It would explain why the pirate Zathdar never tried to ransom her, or use her as a threat or lever in any way. She got free of him, then was, I believe, briefly held by the prince. Escaped him, too, which argues she knows magic."

"What?" Damedran demanded. "Princess Atanial's daughter?"

"I think so. The descriptions are very brief, but what we do have all seems to fit. It's that banner, mostly." Randart snapped his fingers. "There is another matter. Increasingly I find that reports are indicating unexplained lags in messages or messages not being delivered at all. Anomalies between what was sent and what was received. I believe we have moles in our own information relay, and possibly traitors in important places or close to important people. It will be my immediate job to investigate the most flagrant of these. In the meantime." Randart turned in the saddle to face Damedran. "You are to pick six of your most loyal cadets, and the strongest, and track down the Zhavalieshin girl." He pulled from his pouch a much-folded paper and handed it to Damedran. "Here's the best description we have."

"But—a princess? I don't understand. I want to stay here with the war game—we planned this all summer—"

Randart said softly, "Are you by any chance arguing with an order?"

That voice, terrifying since early childhood, chilled the back of Damedran's neck. He was too old to be beaten, he knew that. So the punishment would only be worse. "No, War Commander."

"You aren't cavorting with that Valleg girl, are you? I thought you'd gotten past that foolishness."

Damedran suppressed a surge of anger. "No."

"The Vallegs are a good service family. Always have been. For generations. I envisioned that girl holding one of the castles in Jora, once we retake it. But if," Randart said in that voice again, soft with threat, "I thought she was suborning you from your duty, I'll have her given a dishonorable dismissal."

Damedran thought wildly. "Oh, it's only that we had a wager. About who'd get their patrol flag to the castle wall first. I hate losing. You know how the seniors gloat. We do that a lot, Ban and Wolfie and the rest of us. Wagers, I mean." That much was true. But Damedran knew he was babbling, as if to cover over his lie. He'd never dared to lie to his uncle before.

Randart's forehead cleared. "Well. I made such wagers, too, when I was a boy, but you know, it is time to grow up. Face your adult responsibilities . . ."

Damedran had guessed right. His uncle, launched down that familiar path, could be safely ignored for a breathing space.

He had to think. These new orders were a disaster! He remembered vividly the lie he'd carelessly tossed off about that stupid princess. And how Ban Kender had reacted. Maybe he'd forgotten, but no, Ban never forgot anything. Damedran scowled. If only Wolfie's leg was healed. Ban was definitely second strongest after Wolfie, and far smarter. Well, as for the lie, he'd say he'd been told it. Yes, that should work. Damn lies anyway, they were too much trouble.

"...so I want you and your six mounted and ready to ride by the watch change," Uncle Dannath said, his tone sharp with finality. "You'll have to begin at this Three Falls Inn, where she is apparently taking a letter, to discover her trail. If you find nothing there, you'll ride the road all the way back to Ellir until someone responds to her description. But you will not halt for more than a single watch until you have her in hand. Got that?"

Damedran gave a stiff nod.

"You'll have the king's sigil, which will get you horses wherever you need them, and supplies. Once you find her, you will bind her against her performing magic. You will contact me, and I will tell you where to meet me. Because she is to be brought directly to me. *Only* to me. I will be giving you a magical case and the code to use to report, in case those damned mages are intercepting our messages. You are to reveal her identity to no one."

Damedran saluted. "It shall be done, War Commander."

"Questions?"

Damedran did not dare, not when the word was barked in that tone, but Orthan said, "I take it this is the king's personal errand?"

Randart hesitated. "I deemed it better, after a night of rest, not to tell the king. It will be far better in a number of ways if I have her first. Once I know what manner of person we are dealing with, she can be surrendered to the king."

No one spoke. But Orthan pursed his lips when his brother turned to survey the camp, and sent a glance at his son.

He's used to being king.

SEVENTEEN

Whammo! Now back to me.

When I left off, I was gloating over the ease with which I had gotten away from the military people, who had not only housed and fed me for free, but who had checked the shoes on my mare as well as curried her. They'd even cleaned and oiled my sword.

My gloat lasted, oh, about two hours, as I recall. Long enough for the next rainstorm to move in.

The civilian roads were soon quagmires at every dip. Once again the horse slogged up to her knees in muck, but this time at least I'd found a wagon to follow, and follow we did, until the wagon got stuck in the mud. I helped, the horse helped, but the big, strong workhorses pulling could not get those wheels out of the mud.

The owners, a pair of sisters, offered me space under the wagon. I took it while my mare joined the two big workhorses, all three animals apparently too wet to bicker. There was as much mud under the wagon as there was outside, but we were out of the rain.

I will pass quickly over that long, miserable night, everyone gritty and shivering, sharing soggy bits of food, while one of the women worried almost constantly about their baskets of fruit—until her sister begged her, eyes closed, to *please* stop asking what they were going to do.

We all finally fell asleep in a kind of exhausted dogpile, waking stiff, creaking, in vile tempers. I rode on, promising to send anyone I saw to help; they perforce had to stay until the mud hardened enough to roll out.

That week there was a series of rainstorms coming through, nothing ever as spectacular as the first, but definitely enough to keep the road soggy and impossible to travel in, unless you're a frog. I got lost not once, not twice, but several times, ending up in fields, in a forest, and once in a bog. Then I'd have to laboriously retrace my steps, always watching for signs of a road. I looked for the muddiest, most puddle-washed stretches and was usually right.

I tried to keep my temper. I did not look skyward and demand *What can be worse than this?* because my mother had trained me well. Ask the universe that, and it will happily show you just how many ways things can get a whole lot worse.

I said once, "What about asking 'What can be better than this?'"

She smiled and patted my knee. "That you have to do on your own."

As a philosophy it probably left much to be desired, but as a rule to go by, it worked. I hunkered over my horse and endured, glad when at last I reached a village with an inn.

They had a map on the wall as decoration, with all the nobles' castles and flags drawn in. Ignoring those, I did some mental math and discovered my slogging had probably advanced me all of a couple hundred miles. The key word there, you notice, is *advanced.* I'd probably covered three times that in false trails and back-tracking.

But I finally reached Zhavlir, and asking around got me to the Three Falls Inn, the sight of which cheered me immediately. Barliman Butterbur couldn't have run a cozier-looking place, opened in a V, at one side a stable, at the other a garden, big windows, the entire bottom floor golden-lit, the sign a big painting of three waterfalls.

The owners, a tall beanpole of a man and a tiny woman with wispy hair, were delighted to receive the letter, waterlogged as it was. I explained that I'd done my best—carrying it next to my skin, along with the remains of my journey food—but they hardly stayed to listen, the man was so anxious to read his letter, and the woman to get me to a bath, to hot food and to bed. I cooperated fully.

Trying to recall the lies I'd told at the first inn, I deflected their friendly questions as best I could. I departed the next day, armed with a carefully hand-drawn map with all kinds of landmarks on it to help me get across the mountains and through the dangers of Locan Jora to Tser Mearsies. Lovingly made—and quite useless. I did try, ever so casually, to ask about landmarks leading to the Bar Larsca Valley, inventing a shipmate from there, but no one seemed to know much beyond the fact that the lands south of the Northsca River were reputed to be wild.

Great.

I tried to remind myself that the worst of the journey, distance-wise, was over. I had to cross a river, pass the city of Barlir to the southwest, and there I'd be.

Well, the day's ride out of the city to the great bridge over the Northsca was about as pleasant as I'd had yet. Cool, clear, the autumn colors stippling the hills to the west with glorious reds, russets and about ten shades of gold. Even the neon orange leaves were beautiful, like little tongues of flame, highlighting the autumn shades with brilliant color. In the distance jutted up purple dragon-toothed mountains—the border dividing Khanerenth from Locan Jora. I was riding into my favorite kind of scenery, mountain forest, and my spirits soared.

The road was crowded the last half of the day, as it narrowed toward a massive bridge. I found myself near a small group of early high-school-aged kids training to be minstrels. I kept hearing their voices rising and falling over the sounds of talk and laughter and the snufflings, whinnies, and brays of animals. The voices were high and sweet, the songs complicated rounds and interlocked rhythms that I could have listened to for days without ever getting tired.

I crossed the bridge sedately behind the singers, looking at the rushing river below, and the sturdy, magic-protected bridge around me. Bridge structure wasn't much different from Earth, only the materials varied. But those mighty braided chains, the iron-banded timber supports, were all reinforced by magic spells, the wood hardened into something that almost looked like stone, the chains glowing with a dull metallic gleam and no speck of rust.

The bridge was maybe twenty feet wide, ten feet for traffic in each direction. No one rode over. Everyone walked their horses. Bored warriors in brown waited at either end, on the one side with wheat stalks sewn onto their tunics, and at the far end roses: ducal sigils.

When I neared the last of the bridge, I followed the motions of people ahead of me, thinking *I'm nearly there.*

That lasted, oh, thirty seconds?

A woman my age and height in brown with a rose waved me over to one side.

Surprised, I went. I was not about to call attention to myself, not without good cause. I joined the group of people waiting for questioning. Behind me, people showed papers to the woman and passed. Those were all people with wagons or people dressed as runners.

My crowd moved briskly; the young singers barely spoke to the guards. They waved, laughed, said something or other I couldn't catch, and ran down the hill to join the crowd of people at the foot of a well-kept road, most climbing into a long wagon waiting there.

It was my turn. "Business?" asked an older fellow, stout, with a ducal coronet stitched over his rose.

"Travel," I said.

"Join," the man replied, pointing.

"Join what?"

His eyes narrowed from boredom to mild interest.

I said, quickly, "I'm a sailor. This is my first journey inland."

"Oh." He shrugged. "The Duke of Larsca's law states that anyone on the road during harvest time not on king's business or delivering goods puts in a week of harvest duty for ducal lands."

A week! Annoyance flushed through me, and I gauged the situation with a quick glance. Maybe ten of them in various jobs all over the bridge foot. Then I turned back to the man, who was now regarding me with more wariness than curiosity.

"Oh." I swallowed, my throat tight. "What do I do next?"

His expression cleared. "Go down there. Wagon will take you to wherever they need. You get housing and food during the week, and extra over quota gets pay. Your horse gets stabled free of charge."

I bobbed the way I'd seen people salute the warriors and followed the young singers, who had jumped into a wagon and commenced a splendid round. A brown-liveried stable hand took charge of the mare, leading her to a string of animals.

I climbed into the wagon thinking sternly: *Lie low, go along. Let's not get search parties and arrests and descriptions going out, shall we? If you need to, you can always run off.* People clambered in behind me, their ages roughly from about fourteen or fifteen, like the minstrels, to maybe early thirties or so. When the wagon was full, someone up front yelled, "Here we go!" and the team of six big plough horses started moving—an empty wagon almost immediately being guided into our place.

When a rainstorm boiled up over those hills to the northwest and bore down on us, everyone in the wagon helped put up a canopy, laughing and joking, and we rode dry while rain drummed the canvas overhead, cascading in silvery fringes all around. The minstrels sang rain songs, many joined in, and I sat there safe and smiling.

There's no use in going into the daily details of my career as a farm worker. I decided by the end of the first day to dutifully put in my week without drawing attention to myself. The place was comfortable, the food was plain and plentiful, the work easy. Here was my chance to hear gossip that would be useful. Or at least learn how people were feeling about the government, so I could tell Dad when I saw him again.

Human nature being what it is, mild fun—though we live for such moments—is really boring to read about.

The ducal farm was a series of long, low buildings, sturdily built. The crop we'd been chosen for was olive picking. I was surprised there were olives growing here at all. The single thing I knew about them was that a Mediterranean climate was needed. But these olives had adapted over the countless centuries since being brought over. The hot northern sun during the summer ripened the olives, the way the hills were sheltered by the mountain ridge looming to the west apparently kept off the worst ice storms in winter, and so these gnarled, rough-barked trees had been steadily producing olives for centuries, while all around Khanerenth's crazy history raveled and unraveled itself.

I learned about olives' growing cycle and that the right time to pick them is an exact science. I also learned that for maximum value they have to be pressed within a day or so, depending on the outside temps.

The work was mostly a lot of reaching overhead, as I was tall. I did my picking as far from the others as I could, carrying on long mental conversations—okay, arguments—with Jehan, justifying the distrust I'd felt so strongly that I wouldn't listen to him.

But I couldn't quite get past knowing how very much I'd hate it if he'd refused to listen to me.

So then I'd try to distract myself by watching the others. That was much more entertaining than my bleak thoughts. I observed the girls noticing the boys who ogled the girls as we carried our bucket loads down to be washed and pressed. Big guys mostly handled the presses, which is why the more flirtatious girls were really enthusiastic about filling their buckets in order to make the trip down the hill. In fact, I am pretty certain that our work boss, a tough grandmotherly woman, deliberately put the cutest guy on the first press, tall, buff, with long curling reddish gold hair and a wickedly flirtatious manner. He *always* had a crowd around him, after fast, enthusiastic picking.

As soon as the sun went down, we were off work. After dinner there was equipment to ready for the next day, then we were pretty much on our own. Every night people who had learned some sort of instrument (some good, some not so, but they could all more or less follow a tune) and the singers got up some sort of concert or dance, and tired as we were, we found energy for dancing.

So did I get a romance going?

Either I tell the truth or toss this thing in the fire.

Easy answer first. Tavan, the cute guy, took no notice of me. He seemed to prefer the shorter girls. But there were other guys, nice ones, cute ones, who seemed to like my looks as much as I liked theirs.

Did I flirt? Jokes and comments, yeah. The easy stuff. But ardent eyes, the narrowed gaze of interest, personal questions, that subtle shift from general interest to individual—whenever I sensed those things, I found somewhere else to be. My favorite retreat was the women's baths, a long room with a hot spring diverted to run through, carrying endless clean water in a natural Jacuzzi. Wow, did that feel good.

Anyway, back to the guys. Why didn't I respond? I'll get there in a sec.

At the end of the first week, which was all I owed as a traveler, the work boss called me over and asked me if I'd put in a second week as the crop was ripening fast, and I'd be paid. They didn't have enough tall women.

I thought, why not? I was having fun. I didn't feel any hurry, except a vague sense of unease when occasional bits of gossip radiated out from Vadnais's royal castle. When my mother's name came up, the rumors were all about how the king and Princess

Atanial were constantly giving parties and balls. Sifting that, I figured my mother was at least safe. She'd been guarding herself a lot longer than I had been guarding me, after all.

In fact, there is one conversation I'll report. We were all sitting on the plain plank porch outside our dorm, the evening cool but still, the air faintly blue everywhere but the forest, which was a vast black silhouette. Insects chirruped peacefully, and in the distance a couple of the horses whinnied at one another.

They'd passed out letters brought in by a runner, and someone mentioned the king and Princess Atanial.

One woman said, "So is she gonna marry him? I mean, she must be after him."

"She's a prisoner," I said, but under my breath.

The woman next to me, who was sewing a hole in the armpit of her shirt, glanced over. "She is?"

"Ribbons for chains. But she can't leave. Remember whose wife she is," I said quickly, wishing I'd kept my mouth shut. I'd gotten into the habit of carrying out those arguments under my breath while picking.

A thoughtful silence settled, and one of the younger women, sitting on the ground leaning against the rail, murmured slowly, "I never thought about it before, but what does a princess *do*?" At the laughs and expressions of scorn, she added hastily, "I know! Balls, gowns, flirt with princes. But, is that it?"

"Practice to be queens?" said the sewing woman. "You would have to know how to read, for example."

The younger woman stirred at this sarcasm, so I said hastily, "I never thought about it, either, but you're watched all the time, I expect. Everyone wants a piece of you. I don't mean that necessarily in a good way."

"'Piece of you'," the sewer repeated. "A strange way to put it. Yet it seems right, from anything I've ever heard."

The younger one laughed. "You can't be serious. How much work is going to a ball?"

They broke into chattering groups, but at least the subject of

Princess Atanial was forgotten.

So now the subject I've been avoiding. The real reason I didn't flirt was because of Jehan.

After those mental arguments I worked hard to shove him out of my mind. But if memory didn't intrude, occasional bits of gossip brought him right back to the forefront of my attention.

I worked so hard to forget him that one afternoon I accidentally broke a branch by yanking too hard, but luckily the olives on it were all ripe and I hastily stripped them off and stowed them in my bucket.

I took my three-quarters-filled bucket away so I wouldn't hear the chatter about Prince Jehan and the Sartoran ambassador's beautiful cousin dancing all night in some marble hall. I didn't care about his flirts, no, not me. He could double-talk anyone he wanted, yessiree-Bob.

Despite my determined efforts Not To Think About Him, I always ended up in those long, exasperating imagined arguments with him. They were exasperating because I didn't know the truth. So when I was mad at him, I imagined him admitting to being a liar, traitor, and all the rest of it, lower than the lowest slug . . . and I'd think, why fool yourself? You were a total IDIOT to have dusted out without finding out the truth.

But how was I to find out the truth while his prisoner and surrounded by his people?

No, I had to stick to my plan. Find my father. Dump the entire mess into his lap. He'd know what to do about Prince Jehan Jervaes Merindar.

I wished—oh, you have no idea how hard I wished—that I hadn't kissed Jehan.

Because my subconscious, who is about as stubborn as a corral full of hungry mules, didn't care about politics, promises, power, princes or princesses. Her needs were direct. Despite how hard I fought during the day, every night when I had to surrender to her realm she adored pressing the backtrack button over and over to replay in my dreams every moment of that sweet, breathlessly intense, absolutely glorious experience.

Me: *Subconscious, please don't do that.*

Her: *I want that one.*

Me: *You're being a total cow. I mean, anybody with half a brain does not mistake lust for love.*

Her: *I want that one.*

Me: *He's a liar. He cheats his own father! He says what he wants me to hear, just like dear old dad.*

Her: *Oooookay, you wanna be like that? Just wait for your dreams tonight, sucker.*

Despite the fact that in this culture, as long as you have not married with the ring ceremony, it's expected you'll shop around before finding a mate, I couldn't head for the sweet-smelling shadowy glades where insects softly chirruped and autumn leaves rustled, to enjoy some recreational kissy-face with one of the nice, cute, pleasant young men I met there, who had no possible interest in politics or power or any of the rest of it, only in me. Because my subconscious promised stubbornly that if I did, I'd have about as much fun as kissing a fence post.

There I was, almost three weeks later, when the last of the olive crop was pretty much down and we were doing a second run for gleanings.

I was a day from finishing the job, so I put in some time that morning asking easy questions here and there about the main landmarks that would lead me to Ivory Mountain.

We were about to break for the midday meal when the entire camp was surprised by new arrivals.

We Got Males.

EIGHTEEN

ONCE THEY WERE ACTUALLY on the road, Damedran and his princess-hunting posse enjoyed the ride. The second morning, as they relaxed around the campfire in their bedrolls while the two servants saw to the horses and cooking, they gloatingly counted up the toilsome chores they *weren't* doing, unlike the other senior cadets.

When breakfast was ready they climbed out of their bedrolls, and after the servants cleaned up, they took to horse. Through the remainder of the day's ride, they wondered aloud from time to time what their own group was doing right at that moment, but Damedran and Ban both noticed that once you were actually out of sight of the game, most of the fun was gone. You had to be there.

Adjusting to what they were missing was a whole lot easier when they remembered that they had the king's sigil. They could change horses whenever they wanted, and could eat anywhere they wanted, what they wanted, and that included drink. And no one made a peep. The shot would be sent back to Vadnais to be paid by Uncle Dannath's paymaster.

Ban Kender and Bowsprit Lanarg hadn't much liked being pulled from the war game, but that was because Damedran hadn't told them why until Castle Cheslan was far behind them. Their first reaction to *We're going to intercept Princess Atanial's daughter* was surprise. Then both of them thought philosophically of the fact that success meant early promotion. Their families counted on their doing well in the military, and if finding and escorting a princess's daughter to the royal city got them made patrol leaders way ahead of the other seniors, well, see the tears?

Except for one bump, the good mood lasted until they reached the outskirts of Zhavlir a few days later. The bump happened midway through the ride, when they reached Barlir and visited an inn. There they were, with no glowering captains, masters, or war-commanding uncles to order them around. They didn't have to spend, or account for, a copper dunket of their own. And the dark ale here was famed throughout the army. What a perfect opportunity to get snockered!

. . . except they had to ride the next day.

Well, all right, so you learn something about how unfun it is to get drunk anywhere but at home, and not with duty the next day.

After that never-too-soon-forgotten ride, things went right back to first rank. Even the weather cooperated, turning from cold with occasional bands of rain to a stretch of sunny, warm days.

The moment finally came when they cleared the last hill above Zhavlir and saw the fine, smooth military road curving gently down between hedgerows toward the city gates.

Damedran cleared his throat. "Getting sick?" Red asked.

"No." Damedran did not look at any of them. Of his six companions, Ban, Red and Bowsprit rode close. The others had formed in a row behind, and could only hear the murmur of voices ahead. Behind them rode the two servants with the equipment packed on the remounts, talking quietly to one another; they didn't even try to listen in on the toff cadets.

Damedran said quickly, "Our orders are, we grab her, and report to my uncle. Then we take her back to him, wherever he is."

Red shrugged. "Sounds easy to me."

Bowsprit turned to Ban, who sent him a grimace.

Ban eyed Damedran. Something was wrong. "We're not taking her to the king?"

"No."

Bowsprit whistled.

Damedran flushed. "My uncle is the war commander. He's the king's voice, his right hand—"

"This isn't a military matter," Ban cut in. "It's a royal one. Why aren't we taking her straight to the king? Or at least contacting him?"

Damedran snarled, "Shut up. Just shut up. You want to be reported for insubordination? In case you have forgotten, *I* am patrol captain for this mission, and it's *I* who has the communication relay." He dug the gold case out of the pouch at his belt and brandished it.

Ban's jaw tightened, his eyes narrowed, and he faced forward.

Bowsprit sent Damedran one last, unhappy glance, then he too faced resolutely forward.

Red jerked his good shoulder up in agreement. When the three behind started in with variations on "What did he say? We can't hear!" he explained in a few terse words.

Two of them shrugged. They were used to Damedran's ways. But the third burst out, "I don't like this."

Ban drawled over his shoulder, "*Lord Damedran Randart* is the *patrol leader*. Oh, I beg your pardon. Patrol *captain*. Haven't you heard? *He* has the communication relay. *He* can snitch, I mean, *report*, us for insubordination. Just for asking honest questions."

"Shut up, Ban."

Ban lifted his voice. "But *we're* not to think. We're here as muscle. Our next order will probably be to beat her up. That doesn't take any thinking. Six of us! Six and no thinking allowed—"

"*Shut up, Ban!*"

"Is that an order, *Lord High Patrol Captain?*"

Damedran burned with fury, and his fists bunched. He longed to fling himself on Ban and pound his face into the dirt. But they weren't behind the stable where cadet fights were carried out with friends on watch. They were here, they were supposedly on their first mission as men, and not cadets.

First mission. As men.

He groaned, remembering his uncle's softly uttered threat, and his anger doused like water on flames. "*My uncle* ordered this secret mission. Want to know what he said when I dared one single question?"

Instantly sobered, Ban shook his head. He'd only seen the war commander lose his temper once, but he'd seen the results of it many times. Not only terrible floggings before the entire assembled academy and garrison, but he'd heard of people vanishing altogether.

As for Damedran, Ban had never actually envied him his exalted position, not after the first time he watched his fellow ten-year-old leave his uncle's chamber after a thrashing. Though Damedran's father was the head of the academy, everyone knew he obeyed his older brother in everything, including how to raise his son.

Red said in a make-peace voice, "King or war commander, what's the problem?"

Bowsprit slewed round in his saddle, studying Ban's long face, then he slewed back. "When Red puts it that way, what *is* the problem?"

Ban hunched his shoulders, glowering between his horse's flicking ears. She was aware of the animals on the civilian road on the other side of the hill, though none of the humans were.

Ban said slowly, working it out as he spoke, "I think it's the secret part of the mission. And the fact that it's *us*. And not any of the guard. Think of it. Your uncle could send any of the top scouts, any of his honor guard, who are all picked for skill and speed and all that. I mean we're about the best in the academy, with one or two exceptions—"

He paused for the hoots and scornful comments to die down, then continued. "—but we're still academy. Why isn't he sending any of them, when they are so much better?"

"Yeah." Bowsprit slewed around again. "Yeah!"

"We don't have orders to, ah, kill her, or anything?" Ban asked in his most surly voice in an effort to hide his anxiety.

Not that it worked, because Damedran felt the same way. "No! No. We're to capture her in secret. No one to find out who she is. Tie her up so she can't do magic. Report to my uncle via message box. And then take her to wherever he says. Only to him, he kept repeating. Not to anyone else, and not a word to anyone, either."

Silence fell between them as they reached the bottom of the hill. They were in arrow shot of the city gates, and the military road was about to blend with the crowded civ road.

"I don't like it," Ban said as the two roads converged, and Damedran made a short gesture meaning *shut up!*

This time Ban obeyed, and they fell in just behind a wagon full of bushels of vegetables, driven by a very shapely girl who kept looking round in a pretense of checking her cargo.

Bowsprit and Red sat up straighter, sneaking peeks at the girl, who scoped them out pretty thoroughly from under drifting black curls. The boys tried to catch her eye when she looked their way. The rest of the time they were checking out her figure instead of watching the road, until Damedran caught them at it. He pulled his riding gloves from his belt, leaned out and whapped Red.

"Pay attention," he snarled. "What if that pirate has spies tracking us?"

They all looked around, radiating furtiveness.

Satisfied that the passing farmers and merchants were not secret spies, Damedran said in a low voice. "Now, here's what we'll do . . ."

None of them gave a second look to the scruffy, scrawny red-haired man slouched on the back of a tired horse, who plodded two wagons behind them. The kingdom seemed to be filled with plain, wiry red-haired men who served in stables or at table or sewed or cobbled or did masonry.

The same was not true of this scruffy red-haired man — known at this end of the continent only as Owl — who was finally close enough to identify them.

He'd first spotted them as the military and civilian roads

topped separate hills and started down toward the fork. He always watched for military roads and who might be on them, going where.

His glimpse of a patrol of cadets had taken him by surprise. The boys looked familiar. He'd ridden along in frustration, peering as they vanished and reappeared again, hidden by hedgerows and the last hill, and then never-to-be-cursed-enough wild ferns growing alongside the roads.

He dared not gallop or in any wise call attention to himself. If that really was Damedran Randart and some of his pack of rats, they might possibly recognize him from his menial labors around the academy. Unlikely, but he wasn't going to take the chance. It was too strange to encounter them here, so far from Castle Cheslan and the rest of the army. Surely they should be at the center of the war game.

Everything seemed to conspire against him, including the angle of the bright sun turning them into silhouettes, until at last the two roads merged. A few moments later the one riding point turned his head, long blue-black hair swinging, as he whapped the red-haired boy with gloves—and Owl stared in amazement. That was indeed Damedran Randart.

Why? The only thing Owl was sure of was that Randart was behind it, for some purpose sinister and sneaky. Surprise inspection for the local garrison, maybe?

The urge to write a note to Jehan gripped him, to be fought off. One thing that would call attention to him would be scrawling a note on horseback, and whipping out a golden case to put it into. Owl knew that he'd be seen. Circumstances were lamentably predictable that way.

So once they were through the city gates, he deliberately turned his horse up a different street than the main street, which led straight to the garrison. He dismounted when he found a quirk between two old alleyways, moss growing between the bricks. He slid off the horse and kept it between him and the alleyway intersection as he pulled out his chalk and a scrap of paper from his pack, and wrote:

Damedran here. Know why? Should I do anything?

He tucked it into the notecase and leaned tiredly against the horse to wait. Jehan might answer right away, if he was alone. But if he wasn't, it could be half a day. Or longer. So he'd give himself a breather. If nothing came, it meant Jehan was away from his rooms.

As he stood there absently running his hands over the neck of the drooping animal, he thought back over the exercise in frustration the past weeks had been. Like losing the princess during the very first storm that ended the summer and discovering she'd vanished. He'd ridden as hard as he could along the river road, pausing only to arrange for changes of mount, until he reached the foothills below the border mountains.

Here the road narrowed, leading directly to Moonsky Lake at the border. He'd asked at the inn where absolutely everyone stopped, and despite coins and exhaustive questioning, discovered no trace of any tall woman fitting the description of Sasharia Zhavalieshin.

So he'd ridden all the way back to the last inn he'd seen her at, wishing he'd dared sleep inside the first time. But that enormous wedding party and all those harvesters had convinced him to ride on to the next inn and wait for her to catch up. That was before the big storm.

He hoped that the inn folk remembered her. A description, some added coin, and the innkeeping pair told him they did indeed remember her. She'd helped that night, and further she'd carried a letter for them to the Three Falls Inn in Zhavlir . . .

Zhavlir? On the other side of the river?

Owl got a room, sat down, wrote a bitter letter, tore it up. Wrote another saying only that he'd found the right road. Sure enough Jehan wrote back: *Waste no time. Find her.*

So here he was again, after another mad dashing ride. Now he only had to locate the inn.

He yawned, leaning against the horse. "Just one more ride, old friend," he murmured, making a mental promise of bran mash as he himself thought longingly of a good pull on some fine dark ale . . .

While he was trying to find the energy to get himself back in the saddle and seek the inn, Damedran and his posse had ridden straight to the garrison in the middle of the town, sent a servant in to get directions to the Three Falls, and rode the few blocks to reach it.

They dismounted in the stable yard, Damedran saying, "The trail is at least a week old, so she can't still be here. But in case, I want a perimeter. Make certain you can all see one another. No yelling, no attention."

The others obeyed while Damedran walked into the inn. A teenaged girl clearing a table took in his long stride, his swinging black hair, the sword at his side, blushed and ran into the kitchen. He never gave her a glance, but made directly for the tall man at the counter.

He said, "Master Innkeeper? I'm looking for an old friend I was supposed to meet on the road. A woman with honey-colored hair, one of her names being Lasva. Very tall. Carried a letter for you."

Until the mention of the last, the innkeeper had looked puzzled, for he'd served plenty of tall women with honey-colored hair, and Lasva was a very common name. But the letter?

"Ah, the sailor! Very nice person. You come from the west, then? Your accent is good. Are those not guard colors?" He indicated the brown tunic.

"West?" Damedran repeated, as confused as the innkeeper.

"Yes. What was it . . . somewhere west of Colend . . . Bermund? Hanbria? No, I think it might have been Tser Mearsies. Yes. My wife made her a map, see. She can draw a mighty fine map. She puts things like rivers and forests and mountains in it, little tiny ones. Not like real ones, if you get my drift, but to represent—"

Damedran waved a hand. "I comprehend. So she rode west, did she?"

The man shrugged. "One can only assume so, if she asked for the map to help her get home again."

Damedran bit his lip against letting out any curses, turned away, then turned back. He pulled out his coin purse and laid several heavy golden six-sided coins on the counter, but kept his hand on them. "Did she happen to mention any other places?"

He shrugged again, but his wife appeared, drying her hands, glanced from the coins to Damedran. Her tired face took on a wary look. "Is there a problem? She was a very nice young woman. Even neatened her room when she left. They don't always, the young."

"I think someone we know sent her wrong," Damedran invented desperately. He'd never been good at lying on the spot, he always had to think them out first. "But she was going to meet me, and I was east, see, not west."

"You don't look anything like her." The wife smoothed stray hairs off her forehead and narrowed her eyes. "Family, you say?"

"Friends. Ah, my older sister is a sailor too, see, and they got to know each other. And, well, I'm trying to find her." Running out of ideas, Damedran fought against losing his temper again.

The wife looked up at her tall spouse, who gazed down with an air of helpless question, and when a customer yelled out, "Innkeep! Is that ale ready, or must I fetch it myself?" the man whirled away and the woman gave a tiny shrug. "Well. Not my business, I guess you could say. She did ask a bit about Bar Larsca Valley. Said she was looking for a friend. I think she might even have said a sailor, come to think on it."

Damedran grinned. "Ah. Listen, I don't want any more mixed messages. It's not likely anyone else would ask. But if they do. You've forgotten, yes?" He took his hand off the coins.

She smiled, sweeping them into her apron. "I'm always happy to help a nice young woman like that. Indeed, sir."

Damedran almost ran out, signaling to Ban as he did. Ban waved at the next cadet down, and they soon assembled in the courtyard.

"Bar Larsca Valley," Damedran said. "Right back where we started out!"

"Unless she's at the other end," Ban put in. "You know, at the mountains."

"Why would anyone go to the mountains?" Red asked.

Damedran ignored them. "Or she went to Tser Mearsies. But why would she go there?"

"Escape us," Ban said dryly.

"Not in Bar Larsca." Damedran shook his head, thinking of Castle Cheslan sitting at the southeast end of the valley. "Anyone would tell her about the siege game. You'd think. So maybe she did go to Tser Mearsies after all."

"And leave her ma behind?" Red put in.

They all looked thoughtful at that, turning to Red with expressions very close to respect. Red blushed. "Well, I wouldn't. Leave my ma. If—" *If I knew she was a prisoner of the king.* He might get himself into trouble if he said any more, and so he flapped his hands out from his sides, looking skyward.

Damedran was done with the conversation anyway. "Back to the garrison. New mounts, and we're on the road. Remember, we're at least a week behind her."

They returned to the servants, who had been holding the reins of the horses all this time. They remounted and rode sedately out, remembering the order not to call attention to themselves.

One they reached the open road, they could loosen the reins and gallop with the wind.

They reached the garrison at the same time as Owl reached the inn. He walked up to where Mistress Innkeeper was polishing the counter, her expression distracted. The common room was empty except for a table of drunks at one corner, with whom Master Innkeeper was obviously trying to reason. In the kitchen a pair of young teens were busy frosting pastries. Both glanced at Owl, then went back to work, obviously losing interest.

Owl felt the inward tingle of magic—an answer from Jehan.

He laid a silver coin on the counter. "I was told that your

relations sent a letter via a young woman, tall, wheat-colored hair probably in braids. I would like to know where she went, if you remember?"

The woman glanced from the coin to Owl's face, her jaw tight, her hands thrust into her apron pockets. "Couldn't rightly say," she finally replied.

Owl sighed. "I may as well get a room, then. Send word to the stable I'll pay for a bran mash for the mount. Name's Owl."

He sat in a corner, looking about. The man was dealing with the drunks, the woman had vanished, the teenagers were busy in the kitchen, talking and working.

He pulled out the golden case and found a rolled paper on which Jehan had written:

I know nothing about Damedran and some mission. Will try to find out. I don't like this coincidence.

Owl turned over the paper, took from his pouch his drawing chalk, and wrote, *I'm at the inn. They say they know nothing. Do you really want me riding on, weeks behind the last sign of her?*

He put the note in the case, sent it, stowed the case, and then ate supper while one of the teens brought in his gear from the stable and carried it upstairs.

He'd expected an answer right away, but none came. One never knew when Jehan could get the freedom to visit his rooms.

At sundown four young musicians came in, bearing instruments. Mistress Innkeeper opened all the windows and set lamps on each sill. The music drifted out onto the streets and before long the place was filled with custom, drinking, eating, dancing, singing, talking. Owl sat in isolation, too tired to care when the dancers, maneuvering for space, bumped him with hip or elbow. When he caught himself falling asleep right there in the chair, he trod upstairs to the third floor and down the hall to where someone had chalk-marked "Owl" on the door.

The door shut out most of the noise. Someone had lit a lamp, which cast weak light on a bed, a small table with his saddlebag directly below it, a window opened to the cool night air below the slanting beams of the roof.

He pulled the gold case out and removed the tiny scrap of paper on which Jehan had written in careful letters that betrayed not haste but a long period of reflection:

Return to Vadnais.

Though he suspected Jehan was bitter with disappointment for several good reasons, Owl sighed with relief and fell into bed.

His mood was as sunny as the weather the next morning. After a long sleep, a long soak in the bath and a long breakfast, he slung his gear over his shoulder, paid his shot and sauntered out to the stable to retrieve his mount and start the journey south. This time he needn't hurry.

He was smiling to himself, mentally planning a route that would include as many good inns as possible, when he noticed the head stableman watching him in an uncertain way. A stealthy way, even.

Owl checked shoes, saddle, feedbag, then mounted up, and couldn't resist a single glance back. The man shook his head slightly and turned away.

"What is it," Owl said, suspecting he would hate whatever he was about to hear.

The man turned around again, this time scanning in both directions. But all the stable hands were busy, out of earshot.

He stepped to Owl's stirrup. "The mistress is a good one, few better. But she does like a gold coin, and she also is partial to a young, handsome face."

"What?" Owl knew this could not possibly refer to him, as he had offered no one gold, he was no longer young, and had never been handsome.

"Boys in cadet gear here yesterday." The man looked around. "Girl told me they offered six golds for information, and for Mistress to keep quiet. But no one saw fit to pay *me.*"

At that subtle hint, Owl dug into his pouch. "Guards?" Damedran? *Here?*

A nod, then the man leaned up and muttered, "Lookin' for a

tall woman. Light hair. Named Lasva. Carried a letter from Master's cousin at an inn downriver. Girl in the kitchen overheard it all."

Owl gaped. Damedran Randart had been *here*. Not at the garrison, on some fool army task.

There was only one explanation for him being here. He was hunting Sasharia. What had happened? Owl could have sworn Randart had no suspicions when he left the *Dolphin*. Well, of course not, or he would have used that force to take her.

The man sneaked another look around. "I'd swear that boy on point was a Randart. To say no more, a certain relation o' his being one of the reasons I no longer serve in the guard," he added sourly.

Owl handed down a fistful of silver coinage, which was the highest worth he carried. "She say where she was going?"

Another look. "Mistress drew her a map to go west cross-country. They said west of Colend. But she asked about Larsca territory. And when she rode out, she didn't turn west or north, but right down the south road."

Owl slapped the rest of his silver into the man's hand. "Thank you," he murmured. "And . . . I'd not mention this conversation."

The man gave him a wry smile. "I never even saw you."

Owl paused once, again at a corner where he couldn't be seen, and wrote a fast note to Jehan. Without waiting for an answer he started galloping down the south road.

NINETEEN

"LASVA, THERE'S A COUPLE of lookers here to see you," one of the younger girls said to me, eyes wide with interest and curiosity. Probably the more-so since I hadn't been among those going off for long walks in the woods during those evenings, or dancing until past midnight.

"For me?"

My first thought was Jehan.

I scoffed at myself. How would he possibly know where I was, after all these weeks? And second, more to the point, if he was here, they wouldn't say "a couple of lookers," not with that white hair, and the inevitable outriders and hoopla. They'd be going nuts over the sudden appearance of a royal prince.

So I shrugged, and hefted my bag as I'd been heading toward the stable anyway. Probably someone who wanted to hire me for my great reach. Like for apple picking or something.

When I reached the stable yard, two of the younger of my dorm mates were flirting with a pair of teenage guys. The one with the red hair was flirting back. I couldn't hear the words over the noise in the yard, what with horses coming and going, shouts of workers, and conversations everywhere as our former olive-picking mates began their departures.

The redhead laughed, leaned down, and tugged teasingly at one of the girls' braids, to get his hand slapped away with a pretense of anger. The other one, cuter by far, was tall, with a long, serious face and thick waving brown hair worn clipped back. Both wore ill-fitting summer tunics over their shirts, and brown riding trousers tucked into blackweave riding boots much like the military wear. They each had swords at their saddles and knives at their belts.

I walked up. "Looking for me?" I asked, relieved I didn't know them.

The dark-haired one regarded me with an expression impossible to interpret, but the redhead wiggled his brows. "Oh, I do hope you are Lasva."

The girls laughed, and the shorter, blond one (the biggest flirt in our dorm) cast me a mirthful glance. "Good luck winning a kiss out of Lasva! She's far too picky. You're better off with me."

"If they're hiring for kissing, you are the expert. But if it's apple picking," I said, making a show of looking down on her, "you're hopeless."

The girls and the redhead laughed. The other boy leaned forward to pat his horse's neck, as the animal was restless, ears flicking, weight shifting from one leg to the other, head tossing. His hand was big, strong, and callused across the palm.

"Apple picking?" The redheaded guy pretended surprise. "How ever did you know?"

"Because I've already worked a week over the quota on account of my size," I retorted. "What did they give you at the front, a name of all the tall ones who don't spend their time chasing after kisses?"

"Hey! I was a good presser," the blonde protested.

"Yeah. When Tavan was around," her friend retorted, rolling her eyes.

"Am I as handsome as Tavan?" The redhead smoothed back his tousled hair.

"No." All three of us women shook our heads.

Both of the guys laughed this time.

The redhead said to me, "Well, will you come apple picking?"

"Is it really apples? How amazing is that?" I said.

"How . . . amazing . . . is what?" The dark-haired one looked puzzled.

The blonde said, "She talks funny. But she's a sailor." As if that explained everything.

"We have an orchard." The redhead waved a hand in a vague circle. "Actually, several fruits and things."

I shrugged. "How long and where? I have somewhere to be."

"Oh," asked the redhead. "Where is that?"

The dark-haired one sent him a frown, but the redhead shrugged.

"Tser Mearsies." I gave them one of my lies, surprised a little that they would ask.

"This won't take long. Not a large orchard." The redhead grinned.

"All right." I shrugged, thinking that the fewer of those jewels I had to use on my journeys, the less attention I garnered. And anyway my father might need them back. "Let me get my mount."

The blonde grinned at me. "We'll keep them occupied. Take your time."

As I trod to the stable, the teasing, flirting, and laughter promptly started up again behind me.

I found my mare. She was fresh and ready to go, her head tossing, eyes alert, nostrils flaring. The stable hands had already saddled her, and my sword was intact, so all I had to do was tie on my gear and lead her out.

The short time I'd been gone, several more of the younger girls had gathered round. As I led my mare up, I was informed by the girls that my escorts were named Red and Ban.

"Call me Lasva." I mounted up. My riding muscles twinged. Weird, how quickly you lose it if you don't use it.

Everyone exchanged farewells and the fellows led the way out of the place where I'd spent so pleasant a stay. My earnings jingled with satisfying weight in my little belt pouch.

We proceeded at a walking pace toward the crossroads on the

other side of the hill from the farm. They did not angle toward the big main road, rutted from all those wagon runs to and from the duke's row of farms and orchards, but toward a smaller side road. We cut through all the traffic of wagons, riders, and walkers.

The boys had fallen silent. I was fine with that, busy with my own thoughts. Like, how I could get to a map without raising any questions—which meant lying. Which, of course, promptly threw right back at me all the self-righteous yap I'd given to Jehan about his lies.

Of course *my* cause is good, I instantly told myself.

But I could hear him insisting he wanted my dad back. If so, why didn't he just come out and say so, as Prince Jehan—why the purple pirate secret identity? Could it be for the same reasons I was lying? But he was a prince! Princes had power.

Or did he? On the yacht, Randart sure hadn't behaved like . . .

I sighed sharply, causing my mare to sidle.

The boys looked over at me, Ban concerned, Red confused. "Anything wrong? Uh, Lasva?"

"No. Just, next time someone tells me something, I'm going to listen," I said with fake cheer. "Instead of boring myself afterward with trying to imagine what they would have said."

Now both looked confused. I sighed again and looked around. While I'd been arguing with myself for the thousandth time, we'd gradually left the other travelers behind. We were completely alone on a road that had narrowed to something little wider than a worn footpath. "Where are the others?"

Ban said with a tight expression, "Others?"

"Hirelings." I motioned upward, as if picking an apple from a tree. "You cannot tell me I'm the only one hired from that place. I could name you at least a dozen who were faster and better than I. Taller, too." I meant the last as a joke, and belatedly Red laughed, but it was a strangled sort of laugh, and Ban's smile was more of a wince.

I stopped my mare. "Um, what's going on here?" I asked. "You two look like you swallowed glass. There's nobody else around—"

I was interrupted by the thud of horse hooves from beyond a rocky outcropping.

From the other side of the scree, five guys in cadet brown emerged, followed by two more guys with a string of horses. The first rider was familiar—hawk nose a lot like my own, generous, curving lips, black eyes, long glossy black hair—

"Damedran Randart?" I squeaked.

His mouth dropped open. "How did you know that?"

I swung my horse around. "All I know is," I ripped my sword free, "I am not going *anywhere* with a Randart!"

I whapped the mare's sides. Her muscles bunched. She was very ready for a run.

The others closed round me, their faces determined.

None of them were armed. Yet. I whirled around in the saddle, and swung my sword so fast it hummed. Whizz—snap—whoosh! I cut through the reins on three of their mounts. The horses panicked, and the boys couldn't control them.

That was enough to win me a gap in their circle. I gave the mare the knees again. She, rested for weeks, loved the opportunity to gallop, and took off like a rocket. I bent low over her head, bushes whipped past—

A darkish blur thundered up on one side. A flash of silver— Damedran Randart brought his sword down toward me.

I slewed, whipped my blade up. I was already off-balance. I had never fought on horseback and feared my block would be weak, so I rose up in the stirrups the better to brace against his killing blow.

Which was a feint. Damedran snapped his blade to a low flat thrust under my thigh. He flexed his wrist, and whoop! I tumbled right off the horse.

Only my martial arts training in falling saved me from breaking at least an arm, if not my neck. I tucked under, rolled over what felt like 345,679 jagged boulders, and momentum propelled me to my feet.

My sword had tumbled in one direction as I dropped in the

other. I couldn't see it, so I shifted into kenpo mode. When Damedran flung himself down from his horse, I whipped up a foot, kicked his blade clean out of his hand, followed up with a whirl and a sidekick to the knee, and he yelped, falling right in Ban's path.

I ran.

Got about three steps before two big, brawny boys came at me, arms out. No swords. I feinted toward one, and when his hands jerked up to block, I gave him a nasty palm-heel strike to the solar plexus, blocked a reach from the other, and snapped another side-sweep to the knee. He went down first, the other whooping for breath as he stumbled after me.

I whirled, dashed two steps — then two strong hands closed on my shoulders. I twisted, and used an elbow strike.

A teenage-male *whoof* blew in my ear. I grabbed his arm to swing him into his partner — but he planted his feet, and his heavier weight caused me to stumble.

And so the sixth one caught me round the waist. I twisted my hip in order to shift him off-balance, but he gave a grunt and lifted me off the ground. We both fell, he landing on top of me. Crunch. Thud. Three more muscle-bound teenage-boy bodies piled on in a first-class scrimmage heap, with me at the bottom.

Now it was my turn to struggle for breath.

The dogpile shifted, and the boys scrambled up. Two or three hands grasped at my arms, and knees thumped on my back and legs. Though I squirmed and struggled my mightiest, the fight was lost, and determined fingers twisted my hands behind me.

I heard a breathless, "What do I use? What do I use?"

"Who has the rope?" I recognized that voice as Red's. "Nobody brought any? You idiots, we knew we had to —"

"No rope!" The low voice was Damedran's, equally breathless. "Rope is for criminals. You have your sash?"

"We wore belts, remember?" That voice I didn't recognize. It cracked on the word *remember*.

"Here. Use your handkerchief. It's besorcelled, isn't it?"

"Yes."

"Let me do it. I don't want her hurt."

I was struggling with all my might while this conversation went on, not that it did me any good. My hands were effectively bound. Damedran kept pausing to check the knots with shaking fingers.

I heard various versions of fast, heavy-guy breathing all around me as someone stuck hands into my armpits and pulled me up so I could sit.

When the dizziness subsided, I found myself looking into a football huddle of grim faces, as sweaty and dusty as I knew my own had to be. Red's grimness was slightly bemused as he wheezed, and Damedran glowered.

A couple of them exchanged uneasy glances, obviously unwilling to speak first. Damedran kept flicking dark-eyed looks up at me then down at one hand as the other rubbed at his knee.

"Your call." My heart raced. I shifted my weight, knowing I probably couldn't do much besides spring to my feet, but if this ambush was shortly to end in murder, it wouldn't be with my cooperation.

Red gave me a somewhat shaky grin as he rubbed his middle. "Hoo, princess. You really do know how to fight."

Princess. Not Lasva.

So this was a royal hunt.

"Yah. Well. Not well enough to get away."

Damedran glared at me. "How did you know who I was?"

I occupied myself for a moment in trying unsuccessfully to blow a couple of my braids out of my face. My hair knot, so easily made that morning (as the universe had neglected to hint that I should dress for abduction) had come undone.

Though I was ambivalent about Jehan, I had one sure conviction: I did not trust Dannath Randart or any part of his family for a nanosecond. Reluctant to outright lie any more, I said slowly, "You look like your uncle. And I remember him from when I was little."

True, though I would not have recognized Damedran without that introduction aboard Jehan's yacht.

But he seemed to accept it.

"If you're supposed to kill me next, I really would like the chance to fight for my life."

Ban sat back, looking revolted, and Damedran said quickly, "We are not here to kill you."

I sighed. "Nice to know, but you have to see what it looks like to me. The disguises—" I nodded at Ban and Red in their humongous tunics. "The lie about hiring me—"

"Why are you traveling under a false name?" Damedran asked abruptly.

I shrugged. "Come on. Think about it. I'm yanked to this world against my will. My mother is taken prisoner. Am I really going to tell everyone who I am? I want to be left alone."

"To go to Tser Mearsies or to Bar Larsca?" He leaned forward. "I mean, what is there?"

"Nothing except anonymity. I've been a law-abiding olive picker for the past few weeks. I was about to become an apple picker. I thought."

"But you said you had somewhere to be," Red pointed out.

I shrugged. "Conversational gambit. To find out how long I'd be hired."

They exchanged uncertain looks. I suspected they didn't know whether to believe me or not. Time to get the subject from my goals to theirs.

I wriggled my shoulders. "So what next? The noose, war-commander style, or would that be a crossbolt in the back?"

Damedran's splendid cheekbones highlighted even more splendidly with a blush.

Ban said, "Bolt in the back? Why did you say that?"

"Well, isn't that the way he gets rid of inconvenient people? He certainly did to Magister Glathan. I cannot imagine he'd find me anything but inconvenient, or I wouldn't have been ambushed like this."

More uneasy glances met these words.

"Tell me where I'm wrong," I invited, trying again to sling my braids out of my face. I needed to see. I would have expected gloating and bullying, but if anything, these boys seemed if not reluctant, at least ambivalent about their having captured me.

"He wouldn't," Ban said, but I think we all heard the unspoken *Would he?* and he shot a pained look at Damedran.

Who seemed to be totally absorbed in reading his palms. Once again quiet fell, except for the breeze through some autumn red trees, the distant chuckling of an unseen stream, and the snort of a horse.

Finally I said, testing the parameters of this abduction, "Hey. If you're not really going to kill me, how about untying me? You know I can't get the drop on seven of you."

"Yes—" Ban began.

But Damedran put out a hand. "She has magic, remember?"

I sighed, wiggling my fingers. They were tingling slightly, despite Damedran's efforts not to cut off my circulation. I suspect adrenaline had not made him as accurate in safe knot tying as he'd thought he was. "I only know about three spells. Make no mistake, they are powerful, but they are also specific. If I could transfer around by magic, I would have rescued my mother and vanished long ago."

Damedran turned to Ban, who jerked his chin up, then brought his attention back to me. "So you can't use any of these powerful spells and turn us into rocks or something?"

I shook my head. "They are specific, having to do with types of healing, I guess you could say. Like that one your guys saw me do when I was first brought here by Devli Eban. That spell changes . . ."

I thought in English, because I did not know the magical vocabulary. The spell enabled one to "see" a poison in a person and shift what amounted to a dangerous molecule or two, so that they became neutral, and that shift propagated swiftly through the person.

I turned my attention to Damedran, who had crouched down near me, one hand absently rubbing his sore knee as he waited for my answer. It seemed plain that this situation was as important for him as it was for me.

"The spell calls a kind of fire, and not all people can hold it, but it seems I can. So you send the fire in a kind of thread into the person, and it burns out the poison, so to speak, and then is gone."

Ban nodded silently. "My sister said something of the sort once. But she said that kind of magic is only taught when you're at a high level."

"My father was desperate," I answered, glad to speak *some* truth, anyway. "And I guess I had the aptitude. My mother doesn't. She told me once he tried to teach her, but she couldn't hold the magic up here." I tipped my head back and forth. "There wasn't time to teach me all the basics, so he taught me that healing spell in hopes it would protect Mom and me in the other world. Unfortunately, there isn't enough magic potential there for it ever to work."

Damedran rubbed his jaw. "You can't use the spell to, I dunno, change someone's mind about something?"

I laughed. "No. No mood-altering, or mind-altering. At least, I do remember someone talking about the ancient Sartorans, and how they could do that sort of thing. How the villain Detlev can kill with just his mind, without moving a finger. But whether or not that's true, or the exaggeration of rumor, I can't do anything like that."

"Well, remember that Siamis fellow, Detlev's nephew, enchanted us all by talking to leaders," Red said.

Damedran sighed. "All right, but those rotters are four thousand years old, supposedly. Enough about them. What use is magic? I mean, I know, it keeps water clean, and so forth. But—" He shrugged. "Can you use it for much of anything else?"

Ban said soberly, "If you mean for war, my sister says any new spell has to be vetted by the Mage Council. And they find out if you're doing them. Magic is like rain to them. Say you ride into a territory well after the clouds dispersed, but you can smell the wet grass, see puddles, so forth. That's what my sister told me. There's a lot of it at high levels that can do frightening things. But the other mages always know it."

Red said, "Like Siamis spreading that spell just by talking. Of course he didn't care who knew he'd done it."

Come on, boys, see me as a person, not an objective. "Didn't you all pretty much lose a year? That's what I was told. Though I don't get how enchanting leaders of countries got people enchanted, too."

Red pulled off the huge rough-woven tunic and threw it down, leaving him wearing his shirt and brown cadet riding trousers stuffed into his boots. He was the shortest and leanest of them, but that meant he was my size. "If you were loyal to anyone, and he enchanted that person, you fell into it, too. That's what *we* were told."

Ban opened a hand. "My sister thinks time kind of stopped during that enchantment. The way they know is, babies stayed babies. You know how fast they grow. Nobody's baby started walking and talking that year."

That's right, talk to me, boys. Don't let me be the war commander's next crossbow target.

One of the quieter boys spoke up unexpectedly. "There's even bigger magic, in history. Like mages raised all the mountains north of Sartor. My tutor told me it affected weather for a century or more. Yet those spells didn't keep out Norsunder."

That silenced everyone.

I was trying to think of a way to shift the talk from evil mages to evil war commanders when Damedran got to his feet. He looked skyward, then around at the countryside, which was full of russet-hued trees and grass and late-flowering weeds, birds, a stream, and our horses, but no other people.

Then he sighed and faced me, though he wouldn't meet my eyes. "I'd like to untie you. Even if you give us another run." His brief grin was wry and changed his entire demeanor. His gaze touched mine for a fleeting moment. "I apologize for knocking you off the horse."

I shrugged. "Hey, you didn't use the blade on *me*, for which I'm grateful. That was a cool trick."

Cool puzzled them, but they seemed to get the idea.

"As for my part of the fight, well, I'm not going to apologize for anything until I am convinced I'm not on my way to a hasty execution, just because my family name happens to be Zhavalieshin."

Their easy expressions vanished as if wiped by a cloth.

Damedran looked sulky and brooding again. "I can't do anything until I report to my uncle and get orders."

"But—" Ban began.

Damedran swung around. "You know what the orders were," he snapped. Under his breath, though I heard it, "And what will happen if anything goes wrong."

I'd forgotten about fear.

In silence he wrote a note reporting my capture, put it in his magical transfer box, and sent it to the war commander.

TWENTY

IN A LIFETIME OF unexpected blows and tough decisions, Jehan had avoided the toughest of all.

Until now.

As soon as he received Owl's note—*I think I found her, somewhere in Bar Larsca, but Damedran is ahead of me*—he sent Kazdi to dispatch one of his covert teams of guards to Owl as backup.

And then he had to wait.

Days dragged by, excruciatingly slow and meaningless. He stood next to his father to review the palace guard before the chosen wing rode off to participate in the war game. He sat in the royal box during two jaw-stiffeningly boring plays dedicated ostentatiously to the king. Canardan skipped out on the second one, but Jehan remained where all could see him. He attended balls, picnics, regattas, dancing the night away and in the morning he attended trade sessions, but only as a spectator.

Then, unexpectedly, the king said after breakfast one morning, "There's no putting off these hearings concerning this treason-trial foolery. You may as well suffer along with me. It'll look good when these Guild Council fools unload the speeches they've been scribbling for days."

On the ride over (in an open carriage, so they could be seen, but surrounded by armed guards, so they couldn't be touched) Jehan said, "Why are we here? It's hot and stuffy in those halls,

Father. Are you really going to hold a treason trial for those people?"

"Of course not. Treason trials are nothing but an excuse to riot or an excuse to kill off half the populace. I don't want either of those things."

"So why do we go?"

"Because it looks like good faith. I'll whittle 'em down, one or two at a time, while we negotiate the trial. Meantime we'll let them talk as long as they like. It makes them feel good to talk. I want them to feel good. And so they can keep on making speeches and negotiating and feeling good until there's none of the fools left in prison."

Canardan had not meant to say that much, but the question on such a hot morning was unexpected. For some reason Jehan's tone reminded him of Math in the old days, the same dreamy pretense at being reasonable, without any awareness of how kings really did things.

He sent a sharp look at his son, half expecting one of Math's idiotic replies about ideals and loyalty and oaths, but Jehan just squinted up at the sky, admiring a flight of birds flying north for winter. Canardan sat back, wondering irritably why he was thinking of Math, of all people. Maybe he shouldn't eat so many smackerberry tartlets on hot mornings.

At first things began exactly as Canardan predicted.

Jehan stood behind his father's cushioned chair on a hastily made dais as guild masters and mistresses unloosed long, carefully written speeches that were almost comical, how constrained they were to be complimentary to the king and yet make their demands clear.

Another person might have laughed at how the plump, red-cheeked Wood Guild Master bowed every time he made a demand, followed by half a dozen effusive compliments. "As your majesty well knows, your loyal populace appreciates your condescension in . . ." hoola-loola-loo. "But." Bow. "We feel that if we are truly to move past the sad events of two decades ago, as you have often said so gracefully in your Oath Day speeches, then perhaps it might be deemed wise to forgive the, ah, assumed transgressions of these unfortunates in custody . . ." Bow.

Jehan did not laugh. Nor did he find the thin, tremble-voiced Hatters Guild Mistress funny when her good shoes, worn once a year, squeaked as she walked to the front. Her speech had been signed by all the people involved in hat making. As if the king cared for any of those named, but Jehan could imagine the courage it had taken to tramp the hot streets during this unconscionably hot autumn weather, collecting these names, believing that the number of them would impress the king.

Jehan sustained a brief but intense memory of Prince Math's face. He would care. He would listen. Jehan knew it. He could almost see Math listening to the frightened old woman, his head tilted at an encouraging angle.

Pity conflicted with resentment for his father's faint air of endurance, of boredom, the little smile that indicated the king was far off in thought. These people with their wretched speeches so full of clumsy hyperbole were not laughable at all. They were simply out of their realm of experience, but that was evidence of their courage. Wasn't it?

That image of Prince Math nodded emphatically, frizzy hair lifting like a sun corona round his head.

When the Hatters had had their say, they were followed by the Bricklayers and Stonemasons, the Silversmiths, the Ironmongers, the Millers and Bakers and Toymakers and Brewers and Vintners.

After the Coopers' Guild Master hoarsely whispered through his speech, the sea-related guilds were yet to come. Canardan raised a hand, and the old Cooper hastened to his seat as though he feared the sword on the spot.

"Good people." Canardan smiled, lifting his voice so all could hear. "I did say that each of you would have a chance to speak, and I keep my word. Khanerenth's tradition grants that all have access to the king. In turn, the king has access to all. We will not hasten into any decision, be assured, before all you are heard. This has been our civil law . . ."

A flash of warning tightened along Jehan's nerves. He remembered his father's words earlier about whittling down and realized what was coming next.

A moment later Canardan said, ". . . as for military matters, we all know that those are conducted separately."

He's going to cut out Silvag and Folgothan first. Jehan remembered his father's conversation with Randart, and his careless promise to deal with the matter "later." Apparently later meant now.

Canardan paused for the expected agreement, and of course he got it. He'd spoken no more than the truth. They could also feel the threat coming as Canardan said, ". . . and so we can agree that military matters can be effectively overseen by War Commander Randart—"

There was the name, and the implied judgment flitting toward the future, bearing those men's lives, impossible to retrieve.

"—who is, as we all know, a follower of the law." Jehan stood, heart hammering. His gaze slid past his astonished father, to the people.

Canardan stared at Jehan. Once again, this time more distinctly, there was the impulse to laugh. These good people looked so surprised, as if the unlit chandelier had begun to spout poetry. Or more to the point, if a sheep had trotted in from a nearby field and raised up its voice to discourse on law.

He waved a hand to invite Jehan to speak, wondering what the boy could possibly have to say.

"I admire the war commander second to none." Jehan turned in a slow circle, meeting everyone's eyes in turn. "You all will remember how well he reorganized the academy. The new regulations were strict, but all the old favoritism and slackness disappeared. He is an example to us all in how he obeys regulations from dawn to dusk, the same as the smallest cadet and the oldest guard captain."

He paused for breath, got an encouraging nod from his father, and went on in his blandest voice. "So I just know he'll remind us that the two guardsmen are in fact ex-guardsmen, hmm, and though I don't always pay attention the way I should, it seems to me that they might be termed, ah —"

"Civilians, if I may beg your highness's pardon," the guild master said, rising with more haste than dignity. He bowed to Jehan and to the king. "Former guardsmen Silvag and Folgothan are civilians." His voice was reedy with relief. Now he was on sure ground: civilian law.

"That is true," the Heralds' Guild representative said, raising a quill. "They have not been under orders for twenty years —"

"Their oaths were refused," exclaimed a voice from the back, and in the susurrus of *quiet*'s and *shhh*'s that followed, the Scribe Guild's representative said in her soft, mild voice, "If they have not received pay in twenty years, and that is easy to check in the paymaster's books, they are civilians in all points of law."

Someone in the back snarled, "I will not be silent! I'm related to the Folgothans, and I know they didn't do a thing, just talked. Are we all to be arrested for just talking, that is what I want to know!"

Everyone started asking questions and putting demands across one another, with many anxious glances sent toward the king.

Jehan sat down again, affecting boredom as his father sighed loudly. Couldn't he see how anxious people were for reassurance? Couldn't he understand how much they longed to hear the king promise that their way of life would be protected?

Canardan rose to his feet, the guard moving to flank him. The crowd fell silent, everyone there hot and tired, and despite his dismissive words, not there for pleasure. Canardan began to speak, using his humorous voice. He cracked a couple of jokes about the heat and heated comment, and then set out to soothe them.

But underneath every sentence his father uttered, Jehan heard the promise of the invasion. The kingdom would "soon" have land and wealth. There "would be" prestige "soon" for the warriors, the crown, the nobles. And that meant "prosperity" for every single artisan.

As for the promised trial, he assured them that there was no hurry, he granted more time for negotiation, and yes, the conspirators would be kept perfectly safe.

As he spoke, Jehan saw glances returning his way. Thoughtful glances. Jehan suspected his remarks would be repeated in private, maybe discussed, and passed along. The quickest ones had recognized what he had done.

It would have to be enough for now. He knew that this would be his last appearance in public, and not just because his father was annoyed at what he seemed to be choosing to regard as a typically cloud-minded blunder.

The time for all guises to be ripped away was nigh. Damedran Randart was hot on Sasharia Zhavalieshin's trail, and if he caught up with her, the final confrontation would be forced on them all.

"Let's go." Canardan sat back in the carriage, arms crossed, his profile disgusted.

Once again Jehan had slipped just ahead of disaster. Not because of his own ability, he thought as the carriage rattled along the brick-patterned main street, but because his father did not want to see disaster.

As for Jehan himself, his own sense of honor required one last attempt to reach his father. Jehan was not loyal to his father's politics, and never would be, but he remained loyal to the good memories of childhood, the interest, care, and kindness exhibited in their private moments, when matters of state had not divided them. He believed in the possibility of good intention underneath all the vagaries, the series of ambivalent decisions that had slowly led to worse ones.

And he would exert himself to try, even at the risk of his own life, to bridge that chasm of lies between them: to get his father to admit that he was about to break a treaty and throw the kingdom into war.

As the days dragged on, full of noisy parties with too much

food, too many people and far too many empty words chattered in his ears, he became aware that his father was increasingly restless.

Though Randart reported daily via magic to the king, as far as Jehan could determine, there was no mention whatsoever of Damedran's secret mission.

Meanwhile, Atanial was gone, leaving a confusing number of rumors about where she was. At last count, she'd been seen in thirty-eight different villages around the kingdom, including a town five weeks' journey away.

TWENTY-ONE

THE UNSEASONABLE AUTUMN HEAT broke at last.

On a bleak, rainy morning, Jehan stared sightlessly out at the rainwater gushing from a waterspout beyond his window, and vowed that whatever the result, if his father was honest with him, he'd drop all pretense and speak the truth in return. And take the consequences either way — but his instinct was that Canardan, once he got past his anger, would try to find a way to meet him.

That was, if Randart stayed out of it.

Not half a bell later, Jehan felt the tingle of magic. He'd taken to wearing his gold box next to his skin, waking and sleeping.

He had been about to go down to breakfast. He signaled to Kazdi to watch the other servants and took out Owl's note.

Damedran's got her. I'm following. Orders?

Jehan flicked the note into the fire, watched it curl and burn away, snapped the box closed, and stowed it in his tunic.

Kazdi's young face was serious, his brow puckered in question.

Jehan flicked his hand out, palm down. *Wait here.*

He ran downstairs to meet his father.

This is it. He wasn't ready — too soon — such thoughts flitted through his mind, faster than he could move, leaving him tense and filled with regret.

And so the two Merindars sat down at the table in the winter breakfast room for the first time this year. The room had been recently cleaned by the servants, potted plants moved in all around the edge of the room, tall ferny ones before the row of north-facing windows.

To the son's eye, the king was, as ever, big, bluff, handsome, his manner that of a king. The weak light filtering in behind the departing rain clouds shone on his long red hair and on the sides of his jaw, where jowls gradually growing more marked over the years blurred the strength there.

To the father's eye the son—so difficult to understand and so exasperating to control—appeared thinner than he remembered, his slim body tense. Not only that, but his entire manner was *present*, his blue gaze uncharacteristically acute.

Neither spoke as the servants brought in the steaming silver dishes, and so for a time the only sounds were those of clinking metal against porcelain, the whisper of feet on the floor, and beyond the windows the soft, occasional hiss of diminishing bands of rain.

Finally the king lifted his chin. The servants, alert to royal gestures, filed out, and Chas took up station inside the door.

"You have something on your mind, son?" Canardan asked.

"Several things," Jehan replied, toying with a piece of hot biscuit. "Here is the first. I am tired of parties. I want to do something with purpose."

The king tapped his knife lightly against his plate, not really hearing the restless, musical clink-clink-clink. "But the parties are to a purpose."

"Nothing that can't wait."

The king's eyes narrowed. "Wait on what?"

"You tell me, Father. They all talk, but around me. Past me. Knots of people of high degree and low. Innuendo, questions, secrets."

Canardan started eating in a mechanical fashion, frowning at the windows.

Jehan sensed ambivalence and tried again. "What is Randart

doing, Father?"

The king set down his cup. "Presiding over the war game. You know that."

"Why does a war commander need to spend weeks at a war game?" Jehan countered. "Why am I not there instead, if my place is over him?"

Canardan laughed, a forced sound. "No one is really over Dannath, you know that. To the people the king must be seen to command, and that extends to the heir as well. But Randart is far better at military matters than either of us. His eyes are the most discerning, and his report on our readiness for trouble would be more valuable than either of us riding out to camp in the mud to observe a lot of young men and women scrambling around shouting and waving wooden swords, and pretending they aren't watching us to see where we're looking. I'd sit there in boredom, no doubt thinking of all the work lying here undone, and as for your own boredom, you'd inevitably solve that by riding off in the middle of the night with the prettiest patrol leader who had gotten some liberty." Another forced laugh.

"And destroy someone's career? Acquit me of that much stupidity. We know anyone in the army I flirted with would be broken down to the bottom rank as soon as Randart heard of it."

The king lifted his shoulders. "Probably true, but if so, it does attest to his high standards for officer behavior."

Jehan let that pass. "I don't think his eyes are the most discerning. The recent fiasco with the fleet is proof enough of that. Another proof is how late the orders to ride were given, as if no one was aware of the advance of the season. A war game so close to winter? Let me ride out and observe. I promise I will have an assessment as good as anything Randart can give. And I can have them all back in their garrisons before the first snow."

The king set down his knife and fork and regarded his son, who gazed back with unblinking intensity.

Finally Canardan said, slowly, "I want them where they are."

"Why?"

The king's brows furrowed, a quick, irritated reaction. "Because Dannath wants them there. Because—we can move them in any direction if need arises."

"What need do you foresee?"

The king hesitated, then shook his head. "I think we are better discussing this matter when Dannath returns. With his report. We can make decisions much easier when we hear his evaluation."

And Jehan knew he'd lost.

It was not a surprise. Dannath Randart and Canardan Merindar had been friends since their teens, their ambitions marching in parallel. Too far in parallel—Randart having his eye on kingship, if not for himself, for his family. But it was clear that only events would convince Canardan of that. Certainly not his son's talk. Until now Canardan saw only unstinting hard work and unswerving loyalty in his oldest friend, plus a conveniently unflinching ability to make problems go away.

Sharp regret tightened Jehan. He made one more attempt to part on terms of mutual good will. "Let me ride to the academy, then, and consult with Orthan Randart about reorganizing the cadet lessons next spring."

"That, too, can wait on Dannath's return. I know you want to put in some of what you were taught out west, and I do like the idea of some of it. But we cannot plan without Dannath's assessment of their skills. The games were a fluke, we decided. Our cadets got too complacent. Dannath is convinced our training is not at fault."

"Let me ride to the coast, then, and inspect the harbors before winter sets in."

The king shook his head. "Despite the defeat of the fleet, you know as well as I that Randart is familiar with shore defense. And he has adequate captains in place." The king gave an easy laugh. He was back on familiar ground. "You have enough flirts right here, you don't need to be riding around your old haunts, and I don't want to risk any gossip about possible princesses."

"I won't meet any women."

His father shrugged, his brow furrowing impatiently. "Stay here." *Under my eye.* "Those potential princesses are right here in Vadnais."

Jehan laid down his knife and fork. "There is only one princess for me. Permit me to ride out and find Sasharia Zhavalieshin."

This time Canardan's laugh was genuine. "If I thought you could do that, you could go with my good will."

Jehan was about to say *But I can.* Risk everything on a throw and gamble that he could meet his father halfway, as he so badly wanted to do, despite experience, despite reason.

Then the king leaned forward. "You did. Didn't you? Randart boarded the *Dolphin* a few weeks ago. Before he went out to hunt that pirate. He thought you had that girl, for some reason. Did you?"

Jehan's heartbeat raced. "Yes."

Canardan shook his head slowly. "I didn't believe it. I still half don't. Randart was so sure you were plotting treason. But I figured even if you had her—and I didn't believe it—you were going to bring her to me. A surprise. Show me you were doing your job. Which was it?"

Images flitted through Jehan's mind, faster than words. Between one thump of his heart and the next he remembered Randart's disappointment—and heard the import behind his father's question. He was not asking Jehan's reason. He was saying *Are you for me or against me?* There was no compromise.

Taking Sasha to free Prince Math would be seen as treason, because *there was no compromise.*

The shadow of Randart stood squarely between father and son. As always, as always.

And so, hating himself, sick with regret, Jehan said, "Bringing her to you as a surprise."

His father relaxed. "Knew it. I don't mind saying Randart was disappointed. She slipped away, eh?"

"Yes."

The king's amusement was back. "And you think you could

get her now? No, no, let Randart do the dirty work. He's good at it. He *likes* it. Let him bring her here, and you can soothe her ruffled feathers and be the hero. You two marry in spring, everyone smiles, the problems are all solved."

Jehan bowed, low, and left.

He ran back up to his rooms and changed out of his embroidered velvet, pulling on his sturdiest riding gear. He paused and stared down at the gold case in his hand, knowing the next communication in it would be from his father. The temptation to leave it behind was severe. But his road had been laid down as well, the first time he put on a disguise and attacked one of Randart's strongholds.

He opened the case, took out his last transfer token, tossed it up in the air, and caught it with his fingers. Looked across the room at Kazdi, who stood with his shoulders against the closed door.

"Ride out as fast as you can to the resistance mages. Tell Magister Wesec it's time to move her mages into place. There's no more hiding. And if Nadathan and Devli Eban want to help, they're in."

Kazdi bowed, his scrawny neck-knuckle bobbing as he swallowed. His bony teenage face was the last thing Jehan saw before the transfer magic wrenched him out of time and space.

TWENTY-TWO

THE SUDDEN JINGLE OF gear and clatter of many boot steps caused Mirnic Kender to straighten up from the row of buckets she was checking for diminishment of the cleaning spell.

From the siege-camp command tent an arrow shot away, and a stampede of aides and cadets hustled through the opening, dispersing in all directions. She watched them shrug, make gestures of helplessness, and shake heads at the flood of questions. She waited.

Then the cadet on mess duty to the command tent showed up, whistling softly. Mirnic bent over her buckets, making motions with her hands as the boy was met by one of his friends, also on cook detail for the day.

"What was that all about?" the cadet next to her asked the other boy.

"War Commander got one of those magical messages. Told us to wait, opened it, read it, then sent us out on the double. Said something about the king, and he had to answer at once, and he'd be out in a moment, but he did not want distractions."

"Huh. Was he angry?"

"No. Here's what's weird. Most were standing around the map, see, chattering about the siege, and I was collecting the coffee cups. So really I was the only one watching him—couldn't decide if I should touch his cup or not. I mean, if he was done. You know how he gets—"

"Never mind his coffee!"

"Well, so I was watching, see? He grinned. Like this."

Mirnic forced herself not to look. Sure enough the other boy let out his breath in a long whoosh. "I've only seen that grin once. Pret-ty nasty."

"Yeah. If you want to know what I think . . ."

No, Mirnic thought. *I don't.*

She slipped away without either boy paying her the least attention, and sped to the tent she shared with the single other mage student permitted on the run. Her tent mate was asleep—they traded day and night duty—so Mirnic made sure she made no sound as she knelt at her bunk and wrote:

R. received note, said from king. Sent everyone out of tent right after.

She folded it, put it into her case, and sent it to Magister Zhavic, and then sped back to her duty at the cook tent. As she'd expected, no one noticed she'd been gone.

And far away at the harbor, Magister Zhavic read the note, and checked the log of message reports from Vadnais. No messages had been logged either way between the king and the war commander at all that morning. Unless there was an emergency, they always communicated at night, messages duly reported by the journeymages on duty at the royal castle.

Zhavic smiled his own nasty smile.

Time for a talk with the king.

So there I was, no breakfast in me, riding on my mare with my hands tied behind me, surrounded by a bunch of teenage boys who either rode in sulky, nervous or gloomy silence, or else clumped together, arguing in fierce whispers.

At least three times I heard Damedran growl versions of "His orders are to take her there and meet him. Shut up! Just shut up! Or if he doesn't kill you, I will!"

Red shifted his bad mood from Damedran to their lack of food. He got into a short argument with one of the other boys, which made it clear that he'd expected better planning from the others while he and Ban nipped those tunics off someone's clothesline and scouted around my former place of employment.

I think they might have started another fight had not one of the servants spoken up to say that he had a loaf of journey bread that he'd bought the morning before, just in case.

When we reached a chuckling stream with a fall rushing over a grass-covered rocky hillock, Ban said, "If we don't stop here for at least some water, you'll have to shoot me for mutiny. Your bow is right there at your saddle. Here's my back," he added, quite unfairly.

Damedran jerked the reins of his horse, who tossed his head up and almost sat down on his haunches. Damedran flung himself out of the saddle, and the horse stood shivering.

My head panged from hunger and thirst, my shoulders and arms ached, and the sight of that frightened horse snapped my temper. "Someone"—I swung my leg over and jumped from my horse—"has anger-management issues."

"Huh?" Red exclaimed.

Ban mouthed the words *anger management?*

I glanced meaningfully at Damedran's horse, and my irritation faded when I saw him soothing the animal, stroking its nose and murmuring, his forehead leaning against the long, sweaty neck.

He wasn't a complete stinker. But there was the matter of my growling stomach and my aching arms and oh yes. His uncle.

I said kind of generally, to the air, "Every world is different. And places on a single world are different. Where I have been living there are what we call *people skills.*"

Damedran leaned against his horse, but from the stiffness of his shoulders I sensed he was listening. Red made no pretense. He stared at me, mouth open.

I went on as genially as possible, "For example, death threats whenever someone asks a question. That would constitute *bad* people skills. Telling people *why* something is being done, well, that would rank as *good* people skills."

Six pairs of eyes swung from me to Damedran and back again. Red snickered, then looked up at the sky as though seeking the Winged Victory of Samothrace.

Ban's face had gone ruddy from his effort not to laugh. He mumbled, "Garik, I'll help with the journey bread."

A couple of the boys led the horses in two strings to the stream while avoiding looking my way.

Damedran and Red stalked ten or twelve paces in the other direction, facing away and arguing in fierce undertones. Behind some flowering shrubs, Ban and the boy named Garik alternated between growls and whispers.

Ban: "I thought princesses were supposed to act toff. Wear silk. Scream orders so they don't have to get their slippers dusty."

Garik: "I thought they were supposed to be delicate. She's nearly as big as Red. Makes Lesi Valleg look scrawny, and wee-yoo, can she fight!"

"Sh. Sh!"

Whisper, whisper.

Ban: ". . . if we don't follow orders?"

Garik: "I don't even want to think about it. Here. That's her share. You take it over there."

"Coward."

"Yep. And?" Garik retorted promptly and cheerfully.

While all this was going on, I'd spotted a broad rock near the base of the hillock and sat down, since I couldn't run with my hands tied behind my back. Ban rounded the shrubs and came toward me, carrying in both hands what looked like nut-bread, each serving put on a broad, slightly waxy leaf—natural dishes, plucked from the shrub nearby.

He bent and set my share next to me.

"Do I get a feedbag?" I asked.

He had avoided my eyes, but the question startled him, and when he glanced up, I shrugged my shoulders and wiggled my fingers behind me. His face reddened, and he turned Damedran's way.

The Randart heir and Red were still arguing fiercely. "—when we get to Castle Ambais, where my uncle is supposed to meet us," Damedran snarled. "I'll ask him right out."

Ban whistled sharply, and they whirled around, hands going to their weapons. They relaxed their hands, but their faces stayed tense.

"How's she going to eat?"

"Will it make you feel better if I promise not to try to make a bolt during lunch?" I asked. "Which is also my breakfast, I might add. And probably my last meal as well. I'd really like to enjoy it."

"Stop. Saying that," Damedran muttered, pulling his knife out with a faint ringing *zing*.

"Don't cut that kerchief," Red warned. "We don't have another."

"The knots are all pulled hard," Damedran snapped over his shoulder.

"That's because my fingers were going numb." I shrugged. "Had to try to loosen the fabric, though it meant the knots tightened."

A couple of slices and my hands were free, and full of pins and needles. I wrung and flexed them, rubbing them up and down my thighs. When I could grasp again, I wolfed down my share of the journey bread. It was dense, made with about six different kinds of nuts, raisins, and a hint of spices.

When I was done (and had thumb-pressed every crumb off the leaf and nibbled it up) I rose to get some water. All of the guys closed in around me, faces tense and determined.

I washed, drank, then silently held out my dripping hands.

Red offered an old sash. "Found it in my gear. Crumpled but clean."

Damedran sighed, but took it.

This time he did a better job of checking to make sure the bonds were not too tight. He helped me mount up, Ban took the reins of my horse, and in silence the boys mounted. They rode around me downstream a ways, Damedran squinting up at the sun to check direction, until a distant screeching of birds caught his attention.

Everyone's head turned. I looked as well, not comprehending what they could find interesting about a flock of birds rising above the trees, screeling and squawking, until I heard the faint rumble of horse hooves.

Damedran's face blanched. "Ride out!" he shouted, waving at Ban and me. "Ride out. You know where to go!"

Ban used the reins to whack my horse, kneed his own mount, and suddenly there I was, galloping unsteadily—gripping with my legs as best as I could.

Damedran whirled his horse round, pulling his weapons, to face the oncoming threat now raising a great dust cloud. I dared a single glance back. He sat squarely in the path of that billowing grit in which vague silhouettes of mounted warriors could be made out. The five other cadets spread out behind Damedran.

My horse jerked to a stop, and Ban flung the reins back over my leg. "Go," he muttered, not looking at me. "Just—go." Without waiting for me to speak, he whacked my mare on her hindquarter, and she took off downstream.

Ban rode back to face the danger with his mates.

Just as, behind me, Jehan and Owl led their force at a gallop straight toward the boys. The dust thinned, revealing in the lead a tall, slender rider with long white hair.

Damedran raised his sword, then lowered it. "What?" he cried. "Prince *Jehan?*"

Jehan did not halt his sweating, foam-flecked horse. In answer he rode straight at the string of remounts, and as the boys gaped, he leaped from a galloping horse onto the bare back of a fresh remount, who sprang into a gallop. White hair flying, he shot downstream after me, the boys so amazed they didn't comprehend they were efficiently surrounded until it was too late.

"You'll note there are twelve of us." Owl waved a hand. "You might go ahead and sheathe the weapons, boys."

I was galloping about as gracefully as a teapot on a rocking horse alongside a rocky stream, hoping that when I fell off, which I was sure was inevitable, I would manage to hit the water and not a giant boulder.

A galloping horse thundered up behind me.

All I could think of was War Commander Randart. *He doesn't trust Damedran to bring me in. He's here to skewer me personally.* I bent down, as if that would help my poor mare increase her speed.

A hand reached out to grip the mare's reins near her head. Both horses slowed, and I braced myself, angry, fearful—

And stared up into Jehan's face. His pale, grim face. Searching my features to see if I was all right.

"Huh?" I said intelligently.

He leaped off his horse—which had no saddle, I noticed distractedly—and held up his arms. Instinctively I leaned forward, and though I'm not exactly a sylph, he lifted me down as if I were one, and set me gently on my feet. He tightened one arm around me, and laid his other hand along my cheek so I looked up, and there were his lips brushing over my nose, and my eyes, and well, despite the dust, and the pair of us being considerably sweaty and disheveled, the instinct that flared brighter than logic or even laughter locked us together in a long, lingering kiss.

TWENTY-THREE

EVENTUALLY WE HAD TO breathe.

"No—" I began, standing in the circle of his arms. "Wait. You can't."

"Don't," he murmured into my filthy tangle of hair. "Say anything. Just—don't."

I drew in a very unsteady breath, and when I felt the sudden loosening of the sash round my wrists, I fought the urge to hug him back, but neither did I push him away.

I gripped his wrists instead. "Jehan, I don't know how you managed to get here. Or why. In fact I'm almost afraid to ask. But you should know that those boys are scared Dannath Randart will kill them if they don't show up with me at something called Castle Ambais."

"I guessed as much." Jehan whistled softly. "Ambais is a garrison full of handpicked Randart warriors. It's located at this end of the valley, tucked up against the border mountains. If the boys had managed to get you there, it would have been impossible to get you out. At least, without bloodshed that Randart is quite willing to spill."

"Ugh."

Jehan wiped his hair back off his damp forehead and squinted up at the sun's position. "It's one of his staging points for his and my father's war. As near as I can tell, it's also a secret stash for the weapons that are going to conveniently appear for next spring's surprise invasion of Locan Jora."

I saw in his dust-printed face a tension to match my own. I was so full of questions I did not know where to begin, or how to handle any answers I heard. He'd lied before. And so had I. The situation was already impossibly tangled before those kisses made emotional reaction about ten times worse.

"Randart has to know approximately where you and the boys are, which is about half a day's hard ride from Castle Ambais. I figure we have until sunset." Jehan walked away to catch the reins of my mare. "Then Randart will send out rings of trackers to find Damedran. And you."

"And so?"

"And so the days of disguises are past." He handed me the reins and whistled to the other horse, who stood on the other side of the stream a ways away, cropping unconcernedly. It tossed its head and swung round our way. "My first act is to rescue you."

"Here I thought I was going for a Guinness Book of Records for abductions," I cracked. "You being my fourth. Except, does it count when the same fellow —"

Jehan laughed, flinging up a hand. "My second act is going to be to take Damedran hostage." Jehan whistled again, the whistle the stable hands use at the academy. "I think it's the only way to save his life." The horse trotted obediently back toward us.

"And then what?"

Jehan indicated the entire world. "You go wherever you like." He thrust a hand into a pocket in his tunic and brought out a richly gleaming flat gold box about the size of those beautiful cigarette cases that you see gangsters and snobs carrying in old movies. "While I wait to find out what my father says."

I was amazed and relieved almost beyond thought. "You're going to let me go?"

"Did I not say so?" he responded, not without humor.

"Just like that."

"Well, it does seem to me my time is going to be taken up with such small matters as Randart coming after me, with or without my father's orders. As for what he will say—" He opened his hand.

We began walking the horses back toward the others.

I said above that I was almost beyond thought. Actually I wasn't quite there yet.

I turned to face him. "How did you find me? I take it you are not suddenly in Randart's confidence. Damedran made it pretty clear that no one knows about his orders. Except you?"

"I was hoping you wouldn't ask that. But the truth is, I had Owl follow you," Jehan admitted. "Not that he was all that successful. He lost track of you early on and didn't catch up until Damedran appeared on your trail. He showed up at some inn or other. Where you took a letter."

I sighed. "I should be mad. But if he hadn't . . ." I shuddered. "I'd be going straight into Dannath Randart's waiting . . . noose? Sword? Prison cell? Not waiting arms, unless you mean the pointy steel ones. I don't think I'm his type. He sure isn't mine."

Jehan laughed. We rounded the hill where the others were gathered, Jehan's people sitting on horseback, hands resting on sword hilts, chatting back and forth as Damedran's group hunched disconsolately on or around the mossy rock bench where I'd so recently sat to eat my share of the food. Damedran stood a few paces away, head bent, staring at the little waterfall. Even from a distance his profile was strained.

"Busted," I breathed.

Jehan flicked a questioning glance my way.

I didn't answer, but jumped off my mount and ran up to Damedran. Jehan did not stop me, nor did he join us.

"Damedran."

The Randart boy looked my way, his face tight with misery. Then his cheeks reddened with anger, but before he could speak, I flung up a hand in the palm-out sign for peace that I'd seen people use. *Peace* here, and on Earth, *Stop Right There.*

"I wanted to thank you for making things as easy as you

could," I said, not really sure what I was doing, just following instinct. It was that misery in his eyes. "Listen. I've been nabbed by Jehan. A couple of times. It won't be so bad."

"Nabbed," Damedran repeated, the anger fading from his expression.

"You're his hostage. And while I'm trying to sort out what's what, this I will say. You won't hear any death threats from him. Or, if you did, it would surprise me."

Damedran turned his head sharply, and I followed his look. Jehan was busy with the horses some twenty or thirty paces away, though he glanced our way. But not in earshot, which I considered an honorable gesture. A gesture I knew Dannath Randart wouldn't make. "I am a hostage, then?" he asked, his voice lifting at the end. "Us. We? Are hostages? Or prisoners of war? Or what?"

I called out to Jehan, "Damedran has the same question I had earlier. Is he a hostage, prisoner, or what?"

Jehan took that as an invitation to join us. "You can define your exact status at your leisure. All I'm going to say is that Uncle Dannath is not going to get his hands on you unless certain demands are met, and then only with your permission. I can explain on the ride. We're going to have to pick up our feet, if we want to stay outside of Randart's search perimeter, which will be dispatched by sundown, if they aren't riding already. So say your farewells to the princess, because she's presumably going off in another direction."

Jehan held out his hand toward my mare. I saw a new feedbag hooked to the saddle gear. With the other hand, he held out a folded paper. "Here is a map I made last night, to help me orient on you all. Go ahead and take it. I know where I am now. You'll see the major roads, cities, garrisons, and towns marked. Castles as well. You should be able to find several routes out of the kingdom." He gave me a bland smile.

In silence I took it.

I don't know what I might have said or done if we'd been in private. Probably made things worse. But before all those watching guys—both sides in brown uniforms, which was kind of funny and kind of heartbreaking—there was only one thing to do.

I swept as flourishing a bow as I could, turning at the last to include the entire company. Then I said in English, "Gents, it's been real."

And leaving exceedingly puzzled faces behind me, I mounted up and rode away.

Yeah, I managed what I thought a suave exit, but I swore when I first took up my pen I'd tell the truth in this thing, and so I have to admit that within about thirty seconds of choosing a random direction I was snuffling into my sleeve.

Talk about confused. I was sad, scared, angry, mostly at myself for having kissed Jehan again when I knew, I *knew*, I'd feel terrible afterward. Because the kiss itself was so great. Despite everything. And oh yes, what *was* "everything"?

I didn't snivel too long. The sky was clouding. If I lost the sun, I'd lose my sense of direction, and the map would be worthless.

Map.

I unfolded it. There was Jehan's handwriting, in even, slanted letters with slashing curls. It was a dashing handwriting, and I resisted the impulse to kiss the map. Yeah, I know.

Focusing my blurred eyes (this is the last time I wipe away tears, I vowed) I saw he'd marked a place on the map below Ambais, where he wrote: *Should find D. here*. D of course had to mean Damedran.

That meant I could use that point as my orientation.

Tracing my finger straight north, I discovered that Ivory Mountain was not all that far away.

"Papa, I sure hope you are ready to rock and roll," I muttered, kneeing the mare. "Because the house is packed and the band is playing as hard as it can."

TWENTY-FOUR

ALMOST DIRECTLY TO THE west the rain had already begun, a soft plopping of cold drops, when the single sentry at the gate of Zheliga Castle burst into the buttery, where Hilna and Pirie Famid worked alongside their servants, the sisters sharing the title of "baroness" for simplicity's sake as they shared the baroness chores. In this case, pressing butter into the molds and seeing it carried down in neatly wrapped blocks to the cold room.

"Gate," the boy said, his voice cracking.

"Army?" Hilna asked doubtfully, knowing that Orthan and his brother Dannath were somewhere on the other side of the hills to the east, busy with their siege game. She hadn't expected Orthan and Damedran until the siege was over, and it was time to settle in for winter. The sisters had been laying in extra stores for weeks.

The boy shook his head. "Women," he said succinctly.

Pirie and Hilna exchanged puzzled looks. The sisters were not given to needless chatter. They untied their aprons, dropped them onto the table and left, one smoothing back her gray curls, the other brushing flour off her skirts left from the morning's inspection of the milling.

Neither was prepared to see a couple hundred women either riding or walking over the bridge, which two generations ago had been a drawbridge, but had been left down for over fifty years. A couple of hundred? More than that, all strung out in a slow-moving line, as far as one could see.

Hilna gasped when she recognized the tall, tough-looking woman walking beside a horse. "Plir Silvag?"

Plir lifted a hand in greeting, and waved at the woman on the horse. Hilna blinked up at a pretty woman her own age, with pale hair done up elaborately on the top of her head. She looked vaguely familiar —

"You remember Princess Atanial?" Plir asked.

The sisters stared in mute surprise.

Hilna gave a stiff curtsey, her expression changing from blank surprise to a wary question.

Atanial looked down into those faces, seeing yet again the question, doubt, resentment that had been mirrored in variations during her long journey.

They had passed along the old paths, far from the fine military roads and the waterlogged main roads. The worst of the journey had been at first, when Atanial's conversation with Plir was repeated, sometimes with far more hostility than Plir had shown. But Atanial listened, and said the same thing over and over: *We cannot permit an invasion.* A few refused to join. Of those, half caught up later, like Plir herself. With her she brought a number of relatives and old contacts. Since then more were catching up day by day, women of all ages, from girls barely in their teens to women far older than Atanial and Plir.

Women led them to other women who they felt would embrace the cause, and so the group swelled in number every day. The strange thing was, Atanial had realized one night, by now they could hardly be secret, and yet at least so far, no one seemed to have sent word to the king. She did not know if all Canardan's spies were all at the war game, or if some had quietly changed their minds about what side they were on.

Atanial returned Hilna's bow as best she could from the back of a horse, then said, "May we speak privately?"

Hilna rubbed her forehead. "I suppose. But what shall I do about all these people?"

"Most of them brought their own journey bread. And we've been buying fruit along the way." Atanial did not mention that she alone hadn't come prepared. Most of the women shared, but Atanial did not like taking too much. She was always hungry.

Hilna shaded her eyes to ward drops of cold rain. Among those faces, most her age or older, and a very few young, were a couple of guild mistresses, a baroness who had inherited her title in her own right, and at least one garrison captain's wife. "I think you all had better come inside." She cast a glance at her sister. "We can fit you into the hall out of the weather."

"And the sun room, too. This way." Pirie gestured to the women accompanying Atanial. "I'll see to food and drink for those who need it."

"Princess, you come with me, if you will." Hilna waited at the door.

Atanial dismounted with a smothered *woof* and tried to be delicate about rubbing her inner thighs as she walked stiffly behind her hostesses. A smothered snicker from behind testified to her success, before the last of the women vanished into what appeared to be a parlor with plastered and whitewashed walls; they moved through that to the rest of the ground floor of the castle beyond.

But Hilna did not crack a smile as she stalked into a low entry of bare swept stone, the enticing smell of baking apple tarts drifting from somewhere. Atanial's stomach rumbled.

A sharp turn, up a short stairway to a room off a landing, and the smell was cut off by a thick wooden door swinging shut. Hilna indicated a massive wing-backed chair that had to be a hundred years old at least.

Atanial winced at the prospect of her aching hips dealing with that ungiving wood. She sighed in relief when she spotted a newly stuffed cushion on its seat, embroidered somewhat crookedly with tulips and bluebells. There was another such chair, both angled toward a fireplace where a good fire already burned.

Hilna perched on the edge of one and Atanial collapsed into

the other, plopping her cold feet onto the fender.

"I'll try to be brief." Inwardly she resisted the strong desire to sleep right where she was for at least a year. "You don't have to answer. I don't want to put you into a bad position. But Mistress Silvag insisted we should stop here and at least let you know what we're doing. Whatever you decide to do about it, considering who you are married to. Or rather, who your husband is brother to."

"Dannath," Hilna breathed.

"I don't know how much you know, but the evidence is clear that Dannath Randart and the king will be invading Locan Jora in the spring." Atanial braced for—anything. But oh, she did so hope she wasn't going to have to leap to her aching feet and bucket down those stone steps and back onto that horse, sword-waving women on her heels.

Hilna's mouth tightened.

"I know the reasons put forward in favor," Atanial said swiftly. "Locan Jora has been part of Khanerenth for most of recorded history. Though the outer borders have danced about quite a bit from generation to generation. I know there are people who lost their homes when the takeover happened. I know they want their ancestral homes back. I know that there is a belief that the economy will vastly improve, that there will be land and titles for the loyal, that this and that will all make things better. But. I really want you to consider the cost. The real cost. Which is lives. Not necessarily ours, but young people's, like your son's. Because he's supposed to be leading this war, isn't he?"

Hilna's eyes narrowed.

"At least, he'll be right at the front, with all the banners and so forth, but we know who will really be in command." Atanial paused, wondering if she'd gone too far.

Hilna rocked on her chair while rain tapped at the leaded glass window in the deep stone embrasure, and the fire on the hearth crackled and snapped. "If I interfere, I'll never see my son again. It's rare enough I see him now. Either Damedran or my husband, Orthan."

Atanial leaned forward. "Tell me."

Hilna brushed a strand of hair off her forehead with trembling fingers. "What is to tell? I get to see him once a year. If that. Then he pushes me away with *'Uncle Dannath says I'm too soft.' Uncle Dannath says* after every visit home, always something aimed at me. My husband, too. *Dannath says* Damedran has slid back into boy habits, and requires a week of drills to toughen him back up again."

"So you disagree with their goals?"

"If I wished to be known as a traitor," she retorted. "I cannot have an opinion that differs from Dannath's. None of us can. Why do you think I never adopted into the Randart family? It was the one single thing I could keep of my own, my family. Even this barony is nothing but an air title—Orthan saying, often and often, that soon we'll live in Vadnais, we'll have a real title, and this castle, which I have spent the past fifteen years making into a home, is good enough for Pirie and Wolfie."

Atanial had used the past two or three days forming logic chains to argue against every conceivable point of view against an invasion. She had never expected this reaction.

"What would you like to do?"

Hilna dashed her wrist angrily over her eyes. "Is that meant as a jab? No, I see by your face it isn't. But how can you ask that, knowing Dannath? Oh, I knew from the very start that Orthan was loyal to his brother, but in those days the goal was rebuilding the army, which had gotten slack, with pilferage and cronyism and scandalous behavior shrugged at in the upper ranks. That's how we lost half the kingdom in the first place! But after Damedran was born, there were more and more hints about royal vision and royal gifts and . . ."

She wiped her eyes again, frowning down into the fire. "About five years ago, I realized they were not talking about the king. They meant Dami. And at first I conceded, with a mother's pride. I thought he'd make a fine king. I didn't consider how he might get there." She looked up, saying fiercely, "And it's as well I conceded, because I vow as sure as I sit here otherwise, Dannath would have seen to it something happened to me. He's never had any use for women—for anyone, really—unless they can fight."

Atanial nodded. "Or serve. But not think. That seems to go for men, too."

"Yes. Orthan is plenty smart, and loyal, but he's no grand thinker. So what is it you are doing?"

"We are marching across the kingdom." Atanial swept her arm wide. "Where, you shall see. None of the other women know the destination, only that I strongly expect that we will meet the king there, and War Commander Randart. I knew that nothing I did on my own would ever make any difference. But if there were enough of us, maybe we could get them at least to listen?"

Hilna let out her breath in a slow, shaky sigh. "I know I sound like a coward, and perhaps I am one. If I ever cross Dannath, even in a small thing, I will lose my son altogether. And what you are suggesting is no small thing. I shall have to think."

"Fair enough."

"There are two things I will say. First, I will only discuss it with Pirie. And maybe one other friend who I think will be sympathetic. But I'm not sending any messages to Orthan." She gave a small sigh. "I could never force him to choose between his brother and—well, leave it at that. I'm mum. Best that way."

Atanial gestured her thanks.

"Second, if you can convince Starveas Kender to join you, she might bring some of the old Joran nobility over. Her husband loved marrying an old noble family with a title, even if deposed. The Kenders have their title by courtesy, as do all the old Joran nobility. You know that." She scarcely paused for Atanial to assent. "I know that he can hardly wait for the invasion to be over, so they can lord it once again on the other side of the mountains. But she's worried. Not only about Ban. Also about her daughter Mirnic, who will be sent with the mages. Who end up as targets as often as the warriors."

"I would love to, but I don't dare go back to Vadnais. It was too difficult to get past the guard on my way out. I don't believe I'd make it back in without being caught."

"The Kenders don't live in the royal city," Hilna exclaimed. "They live in Ellir. They left that several weeks ago, knowing about the siege running into winter, and how those with castles along the west will all go home, taking sizable portions of the army with them for the winter. The Kenders are staying with her cousin, the Duchess of Frazhan. They stopped here day before yesterday."

"Frazhan on the border," Atanial murmured.

"They have that wonderful old castle directly across the river valley from Ivory Mountain."

"Ahhhhh." Atanial smiled.

TWENTY-FIVE

MAGISTER ZHAVIC WATCHED THE king rub his forehead with tense fingers, the ruby in his ring winking and glittering.

He looked up wearily. "Zhavic. I know you don't trust my war commander. Neither of you has ever even tried to comprehend the other, it seems to me. Yet you are loyal and dedicated. So why can't you see that we must work together now? We cannot afford strife among ourselves."

Zhavic struggled to suppress his annoyance. It wasn't as if this reaction of the king's was unexpected. "Write to him, your majesty," he urged, keeping his voice low, quiet. "Please. If there is a reasonable explanation, I vow I will never again bring forward any suspicions." *Not without undeniable proof, anyway.*

The king let out a long-suffering sigh, and with a spurt of ill-tempered impatience, threw aside a couple of stacks of papers in search of one of the small slips he used for the magic-transfer box.

Zhavic bent, picked up the snow of papers on the floor and returned them, glancing covertly at the top of each. Most were supply lists, but one was from the *Skate*'s infamous Captain Bragail, on which Zhavic glimpsed the phrase . . . *of the pirate absolutely no sign.*

The king extricated a small piece of paper, picked up his pen, dipped it, and frowned at the mage. "What am I asking again?"

"I do not know what questions you deem appropriate, your majesty, but the questions that occur to me are why he considered it necessary to send his nephew and several senior cadets away from the siege on a secret mission, and why he suddenly had to ride off, again without telling anyone."

The king frowned down at the pen, apparently not seeing the slow formation of a droplet of ink. It was about to splash on the paper when he threw the pen into the well and leaned back in his chair. "You know, it really *is* odd, when I think about it. He mentioned nothing of any of these things in his report last night. I thought Damedran was with the other cadets. And that Randart himself was overseeing things at Cheslan Castle."

Zhavic put his hands behind his back lest they betray him. Long years had taught him to keep his face impervious, but the surge of triumph burning through him made him almost shaky.

The king nipped up his pen. He wrote in a fast scrawl, folded the paper, shoved it into the box without waiting for the ink to dry and tapped it. He looked up, eyes narrowed. "If there is a good explanation I will hold you to your promise."

"If there is a good explanation, I shall be satisfied, that is a vow. You know I only have the good of the kingdom in mind—"

"Yes, yes, everyone always has the good of the kingdom in mind, especially when they begin arguing with me." Canardan waved a hand to cut off the flow of self-justification. He uttered a sharp laugh. "If you didn't, you would hardly be alive to argue."

The implied threat silenced the mage.

Canardan felt the inner click of the message-box magic, which was somewhat of a relief. Dannath had, so far, always responded immediately.

He flipped it open and pulled out the folded square. Randart's neat writing filled the entire paper. *For a month we have been tracking Atanial's daughter Sasharia on your orders earlier in the summer. Damedran has her now. I am in Ambais to meet him. Planned to have her in hand before sending my report.*

Canardan laughed, then flicked the paper in Zhavic's

direction. He watched the master mage read it.

"What's the matter now?" Canardan demanded when the mage handed back the paper, his lips tightly closed.

Zhavic looked out the window as rain began tapping the glass. "A month. And you didn't know. I wonder if he really was going to tell you when he did get hold of her."

Canardan threw the pen down. "Damnation, we're right back to where we were! Why not? What else would he do with her?"

"Perran believes that she might be coerced into a match with Damedran. So that he could become . . . the heir."

"That again."

Canardan's grim look sent a spurt of pleasure through Zhavic. The mages didn't believe any such thing. Randart's mind did not run to marriages. But the king's did. And reminding him of the Randarts' suspected plot to put Damedran on the throne was always a good idea.

Zhavic went on in a slow, ruminative voice, as if he were thinking, though he and Perran had rehearsed this interview half a dozen times. "I think Perran's wrong. I wonder if Randart means to assassinate her. The war commander's thinking appears to be of military and political advantage, not magical."

Canardan frowned at the mage. "What are you talking about?"

"Why else would he take so long to secure her, without letting you know? If he wanted to find out where she was going —"

"The cook! She was the cook!" The king snapped his fingers. "Jehan had her briefly. Randart went out to search Jehan's yacht and didn't find her. I assumed because the girl had slipped Jehan's grip before Randart showed up. But now I think Jehan was lying to Randart. And she was there all along. Which changes everything." The king drew in a slow breath. "Only which way?"

"What?" Zhavic's voice, which was far more revealing than his face, lost the smoothness of rehearsed musing and revealed genuine spontaneity. "Princess Atanial's daughter is a cook?"

The king snorted a not-quite-laugh. "You don't remember? I do. I've always had a head for details. Which, one could argue, is what kingship is. The tall female cook on Jehan's yacht, with the flour all over her face so no one saw what she looked like—" He turned his head, spoke sharply. "Page!"

The runner on duty outside the king's study opened the door.

"Request Prince Jehan to attend me for an immediate interview." He turned back to Zhavic. "Finish your point."

Magister Zhavic had been wondering how to get back to it. He smiled. "Well. If you consider she was last known aboard the pirate ship, and presumably managed to escape somewhere along the coast—"

"Or was rescued by a very romantic prince, let us say."

Zhavic blinked, and the look he gave the king caused Canardan to laugh out loud.

"No, I have not lost my wits. Though I might be chasing down the wrong trail. We'll know in a moment. Go on. So Atanial's daughter escapes on the coast . . ."

". . . then turns up in Bar Larsca, what kind of a vector, as the military term it, does that give you?"

The king rubbed his chin, mentally reviewing the map. "Not the siege, though she's close. That makes no sense."

"Think magic, not military," Zhavic urged. "Remember who her father was. Though you were not trained, surely your first wife told you some things about the magical part of our history—"

"Ivory Mountain?" the king asked and watched the mage's face smooth into blandness. "But why? That's an old morvende geliath, empty for centuries. Even I know that."

As usual, Zhavic's voice betrayed him. "If Mathias is alive, it could be that he is hiding there, beyond time."

Canardan rapped his knuckles on the table. "How do you get to that conclusion?"

"While guarding the old World Gate site, Perran decided to do a thorough search of the castle. He found a couple of hidden chambers, and one of them held some of Glathan's old papers. Nothing was astoundingly revealing, or *we* would have reported instantly to you," Zhavic added quickly.

He shifted on his seat. "But in a chest Glathan had stored an old book on morvende geliaths. That book is well known to mages. Most of us have a copy. At first Perran didn't even look through it. But as time went on and he had finished his search, he decided to go through all the books and papers in a methodical way. In that book, the reference to Ivory Mountain had a scribble next to it, in some kind of code."

"So you think this girl might go to Ivory Mountain and free Math? But she's not a mage."

"We know she was taught at least one difficult spell."

Canardan nodded slowly. He was beginning to wish he'd listened to Dannath in those early days. His reasoning was clear, if brutal. A quick, clean death for Math, and the problem goes away. Kill the woman, too, or send her back to her own world. Keep the girl and raise her to marry the heir. The popular but incompetent family Zhavalieshin sinks into memory, along with incompetent royal families of the past.

Canardan ran his thumb back and forth along Randart's note, remembering how he'd steeled himself to see it through. All those clear reasons Mathias should die: most important, his incompetence as king. Except at this remove, Canardan knew that most of Mathias's supposed incompetence had actually been attempts to cope with the mess the old king had made of things.

He gave his head a shake. The prospect of Mathias walking back in suddenly had ceased to worry him a few years ago. Now it was back.

Canardan turned in his chair, as if physical movement could shake certain other more uncomfortable memories, and he frowned at the mage, who was studying his hands. Underneath all this hinting and innuendo about Randart's secret plans lay the old question again. Why did the mages *really* want to find Mathias? The mages always seemed to have their own plans, which may or may not quite be the same as his. Mathias had been raised to magic knowledge, not to military. Maybe they thought if he returned, mages would gain the political ascendance that Randart thwarted with vigilant energy.

A tap at the door caused Canardan to lean forward. "Enter."

The page stepped inside. "Prince Jehan is not in the castle."

Chas appeared directly behind him, face slick with sweat.

The king locked his jaw hard against a surge of rage. He twiddled his fingers in dismissal, and the page ducked round Chas, obviously relieved at being able to escape.

Chas walked in and gave the mage a poisonous look. But the king did not dismiss Magister Zhavic.

So Chas said, "He's gone. So is that boy he kept as personal servant. And—"

"There's always an 'and', these days," Canardan murmured, waggling his fingers again. "Yes, get on with it."

"Certain among the guard are missing as well, all without leave."

Canardan smacked his hands down on the desk, stood, and dropped back into his chair. This time he swept everything except the inkwell off the desk in one angry motion. Papers hissed to a snowdrift on the floor as he pulled a small communication note from inside the desk, and wrote:

Jehan, where are you and what are you doing?

He shoved the paper inside the magic box and tapped out Jehan's signal.

No one spoke, or moved, until the king twitched. He'd received a magical signal, which meant an answer had arrived. He pulled out and read a paper, then tossed it onto the desk, the inscription toward them. "What d'you make of that?" he asked, grinning.

They leaned forward and read:

I am here to rescue Sasharia Zhavalieshin from Dannath Randart.

"My son might be an idiot, but he's a romantic idiot," Canardan said, almost buoyant with relief. He'd feared treachery. He couldn't even bear to think about that. Here was the real answer, even if it wasn't quite reasonable. But Jehan had always been like his mother, romantic and idealistic. "I don't know why he didn't tell me. Maybe more romantic that way. Wait. He did tell me the other day that he wanted to find her . . . and yes, I told him to sit tight. Well, well. Maybe he's not such an idiot after all. At least, not when it comes to romance."

Laughing, he bent over the paper, crossed out the former words and wrote below, in small letters: *So who has her?*

And the answer came back: *No one, right now.*

Canardan did not show that response to Zhavic or Chas, who tried to sneak peeks at those upside down letters, but the king kept using the same scrap of paper, as did the prince, the writings tinier and tinier.

And if I order you to come home? Saying that I will deal with Randart as I see fit?

This time the wait was longer. The king was aware of his own breathing sounding loud and harsh, his heartbeat thrumming in his ears as he stared down at his thumb prints on the gleaming golden box.

Zing! An answer. Jehan's print was small, the letters carefully formed. *I have to do what is right. I don't think you can protect her from Randart. I think I can.*

The king sighed, ripping the paper into tiny bits. Then he got up from behind the desk. The other two wheeled to face him as he paced the few steps to the fireplace and cast the note into the fire. But he kept his back to the two men as he sorted his reactions. Some relief, much exasperation. Jehan was a romantic, but it seemed he'd chosen to grow up at last. And typical of sons, with terrible timing and headlong foolishness.

Canardan sat down at the desk, pulled out another note, and wrote: *Dannath, whether you have the girl or not, return to the siege.* He shoved it into the case and tapped out Randart's pattern.

Silence again, the mage and the spy standing, the king neither speaking nor looking their way as he waited for an answer. Again there was a wait. Then:

With all respect, sire, are you not losing sight of an advantage? Permit me to secure then bring to you this objective. You can then decide what to do from a position of strength.

Canardan sat back. Another day — yesterday — before the mage came, before the note from his son, he might have shrugged and accepted that. As he always had in the past. But. He stared down at the piece of paper and Randart's strong, assured handwriting. Despite their long friendship, despite the reasonable wording, the implied service, the truth was, Dannath Randart had refused an order.

Canardan tapped his fingers on the magic box. His first impulse was to demand that Dannath return at once and face him. But even if he said he was riding back, how many of those damned transfer tokens did he possess? Unless he was directly under Canardan's eye, he could go anywhere in an eyeblink, do anything, while saying he was on his way back.

Canardan swung around, glaring at the fire. Did he distrust Dannath, after all these years?

Tap, tap, tap.

Randart had made no mention of Ivory Mountain. If he did capture that wretched girl and promptly ride either for the siege or for the royal city, Canardan would know everything was as it should be. Least said, the better.

The king looked up at the waiting men. "Have my guard saddle up. Say nothing of the destination, only that the king wishes to ride on inspection." His smile was unpleasant. "We're riding for Ivory Mountain, but as yet only the three of us know that. It will be interesting to see who else shows up, eh?"

TWENTY-SIX

War Commander Randart counted out his paces. Fifty . . . a hundred. Still no answer.

Relief. If the king was going to answer, he would have by now. Why had he suddenly took it into his head to interfere at this moment, when matters were the busiest? But wasn't it always that way? You are presented with a crisis of events, and that's when one and all choose to interrupt.

Randart looked out through the tower window at the rain, already receding eastward. Rain. Another disruption. If Damedran hadn't managed to reach one of the military roads, he was no doubt bogged down on some civilian mud track, and that would slow him down.

Randart threw his gold case with a clatter onto the desk, then remembered he was at Ambais. This was a loyal garrison, but they were not used to his ways, and he didn't want to have to shoot someone who touched his things.

So he picked up the case again, thrust it into his pouch, and began pacing, glaring periodically out the window at the court-yard as if he could mentally pull Damedran and those boys in by force of will.

Elsewhere in the castle he could hear the orderly march of events—sentries at their duty, some noise from the mess hall at the bottom of the stone stairway. This was an old fortress, small, inconvenient, but easy to defend and tough to attack. Not that he expected an attack.

Pace, pace, glance out the window. Was that a speck on the road? More than one speck?

He wrenched open the ill-fitting glass, which was befogged with steam. Cold air blew in drops of rain as he peered down the gentle slope below the castle. Sharp disappointment. Yes, two riders galloping up the military road.

Not Damedran, only the trackers he'd sent out to meet the boys and reinforce them for the last leg of their journey. He'd known Damedran would be disgusted with any reinforcement on his first mission, especially a successful mission. Randart would have been at his age as well. But this vile female was far too important for any prudent commander to consider mere boyish emotions.

He resisted the impulse to run downstairs to the court—as if hearing the trackers' bad news that little measure faster would make much difference.

Instead he sat, forcing himself to review the pile of reports he'd thrust into the dispatch bag before riding away from the siege, until the sound of footsteps caused him to look up.

His trackers dashed in, muddy to the waist. "War Commander, they were intercepted."

Fury flared through Randart. He kept his lips tight for one breath. Two. "Report."

The older, more experienced tracker said, "We are reasonably sure we located their trail. Valgan here rode back down it to make certain, and said it definitely led to the farm where the cadets had tracked the target. We even found the place they had to have ambushed the target."

Faint question infused the man's face and voice on the word "target". Randart had not told them who the target was, only that Damedran had been sent to this specific olive farm belonging to the local duke in order to arrest a traitor.

"Looked like a pretty good fight," he added, obviously hoping to provoke some information. "At least, as far as we could tell, as the rain was already beginning to obliterate the tracks."

He paused. When Randart did not respond, he shrugged and went on. "There was another ambush say half a watch's ride from here, twice as many hoof prints. They all rode northwest, cross-country."

"Where did the ambushers come from, could you tell?"

"Their prints began at the military road," was the answer.

Military road? Who could possibly have betrayed him? Who even knew where he was? Not the king. Not even Orthan. Only Damedran—

Randart jammed the reports back into the dispatch bag. "You two. Ride ahead, find their trail. Get a communication box from your commander, Valgan, and report the signal to me before you depart. I am going to follow you with my entire force. So you had better ride at the gallop."

Damedran did not know what to think.

Jehan, the sheep who had quite suddenly changed into a wolf, did not ask for parole, nor did he bind up his prisoners. In fact, he said nothing at all about who would ride where. He didn't even take their weapons.

And so Damedran rode next to him, silent at first as they put in a gallop. His knee throbbed where the princess had kicked him, but he could ignore that. He could wait. You don't gallop horses for long unless you have a lot of posting houses or garrisons with ready mounts. Well, the garrisons did, but the prince seemed to be avoiding them.

They galloped on the flat, smooth, well-maintained military road, and once their trail was thus thoroughly obliterated, they took a side trail over a hard-packed road, one of Jehan's people being detailed to smooth their tracks after them. Then they slowed, walking the horses until they'd cooled, and stopping at a trickling stream to water them.

Jehan squinted at the western sky above the mountaintops. The sun rimmed a uniformly dense gray bar of cloud that covered the entire western horizon, the upper edge of which lit with fiery oranges and reds and yellows, colors that warmed the sky and echoed in the vanguard of cloud patches overhead. A spectacular sunset, but it meant heavy rain on the way.

Red snickered. "They'll be up to their armpits in mud at the siege," he muttered.

"Wonder who's got the night run?" Bowsprit whispered back. "They may's well take boats."

The boys' laughter was subdued, all the clearer because Prince Jehan's men—all wearing warrior brown, but not a one known by sight to Damedran—worked in silence, switching gear to the remounts.

A last ochre ray of sun shone on Jehan's white hair, making him easy to pick out from the others. Damedran waited until Jehan was done talking with one of the men, who promptly rode up the trail and vanished into the woods.

The last of the sun disappeared. The warm sunset colors bleached to cold grays and blues as a wind rose, rustling through the grasses and moaning through the distant trees.

"I don't understand," Damedran said, when at last Jehan turned his way. The words seemed to wring from somewhere inside his chest. "I thought—I thought—"

"That I was a sheep," Jehan said with a quick grin.

Damedran's face burned.

Jehan raised a hand. "Don't fret. I wanted you to think that. I needed you to think that. But the time for lies and disguises is over."

Damedran's lips parted. He didn't want to say *I don't understand* again, though that was what he was thinking. It sounded, well, too sheep-like.

So what he did say was, "What disguises?"

"Zathdar the pirate being one. Besides the Fool your uncle really wanted me to be."

"Zathdar?" Damedran squeaked. He'd thought he'd had enough shocks lately. Not true, obviously. "You? But—" His mind flitted from memory to memory, then formed a question in the way that best fit his experience. "I can see how you can ride like that. Leaping horses. They do that in the west, at their academy, don't they?"

"By the time you're twelve. With your hands tied, by the time you're fifteen."

Damedran whistled soundlessly. "But they don't teach anything about the sea. I know they don't. Do they?"

"You're right," Jehan said gravely.

"Yet you have to have learned something about the sea. I mean, all the stories about Zathdar. You know ships. How did that happen?"

"Not by design. Imagine me, sent away as a small boy to Marloven Hess's military academy. Mathias thinks we need new ideas. Really, he wants to get me away from the corruption in our own academy, which, to attest to your uncle's credit, was largely gone within ten years. My father wanted me to go for different reasons. So I went west, leaving behind everyone at home who I believed were living happy lives. The letters slowed down. Then came the bad news, like my mother and father parting. My mother invited me to move to Sartor with her, but I liked my life, so I stayed."

Damedran nodded. He would have stayed too.

"Life there was good at first, but then it turned dangerous, when a good king was assassinated, and a very bad regent took his place. More news came. My father had married Princess Ananda. Not that that was bad, it just made my life seem unmoored. The old king died, and my father became king, and then the real bad news started coming."

Damedran looked subdued, but he was listening.

"The morvende have access to certain kinds of magic that

delays aging for a time. I used that while I tried to reassemble the pieces of my life, but the news just got worse. Princess Atanial vanished, along with the child I never met. So I took ship for a few years to consider what to do, and ended up as a privateer on the other side of the world. When my father summoned me home, I found myself constantly surrounded by your uncle's men for my protection, but they wouldn't let me go anywhere without permission. I put together Zathdar's fleet to break your uncle's increasing hold over the kingdom, since I knew I wouldn't be able to do anything as Prince Jehan."

Damedran frowned in perplexity.

Jehan wondered if he should let the boy have time to think, but it felt so good to tell the truth. "When you're away and come back, you see differences not apparent to people at home who experienced the changes more gradually. Khanerenth is full of restrictive laws. Rumors. Strife. Killings. I dedicate my life to restoring things to the way I knew Prince Math would have wanted."

Damedran flushed again. "So *I'm* the sheep. That's what you mean. But you're not saying it. I take orders and don't think. It's why Lesi Valleg hates me," he added, looking like the miserable boy he really was.

"We both had to take orders and not think. Or not appear to think." Jehan gestured, now exhilarated. Whatever happened next, he had told the truth. "The crisis came this summer when I discovered the rumors of invasion were a little too detailed to seem just rumor."

Damedran's chin jerked up. "You know about that?"

"I have suspected ever since my pirates intercepted a weapons shipment. Think, Damedran. Past the promise of glory, rank, and land. That invasion would break the treaty. People on both sides of the mountains will get killed. Those plains clans of Locan Jora are not going to let their land be overrun without a vicious fight. But I don't think anyone can stand up to the king and Randart except Prince Mathias."

"*Prince Mathias?* How? I don't understand."

"I have reason to believe that Sasharia knows where her father is, and is on her way to free him. We're going as backup."

"But you let her escape! Did she tell you all that?"

Jehan smiled. "No. She's doing her valiant best to protect her father the only way she knows how. But you forget," he said gently, indicating they mount up, "who my mother is. Though I did not move to Sartor's morvende geliath with her, I never lost contact."

TWENTY-SEVEN

Valiant best.

That's what he said, but I sure did not feel valiant.

Does anyone ever feel valiant—bold—intrepid—*I am courageous, ha ha!* Well, not Yours T, anyway. I felt sulky, depressed, angry and worried by turns. Not to mention hungry and tired, for though I had earned plenty of money, and had my jewels besides, there was nowhere to spend any of it.

My trail was the straightest line to Ivory Mountain, which is not an area boasting a lot of population. I saw why when I reached the hills below the mountain: narrow trails slanting steeply upward, past waterfalls and rushing whitewater streams hidden but recognizable from their roar.

Thick forest surrounded me, layers of complicated, deep green, leafy shrubs and trees. Sunlight penetrated in dapples and shafts of hazy gold. When the sunlight was strongest, sparkles of light danced on the water and gleamed in the pearl drops of moisture hanging from the edges of the leaves.

When the sun vanished, I found myself abruptly closed in uniformly greenish blue shadow, guided mostly by sounds rather than by vision: unseen birds, quick thrashings of animals dashing through the underbrush, and always the trickle, drip, roar, chuckle and hiss of water. I was soon hungry, but never did I go thirsty. The water tasted sweet and cold, and even my mare (who did have her feedbag, and I mentally thanked Jehan several times a day for that) seemed to perk up despite my rotten mood.

So it was a long, tiring slog, though beautiful. But I was in no mood for beauty, because the density of the forest meant I would not see any enemies until they were on me. Shelter was also difficult to find. I spent a couple of miserable nights with all my clothes on and my firebird tapestry banner round me as I crouched under mossy rock outcroppings never quite large enough to be a sheltering cave.

I was on the watch for the sign my father had told me about so many years ago—three bluebells in a row, carved into stone. I'd always thought this symbol would be clear, like some kind of natural road map. As I climbed ever higher, examining every rocky scree, cliff, palisade and what have you, I began to wonder if weather and age would have defaced the carvings. That is, if they weren't overgrown by shrubs, trees or even moss.

But I kept going.

We all kept going, everyone converging on the mountain at pretty much the same time, though from different angles. Canardan's force found the tracks of the women—mistook them for warriors—and sped up their pace.

Jehan knew a wood scavenger who knew where the lower cavern passages were. He and his riders made sure they left no signs behind.

Randart's scouts, under threat of punishment, scarcely ate or slept until they discovered my tracks. Remember I said few live there? Randart didn't know magic, but he was far from ignorant about history. Didn't take long for him to figure that Ivory Mountain had to be my destination.

I was unaware of him on my trail until the last morning, when I woke from a miserable sleep to a misty-blue dawn so cold I could see my breath. Time to do my martial arts stretches and warm up a bit. But I forgot my morning routine when sounds echoed up the narrow valley below me.

I scrambled up, inched out onto a promontory and peered over a tumble of moss-covered stones. Down below on the trail snaked a long trail of armed men, blurred by a long grayish drift of mist, but the brown uniforms were frighteningly visible.

At their head, his dark hair and stony profile clear between dissipating wreaths of fog, was War Commander Randart.

Hunger, everything fled my mind. As Mom would say, *It's time to beat feet.*

The Duke and Duchess of Frazhan rode out with Lord and Lady Kender to meet the women.

They met on a high bridge built over a cascading fall down the side of a mountain. The road had brought them within sight of Ivory Mountain, on the other side of the river valley. It was a beautiful sight with its white crown of snow even in summer, the highest peak shrouded in cloud.

Journey's end.

Atanial straightened up as the ducal pair rode toward them. The duke and duchess were both quite old, white-haired, hard to read as aristocrats typically were. Lord Kender was a tall, lean, handsome man, but Atanial's attention focused solely on his wife, a short, round woman with an intelligent dark gaze framed by wispy silver hair.

Like the ducal pair, Lady Starveas and her husband wore Colendi-style linen over robes, paneled up the sides, with ornamental long sleeves dagged back at an angle. Hers was pale mauve over violet; the duchess and her duke wore white over gray. Lord Kender was the most brightly dressed, his over-robe a rich green with stylized golden rye beards along the hem.

The duke's voice was thin and reedy as he introduced them all.

"Your highness," Lady Starveas said then, somehow making her bow graceful, though she sat on the back of a horse. It was clear that she intended to be the spokesperson.

Atanial copied the bow as best she could, hoping she wouldn't fall out of the saddle. Her hips twinged; the flare of a hot flash burned through her chest, tingling outward to the backs of her hands. Her face broke out with moisture. "My lady."

"We have heard word of your mission. We wish to hear the truth from your lips."

Atanial cleared her dry throat and straightened up, resisting the impulse to wipe her sleeve over her hot face. She gave what by now had become a speech, a pattern of words she could utter without thinking, as she watched for reactions.

The four betrayed little during the speech, but at the end Lady Starveas said, "Thank you. For once rumor was not far wrong, then."

Atanial ached, and itched with the clamminess that followed a hot flash. She longed for a bath and for an end to this endurance test. But the cause was right. Whatever happened.

"We have been granted time to consider." Lady Starveas indicated the four of them with a graceful gesture. "For you must know that my family lands were taken by those who call themselves Locan Jorans now."

Atanial dipped her head in the half nod, half bow she'd seen the aristocrats use to one another.

The duchess pulled from her inner sleeve a golden case. She held it up.

Atanial recognized it as a communications case, which sent messages instantaneously by magic. She swallowed tightly. *Here it comes.* The only surprise was that they had made it so long without discovery.

Lady Starveas had also retrieved her own case. "We waited only to hear the words from you. We have written letters to certain friends and will send them, with your permission."

Now Atanial was surprised. She managed the half bow again, because she had no idea what to say. A trickle of sweat ran down her temple and into her ear. Ugh.

Lady Starveas smiled a little. "I cannot speak for everyone. There are some who will shut their eyes to violence in order to regain what they think was once theirs. My family . . ." She looked away at Ivory Mountain, crowned with snow. "We have morvende in our family. We know that land is land, it stays when we are gone. Our sense of permanence is imposed on land, it is not granted by any but other humans."

Lord Kender stirred, and the lady sent him a fast look. Atanial wondered just how much fraught emotion lay behind those subtle reactions that she could so easily have missed.

A fly buzzed by her mount's ear, causing the animal to twitch and bob. Atanial leaned forward to shoo the fly away and stroked the horse's bony neck ridge. As she did, she surreptitiously wiped the side of her face on her shoulder.

"There is the matter of holding what we'd regain by violence," Lady Starveas went on, as if Atanial had spoken.

Atanial then wondered if the lady was not talking to her at all.

"Some might look forward to years of fighting. I do not. I would rather regain at least some of our holdings by negotiation. I say all this because I believe if your husband, Prince Mathias Zhavalieshin, was to return, perhaps that negotiation would occur. Many of those over in Locan Jora who sit now in our old homes and work our land were loyal to the Zhavalieshins, who once came from that area. But the king is now Canardan Merindar."

The duchess spoke for the first time. Her voice was thin and light as a bird's. "We welcome you to the castle. We extend this invitation to you all. We've been preparing."

Lady Starveas gave one of those slow, stylish nods in her direction, then turned to Atanial. It was very clear they'd planned things out. "But when you move on, we will not be going with you. Honor requires us to keep the oaths we made to Canardan, for he has not broken his oaths to us. Though, now speaking only for myself, my heart yearns for the return of Prince Math."

The duke and duchess made the low bow of accord.

Atanial lifted her voice so the women crowded behind could hear. "I thank you on behalf of everyone here. We ask no more than that."

They crossed the bridge and wound their way to the old castle whose towers were just visible beyond the lacy veil of the cascade.

TWENTY-EIGHT

IVORY MOUNTAIN GOT ITS name from a white stone with peculiar properties, a stone that resembled frozen ice with melted silver mixed in, or so it's been described. Those peculiar properties caused it to be nearly destroyed a few thousand years back or so. The morvende moved from the geliath (which is kind of like a cavern city a couple thousand years old), leaving it empty except for occasional retreats over the succession of centuries following.

That shows about how old the place was.

I galloped up the trail, branches whapping my face and the moisture-laden leaves dousing me with stinging-cold water. I was terrified that Randart and his gang would get me before I could find the access-way, and my fear communicated to the mare, who moved her fastest.

Up and up, the mare's head low to the trail, leaving me to watch the rocks at both sides lest I miss the triple-flower carving, which I was afraid had worn away.

I was wondering what to do if I reached the snowy mountain summit when at last my eyes were drawn to the symbol, weird as that sounds. I found out later, if you're taught the access signals, part of the magic is that image and reality will find a way to match. I mean, we're talking old, *old* magic.

In grateful relief I flung myself off the mare, who was sweating from the steady climb despite the bitter air, and fell to my knees, shaky fingers scrabbling at the smooth stone between a holly bush and a climbing of ivy that had mysteriously never grown over that portion of the stone.

I don't even know what I did, but the entire face of the rock shimmered, and there before me was a narrow fissure reaching up about nine feet, scarcely five feet wide. Dark as it was inside, I figured moss and some spiders would be preferable to a close, personal interview with Randart—backed by a couple hundred buff men and women wearing lots of shiny, pointy things, and probably in bad moods from missing their morning coffee.

The mare sniffed, snorted, then followed me willingly enough. Right after her tail passed the edge of the shadow cast by the sun down the rock face, the shimmer abruptly vanished, leaving us in darkness.

I stood next to the horse, who sniffed some more and turned her head, shifting her weight from hoof to hoof. Thunk, thud. I rubbed my eyes, wondering what the heck to do next.

When I opened my eyes, my vision had adjusted. A faint glow emanated from the stone in a series of purple blossoms painted impossibly long ago. The glowing signals led down a tunnel.

I stayed on foot, not sure how high the ceiling was, leading the mare by the reins. The stone floor seemed firm and not slimy. Good sign, I told myself.

We wound slightly to the left, always downhill, judging from the pressure on my toes.

We entered a cavern lit by a glowglobe of a kind I had never seen. Most have steady, soft light, faintly bluish, though I understand the light comes from gathered sunlight, stored by magical means. I would swear this globe was spread spectrum, for the light was soft but remarkably clear, picking out glittering bits from the rock all around, showing carvings of vines twining up overhead, and the remains of a painted sky with stars. The soft dirt of the ground glittered with blue flakes, bits of paint that had fallen over the centuries.

Below the glowglobe's niche was a trough with running water. I could hear it rushing down from somewhere above. The horse and I were thirsty.

I cupped my hands and dipped them. The water hurt, it was so cold, but it was clear and tasted good. The horse shouldered me aside and got a good long drink.

When we were done, I looked around. Several tunnels led off in various directions. I felt the faint ruffling of an air current from somewhere and almost instinctively turned in that direction.

Why not? Before I'd spent a couple days climbing the side of this mountain I'd thought it would be easy, like entering a big building. There's your directory, you get into the elevator, and whoosh, there's your suite. The vast size of this place was daunting. I kept trying to remember everything my father had told me when I was taught the magic, but all I could bring up was a vague sense of glowglobes, light, gleaming painted stars that looked real to my young eyes — and the spell.

So I followed the fresh-smelling, cool air current. I figured there had to be a hot spring somewhere down in the honeycomb of caverns, the air funneled upward. Anyway, I was grateful that I could see, that the tunnels were clean, no slime, no giant webs.

When I reached the right place, there was no warning. No trumpets, no sinister barriers or portents, no mysterious guardians. Nothing but the two of us emerging from the tunnel into a chamber with a pair of entrances opposite one another.

But I remembered it.

Here the painted ceiling was not flaking off. It glimmered pale blue in the brilliant light given off by hundreds of tiny glowglobes no bigger than a pea, the effect like the twinkling lights some people put in trees, back on Earth. The blue intensified in grada-tions up the dome of the ceiling, becoming a deep, cobalt glow directly overhead, the constellation depicted there glittering like a real sky.

My throat squeezed up when I recalled standing there once before, a scared little kid transfixed with wonder. I'd thought the top of the mountain had opened, leaving me staring straight up at the night sky.

But I knew it was day, and I stood deep inside a mountain—and that an enemy rode hard on my trail.

I had a job to do.

I dropped the reins. The mare watched me, the glowglobes pinpoints in her patient eyes. I dug through my bag and pulled out the little seashell wrapped in its homespun.

I opened the cloth and held out the shell, which began to glisten. There was enough ambient magic—or maybe it was the right magic—for the spell I'd been taught so long ago.

I stepped into the middle of the room, rubbed my damp palms down my grubby clothes, drew in a couple of *chi* breaths, and began the spell.

Magic potential rushed inward through me, a feeling akin to channeling a lightning strike. I shut my eyes and concentrated on the shaping words . . . and finished.

Light snapped on my palms and the shell vanished.

A current of air rushed round the chamber, and the horse tossed her head and stamped as a tall man with wild gray hair appeared. His thin body was clad in a long tunic down to his knees and baggy riding trousers. He had bare feet.

My astonished eyes flicked back to his face, that hawk-nosed, kindly face I'd remembered in dreams and in waking, and then it blurred as hot tears welled up.

"Dad!"

His arms opened, and I hurled myself into them.

When Randart realized he was going to have to deal with a magic mountain, he used one of two transfer tokens the king had insisted that Zhavic make. They were instant summons, pulling either Magister Zhavic or Magister Perran willy-nilly from wherever they were.

Randart had possessed these two tokens for years. He'd never thought he'd want a mage, but the time had come. The one he chose was Magister Perran, who had been guarding the old tower in case anyone tried a World Gate transfer. It was far too late for that.

Magister Perran arrived abruptly. Before he recovered from the transfer dizziness, Randart pointed at him and three of his men seized the mage, who was older, stocky and not exactly in fighting shape. They searched him thoroughly, taking away his magic case, paper, a writing chalk, several transfer tokens, and the book he'd had in his hand.

In silence they handed these things to Randart, who tossed the book off the trailside cliff without a second glance and put the rest of the items in the pouch at his belt. He glared down at the mage, ignoring his faint cry of dismay. "Atanial's girl is farther up the trail here on Ivory Mountain. You will get us inside, without any trickery, or I will cut you down myself before you can gabble one of your spells." He drew his sword from the saddle sheath and kept it gripped in his hand.

Perran shook his head once, and began walking.

Randart glanced back and motioned to two of his very best trackers. They came forward and saluted. "String your bows. Be ready to shoot the girl on first sight. Do not wait for an order. Do it. The one who drops her—and anyone she's with—will get land and a title to match."

They saluted again, the fervency of their emotions expressed in the gesture. The white-lipped rage in their commander's face made it unsafe to speak.

So this is how they wound their way up the mountain, Magister Perran walking, the trackers at either side, the others riding. The mage desperately looking for some way in. He had not been taught the access-way, and if you haven't been taught, it's going to be difficult to find. He knew that much, if nothing else about morvende geliaths.

As they climbed higher, woman and horse tracks fresh before them, his anxiety changed to despair and he wondered if he should jump off the mountain. One glance at Randart's angry face made it clear he was going to get no sympathy or understanding. If the tracks kept going, and all they found was a horse without a rider, Perran knew he would be murdered.

When they reached the place of the carvings, the tracks seemed to lead directly into a wall. How to get in? Magister Perran began searching for any kind of illusion, magical lock, whatever he could find.

Randart shifted impatiently, reminded yet again how much he loathed and distrusted magic and mages. The warriors watched the mage rustling desperately through the holly bushes that grew with profusion all along the cliff face. Perran's hands were soon pricked with scarlet, and his robe tangled constantly on the sharp-edged leaves. But he kept at it until Randart snapped, "Either you find a way in or die right now."

Perran turned around, flinging his bleeding hands out. "Then kill me," he cried. "Because you won't believe anything I say—"

A shimmer at the edge of everyone's vision caused Randart to start violently. The mage stumbled back. The trackers raised their crossbows.

The leaves rustled, and a small boy emerged, seemingly from the stone. He was no more than nine or ten, with brown hair and a considering hazel gaze. He wore ordinary riding clothes.

Randart stared in amazement, as a whisper hissed back down the line: this was the boy who had won at the games.

My father staggered, laughing breathlessly into my filthy hair. "Careful! I'm afraid I'm going to be a bit on the weak side until I learn to live in my body again."

I gave him a gentle squeeze then let him go, knuckling my eyes. "What? Where were you?" I looked up into his face. He had aged along with the rest of us.

He touched my cheek and gave me a crooked grin. "I had a

choice. I could go right out of the world, someplace where time stops, and I would not age, nor would I know what was occurring at home. Or I could sleep in body, but in mind I could learn how to watch. I chose the latter, though my body aged, and though it took me a long time before I could master the art of wandering in the . . . the realm of the mind, I guess you would say."

"Then—you know Randart is after me?"

"Yes." Papa winced. "I have been watching him for several years, now. I eventually even learned to hear his thoughts, a little. However, this summer suddenly I could hear them all, as plain as if I were with him." He shut his eyes and cocked his head. "*Could* hear his thoughts, and anyone else's I wished to. But those voices are fading. His is already gone. Perhaps it is because I'm back inside my own skull, so to speak. How limiting it is! Soon all I'll hear is my own yammer. I'm yammering, aren't I, Sasha?" He gave a wheezy laugh. "Never mind. I do know where we had better go, because there are two others I've been listening to, and they are also here, as it happens."

"What do you mean?"

"I think I'd better show you." Dad drew in a deep breath. "But I don't know how fast I can walk." He peered down and wiggled his toes. "Especially barefoot. When I chose to sleep, I made myself as comfortable as possible and that meant kicking off my shoes. They're back wherever Glathan hid my body while I slept." He waved a hand vaguely.

"Well, why don't you ride? I'm tired of riding. I'd as soon shake out the kinks in my muscles." I handed him the reins to the mare. "You point the way, and we're outa here."

Dad gave me a pensive smile. "This way."

Some of the men reacted with questions, but Randart raised his sword. "Are you some kind of damned mage spy? What are you doing here?"

"I was sent to this mountain this summer, to further my studies in history," the boy replied. "You saw me at your games with some friends. Just now I discovered that other humans were approaching. You can see the outer accesses from certain vantages within," he explained, pointing behind him.

"Other humans, like a tall girl who has no business being on this world at all?" Randart was angrier than ever at the unsettling situation, the sense that he was swiftly losing control. When the boy did not answer, he snapped, "Get out of my way."

For a long moment, as the boy gazed steadily up at Randart, the only sounds were the plop-plop of moisture from the trees, the snort of a horse, and in the distance, the sweet, melodic song of a lark.

The boy said, "I really think you should reconsider. Return to your royal city, as you promised. There is no cause for you to meddle here—"

A low growl of inarticulate rage began in Randart's chest and came out as a cry. He flung the sword like a spear straight at the boy.

Who sidestepped, raising an arm from which the loose sleeve fell, revealing a metal-linked wrist guard. Swifter than sight his arm whirled in a circle, deflecting the blade, which rammed into the twisted holly trunk, vibrating.

Randart gasped, "Who *are* you?"

"My name is immaterial to your purposes, but for what it is worth, it is Sven Eric."

The mage gasped, his cheeks blanching.

The boy looked his way, saying quite kindly, "Not a modern version of *that* name. I would hardly be named after a fool. It's a modern version of my Aunt Svenrael's name." He turned his attention back to Randart. "Will you return to Vadnais?"

The war commander, goaded by his own action as well as the result, by the implied secrecy of some name he'd never heard but which the mage obviously recognized, said distinctly, "I will not permit anyone to interfere with a lifetime of work. *Any*one. And if you do not get out of my way I will kill you or this mage or whoever is in reach, and not stop until that access lies open."

The boy stepped aside. "Then ride within."

When they passed the shimmer and their eyes had adjusted enough to reveal purplish blotches along the tunnel walls, they discovered the boy was gone.

Randart turned to the mage. "What name was he talking about?"

The mage said flatly, "Sfenaraec. The one who Norsunder was . . . founded on, over four thousand years ago. A name not used since."

Silence.

Randart said, "Be ready to shoot."

Dad and I and the mare walked in silence until cool air currents wafted up the tunnel, bringing the smell of running water and the low, steady rumble of a waterfall. Above the sound we heard voices.

Dad put out a hand. "The last thing I heard from Randart was his order to have us shot on sight. We cannot be seen."

I gazed at him in surprise. "Randart is already ahead of us?"

"I think he's near. There are some others as well."

We walked the last few steps and stared down at a vast lake under another domed ceiling, this one about the size of one of those super sports domes in the USA. Again, it was painted with gleaming, even glittering stars, in constellations so specific I had a feeling they were astronomically correct, and I blinked back in memory to childhood, standing on the stone edge of the lake, looking up and thinking I was outside.

Then memory was gone—thought was gone—when I recognized two of the voices.

One was my mother.

The other was Canardan.

TWENTY-NINE

DAD SLID OFF THE mare, wincing when he landed on his bare feet. He leaned against the animal's neck, his face hidden behind the wild tangles of his hair, which, uncut for at least ten years, frizzed out spectacularly, ahem, almost as wild as mine.

The eerily perfect acoustics carried the voices up to us as if they spoke from a few yards away.

Canardan exclaimed with a surprised laugh, "Is that really you, Atanial?"

Mom replied, "I could say the same to you." She wasn't laughing.

I laid my hand on my father's bony shoulder. "Come on, Dad, we gotta tell them we're here. *You're* here."

He turned his head. "I've been out of her life all these years, darling. What I owe her now is a clear choice, not an impossible one."

"What do you mean?" I asked, but my voice collided with Canardan's. "Who are these companions you've gathered about you?"

My mother stated in her Parent Night Voice—pleasant, even bright and social, but quite determined. "Canardan, we have two missions. The first, I am searching through here in case there is any chance, any possible chance, I might find my husband. Yes, you may laugh, but at least we're out of the rain. Our second mission was to confront you. Once we'd made a circuit of the kingdom gathering more women."

"Confront me?" His laughter sounded forced. "What is this? War in the bedroom? Except we are not quite there, are we?"

She said in a loud, clear voice, "The mission is to prevent you, if we can, from creating a war in spring. Everyone here has children, or nieces and nephews, or brothers and sisters, friends and lovers who enlisted in the army in order to protect Khanerenth. Abrogating the treaty with Locan Jora by invading it is not protecting the kingdom."

During the silence that followed, Dad moved slowly the last distance, with me at his side. We found ourselves on a kind of cliff, really no more than a slab of granite forming an outcropping, directly opposite the waterfall. There was a jumble of rock below it, a scree slanting down to a lower natural balcony.

Dad stood well back, in the shadow of the fissure that made our tunnel.

Canardan and his force were ranged up alongside the lake, a huge broken-walled cavern behind them with the faint glow of day stippling the rock. Apparently the lake was not part of the geliath, or at least not any more. An ancient avalanche had opened it to the outside, so people could come and go freely. During that long silence, I noticed that most of the surrounding walls had been shored up, built, torn down, temporarily housing all kinds of people, from thieves to political opponents—"people" constituting what the morvende called sunsider humans, like us. The morvende had abandoned this lake cavern way back when, leaving only that marvelous ceiling.

Mother's army appeared to be in the hundreds, far outnumbering Canardan's force, but they were unarmed. They spread all along the edge of the lake until they were quite near the waterfall, which thundered directly into the lake from a fissure high above. The women seemed to have reached the place within the last day or so, for I saw signs of a campsite, and many had wet hair, and clothing spread over flat rocks.

As Mom spoke across that leg of the lake, they gathered behind her in silence.

Canardan said, "Who is there? I cannot make out faces. The light from this end runs reflections upward, making it difficult to see you."

Mom said, "Never mind who, if you're thinking of removing people from their places in life, for there are far more of us even than you see here. Some are on the way, others are gathering ahead, waiting for us to catch up. I can assure you, if something happens to any of us, your troubles will only begin. And that's before you start your war."

Canardan laughed again.

Then he said, "Atanial sunshine dancingstar from the far-off world, will you marry me?"

I nearly choked, but Dad did not react at all.

I whispered to him, "Speak!"

"She has to have free choice, darling. If I pop up right now, the choice is not free."

I tried not to groan as I peered down. Canardan stood among his warriors, tall, strong, with long waving hair. From the distance across the lake he looked as handsome as I remembered him—unchanged.

"Did you hear me?" he asked, his voice the warm, kingly voice I remembered from childhood, and had learned to distrust and even to hate, with all my single-minded childish passion. I'd thought Mom hated him, too, but obviously I'd not perceived a lot of things. "Marry me, Atanial. Marry me and show me your right and my wrong. There's never been a queen like you, and maybe that's what the kingdom needs."

"I am already married," Mom said, her voice high and tight.

"To a ghost? If you really believe Math is alive, then set aside the marriage. You've waited longer than most would have. He'd understand, especially if it was for the good of the kingdom. Come! Come, I ask you before all these people, make peace and take your place beside me as my queen."

Mom's voice caught. "Canardan, that is probably the most generous offer I've ever heard from you. But it is impossible."

"No, it's not. That's the fun of being king. And queen. You can do things you want to do. You give the orders, make it happen!"

Mom laughed, a kind of half laugh, half sob. "If you truly want my advice, why not make me your adviser? You could do a lot better with me than with Dannath Randart, I promise you that."

"He's right," Dad whispered. "And she knows it. She'd make a wonderful queen. She might even save the kingdom. If not Canardan." He shut his mouth, frowning down in unhappy intensity.

"As adviser, you'd argue with Randart every day." Canardan laughed again. "As queen, you would give him orders, and he must obey."

"Again he's right," Dad murmured. Adding in a less neutral voice, "Until Dannath has her killed."

I fought against the instinct to yell out, *Mom, he's here!* "Dad, you have to do something."

He shook his head. "Don't you see? The important thing for all is the kingdom. Your mother would make a better queen than I would a king. The second most important thing is her happiness. He does love her in his fashion. And I abandoned her."

I kicked at the rubble in frustration, sending rocks skittering back toward the mare, who snorted and backed up a step or two, tossing her head.

Then Dad's hand gripped my shoulder, and he pointed below us. I heard vague sounds, mostly muffled by the water. Randart and his warriors had arrived through another tunnel which gave out onto the natural balcony right beneath us.

Mom's and Canardan's people were completely unaware of them. They were too close to the waterfall. Its noise covered everything but their own voices.

Most of Randart's force began making their way down to the lake, midway between Mom's group and the king's. Canardan and Mom were too intent on one another to notice.

I could only see the back of Randart's head, but even from that distance it was easy to make out how angry he was. And oh, he was angry. No, he was enraged. When I saw him bend a little to address one of the men following behind his horse, the man's reaction made it clear Randart's words were upsetting.

I couldn't hear it at the time, but he said, "Why did I not know about these women? I will flay whoever was responsible."

As always, he meant it.

He jerked up when Mom spoke. Her conviction was audible to everyone. "It will never happen. I would be your adviser gladly, but I will never be your wife."

Canardan stilled, watched by his men, the gathered women and (though he still did not know it) Randart.

Randart's eyes narrowed. Dad and I could see his profile. He raised a gloved hand, and his men stopped, everyone quiet.

Canardan's force gradually became aware of Randart's men through surreptitious nudges and head tips, but Canardan's attention was divided between Mom and memory. Atanial had spoken in exactly the same tone, the same gentleness, that Jehan's mother Feraeth had used so long ago. Though he'd ended the marriage, he'd tried to talk her into staying—they were still friends—they shared a child. But Feraeth had said, "I must go, Canardan. Your choices are no longer my choices."

Who knows. Maybe he had never really considered Mom would turn him down. Maybe he thought if he could get her to agree to one term, he could convince her on all the others. Maybe he had to seem to be the good guy, in her eyes, in the women's eyes, in his guards' eyes—in his own eyes—but he laughed again, head back, teeth flashing.

We were all watching him now, including Jehan, who had arrived from another tunnel, unseen by any of us.

Canardan threw his hands wide. "Atanial! If you will come back with me to the capital, I promise, my gift to you will be an end to any invasion—"

"You *idiot!*"

The roar of fury was almost unintelligible.

Everyone's attention snapped to Randart—who had yanked a loaded crossbow from one of his men, and fired.

Canardan jerked around, mouth open in surprise. I don't think he even saw the bolt that had been meant for his back. When he turned, it smacked straight into his chest.

Canardan's long silver-touched auburn hair flung back. One hand groped futilely at the shaft protruding from him, until he began to fall, slowly, slowly to his knees as two or three of his men who were obviously as shocked as the rest of us belatedly sprang forward to catch him.

The clang of a sword rang out, the echo ricocheting. There was a flash of white hair as Jehan leaped down from the rock fall from another of the many tunnels, unseen until now by any of us. He flung his way through the warriors ringing Randart and attacked the murderer of his father.

Randart's men had fallen back, shocked at the death of the king, but I didn't trust them. I yanked my sword from the mare's saddle sheath and vaulted down the rocky scree until I ranged up behind Jehan, whose blades whirled.

In the time I'd taken to run up, Jehan had gotten Randart off the horse, whose hooves slipped in the rubble. Randart jumped clear and the animal plunged away, ears flat, as men reached to catch the reins.

Randart backed up two steps under Jehan's furious attack, almost skidding in the rubble as he warded off blow after blow with his heavy cavalry blade. He bumped up against a flat rock and hopped up, now striking down at Jehan, who braced himself in the gravel before the rock, his cavalry sword and someone else's rapier humming.

Randart yelled over his shoulder, "Take him! Take him!"

Randart had chosen his crossbow men deliberately. They were willing to kill in cold blood. The one with the still-loaded bow yanked it up and took aim at Jehan.

"Touch him and you die," I bellowed as I dashed forward.

The man yanked the bow toward me. I snapped off a sidekick to his hand that sent the bow hurtling into the air. It smashed against the ceiling and the bolt fired—straight into the ground in front of the other riders, sending up a spurt of gravel.

Horses panicked, men in the narrow tunnel mouth fell back, some shoving, everyone yelling and slipping and sliding, as Randart glared past Jehan at me. "Kill her!" Randart yelled, with a flourish of his sword.

Most of the nearby men just pressed back, but two came at me, blades raised. I kicked up gravel at one and met the blade of the other, flinging it off. The first lunged in, but I snapped a whirling time bind with my rapier round his heavy sword, and slid the point past it straight into his shoulder. He staggered back, and as the second guy brought his blade down at me I swung inside, caught him by the wrist and used my judo to yank him off-balance. I kicked out his knee and slammed him into the first man.

Two of Jehan's men had reached me and stood over the attackers, swords upraised.

I leaped to guard Jehan's back.

Unfortunately he caught the flicker of motion at the extreme edge of his vision. He glanced back—but just as he reassured himself that it was me and not an attacker, his heel skidded.

In the second he was off-balance, Randart brought his hilt toward Jehan's head in the backswing, and brained him from behind. Jehan crashed to the ground.

Randart's men leaped forward to finish Jehan off. I whirled, sword out, to keep them back.

Randart stepped down from the rock, swinging his blade back and forth. "No, no, keep him alive. He's now the king. And he's going to take orders from me. As for *her*." Randart pointed with the sword directly at me. "Everything, *everything* is her fault. Get away," he ordered the men still ringing us, and they backed up, staring from him to me and down to Jehan. Randart bared his teeth. "This pleasure I reserve for myself."

He swung with a power stroke I could not block with a mere

rapier. He had that heavy cavalry sword, and he was fighting to kill. I backed gracelessly out of the way, slipped on gritty dust just like Jehan had and dropped my rapier.

Randart laughed as he advanced.

"Your mistake," I said, though my voice quavered.

He took another swipe at me. I whirled under the blade and did a sweep kick. He was too well planted, and my feet only bounced off his heavy boots. But he looked down, and in that moment I dove to one side, rolled (Ow! Never roll on gravel!) and came up with Jehan's heavier cavalry sword that had been lying by his hand. Randart's blade flashed toward my head. The angle was too close for a power block. I dropped to one knee and flung up both hands, the tip resting on the flat of my palm, and took the blow on the flat of Jehan's heavy blade.

Shock rang through my bones, sparks flew. "You cheated," I yelled. "You rotten, cowardly slime, you hit him from behind!"

"Die." Randart brought the sword round in a deadly side-arc that whooshed within an inch of my gut. I danced back, though that put me close to the edge of the cliff.

Then something silver glittered in the air between Randart and me.

Thunk.

Randart lowered his sword, staring at the knife in his shoulder.

The men, who had stood frozen, some of them gazing in horror at the king across the lake, others at Randart, obviously unsure what to do, all stepped back as Damedran scrambled over the rocks.

"You broke your promise," he yelled, his voice cracking on the last word. "You *lied.*" And he began to sob, the angry, honking sobs of a teen betrayed beyond endurance.

Randart pressed his fingers over the horrible, spurting wound. "You always had . . . rotten aim," he snarled.

"I don't," came a voice from behind.

Randart whipped round. There was Jehan, rising to his feet, crimson blood trickling in shocking contrast down through his white hair into his face, which was as bleak as I'd ever seen it. His hand gripped my dueling rapier.

Randart shifted his blade to his left, and swung at Jehan. Neatly, without fuss or flourish, Jehan blocked and, without a check, the rapier flashed straight through Randart's heart.

The warriors stirred, some starting toward me, some toward Damedran. Damedran's fellow cadets swarmed over the rocks, ranging themselves in a row, blades raised.

Everyone eyed one another, poised for action—but who was in charge? Jehan swiped blood out of his face, blinking in an effort to see.

"Hold! Everyone, hold hard! Lay down your arms," my father ordered in a voice of authority I had never heard him use.

The older army men stared, aghast, astonished. In disbelief.

"*Math?*"

That was Mom.

"Down with your weapons," Dad said, his voice strong enough to echo back from the far stone walls. "Now. There will be no retribution for those who lay down weapons. But another strike, and you are forsworn."

Clang. Clank. Zhing.

I think, looking back, many of them were relieved to get rid of the steel and the responsibility it implied. Too much had happened too fast. The pair of men holding Damedran stepped away, leaving him weeping quietly, disconsolately.

Dad picked his way down to us, his hair wild, his feet absurdly bare. But he didn't look ridiculous, he looked assured, cool, well, *kingly.*

Jehan flung down his red-smeared blade.

Dad gripped Jehan's shoulders with both hands. "You have done well, my boy," he said quietly.

Jehan squinted into his face past the blood trickling from the blow Randart had given him, and his brow smoothed. Dad was not talking about the fight with Randart at all.

I looked uncertainly from Dad to Jehan, unsure what to do

now that the emergency was over.

Dad let go of Jehan and stepped to me, giving me his funny smile as he murmured for my ears alone, "He told you the truth in everything that matters."

I know it's about as trite as "true love," but I really did feel as if a weight had lifted from my heart.

Before I could cross those last few steps to Jehan, a figure hurtled between the warriors, shoving some of them aside, and then, crying as hard as she had in those early days when we first reached Earth—but this time for joy—was Mom.

She flung herself into Dad's arms, laughing, weeping, covering his face with kisses, stopping only when his arms locked around her as if they would never let her go.

THIRTY

JEHAN AND I HAD only had a single private conversation between that terrible day in Ivory Mountain and our arrival in Vadnais. And it wasn't much of one.

Immediately after Randart's death and Dad's surprise appearance, Mom got everyone organized. She asked the women to help marshal Canardan's men. By that I mean they went to the ones they knew, asking for help carrying things or help with horses or to talk—keeping them apart from Randart's men so they wouldn't get the bright idea of attacking their ex-army mates for some wholesale slaughter to relieve pent-up feelings.

Dad remained with Randart's men, forcing them to stay in military formation, that is under tight control. They were sworn to follow orders, and right now, Dad seemed to be the senior royal representative. At least no one tried to question his authority.

For the rest of that horrible day, Jehan stayed with Damedran and the cadets.

I kept out of their way as we trudged out of the cavern and began the long, dreary journey back to Vadnais. Jehan's and Damedran's faces wore twin expressions of shock; Damedran's grief was terribly close to the surface, fueled by anger and even guilt. Though he kept repeating that his uncle got what he deserved, got what he deserved. No one argued. Damedran was his own judge and jury. Finally, surrounded protectively by his cadet pack, Damedran fell into an exhausted sleep near the campfire that first night.

I eased my way through all the slumbering warriors and stable people, and sat down next to Jehan. He had been sitting alone with his back to a rock, staring into the distant fire, his hands loose on his knees.

His head turned sharply, and he looked searchingly into my face. Though we did not really know one another yet, I suspected he was bracing against an expression of triumph or some other careless dismissal of his father because he'd heard plenty from me about Canardan. And I'd never had the chance to know the king as anything but a villain.

But I'd witnessed that last exchange with my mother, during which I got a glimpse of the Canardan whom Jehan loved, the man Mom had regarded as more of a friend than as an enemy. Despite everything.

So there was no sign in me of the reactions he dreaded. All the tension went out of him, and the look he gave me, the puckered brow of grief, whacked my heart with an echo of his sorrow.

"I'm sorry," I said, and meant it. "Jehan, I'm so sorry."

His expression tightened. "If I'd been faster . . . I should have seen it coming—" He shook his head.

"Can I get you anything?" I knew it was woefully inadequate, but what could I do? What could I say? No action of mine would bring his father back and set everything to rights. "They seem to have got supper going at the other end of camp. I don't know about you, but I tend to eat least when I need it the most."

He half raised a hand in dismissal, then looked away, toward the boys, a couple of whom were also asleep, though most were awake. "I don't think I ate today. Maybe I'd better."

"Right." I got to my feet. "Let me bring it to you."

A quiet tone, practical words and sensible action eased his tension a little. He didn't want soggy sympathy, nor did he want drama. We'd just lived through plenty of that.

I went away to get in line where some of the army men and a

few of the women had set up a cook tent and a kind of instant buffet row. I got a hunk of pan-fried cornbread, some sort of fish cooked in pressed olives and wine, and sautéed carrots someone had gotten permission to pick from a local truck garden.

When I finally reached Jehan, I discovered that he'd fallen deeply and profoundly asleep, his cheek resting on the arm he'd crooked over the rock.

I set the plate nearby and returned to get some food for myself. And then I went and sat with Damedran's friends, who looked like a bunch of scared pups. Husky ones, to be sure, but pups all the same. I asked them easy questions—about homes, families, favorite activities. Things they could answer without reference to so-called Great Events.

Why do bloody events get translated into Great Events in histories? Probably because they force summary change. But here was the real effect of sudden change—the wrenches in the lives of those who would never leave behind records, the people who lived and breathed and hated and loved, feared and fought, the everyday folk whom the balladeers inevitably overlooked. They might go home and tell the story, and perhaps the sword Ban Kender gripped would be handed down to a grandson, along with the story of this day. Maybe he would even figure as a hero.

The next day Jehan rode in the wagon with his father's body. He didn't ride with me partly because he needed time alone, but also because Damedran stuck to me like glue.

From his occasional, uncharacteristically shy questions or comments, I finally realized Damedran was crushing on me, but it was a dazed crush, I think more gratitude than any real admiration for my great looks or stunning abilities. Making me into a kind of heroine probably felt better than the emotions of disgrace, defeat and attempted murder, no matter how justified everyone told him his action had been.

So passed a few days.

Before we reached Vadnais, we paused at a crossroad, and my father rode a little ways apart with Damedran and spoke to him alone. The boy separated off with a small guard leading the wagon bearing Randart's body that would be taken to his family castle, where they could have a private funeral. Dad was not having any sort of shame ceremony, too often held in the past. Those caused nothing but bad feelings.

Jehan and I traveled together after that, for the few days remaining, but he almost never spoke. From time to time he looked ahead at Dad. It was pretty plain to me he was wondering what kind of disgrace lay ahead for him, but he didn't say anything.

Mom and Dad were nearly inseparable, and from the looks of things, they didn't stop yakking except to eat when we camped. A few times they invited us to join them. Jehan refused politely; he seemed to regard himself if not as a prisoner, in isolation. So I divided my time between them, feeling like this could be over ANY time and no one would hear me complain. I mean, the bad guys were gone, where was my happy ending?

Where was Jehan's?

We *finally* reached Vadnais in a kind of procession, Dad and Mom riding at the front, me behind them, an honor guard with Jehan accompanying Canardan laid out in the wagon. Along the trip some of the women had gone home (with their men) but everyone else trailed after, including some lookie-loos who'd invited themselves along now that the danger was over.

Dad had sent riders ahead. The entire city had gathered along the main street leading to the great square between the castle and the guild buildings. Whatever their private feelings, people united in throwing down white blossoms. Canardan was quite covered with a fragrant snowdrift of flowers when we reached the great square, where a quiet, orderly crowd had been waiting since morning.

There, at a gesture from Dad, Jehan stepped up. He did not give a speech. No one made a sound as he passed a torch three times over his father's still body. Magister Zhavic, with trembling hands, performed the Disappearance Spell.

Then my father lifted his voice. "I, Mathias Zhavalieshin, claim the throne of Khanerenth. My first order is to appoint Prince Jehan Merindar as continuing commander of our guard, and he is also to take command as High Admiral of the navy."

Jehan's face blanched nearly as white as his hair.

"If he accepts these tasks, I further order him to ride immediately to Castle Cheslan to lead the army back to Ellir for winter quarters. There, he will preside over a smooth change of command as he sees fit."

I was astonished, but the relief in Jehan's face made it plain to see that this was exactly the right thing to do. He bowed low to my father, setting off a group bow that rustled (with a few creaking and crackling of joints here and there) through the crowd.

After that they sent up a huge cheer.

Jehan said something to Dad. I couldn't catch the words. He turned a twisted smile to me that was so much a mix of unhappiness and desire my throat ached. Then he strode away through the crowd, his white hair floating on the cold autumn breeze, and vanished in the direction of the stable.

"I never got to talk to him," I said, hardly aware of speaking.

Mom squeezed my hand. "Let him get some space. Let people see him trusted by your father."

Space. Yes. I'd asked it of him when I left the yacht, though it had hurt me terribly. I had to give him the same chance. So I bowed my head and followed my mother toward the castle looming over us.

Mom stopped in her tracks. "Where is everyone going to stay?" She stared up at those towers with (I suddenly realized) somewhat wrinkled Zhavalieshin firebird banners hanging down.

Dad looked over at her, brows lifted mildly. "Oh. I didn't think of that."

Mom gave a short nod. "I may as well go right back up to my rooms, and you come with me, dear. In about five minutes you and I are going to be in that bath. I can think of plenty of things to do."

Though I felt closer to tears, I laughed. "Mom. There are about thirty people earing in."

"I'd invite them to join us, but the fashion for hot tubs doesn't seem to have reached this part of the world yet. I'll fix that." She patted my hand and turned around. "Well! Since we have quite a crowd, why don't we get those with nothing to do started on cleaning up this castle?"

She began handing out jobs. Those who didn't backpedal fast enough got assigned to broom and scrub squads. The surprising thing is, most of them actually went out and did the assigned jobs. A lot of them were castle servants hoping not to be fired, it turned out. Having work to do was a good thing, it helped establish a semblance or normality.

Mom then turned on me. "And you, my dear, are going to have an appointment with the royal seamstress. You have to start dressing like a princess."

"Nooo," I howled, hovering in that unsteady state between laughter and a flood of tears. "Not a big dress!"

"If *I* can get used to it, *you* can."

Despite her determination to polish me up before Jehan returned, when he did arrive, I wasn't in any of my new gowns. (Which I have to admit were stylish and easy to wear.) I was out in the court doing weapons practice with the guards, wearing my workout clothes, when one of Steward Eban's nieces came to fetch me. "Prince Jehan is here!" she cried, grinning with excitement.

I ran inside and straight to the side parlor that Dad and Mom had taken over as our central HQ. Dad had insisted that the servants not disturb Canardan's rooms, and Mom couldn't bear to go near them. They had agreed to let Jehan decide what to do about his father's things.

Jehan arrived just after I reached the parlor. He still wore his brown tunic uniform, now dusty from the road. He bowed to Dad and Mom, and turned to me. He no longer wore that look of pain that had so wrenched my heart on the long, awful ride. I grinned at him.

He flashed a subdued version of his old smile before turning to Dad. "Sire, would you like my report?"

Dad waved a hand. "Sit, Jehan. I sent for something to eat and drink."

Jehan dropped down next to me. Our shoulders touched; I held out my hand. His face relaxed, and his fingers gripped mine.

"Did Orthan Randart assist you as I required?" Dad asked.

"He did." Jehan's tone was grim.

Servants came in, bringing hot food and drinks. The slanting rays of late autumn touched the table where we all kept our own stacks of to-do things, striking into gold the tea as it was poured into the fine blue porcelain cups.

Kreki Eban had gone straight from the dungeon to the steward's chambers. Mom and I had been trying to figure out how to help Kreki Eban reorganize the staff, for a lot of Canardan's servants had quit. Some had vanished when the news of Canardan's death reached the city, along with a sizable amount of silver, plate and other valuables, Chas in the lead—ahead of a pack of guards who badly wanted to scrag him.

But Kreki had unearthed a lot of the old servants, who were quite eager to have their old jobs back.

Mom sighed, rubbing her temples. "Zhavic searched Randart's office down in the garrison at Math's request. He didn't find any wards or anything."

Jehan dropped his biscuit onto his plate. "I searched his office at Ellir, as you required, sire. I didn't expect to find anything like 'Future King Plans' but Orthan, who really seemed to want to cooperate, kept telling me his brother was fond of lists. Randart had had his own section of the academy archive room. We opened those chests and found the files scrupulously neat, arranged according to year, supplies, reports on personnel and exercises, for the entire army. He even noted down interrogations and the type of, um, coercion, let's call it, that was most effective for that person."

"Yuk!" Mom and I said together.

"I burned that one." Jehan grimaced. "Research I'd as soon no one ever uses. For the rest, we had to go through it all, but in the end it was worthwhile. He kept two kinds of open lists, we finally figured out: immediate goals and long-term goals."

"Ah." Mom leaned forward and pushed the biscuit back into Jehan's free hand, for his other still held mine tightly. He obediently took a bite.

Mom smiled fondly at him. "Let me guess. Long-term goals would get shifted to immediate and when accomplished, were filed as done."

"Exactly. The outstanding ones were mostly various contingency plans, but there was one single sheet, and from the looks of it quite old, on which he'd written *hypotheticals*. All of them expressed as ideas. But if you read them mentally prefacing each with *If I were king*, they changed in meaning. It looks, from that paper and some other hints, as if he'd first considered the idea of assassinating my father within the past two or three years, if he didn't get rid of me. He was only waiting for Damedran to leave the academy and gain some sort of military triumph before acting."

"So his killing Canardan wasn't impulse so much as a long-term plan inadvertently carried out too soon," Mom said.

Jehan said, "I really believe the intention had always been there. Instinct took over."

"And he hadn't shared it with his family?"

Jehan shook his head. "Damedran made that clear enough back at Ivory Mountain. And his father was equally appalled. Almost tearfully so. I believe he was afraid he would be summarily condemned for a family conspiracy that hadn't actually existed. The invasion, yes. But Orthan and Damedran had really thought that the king would then be convinced to set me aside as heir, appoint Damedran in my place, and everyone would carry on happily ever after. Except for me," he finished wryly. "But even then, I'd no doubt run off chasing artists and bards."

"You did well." Dad rose. "No. Sit there and eat. I have to get back to the mages and see if I can get them sorted out." He winked at me, and left.

Mom leaped up, rustled over in her long blue skirts and cupped her hands round his face. She leaned down and kissed his forehead. "So glad you are back, dear boy."

She whirled around, the fresh herbal scent from her skirts wafting through the air, and she was gone.

"She seems happy," Jehan said as the door closed quietly on us.

"She's happy with Dad." I hesitated, then shook my head—which set our hands to swinging.

Jehan gave me a brief grin. "Promise me. Don't hide things. Spit 'em out. I will, too."

"Promise." I turned his hand over and rubbed my thumb over his rough, callused palm. His skin so warm. "Mom is happy when she's with Dad, but that's not nearly often enough. She was happy, oh, the first day or so here, but the talk about Norsunder and possible war worries her. A lot. She likes being social, when everyone gets along."

Jehan drank off his tea. "I sensed that, when we were here in the summer."

"Speaking of the past. I never saw your father with her, but I'm wondering if she had a kind of weird love-hate thing going with him."

"I saw them together. That's pretty much it," Jehan responded.

I nodded. "Dad won't say anything at all, but he looks worried sometimes, when he watches her, and he doesn't think anyone is looking. Not about her feelings for Canary—Canardan, sorry." I sighed. "But about these future threats, and how that relates to the queen gig."

"Gig," Jehan breathed, smiling at last. That smile, so pensive, so sweet, melted me right down to the socks I wasn't wearing.

"Jehan. Speaking of no one around. Who knows how long that will last. I have something to say."

Jehan gave my hand a brief, tentative squeeze. I got to my feet then pulled him up. We stood there in the golden shafts of sunlight, his white hair gleaming, pinpricks of light in his blue eyes.

He looked into my face and grinned. "A prepared speech, eh? If it's self-condemnation, don't do it. But if it's something you will feel the better having shed, well, let's have it."

"We call it clearing the air." I leaned up and kissed him. "And yes. I mean, I don't think I'm Princess Perfect, and I want to apologize. For not trusting you. See, I wanted to trust you, oh, way too much. So I didn't trust myself."

"Or Merindars," he murmured.

I groaned. "That sounds so awful."

"But it's true." He watched me closely. "Isn't it? Truth is, if my father were alive, where would we all be? Would he be in prison, or halfway across the kingdom drawing as many to him as possible for a civil war? I don't think he could have brought himself to give up being king. He probably expected, if your father really did turn up alive, that it would be Mathias who would conveniently go away with a cheery farewell. I am convinced it would have grieved your father to put him on trial, much less anything more drastic."

Echoing what Dad had said to Mom and me in private, two nights before: *I don't think I could have borne putting Canardan on trial, despite everything he's done. And I know what he's done, I've been inside his head a great deal this summer. Yet I also know his motives, and he was not at heart an evil man. But he was evilly educated and easily influenced to talk himself into what he wanted, and shutting his eyes to Randart's goals.*

I said, "All true."

"So where does that leave me, I am beginning to wonder? There were some at the academy who did not like seeing me free and not in prison. Others assured me of their continued loyalty. I mislike the division between people that these attitudes imply. For surely, if there is so broad a range there at the academy, does it not hold it would be much the same across the kingdom?" He looked away, then met my eyes and said in a low voice, "In truth, I wonder if there is a place for me here at all."

What ever happened to "happily ever after"? I thought, trying not to show my dismay. "Please don't decide anything without talking to Dad."

"I can't begin to decide anything." His gaze was steady. He'd tensed up again, and I could feel how important this conversation, this moment was. "Not until I know where I stand with you."

"I have been considering that. Trying to be practical. And adult. But I don't know what to think. I mean, we have an attraction thing going on that would fuel suns. We seem to know where we are with trust. What we haven't yet is a relationship."

"We have a friendship." He gave me a whimsical smile. "Or we did. Beginning on board my ship."

"Oh, we got along great when I thought you were Zathdar. Soon's I knew the truth, there was your name right there between us, like some kind of shadow. Merindar. You know, Dad asked me to do something for him. He wants me to write everything down from the beginning of the summer, when he could hear everyone's thoughts. I hadn't meant to tell you, but I think it important that I do."

"He even heard mine?" Jehan winced.

"Yes, but he hasn't told me any. That's for you to do. If you want. He not only knows what happened, but why. What people were really thinking, though he can't do it any more, and he says that what he remembers is already beginning to fade. Will you tell me your side? Maybe, I don't know, maybe I can put it all together and understand some of what happened."

"I will do that."

"Thank you. But that's for me. So what do *you* want to do?"

Jehan let go of my hands and pulled me into his arms. "I want to begin all over again, courting you," he murmured into my hair. "I want to spend the rest of my life courting you."

Whee. Even if we hadn't gotten any convenient fairy god-mothers wand-waving us into happily ever after, hearing those words came pret-ty close to making up for it all. I flung my arms round his neck and this time the kiss was long, satisfying, and didn't end with sorrow, regret or distrust.

So we did it again. And, oh, a few more times.

When we did talk again, I said, "What's next?"

I meant it as a joke but Jehan let go and took a few steps away, as if proximity would restore rational thought. He looked over his shoulder. "Back to where we were. Which is deciding where my place is. Sasharia, what if the best thing for the kingdom is my leaving?"

I shrugged. "If you and I get on the same page, and I think we're going to, Mom and Dad would understand. I'm too old for them to stop me and they know it. So if you're worried about the whole princess thing, well, it was never real to me anyway. I don't hate it, but I'd rather be with you than wearing diamonds in my hair and making nice with duchesses. In short, if you've got to leave, let's pack a hammock for two."

He closed the distance again, searching my face. "You mean that?"

"Of course I do." I laughed. "Heck, when I was a girl I never wanted to be a princess even if we did come back here. Princesses were small and dainty and neat, and I was too big. What I wanted to be—" I stopped, and felt my face redden.

Jehan's eyes narrowed. "Come on. Say it."

"You're gonna laugh."

"I won't."

"You will. I know it. One snicker, and I'm outa here."

He raised his hands, smiling.

"All right. I wanted to be . . . a pirate!"

How he laughed. I whirled around to march out, he caught me, we wrestled, then fell laughing onto the couch, where I kissed away his laughter.

And when we were both breathless, he caught my hand. "I

think it is time to talk to your father."

The result of which was today, New Year's Week Firstday.

This morning dawned gray with impending snow, but despite the prospect of dreary weather, the bells of the castle, echoed by the bells of the garrison and the guildhall, all rang the rarely heard full royal wedding and coronation carillons. Bell ringers crowded into the towers, wakening the big bells and the small ones that usually hung silent. They played wonderful patterns as two carriages, drawn by pairs of white horses, rolled slowly on a circuit of the royal city.

This was New Year's Firstday, the day Mom and Dad would officially become king and queen, and Jehan and I would marry.

Mom and Dad sat in the first carriage, dressed in the crimson and gold and silver of Zhavalieshin. Dad wore a fabulous tabard embroidered long ago with twined firebirds, hidden by Kreki Eban and triumphantly brought out last week. Mom's hair was done up elaborately with pearls and beautifully cut stones that gleamed with amber highlights.

In the back carriage, feeling very weird, I sat beside Jehan. I looked down at myself, wondering who was sitting there in the white brocade gown with the emerald green embroidery down the sleeves, round the neck and hem. Under the brocade I wore a green silk gown, which would only show when I moved.

My hair had been done up by not one but two hairdressers (one joking, when she discovered the princess liked jokes, about how her arms were going to fall off, making all those little braids), each braid with a single tiny diamond fastener at the end before being looped up into a complicated coronet atop my head. Fitted against the coronet of hair, a tiara with diamonds and one single whopping emerald whose price would probably have netted me a brand new BMW, back in L.A. Nobody knew it, but I'd hauled that gem around all summer in my bag. It was left over from the bad old days.

L.A. seems unreal now, a dream—endless hot days, cars, TV and palm trees. Reality was winter slowly closing in on days of hard work, in-between all these fittings. But the good side of reality were the evenings when the four of us would gather, tired from a day of labor, talking as we ate dinner, and relearning to laugh.

Jehan told me his story privately, before he had to leave for his tour of inspection. Our going over all that old ground together— what did I think, what did he think—somehow cemented the bond that we'd always felt between us, even back on the very first day, when we'd fought side by side. We could say anything to the other, which helped us both get past all the bad stuff.

He said he didn't want to hear Dad talk about Canardan's inner thoughts, at least not until some time had passed. So it wasn't until he left us to ride around the kingdom inspecting castles that Dad described Canardan's and Randart's view of events, and I wrote it all down as you've seen it here.

Then it was Mom's turn. When she had finished and read over what I wrote, she hugged Dad and me, saying, "It's good to get that out of my headspace. The whole thing finally feels done. Finished business."

Jehan had not been able to decide about his father's effects. Mom helped the servants clear all Canardan's things out of his rooms, so Jehan would not have to do it. The rooms were clean and empty by the time he returned, his father's personal things put into carved chests for him to keep or sort as he wished, whenever he was ready.

Mom and Dad stayed up in Mom's rooms, and I'll get to why in a minute.

When he returned a week ago, ahead of a huge snowstorm, Jehan was able tell us how Damedran was doing. By then he'd completed his month's thorough tour with Damedran at his side, inspecting garrisons, handing out orders right and left "in the name of the king" and generally being In Charge.

Because this is what Dad wanted. Just as he'd wanted the record. Just as he wanted the wedding today—Jehan joining our family, which would add Zhavalieshin to his name—the same day as the coronation. Emphasizing how the four of us were a family.

The carriages stopped at the royal castle's grand entrance as the first flakes began to drift from the sky. We walked into the great hall, glad of our heavy clothes, our breath puffing in the cold air. All the court was gathered, the smell of beeswax candles, and personal scents made of wildflowers and herbs, a kind of echo of summer.

It's strange, how sharp my memory is with some details: the pale light glowing in the long windows, a soft bluish white light now that snow was falling; tears along my mother's eyelids, and the corner of her mouth where the skin had softened over time, trembling even as she smiled; my dad's hand holding hers tightly, his thumb rubbing absently over her palm the same way I liked to rub Jehan's palm.

The glow of that snowy light on the white hair of a woman with a curiously ageless face and Jehan's blue eyes, who had slipped in among the mages in their fine, light gray robes. She was Feraeth Jervaes, Jehan's mother. She stood side by side with the former Queen Ananda, who smiled fully now, for the first time in many years.

One of the clearest and most precious memories was the look in Jehan's eyes when he saw his mother, before he turned to me, smiling that smile with the deep dimple down one side.

And one of the dearest memories was the slight huskiness of emotion, the conviction in his voice as he said, "I offer you this ring, which has no beginning and no end. It is a symbol of our love . . ."

The funniest memory was the way I heard myself gulping for air almost every phrase as I echoed the same words and shoved the golden ring, all embroidered with intertwined leaves, onto his longest finger.

"Your prosperity is my prosperity . . ."

"Your hardship is my hardship . . ."

". . . and we call upon all who are gathered here to witness the joining of this family, as long as we shall live."

And then my memory grays out, but at some point I became aware of standing at my mother's side, as Jehan stood at my father's, and how their vows to the kingdom curiously echoed the vows of marriage.

Three things my father had asked for: that I write the record, that Jehan take his name. That's two.

The third? Within the next three years, when the kingdom has accustomed itself to all of us, my father and mother will abdicate and go to Sartor as ambassadors, Mom to stay in a court she knows she will love, Dad to study magic with the most powerful mages. He thinks that's the best way for him to prepare for the troubles ahead. He says that being king requires youth and strength. So he wants Jehan and me to take their place, and make those very same vows.

But the whole idea of me and queenship doesn't yet compute. I'm not really accustomed to the princess gig yet.

So back to memories. Like the tenderness apparent in both as Jehan and his mother met again, after years of contact only through letters. She stroked my hair, whispering how welcome I was in her life.

And the last memories are a montage of music, and dancing under the glittering lights illuminating the castle.

So I sit here now, writing it all down—

Jehan just leaned over my shoulder. "Are you not done with that thing yet?"

"I have to put in our wedding." I looked down at myself. "I have to describe me sitting in this ridiculous chair—who *is* the twit who put silk knots in the seat cushions? *What* were they *thinking*? And my first waltz in my wedding gown. Shall I put in how I tripped on my train? Then I have to get down what everyone looked like, and how your mom and mine got along like a couple of houses on fire—"

"Sasha."

"What?"

"You are not writing down everything I say. Are you?"

"Yes. So speak slower."

I can hardly write, I am laughing so hard.

"Shall. I. Describe. What. We. *Should*. Be. Doing. On. Our. Wedding. Night?"

Okay, he wins.

And here it is the next day, but as you can see, it's going to be short, for very soon all these papers will lie on the desk of King Mathias and he can do whatever he wants with them.

Because why?

Because a little while ago, I was waking up with that happy, sleepy sense that all is right with the world. How rare, how wonderful! Outside it was cold and clear and icy, but inside warm and snug, and . . .

I looked over, but no husband slumbering beside me!

I sat up, peering through the open doors to the wardrobe—for I'd moved into his rooms, which were a lot less gloomy than Queen Ananda's old chambers. And what did I see? Jehan standing before the mirror, trying on the most horrible pink shirt I've ever seen—all embroidered with orange peonies.

"Jehan!" I yelped. When he turned around, I saw that he'd managed to dig up a pair of deck trousers of purple and yellow stripes. "You are not, not, *not* going out into the city in those."

"No." He strode back into the bedroom and preened, then began tying his hair up in a rose and violet bandana with green fringes. "But I am wearing it on board the *Zathdar*."

"What?"

He gave me his old, ironic grin. "Zathdar the pirate has to sail again."

"Today? Now? I thought we'd . . ." I waved my hand around

the room. "Have some time to ourselves."

He flicked one of those magic communication boxes, which was lying on the desk. "I told you Owl rejoined my fleet. And Elva Eban's the new navigator, by the way. He just wrote. He's found Bragail of the *Skate*. Says he not only turned corsair, which doesn't surprise me. But that far too many of the very ones among Randart's old captains that I found had skipped out of Ellir are now poised in time-honored Khanerenth fashion to turn to piracy, aided by that slimy Chas, with half my father's personal treasury. It's time to do something about them, don't you think?"

"But—"

"So it'll be crowded in the captain's cabin. Won't that be cozier?" He wiggled his brows. "Get rid of those papers. You're done."

"You mean you want me to join you? In the dead of winter, chasing a slimy Randart captain and probably his entire fleet and that stinker Chas, all turned pirate?" I yelled, for he'd vanished inside the wardrobe. "What kind of a wedding trip is that?"

He reappeared. "In the dead of winter."

He tossed my winter mocs onto the bedding.

"Chasing pirates led by a slimy Randart captain."

He pitched my sturdy shirt and riding trousers into my lap.

"And desperate duels on heaving decks. For truth, justice and honor."

Next came my sword.

"Against sinister villains. Winning fabulous treasures. You know you want to," he cooed.

And I do!